FESTIVAL OF Stars

EILIS FLYNN

www.ElloRasCave.com

An Ellora's Cave Publication

www.ellorascave.com

Festival of Stars

ISBN 9781419965821
ALL RIGHTS RESERVED.
Festival of Stars Copyright © 2007 Eilis Flynn
Edited by Jaynie Ritchie.
Design by Syneca.
Photography by Coka.

Electronic book publication May 2007
Trade paperback publication 2012

With the exception of quotes used in reviews, this book may not be reproduced or used in whole or in part by any means existing without written permission from the publisher, Ellora's Cave Publishing, Inc.® 1056 Home Avenue, Akron OH 44310-3502.

Warning: The unauthorized reproduction or distribution of this copyrighted work is illegal. Criminal copyright infringement, including infringement without monetary gain, is investigated by the FBI and is punishable by up to 5 years in federal prison and a fine of $250,000. (http://www.fbi.gov/ipr/)

This book is a work of fiction and any resemblance to persons, living or dead, or places, events or locales is purely coincidental. The characters are productions of the author's imagination and used fictitiously.

The publisher and author(s) acknowledge the trademark status and trademark ownership of all trademarks, service marks and word marks mentioned in this book.

The publisher does not have any control over and does not assume any responsibility for author or third-party Web sites or their content.

FESTIVAL OF STARS
ଔ

Dedication

This is for critiquers Angie, Jacquie, Linda, Roberta; for the hapa out there straddling two cultures and sometimes uncomfortably; for Emma and Aunt Yoko for their translation services; for Mike.

And for my mother.

Prologue

It happens once a year in the summer. If you don't look closely enough, you may miss it altogether. If it's raining, it may not occur at all. But if you know where to search the skies and the weather is clear, all you have to do is look. The star lovers will meet in the sky once more.

Gaze up at the evening sky at the right time of the year, amid the stars of the River of Heaven – the Milky Way – and if you're lucky, you'll see the Weaver Princess and the Cowherder meeting in the skies after spending a year apart, reunited on the wings of the star ravens.

Of course, that only occurs if the weather is clear. If it's not – if rain or fog prevents them from finding each other – the star lovers must wait another year. The torrential rains that summer sometimes brings are the star lovers, weeping in frustration.

Astronomers call them Vega and Altair, but those designations are so cold. When the Weaver Princess and the Cowherder finally meet in the sky, mortals on Earth celebrate the "romance of the Milky Way", as the ancient poems refer to the **Tanabata**, or the Festival of Stars.

The legend goes like this. The Emperor of the Sky ruled from his palace wrought of silver and gold and jewels of fire on the banks of the Milky Way, while his daughter, the Weaver Princess, had the task of picking the stars and designing the rich and bejeweled cloth for the gods of the constellations.

One day she met the Cowherder as he tended his herd on the banks of the River of Heaven. They fell in love, and in their rapture, they neglected their duties. The stars went unpicked, the cloth went unwoven and the celestial herd went untended.

When the Emperor learned that the Princess and the Cowherder were neglecting their duties, he became angry and in his fury sundered the River of Heaven, ripping the star lovers apart. Upon hearing their pleas, he relented, decreeing that if they tended to their tasks, they could meet once a year.

Toward this end, the Princess and the Cowherder are allowed to have help in the form of their servants the ravens, who spread their wings to bridge the River of Heaven so the star lovers can meet in the middle. On that day, it is the duty of the ravens to help the star lovers come together. Sometimes inclement weather prevents them from meeting atop the wings of the ravens. The rain and the wind rise and overwhelm them, blinding them and driving each away from the other. If that is the case, they must wait another year.

Sometimes when the stars shift in the sky, the star lovers are a little farther apart than they should be, and they struggle to reach each other. And reach each other they must. Unless they do so, eventually, the stars will shift away from each other, never to meet again.

If that were to happen, the star lovers will diminish, their lights fading from the luminance of the sky forever.

And so, each year, they must try.

Chapter One
First Year:
The rains fell in a torrent, blinding the lovers.

~

The summer rains fell hard that year, blinding those who traveled in it. The storm raged for better part of the day and the fog soon followed.

When Dare Borodin walked into the emergency ward cradling his right wrist, Kristin Olafsson was just two exam rooms away.

Dare was greeted by a clerk, whom it turned out he knew — but then, Pascisci, Indiana, was no metropolis, and the odds of running into someone he knew were high — and the two of them engaged in idle chitchat as he filled out the appropriate forms. That accomplished, Dare went into the waiting area.

He didn't wait long before he got antsy. Waiting was not his strong suit, and particularly not in hospitals. Pretty soon, he had an idea.

Dare glanced around. No one was paying attention. No one would notice if he left. Maybe he could just ice his wrist —

He felt it before he heard it. The back of his neck prickled, the fine hairs stiffened, his muscles tensed, waiting for the —

Boom!

A gigantic clap of thunder rattled the windows of the building, deafening him for a second. The overhead lights in the hallway flickered once, twice, before the incandescent bulbs shattered, spraying shards of glass and spewing sparks into the dimness.

Ignoring the shouts and rush of activity around him, Dare leaned against the wall, staring at the storm outside. The rain hammered at the windowed doors, as though each drop were a tiny battering ram, pelting the unyielding steel in a vain attempt to tear it apart. The flashes of lightning, almost directly overhead, gave him moments of clarity through the darkness, and he watched as all the people who had escaped through that exit came running back in, holding sopping newspapers above their heads. The gusts of wind that came in with them felt almost hot on his damp skin, making his wrist throb.

What he would have given for some ice right then. "Damn it," he muttered. He was stuck. He wasn't going anywhere until the storm eased up or the pain in his wrist eased up. Defeated, he made his way back to the waiting area.

"I don't understand it," a woman exclaimed as she limped in, dripping wet. "It was so slick. The rain came out of *nowhere*! Why didn't they say something on the news?"

Dare looked away, trying to control his smile. *They did, lady*, he wanted to say but didn't bother. The predicted thunderstorm had been the lead feature on the news that morning but it had still taken the locals unawares.

Well, he hadn't been surprised. But the elderly lady who broadsided him certainly had been. And *she* must have been surprised when her Chihuahua, which in turn was startled by the crackle and boom of the early thunder, nipped her ear. The woman lost control and her car careened through the intersection, hitting his own.

The icing on the cake? Apparently the dog had been sitting on her head when it happened. The elderly woman was being examined now—he could hear the dog yipping down the hall.

It would have been funny if it hadn't been so aggravating.

Sidestepping broken glass, he started to pace. With his good hand, he rubbed the back of his neck. The downpour would make the local farmers happy but it didn't help him at all. He had enough to do while he was back in town without dealing with an insurance adjuster—no, sorry, two insurance adjusters, the elderly lady's and his own—the rental car company *and* the hospital.

Not to mention his father. He knew they would have to speak sooner or later, but he had really been hoping it would be later. Say, right before he left town to say goodbye.

The rain was still coming down hard but at least the lightning had eased off. Not only that, there were three—what were they, crows? No, ravens—huddled in the tree right outside the door. He could hear an occasional *caw*, and once in a while, one of them would flap its wings, perhaps to ward off the rain.

"You idiot birds," he muttered. But it wasn't their fault either. It was just…one of those days.

Dare rubbed his wrist. He could come back later, just keep it iced for the time being. Had the drivers been this bad in Pascisci when he was a kid? Worse, had he been one of them as a teenager and he had somehow improved after, say, nearly being crushed by a maniacal driver in Helsinki or Paris or Berlin?

He could just go sit in the car, wait until the rain stopped. Then he could go back to his father's house and lie down. Maybe his nausea would go away after a while. Maybe the pain would abate.

Dare found himself walking down the hall before he thought about it. He walked away from the screaming kids and the babbling, shaken injured people in the dimmed waiting room, away from the smell of sickness, of death somewhere nearby. Better the cold silence of his father's house than the despair here.

From the exit door, it was a quick walk to the parking lot, and he could be back at the house in fifteen minutes tops. And back at the hospital *tout de suite* if his wrist swelled or got any worse. It was the best solution. He wouldn't be putting an unnecessary strain on the ER, and he could get back to packing. Win-win situation, and he was one step closer to leaving forever.

But why did he feel foolish? It might have been those ravens sitting in the tree. He could have sworn they were staring at him. It might have been because he felt as though he were doing something definitely not kosher, though all he had done was decide to leave.

Freedom was so close…another step, a push on the door, and he would feel the rain on his face and hear the hoarse cry of the ravens only feet away. Just another…

Yes.

"Mr. Borbin?"

He froze, his shoulder against the door, the breeze that rushed in already numbing the ache in his wrist.

No!

"Should I wait for you to come back, or would you like us to look at your wrist right now, Mr…uh, Borbin?" he heard.

Sighing, he turned around. "Borodin. With a 'd'," he said.

It was a woman, an attractive one at that, standing a few feet from him. She had to be a doctor, judging by the white lab coat and the stethoscope around her neck.

The look in her eyes…

He frowned. There was something about her, something familiar. Something he knew but didn't know how…

She looked him in the eye and opened her mouth to speak.

Just then, a light bulb exploded above them.

* * * * *

She flinched, stepping away from the shower of sparks and the gust of wind, raising her hand to protect herself even as the dim hallway became bright once again. Outside, the ravens perched on the red oak cawed and, in a flurry of activity, flew away. But she couldn't take her eyes off him.

Who *was* he?

He looked familiar, for no good reason. She knew she had never seen him before in her life. But...

It wasn't rational but there it was.

She stared back at him without knowing she was. He was nothing like anyone she had ever met there in that little town. He wasn't blond, which was a shock for Pascisci, home to generations of fair Scandinavians. His hair was dark — almost as dark as hers, but probably not for the same reason. She guessed he was Finnish. Not a farmer, even in the middle of the heartland — this man dressed like a city boy, had the face of one, his expression guarded, emotions closeted.

He was out of place, just like her. And somehow, oddly, familiar.

A conundrum today, of all days. Not something she needed right now. But there it was.

She took a deep breath and shook her head. "I'm sorry. Mr. Borodin? Are you all right?"

* * * * *

He glanced at the tag on her lab coat. It read "Dr. K. Olafsson", which confused, then amused him. She didn't look like an Olafsson. Perhaps she was wearing someone else's coat by mistake. "That's right," he answered, forcing away that odd, unsettling sensation of — *knowing*. "And you are?"

"I'm sorry. I'm Dr. Olafsson," she said. She smiled and he could have sworn the glint in her eye dared him to make something of it.

He liked that. He liked that a lot.

Aloud he asked, "What did you do, follow me down the hall? I had given up." He willed his heart to slow down, his breathing to even out. Whoever she was, no matter why she seemed so familiar, this was neither the time nor the place for him to pursue it. Especially not with his wrist feeling as if it were on fire.

Oblivious to his internal monologue, Dr. Olafsson—if that truly was her name—glanced at her clipboard. "You've been waiting about forty minutes," she said in answer to his comment. She looked him in the eye, which surprised him. He wasn't used to women being that tall, let alone an Asian. He remembered his mother as having been tiny, though she had probably been average height for her generation. "And I was coming down the hall for you when I saw you leaving. Now, if you could follow me?" She started to walk, looking at him over her shoulder.

That look was almost coquettish—but it wasn't, he knew that. If only. "Sure," he said as he followed her. "You're not from around here, I'll bet. You don't look like an Olafsson."

Wrong thing to say. She had been scribbling away on the clipboard, but at his comment, she stopped, and her back stiffened. She resumed walking, though, and he followed her into an area that was curtained off. She tapped the paper with her pen. "On the exam table, please, Mr. Borodin."

He obliged, still watching her as much as he could without actually ogling. That sense of wonder remained. But he had never met her before, he knew that.

Her dark eyes sparked like fire. Her mouth was just a little too large for her heart-shaped face, turned down slightly at the corners, as if she had to make up for having too lush a mouth for such sterile surroundings. She had a Swedish name, an Asian face, an American height and at the moment, a surly expression that could have scared men anywhere in the world. God bless America, he thought irreverently.

"You hurt your wrist," she said, scrutinizing her clipboard.

Definitely like no other Olafsson he'd ever met. Her voice was husky and he could have listened to it all day long.

She tucked an errant strand of hair behind her ear—silky, black hair, shining in the harsh overhead lights. He wondered how it would feel between his fingers. "Mr. Borodin?" she said. "Did you hear me?"

"Sorry," he said. "Yes. Car accident. I was turning the steering wheel and my wrist was in a funny—"

"Position when the car was struck. Does it hurt?" She reached out and tilted his hand.

He yelped, surprising himself and, apparently, the pretty doctor. "Yes," he gasped after a second. His heart was racing again, but it wasn't her presence this time.

He watched her wince. At least she didn't look annoyed anymore. He would take sympathy over annoyance any day.

He watched as she poked and prodded and did all those doctor-things to determine what he had done to his wrist. "We'll have to take some x-rays to make sure, but it looks like your wrist's going to be in a cast for a while, Mr. Borodin. You're lucky. It could have been a lot worse."

He expelled a deep breath. "Tying a tie's going to be a challenge."

Her reaction made him glad he had said something, because she glanced up, flashing a smile. "Would you like me to write you out a prescription stating you shouldn't wear a tie as long as you're wearing a cast?"

He laughed at that. "I guess you *are* Dr. Olafsson," he said. Summoning the first phrase he could think of in the appropriate language, he ventured forth with, "*Den ar ratt, ja?*" he said, watching her for a reaction.

He didn't get the one he expected. "*Ja,*" she said, sighing. Her mouth turned down a little.

"What did I say?"

She looked up, startled. "What? When?"

"You—looked disappointed, or something. You *are* Dr. Olafsson?"

She stopped cold. "Were you expecting someone Nordic and blonde?"

Hell. One innocuous comment, and he had managed to tick off someone with legal access to drugs and deadly implements. "*I* wasn't expecting anything."

Her expression changed when her eyes widened. All of a sudden, she looked like one of those porcelain dolls dressed in traditional kimono, hair lacquered into position and face in maquillage. "What do you mean?"

"Your bedside manner. Are you like this with all your patients? On, off, friendly, cold?"

She bit her lip, and he almost felt guilty. "I'm sorry," she murmured. She pinched the bridge of her nose, leaning against the counter. "I've heard so many comments since I've been working here, I just overreacted. I apologize."

He stared at her. "That's all right. I understand."

Her mouth twisted as she thrust her hand out. "Let me start over. I'm Dr. Olafsson. *Jag ar doktora Olafsson,*" she said in rusty Swedish, her eyes twinkling. "You must be Darien Borodin. So how's that wrist, Mr. Borodin?"

He looked at her, her eyes glowed with that dark fire again. He liked it. In response, he reached out and clasped her hand with his good one. He liked how her hand felt, slightly cool.

"Was that better?" she challenged.

"Much better." He hesitated for a second then said, "*Jag ar* Darien Borodin. *Goddag. Hur mar du?*" Pleased to meet you. How do you do? Crummy Swedish, true, but in his own defense, he hadn't used it in a while—

He was wrong. Her hand was warm after all. A faint scent of apricot and the softness of her skin touched his senses, not overwhelming them but sliding by, as if they had passed him in a narrow corridor and moved on. Strands of hair curled around her face, making her look as though she were nineteen.

Suddenly, he wished he had known her then.

His blatant attempt to get on her good side apparently worked, because she laughed. "I'm doing well, thank you. Your Swedish is way better than mine."

"I doubt my Swedish is any good." He was on safe territory now. He could feel it. "These days, I only use it in Swedish restaurants. I'm impressed," he said, changing the subject. "You've become much friendlier within seconds."

She smiled again. "I'm a very friendly person. *I* don't have any problems if *you* don't have any problem believing I'm Dr. Olafsson," she answered. Her cheeks were pink as she tucked a strand of hair behind her ear.

No ring, he noted.

"I've had patients who refuse to believe I'm Dr. Olafsson," she explained. "I got tired of it. I am so sorry."

"You have to remember, Dr. Hobaquist was the doctor a lot of folks around here ran to when there was an emergency, back before the town got this fancy hospital. I know I did. And you're clearly not Doc Hobaquist."

"I'm not sure if that's good or bad."

"Well, I think it's great."

"Thank you." She paused. "I need my hand back."

He looked down. Her hand was still nestled in his. His own hands weren't particularly large, but the sight of her hand curled up in his made him feel as though he were a giant. "Are you sure? Your hand feels so good there."

She smiled briefly as she withdrew. "I don't write that well with my left hand," she said. All of a sudden her nose twitched, and he realized he could smell his shirt drying on him after being caught in the downpour. But then she smiled, and he thought perhaps the smell wasn't so unpleasant. It reminded him of the scent of laundry drying on a line, in a home he had once, years ago.

"Are you going to need both hands for work?" she asked.

Back to business. "No. Do I look like I need both hands?"

She glanced at him over the clipboard. "You'll be surprised at how many things you need both hands for," she said, with that glint in her eye again.

"There's a double entendre there, but I'm going to be a gentleman and ignore it," he told her.

He was enjoying himself. Who would have thought visiting a hospital would have been the high point of his day?

She laughed. "You have a sense of humor, Mr. Borodin. You must not be a native."

That made him laugh, but he stopped when she covered her mouth with her fingers. "That was so rude," she murmured. "I'm so sorry."

He took a wild guess. "I'll bet you got tired of being the only non-blond in a ten-mile radius. Currently," he added. "I used to be it when I lived here." Most of the town's longtime residents were of Swedish descent, as blond as they could be, with an occasional Norwegian here or there, or even a Finn.

"Yeah, I do," she admitted. "How did you manage?"

He shrugged. "I got used to it. People thought I was a foreigner. Finnish," he added with a smile.

Her mouth curved. Her eyes were wistful, and he wished he could have been privy to her thoughts. "If only they could have thought I was," she commented. "But no such luck. Now, about your wrist—"

"I forgot about that for a second."

"That's our goal here, to make you forget your pains. If you're ready to be left-handed for a while, just go with this nice man," she said, gesturing to the physician's assistant who had stepped into the exam bay behind her.

Dare watched as his wrist was examined via x-ray and determined to have a hairline fracture. Soon enough, he was sitting in an exam room once more, this time sporting a cast.

When he saw Dr. Olafsson again, he was pleased to note his original assessment of her had been correct—she was still exotic. Now, though, she looked flushed. "Just have your primary care physician take a look at it, and have him call us," she concluded. He could see her pulse beat in the valley of her throat as she scanned her notes.

Not for the first time, he cursed the timing. "I'm going to be packing. I hope I can do that," he said.

She smiled at him and resumed her reading. "I hope you're not planning on doing a lot of it."

With a doleful glance at his encased wrist, he rubbed his knuckles against his jaw...with the wrong hand. He winced. "I've got to." He tried to flex his arm and regretted it. "Damn it," he said under his breath. "That hurts."

At that, she looked at him with a reproving glare. "Don't do that," she commanded. "Just take it easy for a day or two. Isn't there someone who can help you? A relative, a friend?"

"My father, but he's not going to be any help."

"A friend? You must have friends. Two. At least one?"

He gave her a half-grin. "Maybe even three. Maybe there's one who'd help me," he said, reconsidering.

"Well, see if he'll help you."

"I think she will."

"Good for you. Flirt a little. Bat those green eyes."

"They're brown," he corrected.

She leaned in and peered at him. He held his breath for a second. He could see his own reflection in her irises.

"Hazel," she decided as she straightened. She looked away, back at her clipboard. "Well, bat 'em anyway. Your ladyfriend will be unable to resist."

"I'll offer to take her out for dinner. You have more confidence in my persuasive abilities than I do."

She patted his arm, as though he needed comforting. Hell, maybe he did.

"Make an appointment for a checkup," she said. "Come in before you leave, and then we can make arrangements for you to see a doctor when you get back."

"But I'm—" He shut his mouth. He wasn't coming back but never mind. "Fine."

Her smile was professional again, and he found himself disappointed. Not being able to flirt again with the pretty doctor was going to be the only thing he would miss about Pascisci. "But in the meantime, take the day off, ask your friend to help and avoid other cars. And Mr. Borodin?"

He looked at her as he hopped off the exam table. "Yes?"

"Take care of yourself."

The lights flickered again as, once more, there was a rumble nearby. The wind had stepped up again—he could hear it.

Forever after, the rest of the day remained a jumble in his memory. The only part he remembered clearly was the remarkably non-blonde Dr. Olafsson.

Dare finally got up the nerve to call the hospital the next afternoon, after he had spent too much time trying to pack with one hand. He finally begged a favor from his friend.

A news segment on CNN about the Tokyo subway reminded him of Dr. K. Olafsson. His memory of the woman made him marvel. How isolated she must have felt, in this mostly farming community. As isolated as he had felt growing up here.

He picked up the phone but then he put it down. He wasn't used to being nervous. Certainly not over a simple phone call.

The third time was the charm. Dare picked up the phone and balanced the handset on his shoulder. He punched in the number, clearing his throat before he got an answer.

The voice was familiar. He sighed and settled in for the long haul. "Ginnie? It's Dare." Ginnie Venderkash, his late grandmother's dear friend and the hospital clerk to whom he had spoken the day before, was a tad loquacious.

"Dare, my dear!" the voice on the other end chirped. "How's your arm? Are you okay?"

"I'm fine, Ginnie," he said patiently. "I was wondering if I could talk to the doctor I saw yesterday. Olafsson," he added. He felt his face turning red. "I wanted to thank her."

"Dr. Olafsson? Oh, I don't know. Hold on." She came back. "Dr. Olafsson left, dear," Ginnie informed him.

"Do you know if she's going to be in tomorrow?"

"She's not with the hospital anymore, dear. Yesterday was her last day. She's moving home and she's taking her grandma with her."

He tried to be subtle. "So Dr. Olafsson decided to move back home with her grandmother? Where's that, on the East Coast?"

"No, Seattle. I hope Solveig's going to be happy there," Ginnie fretted. "But ever since Ole died, she's been talking about moving closer to her grandchildren, and when Kristin decided to go back, Solveig decided to go with her."

What a coincidence. "Seattle, you say? That's where I'm going on my next assignment."

"So I hear. Maybe you could look her up when you get there, see how she is."

"If she grew up there, I'm sure she's not going to have any trouble adapting, Ginnie."

"Oh, not Kristin, dear. I was talking about Solveig. I know Kristin's not going to have any trouble getting used to Seattle again. I think she was homesick."

"Well, I'll have to do just that. Look her up, I mean," he said. "When I get there. After I settle in."

"That would be nice. Did you need to talk to anyone else, dear?"

"No, it can wait, Ginnie. Thanks."

"In that case, say hi to your father for me."

"Sure," he said. He replaced the phone, musing.

Kristin Olafsson. A hell of a name for a nice Asian girl in the middle of nowhere.

Dare Borodin paused. He would have to look her up. The Seattle assignment was one he had taken because it led to his ultimate goal. Maybe he would have something to look forward to if he was going to be stuck there for a while.

One last thing. Before he forgot, he scribbled a note to his father—virtually the only way they communicated these days. "Ginnie Venderkash says hi," he wrote.

As he put down the pen, he heard a yell, a deafening crash on the second floor and then a thump-thump-thump down the stairs. Then a groan.

He froze. "Dad?" he called out.

Chapter Two
Second Year:
The wind and the rain rose, tearing the lovers apart.

೫ು

A year later, the huge gusts of wind and rain drenched the parking lot in sheets. The murder of ravens shrieked nearby in displeasure as paramedics wheeled Dare Borodin into another emergency room, this time in Seattle.

Not that he noticed. A red haze filmed over his vision and seemed to pulsate with every sudden movement, and all he could feel was the burning agony that encompassed his leg. He wanted to say something intelligible, but he couldn't think, he couldn't speak, he could only feel. His leg was bumped during the transfer from the ambulance to the gurney. His instinctive response was to scream and clutch at his leg. Mercifully, he blacked out.

The next time he opened his eyes, he found he was on a gurney, surrounded by pastel-uniformed personnel. His head was still spinning. He decided not to look around too much.

"What happened?" he whispered to no one in particular.

"You passed out, Mr. Borodin," someone chirped, just out of view. "Someone will be with you in just a minute."

"That's fine," Dare said faintly. "I'll just wait here." He brought his hand up and noticed with only mild surprise that his palm was bleeding. He vaguely remembered using that hand to slow his fall, skidding along sharp pebbles and stones and wet concrete for a few seconds before he collapsed in a heap of pulsating pain, the rain beating against him.

It would start hurting real soon, he thought. In fact, it hurt now. He closed his eyes.

He slowly opened his eyes again when a voice intruded into his pain-induced haze. This voice wasn't talking to him, but it was one he had heard before, he knew it.

He turned his head—or tried.

Someone walked past. A woman.

As it happened, she looked down at the same time.

For a moment, they stared at each other.

Hair so dark and shiny it looked like black satin; her eyes sparked like fire. And that mouth. He knew that mouth.

Who was she? The pain receded as he tried to focus. Then he remembered.

She laughed out loud. "You have a sense of humor, Mr. Borodin. You must not be a native."

The doctor from Indiana. The name. It was something he wouldn't have guessed—

"Dr.—Dr. Olafsson?" he whispered, ignoring the pain for the time being as he struggled to converse. "Aren't you Dr. Olafsson?"

She bent down closer to him. The faintest scent of apricot hit his senses, triggering the memory of a spirited conversation, and—something else. "Do you remember me?" he asked.

Probably she didn't, he thought vaguely, since her expression didn't change. But then her eyes widened just a little. "I'm sorry. I know we've met before, but—"

Dare tried again. The Swedish came back mercifully quickly. "*Mitt namn ar* Borodin," he said, trying to prompt a memory. He smiled, forgetting for the moment he was flat on his back, the human version of a minor car wreck. "Dare Borodin. *Ar min Svenska sa dalig?*" Is my Swedish that bad?

He racked his brain for all the Swedish he could remember. If he weren't in pain, he would have been embarrassed.

But it was worth it. He saw her stifle a smile. *"Jag har brutit armen?"* he continued, recalling lessons learned years ago. I broke my arm?

Well, it hadn't been his arm, but he couldn't recall the word for "wrist". And it had been a fracture, but he couldn't remember the word for that either. He tried to get up, but thought better of it when his head began to spin.

"Don't move," Dr. Olafsson said, pressing him back down. Then she stared at him for a second. He knew he looked like hell—again. He was wet, his face covered with cuts and bruises, and when she reached out and flicked at his hair, he realized he still had some twigs tangled there.

Actually, she would never have recognized him if he had been in one piece, clean-shaven and well-groomed. And dry.

She said after a pause, "Mr. Borodin, right? Pascisci? What happened? How did you get hurt this time?"

His eyes closed for a second. "A car and I had a face-off, and I lost."

That chirpy voice behind him spoke, startling him. "He was riding a bicycle. A passerby said a car that skidded in the rain hit his bike and he went head over heels. But he was trying to get up when the EMT crew got there."

She exclaimed as she cleared the hair off the gash on his forehead.

He could almost hear the sticky ooze of blood slide across his head. "That hurts," he mumbled.

"I'll bet it does, Mr. Borodin," she said, flashing a smile. "We'll take care of that."

Her face lit up. She snapped her fingers. "Car accident, in the rain. Another one. Right?"

"Right," he said, smiling as he took a deep breath. "Your last day at the hospital."

She nodded, brightening. "You're a long way from Indiana. What are you doing here?"

"Here in Seattle, or…here?"

"I can guess why you're in the hospital again. You hurt your wrist before, didn't you? Not your arm?" She glanced at the appendage in question.

He looked too, taking care when he moved his head. His windbreaker, threadbare to begin with, must have ripped when he hit the ground. The sleeve was torn half off, and the pocket hung by a thread, the zipper in pieces.

Summoning as much strength as he could, he tried to explain. "I don't usually look like this." He tried to sit up again.

Of course, that turned out to be a mistake. His head didn't vibrate this time, but every muscle in his body screamed.

He didn't think he had made a noise, but maybe he had, because she was right there urging him back down. "Mr. Borodin, just relax. We're going to take care of you."

"I just wanted to see how my leg looked," he persisted. He started to turn his head.

Her hands came up and stopped him. "Don't worry about that. But if you want to look, move slowly."

He did, and regretted it. "Jesus," he said. "It looks like something out of a horror movie." His left knee was bloody and swelling, coloring with the start of a horrendous bruise. He could feel his stomach roil just looking at it.

"Lie down," she commanded, her hand touching his shoulder.

"I think my helmet absorbed most of the impact," he said faintly as he obeyed.

"Your helmet was broken in two, so we can only hope it did. We'll take a look. You're a dangerous man, Mr. Borodin."

"I'm endangered, Dr. Olafsson," he answered.

"Bay 4," he heard her say, presumably to an orderly. "Dr. Malley's ready to look at him." She turned back to Dare. "It was good to see you again," she added with a smile. "Maybe next time we'll meet under less painful circumstances for you."

He watched her as long as he could before the swinging doors blocked his view. He wished she would come back but she didn't.

It was pouring the last time too, he reflected as he was wheeled into the exam room.

* * * * *

Later—much, much later—as he tried to figure out how to get home with a brace on his leg, he found his wish at least partly answered.

He was checking out cab services at the bank of pay phones when he felt a tap on his shoulder. "We meet again," he heard.

He turned. It was Dr. Olafsson, this time without the white coat, looking like a normal person, dressed in beige slacks and a brightly flowered, hot-pink aloha shirt that almost made him dizzy. "We do indeed," he managed.

She also looked less harried. "I guess you're still in one piece." She looked him up and down.

Once again he knew he looked less than impressive. True, he actually had use of both arms this time, but now he had to deal with a cumbersome brace and a pair of crutches. His windbreaker was history, leaving him in a T-shirt, exposing the scratches and bruises on his arms and hands, and what remained of his jeans after some quick fashion redesign. He could have looked worse but not by much.

"More or less," he said. "But I'll bet my bike isn't."

"You're not going to be on one for a while. How long did they say you were going to be in that brace?"

"Six weeks. But the collar's a short-term thing." Then he remembered. "Remember Ginnie Venderkash? She says hello."

Dr. Olafsson stared at him. He rather enjoyed the expression. It made her look as though she was a little girl, big brown eyes round and puzzled. "Ginnie?"

"Venderkash," he prompted. "Remember her? Pascisci Medical Center?"

Her brow furrowed. He wondered if that had been the way she studied through her medical school years, with that tiny line between her eyebrows. But it clearly helped, because she asked, "Ginnie the receptionist? Short lady, curly blue hair, rhinestone glasses, knows all, tells all?"

"Ayuh," he drawled, sounding like the Hoosier he had been. "Actually," he added, "that 'hello' wasn't for you. Ginnie told me to tell your grandmother hey and to make sure she was getting along okay. So is she?"

My God, she looked fifteen with that surprised expression. "She's getting along fine. She joined the local chapter of the American Daughters of Sweden and she found a Lutheran church near where we live."

"You live with your grandmother?"

"I live with my mother and grandmother. And my little brother."

"Doesn't that—" he paused. "Doesn't that drive you crazy?" The thought of living with his father again wasn't one he wanted to contemplate in any shape or form. In fact, the thought made him shudder.

"No," she said, clearly amused. "Should it?"

He had to ask. "How can you stand living with them?"

She shrugged. "We get along. You're not that lucky?"

"No," he said, and left it at that.

"I see." She looked him up and down again. "So, is someone picking you up?"

"It depends on whether I can find someone," he said, gesturing to the Yellow Pages. At least this time he had both hands to work with, as opposed to the wrist injury the previous year. His palms stung but at least they were both functional.

"Wife not home?"

"Wife nonexistent. Friends not home. Up a creek."

"Lost your paddle?"

He snorted. "Seems like it."

"Disorganized?" she asked, dimples popping out of nowhere.

"Very. Also, I hadn't counted on going this far away from home when I started out. I'm lucky I didn't lose my wallet."

She hesitated, then said, "Where do you live?"

"West Seattle," he said, aware of a flicker of surprise. "It's not far. I can find a cab."

"The faster you go home, the sooner you can relax," she pointed out. "I'll give you a lift."

He glanced out the entrance. It was still raining, but it no longer looked as if buckets were involved, only a steady sprinkler. And he could hear cawing, so at least the birds hadn't been scared away.

Dare looked at her. "You don't know me."

"No, I don't. For all I know, you're a stalker. Or a murderer."

"Do you offer rides to all your patients?"

"Only those who know my grandmother's old friend."

He smiled. "She was my grandmother's friend too. Thank you," he said. "I really appreciate this, considering you don't know me from Adam."

This time, she gave him an appraising look that began at his toes and made its way up to his face. "It's still raining. And you look harmless."

He exhaled. "Looks are deceiving."

"True. But I've also seen your medical reports. I know how to incapacitate you if you turn violent. Are you allergic to anything, just in case I have to sedate you?"

He began to laugh then stopped. Maybe she wasn't joking. "No," he said. He hung up the phone. "I'm at your mercy."

"You are. Why don't we pick up what's left of your bike while we're at it, Mr. Borodin."

"Dare. Call me Dare," he said. He leaned against the edge of the phone carrel. His leg ached again but he refused to admit to it right then. "Mr. Borodin's my father."

"I'm Kristin. And do you?" she asked, looking at him, a smile working at the edges of her mouth.

He met her gaze. "Do I what?"

"Dare," she said.

His breath stopped for a second. "When I can."

He couldn't think of anything to say after that—nothing he could carry through, at least.

The trip across the long bridge to West Seattle didn't take long, but it did take him a few minutes to remember exactly where he had been when he was hit. "Oh *Schiest*," he sighed, his years in Berlin clicking in as soon as he got a look at what was left of his bike.

He had the car door open before she could shift into park. Clumsily manipulating his crutches, he hobbled toward the pile of twisted aluminum and rubber, now sitting in a puddle of mud.

"Be careful! You're not used to dealing with crutches!" she shouted. He waved to indicate he heard but didn't slow down.

He was still nudging the remains of his bike when Kristin stopped beside him. "I hope it wasn't new," she said finally. She prodded at a dented handlebar with her black sneaker.

"No. I bought it at a yard sale." Carefully, he bent down and picked up a tire frame. He teetered, balancing on his good leg, but managed to straighten. "Maybe I can rebuild it."

"If my bike looked like that, I'd take it straight to the dump. You think you can rebuild this?"

He shrugged. He blinked hard to keep the rain out of his eyes. "I won't know until I try."

"You must have some workshop."

The admiration in her voice made him preen for a second, but then his common sense—what was left of it—made him snort. "I have a patio," he corrected her. "I'll spread the pieces out and look at them one piece at a time, renting whatever I need to fix it as I come to it."

"That's still pretty impressive."

He wanted to bask in the admiration but he couldn't do it. "I've got an ulterior motive. Until I'm out of this cast, putting this thing together again is going to be my hobby."

She picked up the second tire and held it at arm's length. "Sounds like you've got your time planned out for a few weeks," she observed. "But don't start today. Take the rest of the day off." She dropped the tire into her trunk.

"I don't think I have a choice."

"True. Why don't you just stare at the TV and wait for the painkillers to kick in? Your prescription's filled, right?"

He tried not to notice the rain was wetting down her bright floral blouse. He averted his eyes as she took the crossbar from him. "I can watch a movie, I guess. *Tak.*"

If she noticed, she didn't show it. "You're welcome. Now that I'm not patching you up, maybe you can tell me where you picked up Swedish."

"I took it in high school." He tossed in the last piece of crumpled aluminum and slammed the trunk shut. "I was surrounded by Swedes, so it made sense."

He paused and tried to gain the knowledge he sought in the most subtle way possible before he realized there was no subtle way. "Is Swedish your husband's language?"

But she laughed as they got into the car. "It was my dad's first language. And my mother's Japanese, before you ask," she added, answering the unspoken question.

What a coincidence. So was mine. But of course that wasn't anything he was going to mention.

He smiled. "And you grew up speaking a little of both?"

"Yeah. And English, of course. How—"

"Just a guess," he said, and left it at that.

His apartment duplex abutted the beach but was not the newest of structures, shabby, in need of some work. The street on which it stood was still mostly lined with bungalows that were pleasant during the summer but bitter cold when the winter winds whipped off Puget Sound. It was only a matter of time before the inevitable wave of luxury condominiums displaced these modest homes, but for the moment, the street had character that appealed to Dare. It reminded him of a home he could barely remember—a little place not far from the water, so long ago.

A trio of ravens attracted Dare's attention as Kristin parked in front of his duplex. They swooped toward the water, then soared up, around and back to land, seemingly impervious to the rain and wind. That in itself didn't strike him as odd. Birds were common around there, with an eagle's nest, even, close by. But this was the first time he had ever seen the birds so active during a rainstorm. Weird.

He was still watching the birds when Kristin came around. "Do you need any help?" she asked.

It was on the tip of his tongue to say no, but he stopped. He fished out his keys. "Could you open my door so I can fall into my apartment? I'm still getting used to these crutches, and it's going to take me a minute." He handed the silver loop of his keys up to her and watched as she headed to his door.

He knew what she would see—a few dishes in the sink, rinsed but not washed, laundry piled at the side of the washer/dryer, washed but not folded, newspapers next to the front door, ready for the recycling bin. Not neat, but not a sty.

By the time he got inside, she had switched on his lamps in the living room. "You need to relax," she said as he shut the door against the wind. "Why don't you sit down."

He crawled onto the overstuffed easy chair in front of the TV and heaved a huge sigh. "Sounds good," he mumbled. He swung his foot up onto the ottoman and removed the soft cervical collar from around his neck. "Man, that feels better. Thanks for everything," he muttered, grimacing as he massaged his neck. "I know what those poor dogs that wear these things feel like now."

He could hear her bustling around. From the various rattles, clangs and ding he guessed that she had found the Sanka and heated a cup of water in the microwave. "No problem. I was going to make you something to eat, but I'm not having much luck here," she called out. "You must eat out a lot. Or know how to make food out of instant coffee."

"I eat out a lot. Thanks anyway," he said, sitting up a little as she delivered the hot cup of coffee. "And thanks for the ride. Considering this has to be out of your way."

"From here to home isn't any more than ten minutes once I get on the freeway. Are you going to be all right? Can you take a few days off?"

He started to shrug then thought better of it. His shoulder was still stiff. "I may take tomorrow off." He swung his good leg up on the ottoman too. "But tonight I'm going to veg out in front of the tube. I'll be fine."

"Sounds good." He heard her start for the door then stop. "Is there someone you'd like me to call?"

He shook his head. "I'll order pizza, watch the tube and fall asleep." The Yellow Pages were next to him, the phone nearby, the TV remote control at hand. He was exactly what he seemed to be—a lonely bachelor. He would feel sorry for himself but he was too tired.

"Get some rest. Will you remember to take your pills?"

He nodded. "Sure." The haze filming his vision was from fatigue this time, not pain, but he tried to smile anyway. "Aside from being temporarily crippled, I'm fine. But thanks."

"Dare?"

"Yes?" He turned toward her, as much as he could without triggering a spasm of searing pain down his spine. He was going to be so sore tomorrow, with or without the pain pills.

She stood at the door, hand on the knob. She smiled, but this time, she looked uncertain. "Avoid the hills in the rain, okay? Next time, you might not be so lucky."

She left after that.

The apartment abruptly became silent. To compensate, he hit the remote control. The TV blared to life, louder than he expected. Suddenly, he heard a raucous clatter rise above the burst of noise from the TV. He looked up.

A raven sat on the windowsill, looking in. As Dare watched, the bird tapped at the painted-over frame. Then it looked at him, tilted its head and cawed.

"What?" Dare asked, amused.

The raven didn't answer. It cocked its head and tapped at the window frame again. Dare looked at the expression in its beady little eyes. He could have sworn it looked vaguely concerned. About what?

He had to be hallucinating. The pills must be working already.

"Thanks for your concern," he told the bird. "I'll see you tomorrow."

Perhaps that was what the raven was trying to communicate, for it pecked at the window one more time, then flew off with a hoarse caw.

Very weird.

That settled, Dare punched in the number of the local Pizza Time, placed an order, and sat back.

He opened his eyes when he heard the sharp rap. He hadn't even realized his eyes had drifted shut. At first he thought it was the raven, back for another conversation. Then the rap came again and he realized someone was at the door.

Groggily, he looked at his watch. "Not bad at all," he said aloud. "Pretty damn efficient delivery."

When the knock came again, he called out, "Gimme a minute," and eased himself up. Balancing on one foot and swinging the other was awkward, but at least he'd fall on his own carpet. He gimped over and opened the door.

He was concentrating on standing upright, so he didn't look up immediately at the delivery guy. "That was fast," he began.

"You expected me to come back?"

It was her again. She still looked fresh and sharp, and in front of her, he felt tired and dirty and infinitely adolescent.

"Sorry," he said, surprised. "I thought you were the pizza guy. What are you doing back here?"

"Professional concern," she answered. Belatedly, Dare noticed her hands were filled with plastic bags bulging with foodstuffs. "I figured you weren't going to feel like going to the store anytime soon."

"So you came back to feed me? You heal *and* you feed?"

"That and I still have your bicycle parts, so I decided to drop them off along with groceries," she explained. "Busy?"

"At the moment? A surprising lack of social appointments."

Her mouth curled. "Well, that's good, considering you're in no condition to go dancing."

He hopped out of the way and closed the door after she walked in. "I'll put this stuff away," she said as she strode to his kitchen. "I hope you like V-8. How about a salad?"

Not for the first time, he wished he were in better shape. "Thank you, but you don't have to do this," he said, his voice fading as another wave of fatigue hit him.

"Well, I didn't want to drag around your bicycle parts anyway. Humor me. I'm building up karma points."

Damn. "I forgot about the bike," he confessed. Or maybe not. At the moment, rebuilding a bike he would get rid of in less than two years was low on his list of priorities. "I hope I'm not keeping you from anything."

"Dinner in front of the tube," she replied. Then her eyes widened, and she looked fifteen again. "I wasn't hinting for an invitation. I'm so embarrassed."

Despite his fatigue, he smiled. "Would you like to share my pizza? If you like mushroom and peppers, half of it's yours."

"I don't want to put you out," she warned as she popped a quart of milk into the refrigerator.

He noticed that. "It was very kind of you to do this, but the milk's one thing I definitely won't use. Why don't you take that home? Do you drink milk?"

"You don't?"

He shook his head. "I'm allergic. Cheese is okay, though."

She nodded, looking surprised. "Fine. I have the same problem. I won't use it but my grandmother will. Are you sure you want me to stay?"

He shrugged. "I could use the company. And the pizza would have been breakfast tomorrow." There was a knock on the door. "Too late, Dr. Olafsson. The pizza's here. You *have* to share it with me now," he said as he hopped to the door again.

By the time he finished his transaction with the delivery guy, Kristin had managed to rinse the wilted lettuce, tear it up, and wash and slice up the apple. By the time he closed the door, she had ready the salad course, such as it was.

Dare paused with the flat, steaming box in his hand. "In front of the TV," she decided without hesitation. "You can keep your foot up. Sit."

Without a word, he slid the pizza box onto the side table and dropped back into his chair, sighing. His leg—aching again, and ready to be prone—went back onto the ottoman. "This is definitely a 'pizza in front of the TV' kind of night."

"That's for sure," she said as she came in, holding two salad bowls. He had bowls? "The rain's stopped, but the wind's kicking up. You're not going anywhere tonight."

"I hadn't planned on it. I'm not the dancing type," he added. He accepted a bowl and a fork and started to eat.

"Typical Y-chromosome," she sneered, that glint in her eye again. "You eat our food, and you still won't take us dancing."

"You never asked me," he pointed out. "Is this dressing? I had some?"

"You had vinegar and oil in your cabinets," she corrected. "I was shocked to see them."

"I'm shocked, too. I wonder how long they were there."

"Am I poisoning us?"

"Not likely. I haven't been in town that long." He snapped his fingers. "I've got it. Housewarming gift."

"So when did you move in? The expiration date on both the vinegar and the oil—"

"I only moved in a few months ago. None of that stuff could have gone bad this fast."

She nodded, kicked her shoes off and curled up into the chair opposite him. They were quiet as they picked at their food. He enjoyed this. He thought it would be awkward to be this intimate with someone he had essentially known for a matter of minutes. To his surprise, it wasn't.

In fact, he could have sworn he had known her forever. He stole a glance as she speared an apple slice. "So what do you do, anyway?" she asked, looking up and nearly catching him.

"Besides end up in hospitals?"

"I gave you a ride home, I made you a salad and I've even seen your medical records, but other than that, I have no idea who you are."

"I've had dates that weren't as informative."

"In that case, I don't want to hear about them. So how did you end up here?"

"Maybe I pursued you here," he suggested. "Maybe I'm a lunatic."

She wrinkled her nose. "Didn't you tell me you were a Hoosier?"

He chewed on his lettuce. "*Jag talar svenska,*" he said after he swallowed. I speak Swedish. "*Ya gavarit parusski,*" he continued. I speak Russian. "*Je parle le francais,*" he said. I speak French. "*Ya*—should I go on?"

"No, I get the idea. Not much translating work in Pascisci."

He shrugged. "I work for a company that specializes in technical translations. Seattle's my latest assignment."

She nodded. "Software?"

"Biosciences. Cattle."

"You translate technical jargon about *cattle*?"

He shrugged. "It's a living. I'm good at it."

"I can speak a little Swedish and a little Japanese, but I'm not any good at either. I can't imagine being good enough to speak in three other languages about cows."

It was on the tip of his tongue to tell her he knew more but he thought better of it. "I like it," he said, with no other elaboration. "I like being able to tell puns in three languages at once. I like being able to tell someone I broke my wrist, if I'm overseas, say."

"How's that doing, anyway?"

Once a doctor, always a doctor. "It's fine. My father broke his hip while I was in Pascisci, so I now know how to say 'He needs a physical therapist' in several languages."

"That must have been hard on your mother."

He opened his mouth, but found he couldn't do it. After all these years, it still wasn't something he could talk about. He shook his head. "It's just him."

He knew the look that came into her eye—a wary one, one that said beware, ahead was treacherous territory, lined with minefields and booby traps. He hated that look.

But he had to hand it to her, because she decided to walk through the minefield anyway. "Divorced?"

The mask he was wearing was turning into stone. He could feel it. He hated having it come over him, every time. "Dead," Dare said after a moment.

As always, the simple truth was the best.

"I'm sorry."

"Don't be," he answered, his voice getting stronger again. "It was a long time ago."

He stabbed at the stray lettuce leaf left in his bowl. He didn't want to look up. He didn't want to see her expression. When he could bear it, he looked up and said, "Thanks."

Her face relaxed. He could sense his own following suit. "I feel better. I guess the food helped."

"Not to mention taking off the collar," she said amiably. "Have some more pizza."

"I will," he said. But first, he watched as she stretched out onto the ottoman.

"My poor feet," she mourned, wiggling her toes inches from his own. "Those sneakers are new and they pinch. But at least my toes aren't black and blue."

He looked at his own and was taken aback. "Good God," he said after a moment. "They don't look good, do they?"

"No. Did they tell you you could put your shoe back on?"

His foot, bare of shoe as well as sock, was a vivid maroon, patchy and splatted all over and around. "He told me not to, but I wasn't going home without it on, so I put it back on after the doctor—Dr. Malley?—discharged me." He tried to wiggle his own toes and winced. "I'm not wearing any for now."

"Your feet will thank you."

Well, yeah, he thought. "You probably grew up with your shoes off. At least that's what I remember when we lived in Japan."

There, he thought. *I told her. No one can accuse me of being secretive about* that.

She lit up. "Oh, you lived there? When?"

"When I was a kid. My father was in the Navy. You?"

"Army," she exclaimed. "Where?"

"Near Tokyo." He was feeling a little queasy now that he had broached the subject. "But you take your shoes off in Pascisci, just like Japan, during the rainy season?"

She didn't notice he was steering the conversation. Why would she? "Yes, but not always. And when I visited my grandparents, they always got confused when I'd come into the house and take my shoes off if it wasn't raining."

He grinned as he imagined her as a little Japanese girl in the Scandinavian town. He tried to imagine her in pigtails and a grubby set of overalls and utterly failed. "In the middle of Indiana farm country? I don't doubt it."

* * * * *

They munched pizza as they watched Sunday night prime time programming, a TV movie involving a baby, a rancher and a woman in jeopardy—the plot of which Dare soon lost track of as the painkillers and the long day caught up with him.

Kristin noticed. Even then she waited five minutes before she quietly stood up, eased the remote from Dare's unresisting fingers and shut off the TV.

She padded into his bedroom and looked around for a few seconds before she found what she was looking for. She saw something that puzzled her, but she didn't have time to dwell on it. She picked up the worn quilt from the foot of the bed, came back out into the living room and covered him with it.

She leaned over and cleared the hair off his forehead. "Good night," she whispered. "And thanks for the pizza."

He stirred, and for a second she thought he was going to open his eyes. But he muttered in his dreams, then subsided.

She slipped her sneakers on, grabbed one of her business cards and scribbled a note on it. Then she left it on the side table and turned that lamp off.

She was already on Interstate 90, heading home, when she remembered she still had the pieces of his bicycle in her trunk.

She had a good reason to see him again.

Chapter Three
✷

"Borodin? Would that be Johnny Borodin's son, Kritchka?"

Kristin brightened, the warm blueberry muffin in her hand forgotten for the moment. "You remember him, Marmar?"

"I remember Johnny Borodin's mother. She was a dear. But Johnny?" Solveig Olafsson, Kristin's paternal grandmother, shook her head, her silver-white curls glinting in the warm morning light pouring into the breakfast room. "Johnny wasn't sociable, ever. I never would have known he had a son if Anneliese wasn't so proud of her grandson. Is he a nice boy?"

Kristin sipped at her coffee, acutely aware of the heat emanating from the sturdy ceramic mug. "He seemed like it. You don't remember him from when you were teaching?"

"*Sonna otokonoko wa dareh?*" Who is this?

Kristin looked up at the quiet voice. Her mother stood at the entrance to the kitchen, a rice paddle in one hand and a rice bowl in the other. Their gazes met, and without another word spoken, Kristin knew her mother had overheard at least part of the conversation and swiftly came to a conclusion. The right one, unfortunately. Her mother knew her too well.

She sighed, knowing that no matter what she said, between her mother and her grandmother, no secret would remain a secret. "Someone I met today at the hospital, Mama," Kristin said, adding in Japanese, "*Pascisci kara.*" From Pascisci.

Moyo Olafsson's eyes opened wide for a second, and there was a hint of curiosity there—but she didn't ask anything else. Instead, she headed for the side buffet, where the rice cooker sat, its contents piping hot. Nearly forty years as the wife of an American had not changed her preference for a good Japanese breakfast. "*Gohan tabetai?*" she inquired of her daughter.

It was a good Japanese breakfast or nuthin' for her mother, yes sir. Her mother was a woman of strong convictions. Unfortunately, because of those convictions, Kristin found herself eating two breakfasts sometimes.

But not today. Kristin shook her head, gesturing to her muffin. "*Iie, hoshikunai,*" she said, taking a bite. She held her breath for a moment, hoping she wouldn't get the two-pronged attack, from her mother and grandmother both, about a decent breakfast.

"So you don't remember him?" she asked her grandmother, avoiding her mother's gaze and turning the subject back to one that wasn't centered on *her*. Not this early, thank you.

Her grandmother shook her head again. "I don't think he took Social Studies from me, Kritchka. Wait, I think I do remember him!" she exclaimed. "Dark-haired boy? Tall? Quiet? So that's Johnny's son? Huh. I don't remember him looking much like his papa. He and Sven, they had a fight and Johnny's son took Social Studies from Mrs. Houderin after that."

There was a hush and Kristin glanced at her mother. Sven was a family story best left unmentioned. Moyo, however, said nothing, other than murmuring a soft "*Itadakemasu*", the traditional Japanese thanks for a meal about to be consumed, to eat her own breakfast of hot rice and fish. She wasn't going to get involved in a conversation about the family shame, Kristin guessed, at least not this early in the morning.

Nor was Solveig, who shook her head. "That Sven."

"*So ne.*" Moyo said nothing more.

Laconic as ever, Kristin thought. "He seems nice," she said, adding, "Mr. Borodin's son. And he knows Ginnie."

"Ginnie! Oh, how nice!"

Moyo glanced at her mother-in-law. "*Tomodachi*?"

"Friend," Kristin confirmed. "Good friend, Marmar?"

Solveig reached over and patted her daughter-in-law on the arm. "You remember," she said with a smile. "With the glasses?" She pantomimed a pair of harlequin-shaped glasses.

Moyo Olafsson laughed, nodding. "Of course," she said, her accent coloring her words. "Very nice. I like those glasses."

Smiling, Kristin let the conversation in fractured English flow past her as she sipped her coffee.

Not for the first time, she marveled at the similarities and differences between her mother and grandmother. They were both pretty much what they seemed—her grandmother Solveig a Swedish emigrant, married in the Midwest. Moyo, Kristin's mother, was a native Japanese born in Tokyo, but in her case she had come to the US only after she had met and married an American serviceman. And what they had in common essentially fit into this house.

Which included her. Kristin knew that paradoxically, she looked like both her parents and neither, making her background a challenge for those who met her for the first time.

She yawned, which she tried to stem, but too late. Her grandmother saw it.

"Do you *have* to work today, Kritchka?"

Kristin took a deep breath and rubbed her neck. "Yes, Marmar, I do. In fact, don't hold dinner for me."

"But you got home so late last night."

"I know. Today I'm covering for someone. It's going to be a long day." She pasted a smile on her face, knowing without a glance that both her mother and grandmother wore identical looks of concern. There were times when living on her own would have been far simpler, and this was one of them.

"Nobody likes putting in double shifts, but sometimes you have to."

"But you'll be sick too," Solveig said.

"I'm not that fragile." Now, at least.

Her mother frowned. *"Zuibun hataraiku ne,"* Moyo exclaimed.

"It's not so bad, Mama," Kristin said, and this time the smile on her face was unforced. "I can help people."

"But you could help and not work so hard," Moyo argued, switching to English to enlist the help of her mother-in-law.

As much as she loved them both, Kristin hated it when both her mother and grandmother, separated by upbringing and ethnicity but united in motherhood, ganged up on her. Invariably, it happened when she was barely awake, when she had to go to work bright and early in the morning.

This morning, she was tired and she was going to be grumpy if they didn't stop. So she simply said, "I do it for Dad," and took another bite of her muffin.

The silence that followed was of her own making. It had been her decision, no one else's, to specialize in emergency medicine. She was good at what she did. She just didn't like it very much, but that didn't matter. She had made a promise to the memory of her father, and she was going to keep it.

She ignored the familiar, faint prickle of tears. The image of her father, slumped over in his garden, no longer came to her unbidden. What did overwhelm her on occasion, however, was the helplessness, that feeling there was nothing she could do except watch as life seeped out, as it had with her father.

She had been too late to help him, but she had helped others in similar circumstances since. She was proud of that. She just wanted to be proud more often, without feeling as though she had something to prove.

Note to self—Avoid these cozy breakfasts when she had double shifts. The guilt on top of the work was too much. "I'll have tomorrow and the next day off," she said, closing the subject. "I can sleep in then."

The chandelier above the table started to sway when a distant crash startled her. The golden-yellow dahlias on the table trembled, but after the first jolt, she didn't react.

"He's up early," Kristin commented to no one in particular.

The French doors to the breakfast room swung open, deftly caught before they crashed into the walls. A dark-haired young man came running in, still buttoning his shirt as he slid into a chair. His dark hair glistened in the morning light as he reached for the jug of orange juice.

"Good morning," he said cheerily. "How is everyone?"

"*God morgon,* Eric. You're up early," Solveig observed.

Kristin's younger brother nodded as he reached for the bowl of hot rice that his mother had placed in front of him, picking up the raw egg in his other hand. "I've got to go over to the university. I need to get the books for my classes."

"*Baiku ni noranai de!*" his mother exclaimed immediately, a fine line appearing between her eyebrows.

"It's okay, I'm going with the guys, Mom," he protested. "I'm not taking the bike. It'll be fine." He tapped the egg on the side of his bowl and broke it open onto the rice, mixing it all together, with a splash of soy sauce.

Kristin barely noticed. *Tamago kake* was a typical Japanese breakfast, and it didn't occur to her until she was in her teens that raw egg over hot rice wasn't a breakfast that everyone ate. Even her grandmother, good Swede that she was, barely reacted, having seen it often enough over the years.

Her mother's quiet voice cut through the inane conversation. "Why don't you invite him dinner?" Moyo asked, enunciating.

"Mama?" Kristin looked at her, surprised but pleased. But her mother had to mean it. She had made a point of using

English instead of Japanese, so there would be no misunderstanding. "*Ii?*" Would it be all right?

She knew the American habit of inviting virtual strangers into private domiciles still startled her mother after all these years, as the Japanese kept their homes private. This was the first time her mother had suggested inviting to dinner someone she had never even met or heard of previously.

"*Obaasan ga ai shitai kara,*" her mother said to her, flashing a smile, not bothering to translate for Solveig and Eric. *Because your grandmother wants to meet him.*

Solveig's expression confirmed her daughter-in-law's comment in English. "That's a wonderful idea," she exclaimed.

"I'm sure you have lots to discuss," Moyo said, her amusement getting the better of her.

"Who's this?" Eric said, looking up from shoveling the egg and rice mixture into his mouth.

"Someone I just met at the hospital. Who, it turns out, is from Pascisci."

Her baby brother snorted but managed to keep eating. "That's amazing," he said, the words muffled. "What are the odds? Does Lars know?"

Kristin snorted, a flush creeping across her face at the mention of her ex-boyfriend and, unfortunately, old family friend. "You can scope him out when he comes for dinner. And it's none of Lars' business."

By the time she had the phone in hand later, she found herself regretting her decision.

Why was this different? Was it different because she'd met this man in Pascisci? She didn't know.

Dare Borodin wasn't home—or at least answering the phone—when she finally screwed up her courage to punch in the right set of numbers. His machine picked up.

She took a deep breath. Before she chickened out, she rushed on with her message and babbled something about the bicycle parts still in her car trunk. And before she lost her courage completely, she added, no longer even trying to be subtle, "You're probably not going to feel much like cooking for a few days, so why don't you come for dinner? You can meet my mother and grandmother, and you can gossip with Marmar about Pascisci. Call me when you get a chance. You have my card."

She hung up quickly, just in case he picked up the phone at the last minute. Suddenly restless, she wandered off, wondering if she should straighten up the living room.

She found out later Dare Borodin had called her service, but pulling a double shift meant it was the following day before she called him back. By then her fluttery nerves had subsided. Without hesitation she picked up the phone and punched out the number again—quick, before she lost her courage.

The ringing was cut short. "Hello?"

"Oh, you're home," Kristin said. Somehow, she thought she would get his answering machine again.

She heard him take a breath then chuckle. "I'm on short hours for a while," Dare explained. "The company physician took one look at me and said so. Or were you trying to avoid me?"

"No," she said, laughing. Well, maybe. She wasn't going to admit to it, though. "This is Kristin Olafsson, in case you didn't recognize my voice."

"I figured it out," he answered. She could hear something rustle, as if he had put his feet up. "Are you returning my call?"

"Yes, I am. When are you free?"

"I'm never free. There's always a price."

"I'm off tomorrow night. What about then? Do you like lutefisk?"

He took a breath, but then he said, "It's all right."

She grinned. No child who had spent any amount of time in Pascisci could escape the Scandinavian delicacy. Of course, after the first taste, most children ran and hid before they willingly took a second.

"Have you ever had it with soy sauce?"

"I don't think so."

"You'll love it," she assured him, tongue in cheek.

"I'll take your word for it. What time?"

Maybe he was allergic to lutefisk, she mused the next day as she punched up a sofa pillow in the gracious living room. Of course, most people didn't like lutefisk the first time they tried it, but then they'd never had it with soy sauce.

She was idly dusting the row of dollcases on the credenza when she heard soft footsteps behind her.

"Kritchka? Do you need help?" her grandmother inquired. "I don't want to disturb you, but I know this is important to you."

Kristin jumped. "I didn't hear you. I'm just making sure everything looks good, Gram, it's not that big a deal."

"These slippers your mother makes us wear inside are very soft," her grandmother informed her. "Changing from shoes to slippers still feels funny, even after all this time."

Kristin stopped her dusting, although she was still edgy. "You know it's the Japanese way, Marmar."

"Oh, I know. And this way, these beautiful wood floors don't get scuffed. I'm getting used to it."

"Kritchka, do you like this boy or did you ask him for me?" Solveig asked, changing the subject. She patted her cheek. "Even your mother must think you like this boy."

Kristin's cheeks warmed. "This is the first time she's ever told me I could bring someone home before I even thought to ask," she said, dodging the question.

But her grandmother knew. "It's time you got married, Kritchka," Solveig said, laughing. "Even your mother thinks so. If you're not quick about it, she's going to decide that even Lars might be a good prospect, though he's a doctor too."

"I know. 'Work too hard'," Kristin said, quoting her mother on the subject of doctors.

The conversation was becoming distressingly theoretical, and Kristin decided it was time for it to end. "Why don't we wait until the poor guy gets here before you make any decisions about my future? You might decide he would be the last man on Earth I should marry, and that would be that. I'd have to kick him out of the house, and go find Lars."

To her wonder—again; her grandmother was surprising her, one way or another, today—Solveig shook her head. "Not Lars," she said firmly. "He's a nice boy, but not for you. He wants things his own way and you want things your own way, but he's quiet about it and you're not. But you're a good girl to your old grandma," she added indulgently.

Kristin smiled even as she bristled. "I'm very good at give and take. My way is usually the best way, that's all."

Her grandmother laughed. "Someday you'll learn what compromise is, Kritchka." She looked up then and through the picture window.

Kristin's gaze followed hers. Together, they watched a late-model car move slowly down the street, pause in front of the house, then awkwardly parallel park.

"Is that his car, Kritchka?"

Kristin didn't look at her grandmother. She could feel her face grow pink as she watched the car pull into place. "I guess," she said as casually as she could.

Her heart was pounding. She didn't understand why.

"Well, I'll let you finish up here, dear," her grandmother said. "I'll help your mother with dinner."

"Okay," Kristin said absently. She was still looking out the picture window. "I'll see you later."

* * * * *

Only an hour previous, with a nervousness that both amused and appalled him, Dare had dug into his closet and brought out a blazer and a tie, even though Seattle was smack-dab in the middle of its traditional—brief—scorching summer heat. He was, after all, meeting somebody's mom and grandmom. It was, after all, the polite thing to do. He could do that much.

Dare got out of the car, taking his time as he hobbled to the tall wooden gate.

A pang of uneasiness overtook him, replaced by a rare streak of nostalgia, as sharp as ginger and as bitter as an orange pip. *That life was over and done decades ago, he reminded himself.* That had nothing to do with the here and now.

Grimly, he walked up the walkway and finally found himself at the front door. He rang the doorbell. As he was waiting for the door to open, he looked around. It was a pleasant place, as far as he could see. For someone.

But memory is a persistent thing.

The door opened while he was turned around. He took a deep breath and smiled as he faced the door again. "Hi," he said. He clenched his fist.

"I know you," Kristin said, stepping into the light and looking happy to see him. She looked beautiful, dressed in red and black. She smiled eagerly. "Come on in. *Welkommen.*"

He stared at her, and his stomach started to roil. "I can't do this."

Chapter Four

He watched as her bright, expectant expression morphed into confusion, and then concern. "Are you all right?" she asked.

His stomach was churning, and he didn't know why. Or maybe he did. But whether he could admit it was something else.

He was sweating. It was warm, but he shouldn't have been sweating like this. It was a pleasant evening, and he could feel a gentle breeze against his damp skin. Twilight was approaching, but he could see the gleam of lapping water at the other end of the house, hear the gentle wash of the waves. He willed the tranquil sight to calm him down.

It didn't work.

Gradually, he became aware she was waiting for a reaction. Any reaction. And that look of concern was turning into alarm.

"*What the hell is this shit,*" *he remembered his father growling, throwing his napkin down in disgust.* "*Why the hell would you think this is food?*"

"I can't do this," he repeated. He swallowed and tried to ignore the sour taste in his mouth.

She stared at him. "Do what?"

"I can't. I can't come in."

She glanced down. "Is it your leg? If you can't take your shoes off, Mom won't have a problem. A lot of people come in and don't. She knows it's an American thing."

He stared at her. "My shoes? What do my shoes have to do with anything?" But even as he said it, he remembered—

the Japanese custom of going shoeless in the house. He'd forgotten all about it.

"Taking off your shoes," she said, confirming his memory. "You probably can't bend comfortably. When I was younger, our friends only took their shoes off if they had mud on them."

His brow furrowed. This conversation was not going in the direction he thought it would at all. "I'm wearing loafers for a while. But—" he stopped, confused.

"Let's start over," she suggested.

"Yeah," he answered faintly. "I think we'd better."

"Glad you agree. Hello," she said pointedly. "Come on in. Or do you want to stand there all night?"

"No, of course not. I just don't think I should be doing this." He stopped.

She smiled, and he noticed she smelled like fresh-baked bread. He couldn't be doing this. It was a mistake. "I was just—" He paused. Could he think of a reason, any reason, to leave?

His stomach twisted.

"Isn't the view great?" Kristin enthused, not noticing his reaction. "Most people think it's the greatest view since Mount Rushmore."

He blinked. "What?"

She smiled again, but this time, her smile was a little less certain. "The view. When they see the lake out the back, most people just stare for a second before they come in." She paused. "Once they come in."

He smiled wanly, finally focusing on her. He was there. He was going to persevere. *Gambatte.*

Until the bitter end.

"Thank you," he said.

Gripping his crutches, he took a step forward, at long last entering the house. The first thing he saw were the neatly organized pairs of shoes in the alcove, the little stacks of house slippers on the side, so Japanese.

"When I say I want my dinner, I mean I want my steak and potato," his father snapped at his mother. "Why is that so hard for you to understand? Get that crap away from me. It's not fit for people to eat."

He looked around again but he wasn't seeing the house. "Thank you for inviting me to dinner," he said mechanically.

Kristin glanced down. "Shall I take those off your hands?"

Startled, he followed her gaze. He had forgotten he had arrived bearing gifts. "For the hostess. These are for you," he said as if on cue, to the older Asian woman who came into the foyer just then. "You must be Mrs. Olafsson."

She looked like her daughter and she didn't. Predictably, she looked the way her daughter might look in thirty years or so, but petite, almost classically Asian, tiny hands, tiny feet, her back straight, the way she had probably been taught when she was little. Instead of a dark kimono, however, she was dressed in a royal blue sheath, with a frilly apron over it. He guessed she was dressed for the occasion.

His stomach twisted again.

Shifting his crutch, he held out the bouquet. The flowers were a gorgeous riot of color, picked out at random at the florist. Stargazer lilies fought for attention with white and pink roses and orange bird-of-paradise and it was all wrapped in baby's breath and greens.

She smiled and bowed. "Thank you," she said formally, accent thick. Then she turned. "Kristin?"

Kristin took the hint. "This is my mother, Dare. This is Dare Borodin, Mother," she said formally.

Mrs. Olafsson bowed, and he nodded back, barely stopping himself from bowing. He was an American, after all. No bowing. She was polite and formal and now she had to be gracious, didn't she? Of course she did. This was her home and he was a stranger her daughter had picked up somewhere, out of the gutter. He blinked, trying to ignore the flood of unexpected, unwarranted bitterness.

His father's voice came out of nowhere again, twisting his stomach. "Americans don't bow. What am I, an opera singer? Damn stupid."

"How is Seattle compared with your home?" Moyo asked. She was the very model of a modern Japanese matron, wasn't she? Of course she was.

He said the first thing that came to mind, which was, "Seattle's a lot hillier, ma'am." After the words came out of his mouth, he could have cursed himself.

"Yes, that's true," she replied, but by now she had turned and he couldn't see the expression in her eyes. Then she looked at him and he froze, startled she would have caught him looking at her.

Again, she didn't seem to notice anything was amiss. "*Ochawan motte kiteh,*" she told Kristin.

He started to nod before Kristin said quickly, "Why don't I bring out some tea?" Without waiting for an answer, she turned and slid down the hallway, skimming along on the polished wooden floors with her house slippers.

Dare watched her go. "Should I take off my shoes?"

Kristin's mother looked up, startled, looking like her daughter in that instant. "Oh, no, not necessary," she said. She smiled reassuringly. "Come in."

Dare followed her into the living room and carefully sat down, his hands clasped in an unconscious gesture of supplication as soon as he put aside his crutches. "Thank you for inviting me to dinner, Mrs. Olafsson," he said again. He could feel a bead of sweat at his temple. "Are you sure I shouldn't take my shoes off?"

"Oh, no," Mrs. Olafsson said again.

"This is an American home, Mr. Borodin," a new voice said.

He looked up. An older, silver-haired woman, of European origin, had joined them, with an apron that was exactly like the one the younger Mrs. Olafsson wore. Again, he could both see and not see Kristin in her face. "You must be the senior Mrs. Olafsson, Kristin's grandmother," he said as he stood up. Or he tried. He got halfway there before he lost his balance and sank into the sofa again. "Sorry," he muttered, reaching for his crutches.

The older woman was the very heart of the American Midwest. She was wheat and corn and even soybeans. If Dare had liked his father's hometown at all, he would have been nostalgic.

She smiled, and Dare could see which side of the family Kristin's dimples came from. The knot in his stomach eased a little. "No need to stand, Mr. Borodin. You're Johnny Borodin's son?"

He nodded. His gaze shifted between the Asian woman and the older, Caucasian one, and raised his hand. "Ginnie Venderkash says hi," he said, finally delivering the message that had taken him all of a year and two trips to the emergency room to pass along.

The elder Mrs. Olafsson smiled delightedly. "Ginnie!" she exclaimed. "How is she doing?"

"Last time I heard, she was fine," he stammered. He hadn't expected to be quizzed on details. In fact, her information was probably fresher than his was. But he didn't see the point in telling her that.

"Mr. Borodin brought flowers," Kristin's mother said, gesturing to the array of blooms. "If you excuse me, I will arrange these in a vase," she said to Dare, bowing again.

"Of course," he said hastily. "I hope you like them."

"They're very pretty," Kristin's grandmother assured him. Out of the corner of his eye, he watched as Kristin's mother disappeared around the corner.

Dare turned and met the gaze of Kristin's grandmother. There was something of Kristin in her, all right—not the coloring, but the cheekbones and the slant of the eyes echoed her granddaughter's. Searching for a topic for conversation, he asked, "Do you miss Pascisci?"

She looked back at him and smiled. "Sometimes. You don't favor your father," she commented. Quietly, Kristin's mother reentered the room, holding the flowers, now arranged in a cylindrical black vase. She knelt in front of the coffee table with a grace that belied years of practice in a kimono, and placed the vase in the center.

Dare nodded. "I know. Thank you, Mrs. Olafsson," he said to Kristin's mother. She nodded, and just as graciously, rocked off her knees in a smooth motion before sitting on the club chair behind her.

He watched her do it, and this time it was his heart that twisted. So familiar. And yet not.

Just then, Kristin came in with a tray. The teapot was a traditional American silver one, and the teacups made of delicate china and matching cream and sugar pots. Very Western. Wordlessly, she started to pour, her hands carefully cradling the pot. Very Japanese. She handed him a cup.

"Coffee. Coffee's a man's drink. Why the hell would you serve me tea? I'm not one of your pansies you got over here." *He could still see his father's face twist in disgust at the sight of the light green steaming liquid. And then he didn't see the tea, because his father threw the delicate cup across the room, shattering it against the wall.*

"Milk for your tea, *ja*?" Kristin's grandmother asked. "Sugar?"

"No, thank you. Neither," Dare said quickly, nodding to Kristin and then at her mother, who didn't say anything. She sat and smiled, withholding judgment. "So how long did you live in Pascisci?" he asked the senior Mrs. Olafsson, willing his mind to stay away from the memories and concentrate on the present, only the present.

She cocked her head. "Nearly sixty years."

He nodded. "That's a long time."

"It certainly was," she agreed cheerfully.

There was a pause.

"So how is your father?" she inquired again.

Another question he should have expected but hadn't. He opened his mouth again and almost told her it had been months since he had spoken to his father, but decided not to. "The last time I spoke with him, he was fine," he finally said.

"Is his hip hurting him still?"

"The last time I spoke to him, it was still aching some," he said, stammering slightly. For all he knew his father was turning cartwheels on his way to recovery these days.

He looked around, trying to think of a topic. At that point he realized he was still holding a plastic shopping bag. And if he weren't careful, he could accidentally hit it against something and it would burst.

Kristin noticed it too. "Would you like me to take that?" she inquired. Like her mother had, she knelt, and like her mother, she rocked herself to a standing position.

It was an art and it was a skill and he had not seen it in such a long time.

"Yes," he answered, trying to stand and not succeeding, holding out the bag and not falling back onto the sofa, all at once. "It's the milk you got for me," he explained.

"You brought it?" Kristin asked, surprised. "I'd forgotten."

"I'm allergic," he said, looking her in the eye and ignoring her mother's expression. "I use a soy substitute."

"Allergic to milk? You must have had a hard time in Pascisci," the elder Mrs. Olafsson observed. "All that milk."

He shrugged. "You get used to it." He took another sip. He couldn't tell what kind of tea it was. It didn't matter.

"Why don't you go for a walk before dinner?" the junior Mrs. Olafsson suggested.

Kristin nodded. "As soon as I put this away," she said, gesturing to the milk. She disappeared down the hall, sliding on her slippers again.

Dare was reaching for his crutches as his eyes met those of the senior Mrs. Olafsson. He was curious. "Do you understand any Japanese? Any Swedish?" he asked Kristin's grandmother and mother, respectively.

The elder Mrs. Olafsson smiled. "One or two words. That's about all." The younger Mrs. Olafsson shook her head, smiling faintly and watching him intently.

"Doesn't that frustrate either of you?"

"Not really. Of course, when my husband was alive, I would speak Swedish with him. Now that he's gone, I speak it with my granddaughter."

"So you and Kristin's mother only have English in common?"

"Moyo and I have known each other for many years," Kristin's grandmother said. "We don't need that much to understand each other."

He thought about it for a second, glancing at Kristin's mother. She met his eyes, but he couldn't read their expression. "It must have been tricky," Dare ventured. "Painful sometimes."

"Life is a series of balances," the elder Mrs. Olafsson said. "We get by."

"I'm sorry to interrupt, Marmar, Mom," Kristin said, coming in again. "Dare? Would you like the tour before dinner?"

"What a nice idea," Kristin's grandmother exclaimed, standing up. She nodded to Dare then, a gesture as Japanese as it was anything else. Kristin's mother followed suit. "We'll see you soon, young man."

The house was spacious and surprisingly airy, almost as much window as it was wall. Kristin gave Dare a short tour of the ground floor before she led him through the back door.

It wasn't what he expected. He could see the shining waves of the lake, but at the end of a path lined by tall wooden fences on either side. His puzzlement must have reflected on his face, because Kristin smiled. "Daddy and Mom—well, *Mom* has fenced gardens," her voice faltering momentarily. "Here, I'll show you."

She placed her hand on his elbow—he looked at her in surprise, the churning of his stomach forgotten for the moment—and led him over to a wooden gate that was almost hidden in the fence. Even before Kristin opened it, he could hear the soothing sound of water bubbling from within.

Once they had slipped inside, the minute sounds of civilization from without the walls abruptly vanished. The bamboo trees and the high wooden fence acted as insulation. Within the confines of the walled garden, all he could hear was the peaceful gurgle of the pond.

He looked around the small enclosure. "It's so quiet here," he said, his words almost instantly absorbed into the silence.

The area was small, manicured into a Japanese garden. The walls themselves were almost hidden by the thickets of bamboo, and in the center of the garden was the pond he had heard, with water lilies floating on the surface.

He was surprised to see a cluster of golden and orange koi suddenly heading toward them, disturbing the stillness of the water. He smiled. "They must know you," he whispered.

She nodded. "I like to sit here sometimes," she said, her voice a little closer to normal.

Dare looked around. "I can understand why."

She led him outside again. This time he took her hand first, never mind his crutches were in the way or his regrets.

By then, the sun was sinking into the horizon, suffusing the sky with the colors of fire. Dare had to squint. After the tiny, manicured garden, the waterfront was broad and bright in contrast. There were the remnants of a dock there, but it had fallen into disrepair.

There was an abutment of stone next to the remains of the dock. The rock was flat and looked as though it had been worn smooth. Dare guessed why that might have been the case, as Kristin sat down on it, legs dangling over the edge.

She patted the space next to her. "This is my favorite spot," she told him as he carefully settled in beside her, sliding the crutches behind him. "You can look across the water and almost make out what the people on the other side of the lake are doing. When I was a kid, I always wondered what they had for dinner. I knew they didn't have rice and fish every night, like we did."

He smiled. "Did it occur to you that they might have been looking across the water and wondering about *your* dinner?" The water lapped against the shore, the soothing sound masking the noises of the city. "They probably knew you weren't having hamburger casserole every night, the way they were."

She laughed. In the twilight, it sounded like a bell, wrought from silver and shaped with patient, loving care. "I think that finally occurred to me when I was in high school."

"That occurs to everyone when they're in high school," he said. Tentatively, he put his arm around her. Much to his delight, she nestled into the curve of his arm.

It felt natural. It felt good. He liked it. His stomach didn't feel as though he were going to lose it anymore.

They were silent for a while. He became aware of her even breathing, the rapid beat of her pulse echoing in him.

Then Kristin broke the quiet. "Can you figure out what that light over there is?" she said, her voice hushed.

She pointed. There was a steady light, brighter than others around it. He looked at it for a second, then at her.

The evening was cooling, but he couldn't tell that from the way he felt right then and there. Her breath was sweet. Her hair smelled faintly of apricots. "I have no idea," he whispered. He stroked her cheek.

He gently turned her head so she faced him. "May I?" he asked. His lips paused in front of hers, awaiting an answer.

In the twilight, he couldn't see the expression in her eyes, but he could feel her breathing pause. "Please."

He touched his lips to hers. The rush of adrenaline threatened to overwhelm him at first. He tried to concentrate, exploring her trembling mouth, then feeling an echo of triumph as her lips parted and a murmur rose from her throat. He brushed away strands of hair to expose the curve of her cheek and her temples. Her skin was exquisitely soft.

But then he remembered where he was. He asked, "How many of your dates have you taken out here?" as he dropped his hand from her face. He glanced up at the house. The walls of glass on both the first floor and the second were ablaze with light, but as far as he could tell, no one was silhouetted in them.

Kristin smiled. Her lips were swollen and her hair slightly mussed, but aside from her half-closed eyes, she looked—

She looked as if they had just participated in more than a kiss. She looked as if they had just made love for hours.

The idea, while immensely attractive, was not conducive to an evening with her mother and grandmother.

"Why do you want to know?" she asked, interrupting his thoughts. She followed his gaze up to the house. She grinned. "They're not going to be looking. When I was sixteen, you bet they were. But I'm not sixteen anymore."

Tempting. "In that case—" With another glance at the house, he leaned over and kissed her again, this time making it quick and cool.

Then the sun gasped and disappeared over the horizon, swallowed whole in an instant. A cooler breeze off the lake eclipsed the warmth of the day almost instantly.

Kristin shivered. "Dinner soon," she predicted. "Marmar and Mom have dinner ready by the time the stars are out."

"Can you see the stars from here?" he asked, looking up at the sky. His mouth dropped open. "My God," he exclaimed. He could have sworn that the skies had been clear and empty just a second before, but with the disappearance of the sun, the stars—"It's an explosion up there," he whispered.

"You must be out here every night," he exclaimed. He settled back onto the stone behind him, staring up all the while, all the thoughts he had had about Kristin shoved to the back of his libido for the moment.

"You get used to it," she said. He could feel the warmth of her arm as she settled next to him. "If you're interested, we can dig out the telescope my father set up on the patio."

He propped himself up on his elbows and looked over at her. The sight of her on her back, looking up at him, reminded him for a moment what he had been imagining just a few seconds before, her black hair spread out on the stone. "You must have known all the stars by heart," he told her, his voice hushed in wonder. "I would have."

"Oh, I did. My father taught me," she said. Her voice was contemplative. "During the summer, we would spend most of our evenings out there. Eric was just a baby back then. Daddy would find Orion or another constellation, and he would tell us the Greek myth, and then my mother would tell us the Japanese story behind it."

Dare could see it in his mind's eye, and his heart twisted for a second. Silently, he compared it with the way he had learned about the constellations—at the library.

Kristin looked up. "Dinner's ready," she said. She scrambled to her feet and held out her hands for him.

He looked up. He could hear—what was that, a bell? "What is that?"

"It's a gong," she replied, "and when we were younger, that was how Mom got us to come in." He grabbed her hands and dragged himself up, settling his arms over the crutches she held out for him. "Ready?"

He nodded. Slowly, they walked up the direct route to the house. "So your mom, she called your dad in with the gong too?"

"My little brother. He'll be at dinner." They reached the patio. "Can you make the steps?"

He assessed the flight of steps, broad and shallow. "I should be able to." He hopped up the steps, using the crutches for balance, acutely aware of Kristin coming up behind him. He made sure he was moving with as much dignity as he could. *Considering I'm hopping like I'm Bugs Bunny here*, he thought grimly, *complete with "Doc"*.

The patio door couldn't have come soon enough. Kristin skipped up and pushed it open for him. "Now that wasn't so bad, was it?" she said cheerfully.

"I guess not," he answered, rotating his shoulder carefully. Crutches were not designed to climb stairs, but he managed it anyway.

By the time he had washed up, the twisting knot in his stomach was back, and it was getting tighter and tighter. On his way back to the dining room, he took a wrong turn, and after a moment's indecision, he veered in the direction of the voices he could hear. One of them sounded like Kristin's.

He found himself at the kitchen entrance. There was enough commotion and activity that his presence wasn't immediately noticed. Kristin was there, as he had guessed. So were her mother and grandmother, and they all seemed to be engaged in the cozy activities of getting dinner ready.

As he watched, Kristin scrubbed her hands with hot water and soap. "The table's set," she said, drying her hands on a bright yellow towel nearby. "What's for dinner?" She peered over the shoulder of her mother—not difficult, considering she was more than half a foot taller.

He flushed in embarrassment. He was intruding. This was a family area. He cleared his throat. "I'm sorry. I got lost on my way back."

Kristin turned first, then her mother and grandmother. She smiled quickly. If she was annoyed, it wasn't apparent. Nor did the junior and senior Mrs. Olafssons seem out of sorts. "It's okay. Come on in," Kristin said.

He hobbled in, making sure there wasn't anything wet or slippery on the floor. If nothing else, he was getting tired of visiting the emergency ward. "Nice kitchen," he said inanely once he reached her.

It was spacious and state of the art, and as he watched the two Mrs. Olafssons finish up, he realized it had to have been designed for multiple cooks—or at least two with very different cuisines in mind.

Kristin's next words confirmed his impression. "It *is* nice, isn't it? It's got enough space for both Mom and Marmar, and even Eric and me," she told him. "Take a look at dinner. It's Balls Olafsson."

He quirked his mouth. He was fairly sure that hadn't come from Betty Crocker. "Family recipe?"

"Balls Olafsson" was a combination of Japanese and Swedish cuisine, a true family recipe, Kristin explained as she raised a pot lid for him to look into. Early in her mother's marriage, she and her mother-in-law had accidentally mixed up their dinner preparations. The junior Mrs. Olafsson had been preparing fried chicken balls, a Japanese dish, while the senior Mrs. Olafsson had been preparing Swedish meatballs— and after the accident, they had agreed to cover the result with gravy. The result was surprisingly tasty, and after that, it had become a family favorite.

Kristin's mother flashed a smile, perhaps as she amended the culinary accident with her own memories. "*Kyuri o kitte,*" she said, indicating the cucumbers in the colander.

"Sure," Kristin said as she slid the vegetables over to the cutting board.

"Can I help?" Dare asked.

"Hm. *Pan o tehburu ni motete,*" Kristin's mother said.

He was looking around for the bread when Kristin answered, "Sure," arranging the cucumber slices in a dish. "Where is it?"

Before her mother could answer, Kristin's grandmother wiped her hands on a towel. "Kristin dear. Take the bread in to the dining room, please?"

Dare froze for a moment, but no one noticed. "Sure, where is it?" Kristin repeated.

"I already took it in," a new voice piped in.

Dare turned. A boy who was probably old enough to consider himself a man, wiry and still growing, came in the back door, his arms full of tomatoes. The kid vaguely resembled Kristin's Swedish grandmother, except his eyes and hair were dark.

The little brother, Dare realized.

The kid said, "I took the bread in before I went out to the garden. Where do you want these, Mom?"

"*Soko,*" his mother replied, pointing to the shallow sink. "*Hai, domo. Sore mo kitte, Ki-chan?*"

"Sure, Mom. Eric, this is Dare Borodin," Kristin said, gesturing with a knife. "Dare, this is my younger brother, Eric. Why don't you both go into the dining room?"

"Sure! Let's go, Dare!" Eric said. He blasted through the far doors, presumably to the dining room, leaving Dare to wheel around and make his way at a much slower pace. "Amazing how much noise that boy generates," Kristin's grandmother commented with a chuckle. "He was such an annoyance getting ready for dinner I had to send him out to pick some tomatoes."

"I'm just surprised he's here," Kristin commented.

"Oh, I think he was curious about your date," the senior Mrs. Olafsson said, her eyes twinkling.

Dare's cheeks flared red. He glanced at Kristin out of the corner of his eye.

She rolled her eyes. "I'm going to regret this, aren't I?"

Dare decided he didn't have to be there. With a nod to the older women, he trudged through the kitchen to the dining room.

Again, the room looked as if it had been lived in and appreciated, with a close-knit family. There were memorabilia, including photographs, and if he had been any more comfortable he would have gone straight there to examine them.

But he wasn't comfortable, his stomach was threatening rebellion, and his misgivings were tenfold now. But he was going to get through this. "Any particular place I should sit?" he asked Eric, who had sat down with an ease that spoke of claiming his usual place. The table was generously sized, big enough for a family, mom and dad and the kids and whoever else was around, having their meals together and enjoying each other's company. It was topped with a white tablecloth and tea candles in short fat blue candleholders, with china and cutlery arranged carefully, little swan napkins at each place.

Dare's stomach was twisting in pain by now. The napkins had probably done the trick.

He took a deep breath.

"I think Kris meant that place for you," Eric said, pointing. It was directly across from the younger man, who leaned forward. "So Kris tells me you got hurt riding a bike. Are you a cyclist or just klutzy?"

"Both," Dare said after a moment of surprise. No mincing words with this kid. "But this is the first time I've ended up at the emergency room riding a bike."

"Cool! I've only been at the emergency ward once too. A few years ago, a car hit me and flipped me over," Eric informed him. "My bike helmet broke in two. Mom took me to the emergency ward to make sure I didn't have a concussion."

"Did you?" Dare asked, not sure whether he should ask.

"Nah. So what kind of a bike do you have?"

By the time Kristin, her mother, and grandmother sat down at the table, Eric had managed to drag Dare into a long, drawn-out conversation about cycling. From what Kristin mentioned, the boy's father had died a number of years ago, and it was probably rare for Eric to have another male to talk to at home.

At least the conversation distracted him from his need to get very, very sick.

But when the women came in, Dare decided there was something he should be an example for, and so he stood, holding onto the edge of the table. After a surprised moment, Eric followed.

"Eric! When did you develop manners?" Kristin said as she seated herself. Dare, however, on the other side of the table, did his utmost to try to pull out the chairs for both Mrs. Olafssons and succeeded only in endangering his balance. Eric, taking Dare's cue, raced to finish what Dare had started.

"Thank you, Dare, Eric," Kristin said finally, more than a little mystification in her voice.

Dare looked across the table and smiled at her expression. *I'm polite when I need to be*, he tried to tell her silently.

He felt good about that—or he would have, if not for the growing unease in his stomach. It seemed to be growing to a crisis point. No. *No.*

Kristin smiled, and there was a touch of pink in her cheeks before she broke eye contact and her mother and grandmother started to serve.

He was almost feeling good, almost ready to congratulate himself on keeping himself intact, until he noticed the rice cooker, large economy size, sitting behind Kristin's mother on the sideboard.

That was it. The sight of it took him back, and back and back. And that was it.

It reminded him of something he didn't want to remember.

"God damn it, what is this, bugs? Decent people don't eat shit like this. Why can't you cook anything that tastes decent?"

And that was it.

"Why are you putting insects on the rice?" he heard himself ask, much to his horror, when he saw Eric sprinkle black sesame seeds on his bowl of rice.

"And this looks like crap," he heard himself continue, channeling his father. He wanted to die. "And it smells like it too."

There was a dead silence at the table. He couldn't lift his eyes from his plate. He knew what he would see reflected in the eyes of those around him—pain, embarrassment, dismay. He wished he *could* vomit.

"It's *natto*," he heard Kristin say after a moment, confusion in her voice. "It's fermented soybeans. If you don't want it, that's fine."

"And what is all this, fish bait?" he heard come out of his mouth, compulsively, repulsively. "What the hell is this supposed to be?"

"It's broccoli in tempura," Kristin answered. Her voice was very, very even by then.

His hands started to shake. "It looks like cow intestine. On a bad day."

He couldn't stop. Everytime he opened his mouth, something ill and foul came out. This was what he had been afraid of all evening, that feeling in the pit of his stomach, just waiting to manifest itself.

Oh God, shoot me now, he said to himself.

Chapter Five
And the ravens flew away, one by one.

☙

"You did *what*? Eric, why'd you have to do that for?"

"I didn't think it was going to be a big deal."

Kristin groaned. "Were you at the same dinner *I* was?" She tossed the hairbrush onto her dressing table with a clatter. She glanced at her watch. "I'm late for my shift already, and you have to tell me this *now*!"

She didn't even want the man's name brought up. It had been burned onto her consciousness with a torch, and she flinched when her thoughts wandered and touched on the wound.

"It was such a mistake," she muttered. "It was such a mistake I can't even *fathom* what a mistake it was."

Eric shrugged. He scratched his head, frowning. "I didn't think it was going to be that big a deal. It just occurred to me he lived—"

She wasn't going to listen. It had been such a horrifying experience, and her little brother had to land on the subject and dance on it.

"I just thought—"

"You just *thought*," she repeated, grinding her teeth. "*I* thought Dare Borodin made it pretty clear he didn't want anything to do with us. And you had to go and *call* him?"

Eric's face settled into a mulish expression she would have found amusing if she hadn't been so irritated.

He had wandered into her bedroom, a week after the disastrous dinner, as she was getting ready for her late-night shift. He asked questions that seemed to have no basis in anything, the kind he asked when he had something on his mind and he was talking, just talking, to avoid the real subject. Then to hit her with this —

His naïvete was shining bright. "You know, when you have that expression on your face, you look a lot like you did when you were learning how to walk," she said. "And it didn't matter what anybody did or said, because you were going to do what you wanted to do, how you wanted to do it."

It wasn't the most tactful thing to say to an eighteen year old, and she knew it. She watched as he turned red. "If you're trying to get me off the subject, it's not going to work!" Eric snapped. "I just thought—"

This was a rare demonstration of temper. "Calm down, little brother," Kristin said sharply. "I was trying—"

This time, he wasn't listening. "Maybe something happened that day. Did that occur to you? I'll still bet he's not a bad guy. Anyway," he said, brightening up, "as soon as his leg's out of that brace, we're going biking around West Seattle. I'll find out why he acted like that."

She stood up. "Kiddo—" she began, and she paused. How could she say this? "You never had to really deal with Sven, did you?"

The subject of their Pascisci cousin was an even touchier subject than Dare Borodin was. The cousin who was an out-and-out racist was a subject that no one, not even Marmar, touched on.

Eric shrugged, and for good reason. "I know he's the cousin nobody likes," he muttered. He plucked at the bedspread, not meeting his sister's eyes. "I don't even think I've met him except the one time, at the *Juldagen* dinner we had at Marmar and Farfar's that one time."

Farfar. Their fraternal grandfather was a subject she could work with. "Remember what a good-natured guy Grandpa was?" she asked, prompting.

Eric laughed. "I remember," he exclaimed. "I remember how I could try to be as bad as I could and all he'd do was laugh and say, 'Good boys grow up to be good men.' What about him?"

She smiled wryly. No dummy, her little brother. "He had to spank Sven. He had to yell at Sven. He actually said Sven would never grow up to be a good man. He wanted to give up on Sven."

For a moment, they pondered the extremes to which their cousin had forced their sweet-natured grandfather. "I don't know what this has to do with my bike ride with Dare," Eric muttered.

She sighed heavily. "Remember that organization he was in?"

Eric scowled. Kristin knew he had heard this story before. "So what you're telling me is that Dare's part of a hate group? Isn't that a little farfetched, sis?"

"I'm not saying that," she answered. "What I'm saying is that the things he—Dare—said that night might mean he thinks of things the way Sven and his group does. Did. And I don't want to have any part of it anywhere near me, and neither should you."

"I don't think he's that bad, sis."

Kristin sighed. "According to your logic, Sven's not a bad guy, just misunderstood," she muttered. "If you had been around when I had to spend summers around him—"

He dismissed the thought. "I'm not talking about Sven. I'm talking about Dare. And he said he didn't get along with Sven, either, so that should be something in his favor, shouldn't it?"

Kristin waved him off. "Go, see if I care. I'm not doing much to change your mind."

"What's wrong with you? I thought you liked him. He seemed okay until he started acting like he was allergic to dinner."

"It would have been polite just to pick at dinner, not comment the food was slimy and that there were bugs in the rice," Kristin snapped. "Bugs! I remember Sven using that line! Even you weren't that picky when you were a kid."

"Hey, he said he wasn't used to eating a lot of different kinds of food," Eric defended him. "I remember Mr. Lars Bergen, Mr. 'Pain in the A' Bergen, your boyfriend—"

"He's not my boyfriend."

"Yeah, whatever. I remember Lars looking like he was going to throw up the first time we ate *tamago kake* in front of him."

"Oh, he did not," she snapped. "He didn't say a word. Besides, Lars has nothing to do with this."

"Sure. And then after everyone was done he asked if we weren't afraid of getting sick from eating raw eggs and said that *you* should know better! And did you mention Dare to him, incidentally?"

The smug look on her baby brother's face drove her sharp reply. "Never you mind about Lars. This has nothing to do—"

"Oh, I don't know about that." Eric wiggled his eyebrows. "And where *is* Lars these days?"

"I see him everyday at work. And I told you. The topic of Lars has nothing to do with the topic of Dare Borodin. Got it?"

She should have kept a closer leash on him when he was little, she thought to herself. Or at least threatened him more. She jammed her sunglasses up on her nose before she remembered it was evening and slipped them off. "You started the conversation. Was there a point to telling me you were going to go cycling with him?"

"Well, yeah," Eric said indignantly. "I wanted to know if you were going to be ticked if I went bike riding with him."

They stared at each other for a second before they both started to laugh. "I guess I got my answer," Eric said.

"I guess you did," Kristin replied, sobering. "I assume he said ya-sure-you-betcha, or you would have mentioned it by now."

He shrugged. "He said okay, but I could tell he was trying to get out of it. But I figured he couldn't avoid it forever. I pointed out by the time he got the brace off, he was going to need exercise."

Eric looked so pleased with himself Kristin wanted to bop him upside his head. "Are you sure you don't want to be a lawyer? You're really good about this arguing business."

He guffawed. "No thanks! I figure by the time we're done looking around West Seattle, I'll be able to figure out why he acted like a dork."

"As long as you're open to the fact that possibly he is a jerk."

"Oh, sure. But I don't think so."

Something occurred to her, and she sat back down. "I could have sworn—"

Eric, already on his way out, turned around. "What?"

Startled, she looked up. "What? Oh—" She paused. "I swore I wasn't going to see him again."

Eric shrugged. "You never know, sis. You never know."

* * * * *

You never know, Dare mused, hanging up the phone. He could have sworn he would never see any of the Olafssons again. The embarrassment alone could kill him.

His apartment had been quiet one minute, loud and vibrating the next, after he had picked up the phone and Eric had talked and talked and talked him into this—this tour of West Seattle.

Dare tipped his head back onto his chair. "I'm too old for this," he muttered.

But he just couldn't find the heart to turn the kid down. Eric had been amazingly enthusiastic. He was also annoyingly persuasive. Every time Dare had come up with an excuse, Eric would come up with a counterargument. The kid had come into the one-sided conversation with every excuse Dare could come up with already covered.

"If he ever goes into politics, he's a shoo-in," Dare muttered aloud. His mouth twitched. On occasion when he was younger, he wished he had had a younger sibling. Someone who could have understood his experiences. But he hadn't.

Dare wondered how Kristin and Eric had grown up. He remembered her recollection of how the family had spent summer evenings looking at the starry skies. He wondered how her father had reacted when Kristin had graduated from high school, college.

But by the time Kristin had graduated college, her father had already been dead. Well, his father hadn't been around for his college graduation either. But in his case, he just hadn't bothered. Dare's college roommate had been highly appreciative of the extra tickets to commencement—his entire family, mom and dad and siblings and grandpa and grandma, had all shown up for graduation.

Dare rubbed the side of his nose. *Be fair. He did send a telegram congratulating you. He even got you a gift certificate.*

He didn't talk to his father for five months after that. Dare had managed a phone call on Christmas Day. By then, he was already working overseas. Where had that been? He scratched his head. Berlin. That's right.

Dare shook his head. How he'd started thinking about the Olafssons and ended up thinking about his father, he didn't know. Although they probably held him in equal esteem right now.

Restlessly, Dare turned away from the phone. He could give his father a call, but he didn't see the point. Calling the old man had never been high on his list of things to do.

And of course, he'd give him a call on Christmas Day, same as usual. Why screw with a winning thing, he always said.

* * * * *

When the actual day of the Great Bike Expedition arrived, the weather was mild and fine, the sky filled with big, fluffy clouds.

The bike tour, he told himself, was for purely selfish reasons. This would be his first bike ride since he'd run into that car—or the car had run into him, more precisely—and he was raring to go.

"Hey, Dare! Ready?" Eric greeted him.

Eric was dressed like a biking pro, helmeted and gloved. He shucked his helmet as he walked in and tucked it under his arm.

"Where'd you park?" Dare said, glancing outside and seeing only a BMX mountain bike leaning against the fence.

"I rode the bike over. I don't drive if I don't have to."

Dare's eyes widened. "From Mercer Island? Does your mom know you do that?"

"It's not hard to get around on a bike if you know the bike routes." Eric drummed his heels on the floor. "This is great weather, man! Let's go for it!"

Dare shook his head, still thinking of the freeways and traversing them on two wheels. "It's not safe out there for cyclists."

"I spend a lot of time planning out a route. There are a lot of bike trails around here."

Dare grinned reluctantly. "I'll bet." He wheeled in his bicycle, by now more—or less—restored.

"So you pieced that together yourself, huh?" Eric kneeled and began to look at it with a practiced eye.

Dare shrugged. "You probably maintain yours a lot better than I do mine."

Eric looked up. "If you want the truth, if I were you, I'd scrap it and go out and get something a little newer."

"That bad?"

Eric glanced at it dubiously. "It *should* be okay for today."

"You're real reassuring," Dare said. "Let's try it out."

The weather turned out to be excellent for a bike tour. They didn't have to move that quickly, and they stopped frequently. Dare's leg was getting reacclimated to regular activity—slowly. He could actually see himself doing this on a regular basis again.

As they passed one of the local parks, a familiar sound made Dare look up. Ravens again, swooping and squawking.

He swiveled to call behind him. "Hey, Eric, look!" he said, pointing up. *Snap!*

"Does that look like—*jikushiyo!*" he yelled as he felt the bike beneath him break. He lost his balance and hit the graveled ground, then skidded along a few feet, rolling before he stopped.

The sharp and stinging pain of impact spread over him, this time centered on his knee. *Why do I do this to myself?*

He ended up flat on his back, stunned. He could hear the rush of blood roaring through his ears. He could hear quick, light footsteps coming closer. He kept his eyes closed, willing the world to stop bouncing.

"Dare! You okay?"

Dare took a breath before he answered. "I think so." He opened his eyes. The first thing he saw was Eric staring at him, alarmed.

"I'm okay. I think the bike's shot, though," he added faintly. *Great.* He took inventory, still flat on the ground. He felt sore and sorry all over. But nothing was broken or sprained as far as he could tell.

He brought his hands in front of his face, flexing his fingers. "These gloves actually work," he said, mildly surprised. "The fabric's not even ripped."

"Let me take a look at the bike while you check yourself out," Eric said. He squatted in front of the bike—the large piece, the only piece still intact.

"I'm not going to need the ambulance this time," Dare said, more to himself than to Eric. His hands were intact, his head in one piece, thanks to the helmet. His neck ached, but nothing that a long, hot shower wouldn't cure.

One more joint to check out. He flexed his knees and hissed in pain. "Wouldn't you know it," he muttered. "At least it's the other one this time."

Eric heard him. "Are you okay? Can I do anything?"

Dare finally sat up, his head pounding. "It looks worse than it is," he muttered as he examined his scraped knee. The fabric there had ripped open and he was bleeding slightly, but it wasn't as bad as it might have been.

He winced. It stung like hell. "I'll live. I think my bike is toast, though. Am I right?"

"Well, it's sure in pieces. That axle's gone. It just twisted and snapped, man."

"Oh, *Schiest*," Dare muttered. "Well, sorry, Eric. That's what you get when you go cycling with an old guy."

Eric glanced at his watch. "Kristin's off in a few minutes. I'll have her pick us up." He pulled out a cellphone from his pocket and flipped it open.

Dare stared at him. He didn't want Eric's sister to see him like this. He was tired of having Eric's sister see him like this. "You're going to ask Kristin to come all the way here to pick us up just because my bike fell apart? That's really inconsiderate, Eric. It's not that far to my apartment!"

"Dr. Kristin Olafsson, please," Eric said into the phone. To Dare he said, "Mom and Kristin feel better if I call them when something like this happens instead of trying to get home taking a bus or hitchhiking. Hey, Kris," he chirped into the phone. "You about done? Great! Dare's bike just fell apart. Well, the bike's a wash, but he hurt his knee...I don't know." To Dare he asked, "Is that the leg you hurt?"

Dare shook his head. Somehow, he and Kristin Olafsson seemed destined to meet in less than auspicious circumstances. "I can call a cab."

"The other one. Thanks, Kris. See you in a few," Eric said. He gave her the cross street and then put away the phone. "She'll be here soon."

Dare sighed. He was tempted to run away, but knew he wouldn't get far. "Might as well gather up the pieces." He stood up carefully, putting weight equally on the current hurt leg and the recovering leg. He grabbed the handlebars and tossed it over to the largest cycle carcass.

He gritted his teeth. His knee throbbed. Each time he tried to bend it, a thousand nerve endings screamed, all threatening a riot. "I'm going to sit down for a while," he mumbled.

"You know, that looks gross," Eric observed.

Dare looked down at his knee. It was beginning to well with blood, looking like a *Nightmare on Elm Street* special effect.

Dare waved it off. "As soon as I get home, I'll clean it and put a Band-Aid on it. Your sister will be proud."

"Or you could have her look at it. Here she is," Eric exclaimed. He stood up and waved.

The car slowed as it drew near. Dare could see Eric's sister behind the wheel, her expression more concerned than ominous.

Kristin parked behind them and got out. Again, if not for the fact he was in pain, he could have appreciated looking at her more. She was wearing something bright blue, and it was bluer than the bluest of Seattle skies. It was a good color on her.

"I'm sorry you had to do this," he called out.

She didn't looked irritated, but she certainly didn't look happy. "I was going off-duty anyway. Are you all right, Eric?"

"I'm fine, sis, but Dare got hurt. Could you look at it?"

Silence.

She shifted her gaze over to Dare and looked him over. "I was planning to, Eric," she said. Dare noticed she was looking at him but still talking to her younger brother.

Dare glanced away. "You don't have to."

"I know." She reached out to touch the torn fabric on his knee and then, light as a feather, flicked away some pebbles still clinging to his skin. "There *are* easier ways to get my attention," she said, finally looking him in the eye.

He stared at her for a moment before dawning relief coursed through him. She was going to forgive him. He was getting another chance. "I have to find a way that doesn't involve pain on my part," he answered, watching as she gently peeled away the fabric. His flesh, torn and traumatized, tingled as her fingers brushed at his kneecap. He held his breath, his heart racing at her touch.

"Does it hurt?" she asked, withdrawing finally. Dare felt his bare knee cool, bereft of her warmth. She didn't move from her position, though. Instead of looking at his knee, she focused on his face.

"Not much." He wished desperately, and not for the first time, that the two of them were somewhere private. That he wasn't always in some kind of pain when they met. That he could take back that dinner. That he could have met her as someone else. "I don't hurt right now," he added.

His attempt at machismo was rewarded by a smile. "Do you have a first-aid kit?" she asked. She smoothed the fabric away from his knee again, and this time, she didn't withdraw her hand.

"At home, I think I do," he replied. The touch of her hand on his skin was almost hypnotic.

"Well, let's get you home," she said, standing up finally and reaching out with her hands. "Grab. And be careful how you get up."

Dare did, but his balance was good enough for him to get up on his own. Nevertheless, her firm grip in his was what he centered on. When he stood up, he was reminded she was a tall woman, but somehow managed to seem petite.

She was still focused on him. "Ready?"

"Want me to drive?" Eric volunteered.

She laughed, and it had a genuine ring. "Not right now," she told her brother. "But why don't you get in the back? Dare's not going to be comfortable bending his knee right now, and you said you were all right."

Eric shrugged. "Sure. I just have to get my bike on the car. I don't know about yours, man," he said, looking at the remains of Dare's bicycle.

Dare barely gave a look of disgust at the pieces. "Just toss what you can into the trunk and I'll get rid of them at home. I just hate to buy a new one, considering I never know when or where I'm going to use it."

"Not to mention when or where you're going to get into another accident," Kristin commented while Eric, obviously through long experience, expertly lashed his bike onto the top of her car. "No. You get in the car," she ordered Dare as he started to pick up his handlebars. "Eric and I can do this."

"Let me do this, at least." Dare limped over and placed the handlebars inside the trunk.

"It's a lot faster if I do it," she said as she tossed in what was left of his gearshift and then slammed the trunk lid shut. "Get in," she ordered again.

Dare looked around. That was it. "I'm sorry for all this."

"I told you, it's no trouble," she repeated as he folded himself into the car. "I've picked up Eric before, and we'd rather pick him up than have him get home some other way."

Festival of Stars

For the first few minutes, the drive to Dare's apartment was relatively quiet before Eric's enthusiasm welled up. "The road around the beach is so cool," he burbled. "Have you seen it, Kris? And there's even a little Statue of Liberty. Did you know that West Seattle was where Seattle was founded?"

"Yes I did," she said. Dare glanced over at her, smiling faintly. He met her eyes, and her expression reflected a similar amusement. "And so should you have if you were paying attention in state history class, kiddo."

"Well, I forgot. It must be great living on the beach," Eric said as Kristin parked a few yards from the front of his duplex.

She killed the engine and got out. "Can you manage?" she asked. "Would you like me to open your front door?"

In response, Dare unwound a chain with a small jangle of keys attached from around his neck, handing them to her. "The brass one with the black body."

"Got it. Eric, will you take care of the bike parts?" Kristin tossed her brother the keys to her own car.

Dare limped to the door with Kristin. "Has he always been this enthusiastic?" he asked.

"All his life." She started to sort through his keys.

"He's a great kid, but I feel really old talking to him. That key." He stopped her hand as she paused to examine one. Gently, he took the key ring from her, and with his hand over hers inserted it into the keyhole. The door opened smoothly, gaping to reveal the apartment, dark and cool.

They didn't move. "We should get you in," she said.

"We should."

She didn't move her hand, though.

"Hey, should I just dump the pieces into the garbage?"

Dare turned to see Eric holding various odds and ends of what used to be his bicycle. "Sure." Dare took his hand away from hers and let his arm fall to his side. "Thanks."

"Is your first-aid kit in the medicine cabinet?" Kristin asked. She walked into the apartment, making a beeline for his bathroom. He followed her inside, wincing when he heard the clang of metal as Eric threw out the worn-out bicycle parts.

"Should be in there." He sighed as he sank into his recliner and stretched his leg out on the ottoman—again.

Eric came bounding in, slapping his hands clean. "Let's try it again after you get a new bike!"

"Eric, give him some time to mourn the old bike," Kristin suggested as she came out of the bathroom with the first-aid box and a dampened washcloth. "And could you get the small basin filled with water? It's in the sink."

Dare started to get up. "I'll get it."

"Not you," Kristin said. "Eric."

"Okay," Eric said, bouncing up again and heading for the bathroom. Dare could have sworn he had springs in his feet.

She sat on the club chair across from him. "Move your leg," she ordered. Eric placed the basin next to his sister without being told. Dare guessed he'd played water-carrier before.

"Now let me get this straight," she said as she started to dab around the scrape with the washcloth, her voice softer. "You usually don't have this happen to you, only when you're around me or my family. Is that right?"

Dare twitched as she cleansed the area. "I'd say pure coincidence, except I'm not so sure anymore."

He watched as she spread the first-aid cream on the scrape then covered it with gauze. Her touch was light, and all he could feel was the protective fabric, but he could smell her fragrance as she played doctor.

But he had to remember his manners. "Thank you for picking us up. And for patching me up."

"No problem." She laid the adhesive tape in place, stroking the ends down. Dare's untraumatized flesh tingled.

"As I said, we'd rather Eric call when he gets in trouble. And as for patching you up," she sat back on her heels to survey her work, "again, it's no problem." She looked up, meeting his eyes.

Her eyes weren't quite as cold as they had been. "Thank you," Dare said, his throat suddenly tight.

"Look at this my way," she said as she closed the kit. "This time, you have no broken bones, you won't need a brace, you won't need crutches. This time, all you needed was a little TLC."

She turned to Eric. "Could you take the basin and the first-aid kit back? Thanks."

Once her brother had been dispatched, Dare got up and stood in front of Kristin. He was starting to feel stiff, and his knee twinged. "Thank you again."

She turned away and picked up her purse. "You're welcome. Change that bandage everyday for a few days and don't land on that knee for a while."

Like I wouldn't already do that, he thought in a rush, aware his chance to make up for his behavior was slipping away. "Do you like chili?" he blurted out. Mentally, he kicked himself. *Smooth. Very smooth.*

She stopped and looked at him. "Yes. Why wouldn't I?" There was a touch of belligerence in her tone. Not unexpected.

He took a deep breath. *In for a penny*, he reminded himself. "Some people don't." Dare suddenly became aware Eric had closed the bathroom door, and he had to talk fast.

"I might not because I eat sushi, is that it?"

He could hear the edge in her voice, abruptly razor sharp. *That could hurt*, he thought. "It's possible," he answered, feeling beads of sweat on his forehead. "Or you might not like spicy food. I don't know. That's why I asked."

She shrugged, looking past him at the bathroom door. "Sure."

"Sure you like it or sure it's possible?"

She gave him a look of disdain. "Sure I like chili. The hotter the better. With beef or without. With beans or without. But not if there's something like jelly beans or chocolate in it. That's just too weird."

Dare could hear the screech as the spigots were turned. "There's going to be a chili cook-off here next weekend. Would you like to go?"

She looked him in the eye. He held his breath as he looked back, trying to gauge her reaction. "You know, you don't need to thank me for taking you home."

"I know. You keep telling me," he added. The water stopped.

"Maybe. Eric, what're you doing next weekend?" she asked as her brother emerged from the bathroom.

Startled, the boy looked slightly wary, as if he weren't used to being asked about his plans by his sister. "I'm biking up to Snohomish on Sunday. I don't know about Saturday. Why?"

She turned back to Dare. "What day did you have in mind?"

Dare slowly smiled. His heart began to beat again. "Saturday. I assume you like chili?" he asked the younger man.

Eric nodded. "Sure."

"There's going to be a chili cook-off here next weekend. I just asked your sister if she'd be interested. What about you?"

Even if Eric hadn't said a word, the look on his face would have been enough. Dare guessed the kid probably didn't play poker very often. "Sure!"

Kristin nodded, her chin tipping up. Dare thought she was playing it cool. "In that case, we'll see you next Saturday," she said. She turned back to her brother, who was, Dare saw, shifting his gaze between the two of them, as if he were watching a tennis match between unlikely opponents. "Are you going home, or shall I drop you off somewhere, Eric?"

Eric shrugged. "Home. Some of the guys and I were going to Factoria tonight, and they're supposed to pick me up."

"In that case, would you like to drive us home?" She tossed her keys to him.

He grabbed them. "Sure!"

"If you want to get the car adjusted while I give Dare some last-minute medical advice—"

She didn't need to say anything else. Eric was out of the door before she finished the sentence.

Dare turned to Kristin. "I take it you wanted to say something to me and you didn't want to say it in front of him?"

She looked up at him, her gaze grim. "Got it in one. First of all, I didn't appreciate your behavior toward my mother when you were over for dinner. It was inexcusably rude."

At least she was direct. "I know. I wish I could explain, but—" he stopped. He didn't want to go into this, not now. "I can't begin to tell you how sorry I am."

"Maybe Eric's right, maybe you were just having a bad day or your leg was bothering you. That's possible."

Her glare was as cold as an Indiana winter. And he couldn't deny it. "You're right," he said again. "It was inexcusably rude. And I plan on making the most heartfelt of apologies to your mother when I see her again."

"*If.* I'm not going to inflict you on her if I decide you're a hopeless case."

Dare paused. This was no more than he deserved. He was going to have to work his way back into her good graces again. On the other hand, it sounded as though she was going to give him another chance. "Okay," he conceded. "What else?"

"Second, if you insult anyone in my family like that again, you're going to be *very* sorry." Her jaw was tensed. "Eric and I will come out next weekend, and if you insult him—"

Dare raised his hand. "I agree."

"Fine. In that case, take care of your leg, and we'll see you next weekend. Call me with the details."

"Sure," he said humbly. He felt as though he were five again and for good reason. She turned away and went to the door. "Kristin?"

She stopped and turned her head. "Yes?"

Her eyes could burn through a man's soul. All of a sudden, he wanted desperately for her to stay, but he knew he couldn't say that. It was enough that he had another chance. "Thanks. For everything," he added.

He saw part of a smile. "Like I said, no problem."

Chapter Six

It had been the kind of day that called for a bubble bath and a good night's sleep. She had seen everything from a strep throat case to a messy bullet wound in the lower femur at the ER, and by the time Eric called, Kristin was ready to go home.

Heading home with her brother in the driver's seat, she felt her nerves jangle as Eric dodged other cars on the freeway with the utter disregard for other drivers that only an eighteen year old could have.

"You can get into the carpool lane, Eric," she ventured as he dodged and darted between other vehicles. She wanted to close her eyes, but found she couldn't do it. "Right—there."

"See it, got it, done it," her little brother said. He changed lanes, almost taking the car onto two tires to do it.

Kristin swallowed. She was a nervous passenger, she couldn't deny that, but this time she had cause. She felt beads of sweat gather on her forehead. "You might want to take that a little slower next time," she said, her heart pounding. "Remember, smaller cars don't have the center of balance that larger cars do."

"Yep, I forgot that for a minute. But your car sticks better to the road than Mom's does."

"It's built that way," she said. She glanced down at her hands and carefully unclenched them, willing herself to relax.

What Eric said next didn't help her any. "So you haven't asked me about Dare," he observed as he dodged another car. The other driver blasted his horn. Eric waved.

Her hands grabbed at the armrest. "What is there to ask?" she asked as mildly as she could. How he could talk while he was driving like this, she didn't know—

"You could ask if I had a good time this afternoon."

She looked away, out the side window. She wanted to ask, but found herself reluctant to. Oh, why not? "Did you have a good time? How was Dare? Did he ask why we ate ooky food?"

"Lighten up, Kris. He was cool. Is his knee okay?"

She turned her head to look at Eric. It was, she figured, safer than looking at the way he was driving. She had taught him how to drive. It would have been her father's job, but Eric Sr. had been dead and gone for six years by the time Eric Jr. was taking driver's education classes. Looking back, she couldn't imagine how her father had taught her and her mother without ever, ever losing his temper.

"Dare's knee is going to be fine, as long as he doesn't do anything stupid to it," Kristin answered, taking a deep breath as Eric slowed down for a backup. "Good, that's right, pump your brakes. Let the guy behind you know he'll have to slow down too. Getting rear-ended is no fun. Or being sideswiped," she added as Eric swerved to avoid a car.

"I know he felt really bad about the way he acted at dinner too," Eric went on, tapping the gas again once the backup had cleared. Kristin's head jerked back and instinctively she clutched at the armrest again. "And he really didn't want me to call you, but I wanted to make sure he was okay."

"He probably felt embarrassed asking for help, Eric," she said, sounding more reasonable than she felt.

"So did you make up? Is that why we're going next weekend?"

Kristin looked out the side window again, her nerves at war with her jumping heart. She didn't want to go into this with her little brother. Truly she didn't. "We barely know each other." *Oh, my God, that is the worst cliché in the world. Where is the turnoff? Why aren't we home yet?*

She wished Eric would drive a little faster.

"You don't invite just anybody you meet off the street for dinner," he pointed out. "You didn't bring Lars home to meet Mom until you'd known him three years."

She felt her face get warm. "I told you before, it's not very often you meet someone first in Pascisci and then here, both in the ER. And he knew someone from Pascisci who knows Marmar."

"That was weird," he admitted. "Hang on, it's our exit."

She clutched at the armrest again, but slowly relaxed when Eric stopped smartly at the light off the exit. "That wasn't too bad," she muttered. She willed her heart to slow down.

"No, the traffic wasn't too bad at all," he agreed. "It's not a bad hop over the West Seattle bridge." He glanced at her.

"Light's changed," she said quickly.

Once more she felt herself being thrust back, then buffeted to the side as Eric put his foot on the gas pedal and spun the wheel. "I think he could be an okay guy," he went on, oblivious to her shriek.

"Maybe. But if he decides to get up on a soapbox next weekend and start explaining how America should be all white again, I think we can reasonably assume he's not."

Eric waved her off. "You're too much, sis."

"And don't you have better things to do than to play matchmaker? Shouldn't you be getting ready for your classes to start?" Her cell phone rang just as the traffic light changed. She glanced at the readout, grateful for the break.

"*Moshi-moshi,*" she answered. "*Safeway kara nanika hoshi?*"

"*So ne,*" her mother responded.

It was part habit, part tradition. Kristin called her mother every night on her way home or Moyo called her to make sure she was all right, usually disguised as a request for a stop at the store.

From Kristin's left, she felt Eric lean in. "Hi, Mom," he called out. "Am I stopping at Safeway?"

Kristin smiled. "Yeah, I picked him up," answering her mother's surprised question. "And he's driving," she added, laughing. "*Zuibun kowai yo.*"

She glanced at her little brother. He wrinkled his nose. He actually recognized a few phrases in both Japanese and Swedish, and *kowai*—to be scared—was one of them. "Very funny, Kristin," Eric said. "So am I pulling off?"

"*Nani mo?*" she asked her mother again. "What about Marmar?"

"*Chotto matte.*" Kristin could hear a faint second voice. Then her grandmother came on the line. "Kristin? Is that you?"

The elderly woman always managed to sound fragile on the phone. "Yes, Marmar. Do you need anything? Turn in," she ordered Eric as he prepared to pass by the Safeway. "Marmar wants something."

"Some *brod* crackers. We're out," Solveig announced. "*Adjo.*"

"Is that i—" Kristin began, but the dial tone had replaced Solveig's voice. "Even if she needed anything else, she wouldn't call back," she muttered.

"She'd just do without," Eric agreed as he maneuvered the car into a parking space. Their grandmother's distrust of cell phones was well-known.

"I hope Mom's not going to call to make sure I got in okay when I move out," she said.

"Well, she's not going to do that to me, Kris," Eric said with a laugh, switching the engine off. "You worry about me more than she does."

"You're a boy," she answered ruefully as they got out of the car and started for the supermarket. "She expects you to get into trouble. But I'm a lot older than you are, and she still fusses over me."

He shrugged. "They both remember that accident, Kris," he reminded her. "I wasn't much more than a baby and I remember it. You were in the hospital for a long time, weren't you?"

"Four weeks." Suddenly, she wanted to talk about Dare Borodin again, the weather, anything else. She rubbed her temples. She didn't like this subject either.

"I thought you were pretty brave to move back in after you come back from Indiana."

She shrugged. "I figured Marmar could use the company, get used to living with Mom. But since I'm going to put in for evening shift, now I figure I should get my own place. At least that's going to be my excuse," she added with a smile.

"Well, Lars isn't going to object to your living alone," Eric said, flashing a grin of his own.

She glanced at him as they walked into the supermarket, but decided not to comment. Lars, like Dare, was none of Eric's business. "But who's going to take the garbage out for them if Lars isn't always around to do it?"

They laughed. Sure as clockwork, Lars tended to appear like magic at the back door the night before the trash had to be put out. "You will, kiddo. You're the man of the house."

"In that case, are you sure you want to move out?"

I do, Kristin thought later, after they had arrived home. *I want privacy again. I want freedom again.*

She had had both when she'd gone away to med school. Flush with both, she had spent her first two weeks in New York adjusting more for culture and attitude shock than for schoolwork, thanks, once more, to Lars. He had preceded her to medical school and had shown her New York, and adulthood.

Lars had never pressed. They had dated, off and on, during their undergraduate years, and then, during medical school. He was as familiar as Eric, or Seattle, or even Pascisci.

Lars was her male, Caucasian, socioeconomic doppelgänger, she had told him once when they'd both had too much to drink. They had similar memories, they had similar frustrations, they even had similar ambitions. He could have been a twin in another dimension. Except for the fact he was a Caucasian male, of course.

And which point, she had excused herself and thrown up. That was also the last time she'd thought of Lars that way. Considering she had slept with him, it was a horrifying way of thinking of him.

It didn't happen often. The sex part, at least. Most of the time, they might as well have been siblings. But when she was depressed, or drunk—once a year, by her reckoning—they did—and invariably she regretted it.

Like now. They were adults now, and they were settling into their lives—and he wanted more.

"*Tak*, Kristin. Is Lars coming for dinner?" her grandmother asked as she took the groceries. "We're having his favorite."

Kristin sighed. "He didn't say anything about it when I talked to him today, Marmar. I think he said he was going out."

"Have a problem if I go out tonight?" Eric called over from the phone. "The guys want to go see a movie."

Moyo looked at her watch and then at Kristin, who shrugged. She was familiar with Eric's friends, and they were relatively responsible. "*Itsu kaitte kuru no?*"

"About midnight, I guess," Eric answered. His Japanese was nearly nonexistent, but he could answer some of his mother's questions without a second thought. "Is it okay?"

Moyo waved. "Have good time," she said, smiling.

"Hot damn! Excuse me, Marmar. Pick me up in fifteen," he said into the phone. Disconnecting, he disappeared around the corner. His trip upstairs wasn't hard to discern, Kristin mused. First there was the thunk as he leaped up his usual two steps, and then the run up, threatening to vibrate the paintings off the walls. Within seconds the hanging baskets swayed and the pots and pans on the wall danced as Eric ran to his bedroom.

"I'm not going to miss that when I move out," Kristin said as she shook her head. "Unless I have elephants for neighbors, it's going to be quieter."

Her grandmother touched her arm. "Are you sure you want to move, Kritchka?" she asked anxiously. "Isn't it dangerous?"

Kristin patted her grandmother on the shoulder. Everywhere but Pascisci was dangerous, as far as Solveig was concerned. "I lived in New York, Marmar," she reminded the elderly woman. "Seattle's a picnic in comparison. Even on the evening shift."

She saw the expression on her mother's face, eyebrows furrowed. "*Honto*, Mom," she said.

Kristin hadn't managed to persuade her mother that her moving out was for the best. It was difficult to get Moyo away from the idea that nice, unmarried women lived at home, unless they couldn't—if they lived thousands of miles away, perhaps. Very Japanese, that.

Some double standards were cross-cultural. Her mother and grandmother didn't have any problem with Eric moving to the dorm. They did, however, have a problem with her, even as an adult, getting an apartment of her own.

Nice unmarried women live at home if you're Japanese, but Mom, I'm not Japanese, Kristin said to herself, and not for the first time. "I'd rather live closer to the hospital than have to drive all the way back in the middle of the night," she went on, racking her brain to come up with more excuses.

But the most recent one was a goody, and she decided to work it for all she could. "The place I found is about ten minutes from the hospital, and it's on a very quiet street."

Her mother looked at her. It was an assessing look, one that Kristin was familiar with, had been under the scrutiny of too many times and in too many situations. Did all mothers have that sixth sense when it came to their children, or just hers?

"*Ii* neighborhood *nano?*" her mother asked in Japanglish, using that combination that years of juggling languages had given her.

Kristin exhaled. "It's a great neighborhood, Mama," she assured her. She could feel her blood pressure thrum. She was over thirty, but she still felt as though she needed her mother's consent. It wasn't easy ignoring part of her heritage, she thought, and not for the first time.

"Why don't we look after dinner?" Kristin's mother suggested.

"That's a good idea, Moyo," Kristin's grandmother said. "Has Lars seen it?"

Kristin sighed loudly. *Lars, Lars, Lars.* "No."

"Oh, but Lars would like to know," the old woman murmured.

Kristin controlled a surge of irritation and smiled instead. "I wanted you all to be surprised, Marmar," she said, trying another tack. "After I'm settled in, I thought I'd invite Lars over for a nice dinner with you and Mom and Eric."

"Oh, that's nice," Solveig said, clearly relieved. "That reminds me. Wasn't Eric supposed to see that man?"

"*So ne,*" Moyo said. Kristin didn't like the tone in her mother's voice. By her expression, it was clear she, too, had just remembered what Eric had been doing. "*Daijobu datta? Erikku nanka yutta?*"

"Not really," Kristin said reluctantly, casting about for a change in subject. She could have kicked herself. She didn't want to have Dare Borodin's name to come up, not without Eric there to defend himself.

Her grandmother, not unusually, was echoing her daughter-in-law. "Is everything all right? Did Eric say anything?"

Kristin didn't want to discuss Dare Borodin without having had a chance to think. She didn't want to have to defend herself for accepting his invitation in a moment of weakness.

But the time had arrived. She took a deep breath. "Dare's-bike-fell-apart-and-he-got-hurt-and-Eric-called-me-as-I-was-getting-off-shift-to-come-and-take-them-back-to-Dare's-place-and-I-patched-him-up-and-Eric-and-I-came-home."

"*Doshta no?*" Kristin's mother exclaimed, amid Solveig's cries of concern. "*Erikku wa daijobu?*"

"No, no, Eric's fine," Kristin said hurriedly. She had explained too quickly for her mother to translate. "Eric *daijobu*. Didn't he look fine to you? No, Dare's bike fell apart—it broke. He hurt his leg. I patched him up. That's why Eric came home with me."

Now it was her grandmother's turn to frown. "That boy keeps getting hurt, doesn't he?"

"Who, Eric?" Kristin asked, knowing whom she meant.

"No, that Dare. He should have a doctor give him an exam," Solveig said. "He seems always to be getting hurt."

"Well, we're seeing him again," Eric said, coming back down the stairs in his featherlight way. "Kris and I are going over there for a chili cook-off. Should be fun."

Kristin closed her eyes for a second, knowing that Dare Borodin would be the main topic throughout dinner. And she would be the only one who wouldn't want to talk about it. *Thanks a lot, kiddo.*

"And whose idea was that, *kar?*" Marmar asked. Kristin noticed the glint in her eye and squirmed.

Eric, of course, contributed blithely, unaware of his sister's comfort. "It was his. Sounds cool."

"*So ne*," Moyo said dryly. "*Tanoshi ne.*" She put away the last of the groceries.

Oh no. Her mother was giving her what she and Eric referred to as "the look". The look that said, "You're shaming generations of proud samurai, and for *what?*" The look that made Kristin sigh and wish that she had been born an orphan.

"It's a contest. Dozens of cooks compete. You get to try different flavors of chili, Mom," she added. Her palms were damp. "I've read about these things. It's supposed to be fun. You get to watch the cooks. Maybe I could learn something."

"*So chili cooku ni iku no?*" her mother asked her, her tone familiar to Kristin—a trifle ironic, a trifle tongue-in-cheek. Kristin hated it when her mother got in that mood.

Eric hooted at his mother's suggestion. "Kristin cook? I don't wanna be around!"

Kristin stared at her little brother, who was slapping together a peanut butter-and-jelly sandwich. "Shouldn't you be going?"

A faint toot of a horn interrupted the silence. Eric swallowed his sandwich. "It's the guys. Later!"

After dinner, they piled into Moyo's Camry to look at the neighborhood Kristin would be living in. Kristin chose to drive, with her mother beside her. "Are you all right back there, Marmar?" Kristin asked, glancing in the rearview mirror.

"Yes, *kar*. I'll wave at the populace and pretend I'm the queen of Sweden," Solveig said, with a smile.

Translation—Solveig knew Moyo had something to say to Kristin, and she was staying out of it.

Kristin couldn't wait to move out. These homey tête-à-têtes were going to give her an ulcer.

I can't wait, she thought. Aloud, she said as she drove down the main thoroughfare, "It's not far from the hospital, so I don't have to worry about a long commute. I can walk to the Whole Foods for my groceries," she said, referring to the nearby supermarket. "There's a bus stop a block away if my car breaks down or if I don't want to drive." *I am not eighteen years old,* she shouted within. *I shouldn't have to give this much detail on why I want privacy.*

At least taking a walk in the area would make her feel better. She parked down the street from the apartment complex. "Let's look around," she suggested. "There's a florist down the block, a bookstore around the corner, and some great-looking restaurants. And there's a library down the street. Everything I need. What do you think? Marmar?" she asked, going for the easier target.

"It looks nice, dear," Kristin's grandmother said, looking around as they walked up the steps to the complex's secluded courtyard. "Where does Lars live again?"

Why would I care? But Kristin bit her tongue. "He lives about thirty minutes away. This is closer to the hospital than home, and it's not that far from downtown." She stopped in the middle of the courtyard, a pretty, hidden spot that boasted comfortable benches and planters in front of the garden-level apartments. "Mom? What do you think?"

"*So ne,*" Moyo said, looking around. "*Dotchi na no?*"

"That one," Kristin replied, pointing to a ground-floor apartment that at the moment had open windows, through which they could hear the roar of vacuum cleaners.

"Very pretty," her mother answered in English, with such promptness Kristin almost blinked in surprise. "*Sukoshi rozu wa? Apaato no soto ni bara o uetaho ga ii?*"

"*So ne,*" Kristin said, dawning relief flooding her body. Her mother approved—sort of. "I'll see if I can plant some roses outside."

After that, she relaxed. Her mother had something to say, but she was going to take her own sweet time about it. Kristin forgot about it until hours later, when her mother came into her bedroom as she sorted her laundry, long after Solveig had retired.

Moyo started the conversation innocuously enough. "*Chili no contesto wa itsu nano?*"

Kristin paused. "The cook-off's next Saturday." That feeling of discomfort was rising in her gorge again, but she continued to fold. "Why?"

"*Sonna ni ikitai no?*"

Kristin shrugged. She didn't really care if she went, one way or another. "It would never have occurred to me to go until he suggested it." Some conversations seemed as though they should be in English, and this was one of them. Sometimes Japanese seemed to be right. But not tonight. "And Eric seemed keen on the idea, so—"

Moyo frowned. Kristin recognized the look. It wasn't one that disapproved, it was one that meant she was trying to understand. "*Anohito—*" Moyo paused.

That person. Kristin knew who her mother was referring to, but she didn't want to admit it yet. "Who, Eric?"

Her mother wasn't having any. "*Tomodachi. Borodin-san.*"

Kristin sat next to her clean laundry. It was never good news when her mother referred to one of her friends—her *tomodachi*—by surname. "What about him?" she asked directly. "I think he's more Eric's friend than mine."

"*Kurutteru, anoko.*"

Kristin's eyes widened. "Who? What are you talking about? Who's crazy?"

"That boy," her mother said. "*Dare.*"

Chapter Seven
Second Year:
The ravens watched helplessly as the lovers yearned.

༄

Crazy?

Her mother's words gnawed at Kristin as she got ready on Saturday. Moyo had said nothing more on the subject after that, but now that it was out in the open, the pink elephant in the living room was there for all to see.

After Moyo's comment, Kristin had stared at her mother, aghast. "No, he's not, Mom," she protested, not believing she was defending Dare Borodin, who had insulted them in their own house, at their own table. "He just has—some problems."

Her mother had stared at her dubiously. "*So ne*," she said, irony thick in her tone. "*Zuibun mondai ga aru mitai ne.*"

"Mom, I'm not dating him," Kristin insisted. "He's Eric's friend. I'm just going along."

Of course, Eric was eighteen years old and capable of taking care of himself, but she wasn't going to mention that. Funny how Japanese seemed to be a language of things not said, only implied, while Swedish seemed to be a language of things said, rarely implied. No wonder Kristin was confused on occasion.

"*Chotto hen da,*" her mother said, determined. "*So yu hito to tomodachi ni naritai no?*"

Well, she had to admit, "confused" was fairly accurate. Somewhere along the way, her mother had also used the word for "rude," and once Kristin had looked up the word in her Japanese dictionary—it wasn't one she used an awful lot—"boorish" had popped up as well.

"No, Mom," Kristin said. For conversations like these, she always stuck to answering in English, while her mother spoke Japanese, both leaning on their strengths. "He's not like that, Mom. Really." Maybe he was; she didn't know. But she didn't think so.

He wasn't raised very well, her mother replied, and Kristin couldn't refute that. Moyo was on a roll. What kind of a family does he have? What kind of people are they?

Kristin had shrugged. "*Wakaranai,*" she admitted. Her mother was on a tear. She had never asked these questions about her daughter's friends before. "I don't know." Kristin had had to admit she knew nothing about Dare's family. He never spoke of them. But he did have a father, that she knew, thanks to Solveig.

Moyo shook her head. "*Kimochiwarui.*"

Kristin stared at her. "Like what?"

Unexpectedly, her mother stroked her hair. "Be careful," she said, in English. Then she left, leaving Kristin to stare after her.

The week passed. Kristin woke up early on Saturday with mixed feelings. Should she beg off? Should she cancel, claiming an unexpected cold?

How many colds are planned, Kristin?

She changed her mind, lobbing other plans back and forth with the speed of Wimbledon champions, procrastinating until Eric ultimately made the decision for her.

"Aren't you going to get ready?" he asked, sticking his head in her room.

She looked at herself in the mirror. She was going along because Eric was so enthusiastic, just like she had told her mother.

Her mouth twisted. "Liar," she said to her reflection.

Kristin dragged a pair of walking boots from her closet. She could hear heavy footsteps coming down the hall, stopping at her open door. "What if I told you I remembered something I had to do and you could go on your own today?" she ventured without looking up. She pretended to be examining her boots—for cracks, scuffs, something. "You could use my car."

As little brothers were wont to be, Eric was immediately suspicious. "Are you just trying to get out of going, Kris?" He sat on the edge of her bed, drumming his feet on the carpet. "Coward. And rude. Mom would not approve."

Rude? "I just don't feel comfortable around him, okay?" she snapped. "You're the one who decided to call him. And after what happened at dinner—"

"Aw, geez, Kris!" He bounced up and down. "It's rude," he repeated. He stared at her, an expression in his eyes that Kristin met, stubborn for stubborn.

"It's not rude. I've got to get ready to move. I've got to pay some bills. I promised Marmar I'd help her in the garden. I was going to—"

"Sure, fine," Eric said, his voice as filled with disdain as only the young can. "It's rude, Kris. And Mom would really have a field day with *that*."

"*She* was the one who said he was rude! She'd approve of my skipping out."

"Maybe he was, but it doesn't mean we have to be rude, too."

Kristin rolled her eyes. "No." It was the intersecting Golden Rule of most cultures, trapping her.

She unlaced her boots and picked them up. "Fine," she mumbled. "Let me just find a cap and my sunglasses, and we can get going."

"Great! Does this mean I can still drive?"

She snorted. "In your dreams, kiddo." But she said it with a smile.

It was the kind of day that suckered late-summer tourists into thinking the famous Seattle cloud cover was no more than a nasty rumor. It wasn't a long trip to West Seattle. They were there, as their grandmother would put it, in a jif.

It was only when they were at a stoplight in West Seattle that Kristin realized that Eric was fidgeting. "What's wrong?"

He shook his head. "Nothing. Just thinking."

"About what?"

He gripped the seat belt. "Did Mom—" he hesitated. "Light's changed," he said.

She looked back up and eased through the intersection. "Did Mom what?"

"Did Mom's—comments about Dare seem kinda weird to you?"

After Moyo had left Kristin's room the weekend before, Eric had popped his head in to indicate he had overheard the conversation. "A little," Kristin admitted.

"I don't get it," Eric said, his tone bewildered. "He's no more obnoxious than other guys—"

"But he's the only one who actively insulted her," she reminded him, shaking her head. "What a stupid thing."

"I was just wondering if it was one of those unspoken Japanese things I didn't know and you do."

She shrugged, unsure of what to say. "Not this time. I don't know what was behind her comments, but we'll find out."

Following the street down to Beach Drive, Kristin parked in front of Dare's duplex. "We're meant to be here," Eric commented as he opened the door. "This parking space seems like it's always waiting for you."

"It makes me wonder if it's a no-parking spot and no one's told me yet."

"Always looking for the dark cloud in the silver lining, aren't you?"

She shrugged as she opened her own door, glancing at the side rearview mirror first to make sure there wasn't any vehicle coming. It was clear, save the ravens that were clustered on a nearby power line. "Being practical, Eric."

"We're here for chili, Kris. How practical is that?"

"*You're* here for chili. I'm tagging along."

"I thought I was here as a chaperone."

Kristin gave him a sharp look as they walked up to Dare's door. She jabbed at the bell. "Considering the two of you, I'm here to make sure neither of you break any more bones."

She ignored the fleeting memory of Dare Borodin's eyes, almost golden in the subdued light the previous weekend. His face had been dusty, his sweat-matted hair falling in front of his eyes, his long fingers protecting his gashed knee —

The door swung open. Dare must have caught the end of her comments, because he said, "Don't worry, we won't be able to get into too much trouble." He grinned, but a little hesitant.

"That's good," she said as they walked in. The apartment, Kristin noted, was neat and organized this time. The newspapers were gone, and the dishes had been washed and put away.

"All we're going to be doing, actually, is walking up and down a two-block stretch," Dare explained, shutting the door behind them. "We'll have to avoid running into other people who have exactly the same goal. We'll have to walk slowly not to run anyone over. I defy anyone to get into trouble."

Kristin looked him over with a professional eye, not letting any of her memories interfere with her once-over. He looked hale and hearty, his broad shoulders encased in a Hawaiian aloha shirt over a T-shirt. "You look good," she said without thinking. She reddened.

"You do good work, Dr. Olafsson." He smiled. "My knee's much better."

She looked up at him through her lashes, feeling her pulse race and unwilling to let him disturb her equilibrium any further. "How's your bike?" she asked deliberately. "Did you drag it out from the garbage?"

He looked at her, his smile turning rueful, and she felt the tiniest of triumphs as he tilted his head. "You don't see one around, do you? I'm ready for new things."

Kristin met his gaze. His eyes looked sunlit today, with shades of green and gold and brown. She felt her hand tremble as she tucked a strand of hair behind her ear, feeling self-conscious as his eyes followed her fingers.

She didn't know how long they had stared at each other until Eric interrupted. "So are we walking up?"

Kristin turned away from Dare and looked at her brother. "We'll take my car."

"We can walk," Dare interjected. "It's only a couple of miles."

She turned back to him. So his eyes were gorgeous. Big deal. "It may not be that far, but I don't want to tire out that knee of yours," she said, trying to sound logical. But it was hard to be that reasonable when her gaze kept meeting his.

Focus. "If it's uphill from here, your knee's going to be aching by the time we get there if we walk. Both knees. And you'll have to walk home. This way, we'll have the car if we need it."

"I don't have to visit the ER every week, you know. I'm not that accident-prone. Really."

"It never hurts to be prepared." Their gaze met and held, and she felt a shiver of awareness trail down her back.

Unnerved, she drove, doing her best to ignore Dare, who sat up front with her. In this Eric helped as he jabbered away, nearly parking himself between the bucket seats.

She succeeded only in being distracted. She went through a stop sign as a result, slamming on the brakes and narrowly missing a head-on collision. "Eric, sit back and pipe down," she ordered, now embarrassment overriding any other emotion. "I can't concentrate with you sitting between me and Dare. And put on your seat belt."

"Sorry, sis," Eric said, leaning back.

"He didn't mean any harm," Dare said.

"I know, but I get nervous driving anyway," she said, biting her lip as she took a deep breath.

"Park over here," Dare said quickly, pointing. "It's only a few blocks from here."

They walked up to the main thoroughfare where the chili cook-off was being held at a leisurely pace. Still uneasy, Kristin stayed slightly behind Dare and Eric.

But Dare kept stopping to let her catch up. "I'm just slower than you," she said, waving them on. "Just ignore me."

"Can't. You drove." He held out his hand. After a moment, she took it and kept pace. She tried to ignore the warmth of his hand wrapped around hers. She controlled the urge to withdraw it. Holding hands wasn't anything she should react to, one way or another, she told herself.

But Kristin became acutely aware her brother was, for once, quiet. "Did you ride up these hills when you were here, Eric?" she asked, twisting to catch his eye as he walked on Dare's other side.

Eric jumped slightly, as though he hadn't expected to be spoken to. "Huh? Yeah, I think we did. Didn't we?"

Dare shook his head. "Not here, but not far from here. I wouldn't go up this hill on a bike right now, not with my leg."

Kristin looked up. The hill had to be at an incline of at least forty-five degrees. "I wouldn't either." She stopped and looked behind her. She broke into a smile. She tried to retrieve her hand from Dare, but his grip tightened.

Damn it. "This is lovely," she exclaimed, turning around anyway to admire the view. "I can see why people live here."

The hill was steep enough that they had a clear view of Puget Sound and the peninsula beyond the water, the Olympic mountains in distant silhouette. The sun, bright and clear on the summer day, glittered off the calm waters.

Dare and her brother turned to join her. "Yeah," she heard Eric say. "But it's better-looking closer to the beach."

"But look at what you can see here. Look at that house with all those roses," she exclaimed.

"Where?" Dare asked, looking around.

"Right down there," Kristin said, managing to slip her hand away to point. "Near that cluster of trees. See it?"

"No," he said, turning his head.

She reached up and touched his chin, moving his head in the direction her finger had been pointing. Immediately, she regretted it. The touch brought her in contact with him, her sensitive fingers feeling the rough texture of his five-o'clock shadow, her nose picking up the scent of aftershave. "What is that?" she asked without thinking, curbing the impulse to bury her nose in his neck.

"What, the tree next to the house with all those roses? I think that's cedar," Dare said. She lifted her fingers from his face, but too late. He reached up and caught them.

This was a bad idea, Kristin mused as she met his eyes again, feeling that by-now familiar sensation of vertigo steal over her. *I should have played hooky. I should have let Eric come alone. I should have listened to my mother.*

Her tripping pulse was the least of her problems. "I assume that's what you were talking about," Dare said, the edges of his lips curling into a smile again.

With his tousled hair, he looked disarmingly young when he smiled. He wasn't letting go of her hand again, either. His fingers, warm and strong, were entwined with hers. She could feel the muscles and tendons of his hand shift and play as they wrapped themselves around her own.

She could feel his pulse drumming against hers.

"Actually, I was referring to your aftershave," she said, breathless, after a pause.

"You like it?" he whispered.

"I didn't recognize it," Kristin said. She cleared her throat. "Isn't that your building?" she exclaimed, turning back to the view. "Eric, where did you and Dare ride around last week, anyway?" Her heartbeat didn't slow down any. But she took deep breaths, and hoped it would soon.

Her little brother skittered down a volley of pebbles to stand next to her. He didn't glance in her direction, for which Kristin was grateful, because she didn't know what she would have done to him if he had reported back home that she and Dare had been holding hands.

She felt like an idiot. She was over thirty, and she was worried about what her mother would say.

"I don't know," Eric replied, answering her question. "This is Dare's area, not mine."

"Doesn't anything look familiar?" she asked anxiously. She was desperately aware Dare still had her hand in his. Worse, now he was starting to stroke her palm.

"Not really. Where'd we go last week, Dare?"

Dare brought his hand up—the one without her attached to it—and pointed in the general direction Kristin had pointed. "We went thataway. And we didn't really deal with sharp hills, just really long ones," he added, giving her a sideways glance. "Sort of gentle."

His eyes sparkled tea green in the sunlight now, their color almost translucent. "That's good," she murmured, her mouth dry, turning to study the scenery again. Her nerve endings tingled as Dare caressed her hand. She knew she had to extract herself, but she couldn't for the life of her figure out how—or, at this moment, why.

"That's not my building. We can't see it from here. That's the ridge above Beach Drive," he said, turning to look at her. She kept her eyes forward, pretending to survey the view.

"Hey, guys, get out of the street," Eric called out. Kristin looked behind her. A truck was behind them on the roadway, the driver looking somewhat annoyed there were actually pedestrians afoot.

Kristin took the opportunity to slip her hand out of Dare's grasp again, then headed back toward the sidewalk.

But he was right beside her. She stumbled on a crumbling bit of concrete as she reached the sidewalk. He reached out and steadied her.

Kristin felt her face burn and hoped it wasn't too visible. "I'm fine. I just stumbled," she answered. She straightened, feeling his hand drop away from her back, but his other hand kept hers. "I just lost my footing for a second. I don't know why the city hasn't repaired this yet," she said crossly.

He didn't answer. "Let's go," she said, retrieving her hand from his grasp—again. All she really wanted to do at this point was to go to this cook-off, make her excuses, and then go home. "The top of this hill, right?"

"The top of the hill and over two blocks."

Kristin didn't answer, just walking up the hill, not caring she was outstripping the other two in her determination to make it up the incline—and get her bearings, away from Dare.

Finally, the crest of the hill loomed. She stopped. "Hold on," she finally said, panting. "I want to take one last look at the view." She turned around slowly, making sure her trembling and definitely out of shape legs would support her.

This was humiliating. He was the accident-prone casualty and she was the one who had to catch her breath. She pretended to look at the landscape some more, but it wasn't easy. She found herself concentrating more on her own physical shortcomings than she did on the view.

"You okay?" Dare asked, coming up to her and touching the small of her back again.

She steeled herself not to tremble, not to let him feel her tremble. But she wasn't sure anymore whether that was from her unexpected climb or his touch. "I'm fine," she said again. "Take care of your knee. I'm just not used to hills." She could feel her breathing slow. But the touch on her back didn't go away.

"I'm used to this," he told her cheerfully. "And my knees are used to this. I only hurt when I'm standing still."

"In that case, I guess we'd better keep moving," she said, taking a deep breath.

"I ran on the beach every morning before this thing with my knee," he explained. She could feel his hand finally drop away from her back, and for a moment, she felt bereft. "But I haven't worked my way back up to it yet."

"Running on sand's not the greatest for you at this point," Kristin murmured, finally getting enough composure to turn to look at him. "Try the sidewalks or the running paths for a while longer."

Now that she saw him straight again, she saw what she was afraid she'd see—someone she was attracted to, to her chagrin. Someone she had things in common with, to her surprise.

Someone she was going to see again, much to her shock.

He stood there, dark hair ruffling in the breeze. His light-filled eyes seemed darker at that moment, but she couldn't read them. Her gaze drifted down to his fluid and expressive mouth, and at that moment, it was curled slightly at one end, waiting for her to respond to its implicit message—*Here I am, flaws and all. Am I worth it?*

No. Yes. She had no idea how she was going to respond. But she would have to, one way or another. "Okay, guys," she said, forcing herself to turn away, her heart pounding. "Let's go find out why this chili cook-off is worth my time."

Chapter Eight
Second Year:
Try as they might, the lovers found themselves out of reach.

ಖ

The West Seattle Junction reminded Kristin of Tokyo and New York. Dare seemed to fit in. She was surprised when he greeted and in turn was greeted by shopkeepers. The breeze had picked up, and his hair fell into his eyes, but he didn't seem to notice. Once, one of the little blue-haired ladies who greeted him reached up and smoothed errant strands away from his face.

Kristin fought to maintain a straight face, shaking her head. "If you're so nice to little old ladies, why did you antagonize my mom and grandmother?" she inquired as he rejoined her on their meander past the knick-knack booths and little jewelry stands, drawing ever closer to the smells and spices of the cook-off itself. Ahead of them, she could see Eric at a stand, trying on yet another pair of sunglasses.

Dare snorted. "Because I'm a putz. Is that the answer you wanted to hear?"

"No, but it'll do." Then, "I guess you know a lot of people around here."

"Not a lot. And the little old ladies remind me of my grandmother. And this area sort of—reminds me of home, I guess."

She nodded. "That little hometown feel. Like Pascisci."

"Right." But he hesitated.

Kristin frowned. Was that surprise in his answer? "That's not what you were thinking?"

Dare was frowning. "It's close. Need some sunglasses?" he asked. "Looks like Eric's found a pair."

Sure enough, Kristin's younger brother was paying the girl at the stand as he slipped his newest ones onto his nose. "Didn't you just get another pair last weekend?" she asked him.

Eric shrugged. "Yeah, but I don't have 'em here."

"What about the pair you were just wearing in the car?"

"I left them in the car."

"If you're not careful, I'm going to get a little chain for you to attach the glasses to, like librarians."

"Gimme a break, Kris," her brother said. "I just want to make sure I've got a pair handy."

The breeze shifted. Her nose quivered. She could smell chili and garlic and herbs she couldn't have identified in a million years. She liked this smell as much as she liked the smells of hot rice and *limpa* baking. She took a deep breath. "The chili smells delicious," she pronounced. "I'm starving. When can we eat?"

"It's still in the judging stage," Dare told her. "We can look around until they're done."

She looked around. "If only I had a chili pepper fixation. Some of this stuff would bring nightmares to designers." A number of booths offered T-shirts and sweatshirts with chili pepper designs, and a few even sold appliances with chili pepper motifs.

Images of lamps shaped like red chili peppers in her living room popped into her head. "Yikes," she said, shaking off the images before they ruined her appetite. "I'm pretty good at saying 'no'."

"I'll bet you are."

The vibrations of his voice shot through her, making her look up at him. "I am," she said. "Try me sometime."

His eyelids drooped. "I will."

113

Kristin suddenly became aware of a flood of warmth invading her. *Enough*, she said to herself. *We're in a public place. I have a* chaperone.

She looked around. "Where did Eric go to?"

"I think he went into the music store on the corner. Did you need to talk to him?"

"No, I-I just wanted to make sure I knew where he was."

"How old did you say he was—eight or eighteen?"

She shot Dare a glare. He wasn't looking at her, though. He was surveying the sights. "He's my kid brother," she reminded him. "My mother and grandmother expect me to look after him."

"He was telling me about the bike trips he takes—out to the San Juans, down to Oregon—you don't go along to make sure he's okay, do you?" She could see him tilt his head down to catch her gaze, but she wasn't going to look up just yet.

"That's different," she said, looking toward the music store. "He goes in a group."

"Then what's your problem?" He touched her on her shoulder.

She flinched. "Nothing," she said, but her voice was thin.

"Hey."

She felt, rather than saw, his finger tilt her chin up so she had to look him in the eye.

His eyes were bright. She could smell pungent spices and meat cooking around her, and she could feel his fingers, warm and strong, under her chin, stroking her jaw. Somewhere in the distance she could hear the screams of ravens.

The blare of the country western band at the end of the block should have deafened her, but all of a sudden, the blast of sound seemed far away.

She licked her lips. "I don't have a problem," she said, her voice hoarse. "I—" she trailed off, unable to think of a logical explanation. What was she going to say? *I have an overwhelming urge to renew my acquaintance with the taste of your lips? I want to feel your muscles tense under my fingers?*

What could she say? *I want to know that mind of yours and what makes you say the most appalling things, but I don't want to regret it?* "What can I say?"

"I don't know. What can you say?" His fingers had left her chin but hadn't relinquished contact. She shivered as he traced the contours of her lower lip, smoothing the dimples at the ends, before he stroked the surface of her cheekbones.

"Did I say that aloud?" she whispered. She tried to concentrate, trying not to think of the all-consuming sensation of his touch on her skin. Finally, she did focus.

She cleared her throat. "You interest me. And you disturb me," she said, her voice cracking, marveling his eyes had changed color again. Now they were a golden hazel, like warm, sweet honey. "You make me feel like a kid again."

He smiled, smoothing a tendril of her hair behind her ear. "You don't look much older than one."

She was painfully aware of his touch. She had to remember how to breathe. In, out. In, out. Oh, yeah.

Now that she had figured it out, she could continue. "But I can't get over the things you said to my mother," she whispered. "I don't understand them, or why."

He turned away then, his hand falling. "I'm sorry," he said after a second. "I don't know what else to say. I can't even begin to explain why I said what I did. I could apologize to your mother for a thousand years and still not be through. Should I take a sword and disembowel myself?"

She threw her hands up. "You were doing okay there, until you got to the *hara-kiri* part," she snapped. "I definitely didn't need the sarcasm."

He faced her. "I didn't mean to be sarcastic."

"You weren't being serious, I assume."

"No," he acknowledged. "*Seppuku* was reserved for the upper classes, and I don't qualify for that. I'm sorry if I seemed sarcastic. I just didn't know what else to say."

"Forget it." She started to turn away, her chest tight.

Wait a minute. Why did he know that?

"Don't go," she heard Dare say, disrupting her thoughts. She felt his hand on her arm, and before she knew it, he had turned her around and folded her into his arms.

She looked up at him. "What are you doing?"

He looked as surprised as she did. "I don't know," he said after a moment. "I just didn't want you to think badly of me."

She snorted as she twisted in his grasp. He loosened his hold, but still held on to her. "I don't think that badly of you—yet," she answered, glancing away. She couldn't say the words and look at him. "But I don't understand you at all."

"Listen. Is your heart set on chili?"

Kristin glared at him. "Why are we here? Are you on some medication I didn't see on your chart? *Should* you be on some medication?" Maybe it was the further manifestation of self-destructive behavior. Maybe he was a drug user. Maybe—

"Because I just noticed the sign that the chili from the cook-off's not going to be available to eat for another three hours, and I have a feeling you're not going to tolerate me that long. Hey, Eric!"

Kristin's head turned. Her younger brother was leaving the music store, a package in hand.

"You want to try the sushi bar down the street?" Dare asked as soon as Eric was within range, dodging other festivalgoers.

Kristin shook her head and mouthed "No" to her younger brother, but he ignored her. "Sure! A snack before the chili tasting?"

"Something like that," Dare said.

Kristin stared at him. "Gee, are you sure you want to risk a sushi bar? Shouldn't we go find a Burger King or something? A sushi shop might be serving yesterday's bait."

He met her glare. "For all we know about fast-food joints, they might be too. I don't go for sushi bars a lot, but I figured you might want to try it out."

He grabbed her hand and began to walk, Eric following. She tried to resist, but ended up being pulled along.

The Japanese restaurant was cool and dim after the harsh light of the midday sun. The skylight cast diffused light, but it was still strong enough to make Eric, with his photosensitive eyes, squint. "Geez!" he exclaimed as soon as they entered, abruptly squeezing his eyes shut.

"Sit with your back to it," Kristin told him. Eric nodded, his eyes shut as he fumbled for his sunglasses.

She looked around. There was a corner seat at one of the windows. It was bright enough not to be gloomy, far enough away from the glaring skylight for Eric not to use his new sunglasses unless he wanted to.

Kristin looked over to the register, where a young girl was making change. A glance told her she was full-blooded Asian, and moreover, she looked like a Japanese native to boot. "*Asoko ii?*" Kristin called over to her.

"It should be fine, Kristin," Dare said impatiently. "Let's just sit."

The young girl looked up. Kristin realized then she had been wrong in her assessment. The girl had to be Amerasian, *hapa*, like herself, half-Japanese and half-Caucasian.

The girl's coloring was light, but her eyes tilted in an unmistakably Asian cast. "I'm sorry?"

"*Koko ga ii?*" Kristin persisted.

"Oh, sorry, I don't speak Japanese," the girl said. "But you can sit there, if that's what you're asking."

"Thanks," Kristin said. She slid into the booth and Dare slid in across from her, Eric taking the chair that faced him away from the skylight's glare. "You can probably take those off now," she said, glancing at her brother's sunglasses.

He nodded. "After my eyes adjust."

The young girl came over, holding three plastic-covered menus. "Here you go. Can I get anything for you right now?"

"Water," Dare said immediately. "*Mizu*. And *ocha*, Kristin?"

Confused, she nodded. All of a sudden, he seemed to be very much at ease. "Green tea is fine," she said. "I wouldn't have thought you'd remember the name for it."

He met her eyes and shrugged.

Kristin realized something. "You knew what I said," she said after the young girl had left.

Dare looked at her warily. "What are you talking about?"

His mouth looked set, as though he would deny anything she said. "When I asked whether this table would be okay. You didn't even blink," she persisted. "You just said it would be fine. She didn't understand what I said, but you did."

He sighed. "It was pretty clear what you were asking, Kristin," he said, raising his head. He looked her in the eye, but his face expressed as much emotion as though he were reciting something. "Nobody needed to have that translated. Some statements are obvious in context."

"So how much Japanese do you know?"

"Not much," he said, staring at his menu. "Barely enough to get around in a restaurant. Barely enough to ask for directions to the bathroom. The kind that everyone knows just from watching old movies. My specialty's European languages."

"Depends on the kind of old movies you watch," Eric volunteered. Dare and Kristin stared at him, surprised.

"Did *you* understand what I said?" she asked.

Eric shrugged. "I don't know Japanese like you do, Kris."

That was true. Kristin, by dint of having lived in Japan as a child, knew and understood Japanese far better than Eric, who had been born and raised in the States. But he also understood certain Japanese phrases much the way he understood certain Swedish phrases, allowing him to understand both his mother and grandmother—but not as well as she could. Both her Swedish and her Japanese were better than his.

But he had retained fairly decent comprehension of both languages. And he didn't need to have the largest vocabulary in the world to understand a simple conversation.

Kristin tried again. "So if I were to say to Mom, '*Koko wa ii desu ka?*' like I said to that girl, you would stand around because you hadn't understood what I'd said?"

Eric shrugged again. This time, he was starting to look a little hunted, but she needed to know. "Depends on what Mom said to you when you asked her. But I've heard Mom all my life, too, Kris."

"In that case, you must remember more than you think, Dare," she pursued, shifting her focus again. "Didn't you say that you lived in Japan when you were a kid?"

He stared at her. "Yes." He glanced over to Eric. "Is she always like this?"

"Once she gets on a topic."

"Can she be derailed?"

"Go ahead and try. I'll watch a train wreck if I'm pretty sure no one's going to get hurt."

"No, really, you must remember more than you think. How long were you there?" she persisted.

"Long enough," Dare said. He flipped over the menu.

"It must have been long enough to learn a few phrases you still remember," she said. "And what about that thing that's in your bedroom? What's that all about?"

That thing.

The words fell into an endless silence. Kristin heard the echo of her words die away. Dare didn't look up from the menu. Eric kept his head low.

Until he raised his head. "Why were you in his bedroom?"

Kristin glared at him. "He fell asleep in the living room, and I got a blanket to cover him. Don't change the topic. Really, Dare," she said. "You mentioned you travel light, but that thing has to be awkward—"

Dare raised his hand then, cutting her off. "That's none of your business."

Eric got up. "Gotta use the john," he muttered, but neither acknowledged him. "Excuse me."

Neither Dare nor Kristin glanced at him. She stared back at Dare. "Why?" she challenged. "Why is it none of my business?"

"Jesus, Kristin. Some things just aren't. That's just the way life is. Or haven't you figured that out yet? No matter how curious you get, some things you never understand, no matter how hard you try. Most people realize that pretty early. What's your excuse?"

She stared at him, stunned, unable to figure out who was at fault. He looked out the window. She had hit nerves she hadn't known existed. She had hit the mother lode of nerves—and she had no idea how.

Her initial reaction, of shock and affront, melted in the face of a mystery. But his response was familiar. "That's the tone of voice you used when you were over for dinner," she observed. "The tone of voice you used when you insulted my mother's cooking—"

He turned back, raising his hand slightly, gesturing for her to stop. His jaw was set. "Enough. *I was there.* You don't have to remind me what I did."

Well, she was in for it now. She wasn't going to back away without getting some idea of what she had done.

She leaned in. "All I asked was whether you spoke any Japanese."

"And I told you. I speak enough to ask for directions to the bathroom. I can order from a menu. I can figure out how to get around on the Tokyo subway. What else do you want to know?" he said, his voice rising.

He stopped, his voice echoing in the sudden hush of the restaurant. *We will never be able to show our faces here again*, she thought out of the blue. There were a few diners making a point of not looking at him, Kristin noticed. The sushi chef was creating over at the sushi bar, and a little old Japanese lady stuck her head out of the kitchen to see what the commotion was about.

"I don't want anything from you," Kristin said, her voice low, realizing she had been holding her breath. "I just asked a simple question. I didn't think—"

"Of course you didn't," Dare interrupted, his voice shaking. *Why was it breaking?* Kristin wondered. Whereas it had been angry and forceful seconds ago, now it had lost its strength. "And I gave you an answer. Why do you need to know more?"

"But I d—" Kristin started to reply, then let her answer trail off when she saw the elderly Japanese lady approach them.

She winced. *Oh great. Now we're going to be kicked out. Eric will never let me live this down.*

"*Sumimasen*," the little old lady greeted them.

Dare nodded, took a deep breath. "*Hai*," he started off, his head nodding as he began to apologize. Kristin stared at him. Those old movies he had watched must have included body language, because he was giving all the signs of being a good Japanese boy apologizing to a respected senior.

All-American boy, my foot, she thought. She didn't say a word. She didn't have to. She watched and listened as those few Japanese words that Dare claimed he knew, enough to order in restaurants and get around in subways, exploded into phrases and sentiments, with better grammar and vocabulary than hers.

He apologized for being loud, bowing like a good boy. No, there wasn't anything wrong. Apologies. Great apologies. The little old lady bowed as well, just making sure the restaurant was living up to expectations, so forth and so on.

Then the conversation turned toward a subject that Kristin hadn't expected. Her eyes popped wide, and she turned from Dare to the little old lady. Just then, she saw Eric coming up behind the elderly woman, and he stopped, confused.

Of course he looks confused, Kristin thought. *After everything we've found out about Dare, is his having a conversation in perfect Japanese on the list of possibilities?*

And for Eric it had to be particularly confusing. His Japanese was virtually nonexistent—his knowledge of the language truly *was* limited to ordering in restaurants. And here Dare was conversing. *Truly* conversing. This wasn't anything he learned in the movies. This wasn't anything he would have learned living on a military base in Japan.

Just then, the lady asked Dare a question that made Kristin stare at him. His eyes were wide as he started to answer, glancing once at Kristin, the expression in them almost painful. "Yokosuka," Dare replied. "Zushi." He cleared his throat and, glancing again at Kristin and at Eric, who was still standing behind the little old lady, he repeated, in English this time, "I was born outside Yokosuka Naval Base. My mother was from Zushi."

Kristin stared at him. "Your mother was Japanese," she said, barely getting the words out. How could she not have known?

Dare turned to meet her gaze. Suddenly, he looked old and tired. "Born and bred and died there," he said. "I'm Amerasian, just like you."

Chapter Nine

そ

Kristin stared at him, her eyes round. "You never said anything."

He knew what she was thinking. *How can that be? He doesn't look it. He just looks like a white boy with dark hair.*

After all, that was what they always thought. That was always the first reaction.

Dare shrugged, trapped between her and the little old lady. This poor woman seemed like a nice, inoffensive person, who had only made the mistake of asking one question too many. In Japanese, a language he had claimed he didn't speak.

That seemed like a pretty small lie, considering everything else.

And worse, there wasn't much he really could say at this point. "I never thought it was relevant," he answered, knowing the explanation was inadequate. "It never occurred to me I should tell you right off the bat there was a good reason I didn't look as though I belonged in Pascisci."

"All you said was that you could sympathize with me," Kristin said, her nostrils flaring. There was murder in her eye. Dare winced. He had managed to tick her off again. Maybe it was in his genes. Maybe it was fate.

Belatedly, he remembered the elderly lady standing there, more than a little alarmed. The poor lady shouldn't be forced to stand there as they argued. It was beyond rude. "*Gomenasai,*" he said, apologizing quickly, bowing quickly.

Angry as she was, Kristin got the hint. She too bowed and apologized. As soon as the woman went back to the safety of her kitchen, Dare looked first at Kristin, who was staring at him, then at Eric, who had sat again, looking at him blankly.

Oh, hell. He put his forehead against the cool surface of the table, unmindful he had an audience of at least two.

The day had started off just fine. Now it was in pieces, and it was his own fault. "I'm sorry," he whispered.

Dimly, he wasn't sure who he was apologizing to, or why, and at that moment, he didn't care.

"What for?" he heard Kristin ask.

He raised his head to look at her. "What *for*?"

Kristin's expression was one of curiosity, not of revulsion, or dismay—or any of the other things it could have reflected. "What for?" she repeated. "Why are you apologizing? What did I miss?"

Dare looked at Eric, who shrugged. "I don't know either, man."

"I don't know why you didn't say anything, but I don't think that's why you should apologize, unless you were trying to keep it a secret for some reason," she added. "This makes what you did when you came over for dinner even weirder, but—"

"It doesn't matter," Dare broke in. His hands were on his menu again, but he wasn't looking at it. "Don't you see? None of it matters."

He looked up to meet Kristin's eyes again. He was keenly, painfully aware of the way her eyebrows furrowed, her mouth pursed as her mind raced through the permutations of what he could mean.

It wasn't the time to notice she still had the softest, most desirable mouth he had ever seen. But then, quite possibly, it might never be the time, ever again.

Her eyes flickered warily. "Well, of course it matters," she said. Almost as if she hoped there was a rational explanation of his comment.

"Tell me why it matters."

She took a deep breath. "Because it's you. It's part of you. It makes you who you are."

"No, it doesn't. If I had been adopted, it wouldn't make any difference." His voice was tight.

"If you'd been adopted, you wouldn't speak Japanese better than I do," she pointed out. "And if you'd been adopted, then your family would be your family. But you weren't adopted. You lived in Japan when you were a kid. Your mother was Japanese. You spoke Japanese when you were a kid—"

"It was my first language," he broke in, almost with a compulsion to confess now. "I had a hell of a time picking up English. I had problem with English prepositions and articles, I had accent—"

"So did I," Kristin answered. Dare watched her fingers as they rubbed the edge of the menu. "I had problems with articles and prepositions too. But then we came back to the States and I lost accent. The accent. My accent." She paused. "We're both dropping articles. I don't understand what your point is."

Dare stared at her. "Am I not making myself clear?"

"No. Enlighten me," Kristin said with more than a touch of irony. "I'm slower than usual."

"If I told you, would that have made a difference? Would you have been more or less inclined to look at me in a certain way because you knew my mother, like yours, was Japanese?"

"Probably not. It would have been incidental. But I would have been more inclined to ask you about things we might have had in common—like, say, if you liked living on base. I never did. It was always a little weird, with everyone else staying on base because they didn't speak Japanese but we did."

He didn't hesitate. "We didn't live on base. We lived off. At least my mother and I did." He closed his eyes for a second before he forced them open again. The smell of the boiling noodles in the restaurant kitchen made him remember, for a moment, the tiny apartment where he spent his earliest years—how small it had looked compared with his father, who was an American of average height but looked oversized in the flat. It didn't help that John Borodin's things always seemed to be spread out all over the cramped place, a no-no in those tiny, cramped Japanese apartments, livable only because their residents kept things neat and tidy.

Then there were those newspapers that were always tossed around, both the *Stars and Stripes* from the base, and the Japanese newspapers. Dare's mother had always had to pick them up and stack them neatly in the corner—and how she always reused them, folded them into hats for him, or lined drawers with them, or wrapped lunch in them—

"It must have been wonderful to live off-base," Kristin said wistfully, her mouth curving, breaking into his reminiscences. "Base was so boring."

Those newspapers had been landfill for nearly thirty years now. Those boiled noodles were a thing of the past. They were gone, much as his mother was. "My father didn't want us to live on base," he muttered, staring at the menu again.

"I don't blame him," Kristin remarked. Dare could hear the nostalgia in her voice. He couldn't comprehend it. "I always thought it would be fun to live off-base."

"My father didn't want us to associate with the people on base," he said, compelled to go on. He closed his eyes again, trying to will away those images of his childhood. He had spent too many years—and too much money—trying to forget.

"Well, I can see that, too," she said slowly. He couldn't imagine how many possible phrases she must have picked through to come up with that one. A nice, neutral phrase. "Some of them weren't so nice to mixed-race couples."

He wasn't going to let it go. Not now. "He didn't want us to mix with the people on base," he went on, his voice as controlled as he could make it. The flood of memories were bitter, making him wince as he remembered. "So we didn't."

"Okay," he heard Kristin say after another pause. By this point, he couldn't even hear Eric breathe.

Dare raised his head then. And found that he and Kristin were alone. "What happened to —?"

She gestured toward the other end of the restaurant. "Eric decided to eat at the sushi bar."

Dare looked in the direction in which she had gestured. Sure enough, Eric was on a stool in front of the short sushi bar, talking with his usual enthusiasm with the sushi chef, who presented him with a plate, carefully arranged and decorated. The chef looked over at them just then. Eric must have said something, for he turned around and waved at them.

"Maybe we took too long to order," Dare said after a moment, his throat tight. He looked down at his menu and noticed, with a certain detachment, that his fingers were curling around the plastic-covered menu. The edges of the plastic were cutting into his skin.

"We probably were. *And* he was embarrassed," Kristin added. "I think he assumed, correctly, that the conversation was between you and me."

Dare closed his eyes. "Once I got going, I pretty much forgot where we were—"

"Hey." Her hand covered his and squeezed it. "It's okay. I guess this is something you have some, uh—problems with."

He sighed. Her hand felt warm and soft on his. It made him desperately want to cover it with his other hand, make him feel as if they could work it all out.

Sucker, a little voice jeered in his mind.

He couldn't. "No," he said finally. "I don't have any problems with this." He withdrew his hand from hers, picking up his menu again. He couldn't look at her.

He could feel Kristin's gaze on him. It was everything he could do not to look at her, see the shining hurt in her eyes. "That's funny. I could have sworn you had a *lot* of problems with this," he heard her say. Her voice seemed to quake. He watched as her hand crept back to her side of the table.

"I don't have any problem with this," he repeated. "But maybe you do."

Her eyes widened. "Me? *I* have problems with the fact that *you* prefer not to admit your mother was Japanese? How?"

He raised his head and stared at her. "It seems to mean a lot more to you than it does to me."

"I beg to differ."

"I just don't like talking about it." He took a deep breath. "I don't see any point in talking about it."

There was a pause. "I can see not talking about it," she answered. She pressed her lips together, and for a moment, she bore an uncanny resemblance to her mother at the ill-fated dinner, after he had opened his mouth and demonstrated all too clearly he was an ass. "But your reaction said it all, Dare. And the fact that until this conversation, we have never had any discussion beyond, say, ten words about your family makes me assume you have issues."

He rolled his eyes. "*Issues*? God, let's not get into psychobabble. Are you wishing you'd gone into psychiatry?"

Her cheeks flared red. "No, I do not," she retorted. "Does that make a difference?"

"Not to me. Why should my reluctance to talk about my family make a difference to you?"

She looked around, her hands flat on the table as she leaned in toward him. This woman, almost shaking in frustration at this moment, was a far cry from the focused physician who had examined his wrist the year before.

He wished he could have left well enough alone.

"Why *didn't* you say something?" Kristin asked again.

Dare looked at her for a moment before he could answer. He wasn't quite sure what to say.

He closed his eyes again. He was tired. He wished he were in his apartment, sitting in the dark, avoiding the questions that she had raised.

But he wasn't there. He was in a restaurant with two people he had invited to spend the day with him, and he had to talk to at least one of them.

He opened his eyes. Summoning what strength he could muster, he shrugged and said, "She was out of my life when I was a little kid, before my father and I moved back to the States. And none of it played a part of my life again. The end. *Owari.*"

"Of course it made a difference. How can it *not?*"

The muscles in his jaw tensed. She didn't notice. She sat across from him, her eyes bright. She didn't get it.

She didn't understand he didn't want to talk about it.

She didn't understand he didn't want to talk about it, think about it, or do anything to alleviate the discomfort stemming from it. He was familiar with this section of his mental landscape. He knew to step around it when he was walking a mental walk, the way he would know all the rocks and potholes when he was out bicycling, or when he was out running on the beach. He had accepted it. It was there. It just *was.*

Now why the hell couldn't she leave it *alone?*

"This isn't any of your business," he said, tapping the smooth, slick surface of the menu for emphasis. He swallowed.

She stared at him, the color rising in her cheeks again. "I guess it isn't." The high emotion he had seen in her eyes had been washed away, replaced by a solid, padlocked gate. Those expressive, dark eyes were now flat and dull. "You're absolutely right. I apologize. I'm sorry."

Like hell she was. "I didn't mention it because it isn't any of your business. And it should be clear I didn't want to talk about it. I don't know why I'm talking about it now."

"You're talking about it because you can't *not* talk about it," she retorted. "For someone who doesn't want to talk about it, you're going on and on about it. Make up your mind, Dare. *Dareh desu ka?*" she asked suddenly, switching to Japanese.

Dareh desu ka?

He stared at her for a second. She had taken his name and turned it into a question in Japanese. *Dareh desu ka?*

Who are you?

"I know who I am," he enunciated. "And that has nothing to do with the subject." His heart clenched. He couldn't have said why. Like other matters in his life, he just knew.

She wasn't going to let him get away with that statement. "Of course it does. Don't kid yourself."

Her eyes met his. "I imagine there's no way you're going to let the topic slide."

"I would have before. Not now."

"Why?" The question came out of him sharper than he intended.

Her eyes widened. "Because whatever it is, it's eating you alive."

"Then let it. It's nothing for you to worry about."

She cocked her head to one side. "I'm sorry?"

"I said, 'Let it'," he repeated, more forcefully.

"Why should I?"

"Because it's been there for a good long time and it hasn't bothered me yet."

She shook her head. "Is that what you think? What fantasy world are you living in?"

Finally, he *did* have nothing to say. This was, as he pointed out, none of her business. He could say he was living in the here and now, and he didn't worry about his past—but perhaps his mental landscape might need replanting.

A beeper interrupted them, slicing through the silence, echoing through the restaurant and startling the other patrons. Out of the corner of his eye, he saw Eric look up.

Kristin pulled out a beeper from her jacket and glanced at the readout. "Let me call in."

Taking out her cellphone, she got up and headed toward the door. Dare watched her go, a bitter taste in his mouth. He glanced at Eric, who thrust the last *norimaki* in his mouth and chewed. They both watched Kristin as she spoke softly and rapidly into her phone, nodding once before she hung up.

She caught Dare's eye and shrugged. She caught Eric's eye and gestured toward the door.

Dare slumped in his seat. The day was over. It had started out to be so promising and it had ended in disaster.

Kristin came back. "I'm sorry, but I've got to go in," she said when she got close enough. Expressionless, she picked up her purse. "I'm sorry our day got cut short," she added.

Liar. Dare dropped a bill on the table, to cover not having ordered. "The life of a doctor, I guess," he said after a minute. "I'm sorry your day off got canceled like this."

"You're right, it *is* the life of a doctor," she said. He met her eyes finally. They were cool. Eric joined them, having paid his own bill. "And I'll drop my brother off at the bus stop, so you don't have to worry about him."

"It's a good thing you brought your own car," Dare said as they walked to the entrance. He opened the door and, in unison, he and Kristin bowed to the little old lady who stood guard at the kitchen, and Eric waved. Kristin and Eric walked out, followed by Dare. "This way, I can walk home and let the two of you go straight out of here."

"That *is* convenient," she agreed. They started down the hill in silence. When they reached the car, Dare smiled at Eric. "Thanks, kid. Good luck at the university."

"Thanks," the boy said. Dare noticed his eyes shift to his sister. His sister's expression, however, did not change.

"And thanks for coming out on your day off," Dare said.

Her eyes were blank. "I'm sorry we couldn't stay," she said formally. "We'll have to do this again."

"Sure," he said, knowing they wouldn't.

Dare watched as she edged the car out of the space, and waved back at Eric as she shot down the street. Eric twisted to look back at him. Dare kept watching as they disappeared.

He heard a guttural squawk from above his head. There he saw ravens huddled on the power lines, their wings tucked in, watching him curiously.

Too much. He waved them off. "To hell with you," he said aloud. "To hell with you all."

Chapter Ten
Third Year:
The wind tore the lovers apart.

൞

The street was wetter, Kristin decided, unsurprised. Other than that, West Seattle looked no different than it had the previous year.

A surge of irritation hit her as she huddled in her fire-engine-red rain slicker, pleasingly bright but not necessarily waterproof. "Lars, is there a point to this?" she asked crossly, looking around. She didn't want to be here.

The rain hadn't stopped others, either. All around her, equally sodden festival-goers browsed through the merchandise the vendors offered, chattering and generally having a much better time than she was. "There are street fairs all over Seattle during the summer, and there are four this weekend alone. It's *raining*, Lars! Why are we here?"

Kristin felt, rather than saw, the man beside her glance at her. "I told you. There's an artisan I've been trying to track down who's supposed to have a booth here. She produces some exquisite modern sculpture that would look wonderful in your dining room," Lars said as they edged their way between the booths. It was damp and icky, but that didn't mean festivalgoers moved any faster.

"Oh, Lars. Isn't it bad enough I can barely move in my living room without worrying about getting something dirty in it? Are you going to redo my dining room too?" Kristin could feel the damp permeating the edge of her jeans. Her boots were waterproof but the rest of her attire was not. Home. Home would be nice and dry. Why couldn't she be there instead?

"We'll only be here a few minutes," Lars answered, ignoring the rest of her comment.

Kristin sighed. "Sculpture would look great in your apartment, Lars, not mine. Look for yourself, not me."

"It'll look wonderful in your dining room. In the corner."

"I'm going to put a bookcase in that corner," Kristin said obstinately. "It was enough," bad enough, actually, "you had that designer do my living room. That was more than enough. Really."

Kristin hated her living room. But there was no telling Lars that. The decorator redo had been a birthday gift.

"Well in that case, I'll just look for me."

Kristin grumbled. "I wish I could believe that."

She looked around with a critical eye. Despite the weather, the turnout for this street fair was surprisingly good—perhaps not everyone had her reasons to avoid this part of the city. She had not been back to West Seattle since the previous year, and she would have preferred to keep it that way.

"I don't know what your problem with West Seattle is, Kristin," Lars continued as he poked around.

"It's just not where I want to be at the moment, that's all," she said with a sigh. Something caught her eye, something she could deal with. "I'm ducking into the bookstore over there, okay? Come get me when you're ready to go."

He smiled and kissed her on her cheek. "Of course," he said with approval. "After I hit the booths, we can check out the antique shop around the corner. You'll like that."

She smiled tightly and headed in the direction of the little used-book store. "No, I won't," she muttered.

But otherwise, in general, Lars was an understanding soul, always concerned for the welfare of others and faithful to boot. No wonder she didn't have a dog, Kristin thought darkly. She had Lars.

In the past half year, he had gotten into the habit of hiding a small white velvet-covered box in her apartment. The box contained a diamond solitaire ring. At the moment, it was nestled in a crystal candy dish filled with pastel Jelly Bellies in the living room. She had no idea how long it had been there, since she avoided her own living room.

The bookstore looked as though it would be a quiet respite from the sodden hubbub of the street fair. Kristin stepped underneath the small overhang and yanked at the door.

It didn't budge.

She yanked on it again—and then she noticed the small plastic sign on the door with a cartoon of a clock on it, with the hands set half an hour hence and the words "We'll be back at this time".

She sighed. "Great." Her eyes lit on the window display. If nothing else, she could at least look at the books, organized and divided into hardcovers up on the first row and paperbacks on the second, and she would be protected under the awning. The books were relatively new. She found herself trying to remember whether she had read any of them, something that would take her mind off Lars and his increasingly insistent reminders about the ring.

He could have it back in a second. Now if only she could tell him that gently—

She was only vaguely aware of the footsteps that stopped beside her. She was amusing herself comparing two books with the same title that clearly had nothing in common. Eventually, however, she noticed someone was standing next to her under the overhang, a little too close.

At first, she didn't think anything of it. The weather was wet, the overhang narrow. There wasn't much space but she was willing to share. It wouldn't be long before the store opened up again. Lars would finish traipsing around in the wet sooner or later, and they could go find dinner, and nothing more had to be said or done about the person next to her—and as she became more and more aware of him, she heard his breathing.

The minutes stretched by. The clock on the sign was, clearly, only an approximation of when the store would reopen. Kristin refused to move. The person next to her stood still, facing the display in the window. But she could feel his eyes.

The fine hairs on the back of her neck stood up. She could feel his warmth, even though he wasn't actually touching her. She suppressed a tremor.

No matter how she tried to ignore the sensation of being stared at, it was there.

I am not going to let this get to me, she said to herself. *If nothing else, I will scream.*

When Kristin finally looked up, ready for a confrontation, her first reaction was one of relief. *Oh, good, I don't have to worry.* Her second reaction was one of horror. *Come on, Lars, come get me now.*

The corners of her lips turned up in a semblance of a smile. Then, uncomfortable, she went back to staring at the display.

Dare Borodin. *I knew we shouldn't have come*, she thought.

She looked again. He looked only slightly wet, possibly because of the black umbrella he was holding, now closed. His hair was curling at the collar of his windbreaker, and his denim-encased legs—long, lean, relaxed—looked as though he hadn't had an accident since the year before. Amazing.

"Fancy meeting you here," she heard him say.

Startled, she dropped her purse. He bent down and retrieved it, presenting it to her. "I'm sorry, I thought you'd guess I would say hello," he said.

Right then, the awning overhead decided to let go of the weight of water that had accumulated. Kristin tried to get out of the way, but she got splashed anyway. She yelped.

"No umbrella, huh? Here," he said. He shook his umbrella and opened it, offering shelter to Kristin.

"I'm from Seattle," she muttered, not taking him up on the gesture but not turning it down quite yet. She glanced up at him. At the moment, his eyes were that hazel she liked. "We don't use umbrellas."

She heard him snort. "If you don't mind getting wet." She felt him look at her as he stretched his arm a little closer, bringing her within the shelter of the umbrella.

Tempting, but no. "Seattleites don't." She shivered. It wasn't cold but it wasn't warm, either. It was simply wet. "I'll just wait here, thanks."

"What, for the rain to let up? Is sharing an umbrella with me for a couple minutes going to change your life? Or is someone going to take away your Seattle citizenship?"

She felt him step closer, putting her, without her moving another muscle, directly under the umbrella. "Now isn't that better?" he said, his voice lower.

She could feel his breath on her ear, moving the fine hairs in it. "I guess," she admitted. Her heart started to pound.

She looked at him. He looked much the same, except he wasn't limping, in a cast, in a brace, or even disheveled. "Small world," she said tritely, knowing it was trite. "I almost didn't recognize you without a crutch or a bandage."

Dare smiled slightly, but looked a little wary. She felt her face warm under his gaze. "And I almost didn't recognize you without a white coat. So what are you doing here?"

She gestured toward the booths. "We're looking for one of the artisans who's at this thing," she said, referring to the street fair. "But I got bored, so I figured I'd duck in here for a while. But it's closed."

He nodded. "They'll be back. So how've you been?"

She shrugged. "Not bad." She didn't want to get involved in a discussion of her life at the moment. Her memory replayed the scene from the year before, and she didn't feel comfortable at how they had parted. "Eric's taking summer-quarter classes," she added. "Calculus and biology. He's decided he wants to go into sports medicine."

"Sounds good."

"So what have you been up to?" she asked, looking at him. She cursed her upbringing. If she had been a ruder person, she could have mumbled something and left quickly, disappearing into the crowd. And Dare probably wouldn't have followed her. And that would have been that.

She couldn't get away with that now.

He shrugged. "This and that. I have a friend visiting from out of town at the moment."

"That's nice. Lars, over here," she called out as she saw a familiar figure break out of the crowd. "Are you ready?"

"Almost," he said. He glanced at her and then at Dare. The two men locked stares. Kristin looked at Lars, equally curious. She didn't recognize the expression on his face.

Unfortunately, there were manners to be had all the way around. If there hadn't been, she would have bolted.

Dare was the first to break the mutual stare. "Hi, I'm Dare Borodin," he said, extending his hand. "And you are?"

Lars looked at him and then at Kristin. "I'm Lars Bergen, Kristin's fiancé."

Kristin's eyes bulged. "Lars, we haven't talked about it!"

Lars looked at her with eyes as gray as the weather. "Honey, you've had that ring for half a year," he reminded her. "We should talk about making it official."

"Congratulations," Dare said smoothly. She glanced at him. His face didn't register any emotion. But then, why should it?

"I'm sorry," he said to Kristin. "I somehow got the impression you were here with Eric."

She shook her head. "He's too busy studying. He's taking summer classes."

"So how do you know Kristin?" Lars asked. His expression was back to normal. It was one she was familiar with, vaguely interested, vaguely polite. Vague vague vague.

"From Pascisci, believe it or not," Dare answered, with a smile for Kristin when he glanced at her. "We met when I came in for a broken wrist."

"Ah, the Indiana year," Lars exclaimed. "You know, she hates talking about it."

Dare turned to look at Kristin. "How come?"

She grimaced. *Thanks a lot, Lars.* It was raining, she was wet, and she had to talk about this now? "It was the worst year of my life. I felt so out of place. Grandpa died. It just seemed right to move back here."

Lars reached out and smoothed a strand of damp hair away from her face. "You're just too used to having me there to clear the way for you," he told her.

Kristin felt her cheeks turn red. "That wasn't it," she sputtered. "I just felt out of place. Shouldn't we be getting out of here?" she asked desperately, trying to urge Lars on. She didn't want to be here. She wanted to make her apologies, murmur insipid insincerities and go home.

But Lars wasn't paying any attention. His gaze shifted from Kristin to the source of her discomfort, who was standing too close to her. "So what brings you here from Indiana, Dare? I got the impression that Chicago and St. Louis were the places you Midwesterners ended up at."

Dare smiled briefly. "My job. It takes me all over. Before Seattle, I was in Boston for two years. And I had the choice between Seattle and Chicago this time."

"Sounds like you're quite the traveler. What do you do?"

Kristin cleared her throat. "Lars, you're on duty tonight, aren't you?" She stared at him, willing him with all her mind to read her thoughts. *Let's get out of here. Now.*

If Lars did sense her plea, he chose to ignore it. "That's not for a while yet." He turned back to Dare. "Are you free for dinner?"

Dare shrugged, with a glance at Kristin. "Sure. I'll find out if my friend had other plans, but dinner sounds great."

Kristin chewed on a fingernail. She didn't like the way this was going. "Aren't we supposed to have dinner with my mother and grandmother?" she asked, with a glance at Dare. If he had any couth at all—

Lars smiled. Not for the first time, that indulgent smile was getting on her nerves. "That's tomorrow, honey," he corrected. "Why don't you meet us, once you check with your friend?" he suggested to Dare.

"We were going to a sushi place in the International District, and I don't think you'd care for that," Kristin put in. That was rude, but she was desperate.

On the other hand, she really hoped he'd get the hint.

"And you're supposed to have dinner with your mother and grandmother tomorrow," Dare reminded her.

She glared at him as Dare and Lars exchanged information, Kristin fuming all the while. *This is what comes out of visiting West Seattle. I refuse to come out here ever again.*

"In about half an hour, forty-five minutes?" Lars asked.

"Sounds good. See you there, Kristin," Dare said to her.

She didn't answer him. "Let's go, Lars," she mumbled.

Kristin didn't say another word as she and Lars negotiated the crowds, which seemed to have grown despite the drizzle and the cool. She kept quiet until they found her car.

Kristin unlocked her car door before she started in. "Why couldn't you leave well enough alone? We could have gotten away without having to deal with him," she snapped. She jerked the door open, got in and leaned over to unlock the passenger-side door. She winced. "Ow," she muttered. "Damn it." She broke a fingernail flipping the lock toggle. She rubbed the bent plane of her fingernail, biting her lip.

As usual, Lars said nothing until he was in the car and buckled in. Then he said mildly, "I thought it would be polite. I had no idea you'd mind. Don't bite your nails."

Kristin backed out of the parking space, her jaw set. "How long have you known me, Lars?"

"Twelve years or so. Why?"

"Then haven't you learned by now that when I say 'We should get together sometime,' I'm just being *polite*? Do you listen to *anything* I say?" She put the car into gear and stepped on the gas a little too forcefully. She felt, rather than heard, the tires squeal on the wet pavement.

Lars could feel it too. He grabbed at the armrest of the car door and looked at her reproachfully. "Of course I do."

"I was doing fine getting out of the situation until you piped up," she muttered. She stopped at a red light and took a deep breath. She didn't want to drive too quickly. "But now we have to deal with Mr. Bigot *and* his friend. I swear, if they start ranting about illegal immigrants, I will vomit."

"I've never heard you talk like this before," Lars said, amazed. "What happened?"

She sighed. He had been on sabbatical when Dare had come into—and out of—the lives of the Olafssons the year before. "You were in Baltimore. I bumped into him again last summer, and Marmar wanted to meet him, so I invited him to dinner. All of a sudden, he insulted Mom. He told her there were bugs in the rice, he said that everything tasted as though it was spoiled. It was weird and it was horrible."

"Your mother's cooking? That's odd," Lars mused. "Your cooking leaves something to be desired, but your mother's cooking is quite delicious."

Kristin ignored that. "It gets better. It turns out his mother was Japanese, but he's got a problem with that, and he won't even admit he's half-Japanese. He practically yelled at me when I asked him why. He is just plain bad news, Lars."

"Well, not everyone wears their ethnicity on their sleeve like you do, Kristin."

She tapped the steering wheel for emphasis. "Come on, Lars! He was—he was passing for white!" she said, the phrase dawning on her. She had never thought of it in those terms but it certainly fit.

"He might think of himself as white," Lars pointed out. "He grew up in Pascisci, surrounded by Scandinavians, sweetheart. I must admit, it never occurred to me he might be Asian. It's not the first thing you think when you look at him, but now that you mention it, you can sort of see it."

"And what *is* the first thing you think of, pray tell?" Kristin asked with dripping sarcasm. "A swastika tattoo?"

Lars, for all his good points, did not include a sense of humor among them. The irony was lost on him. "He's got a swastika tattoo?"

"I have no idea, but I wouldn't be surprised."

"We don't have to linger. Happy?"

Her lips pressed together. "It's a start."

By the time they reached the International District, she had calmed down. The restaurant was one of her favorites. It was traditional as far as Japanese restaurants went, with the movable walls between rooms made of wood slats and rice paper, the floors of *tatami*, straw matting, and the servers in real kimonos, the kind that cost the world to buy and you had to be taught how to dress in.

And where no one ever questioned whether she was of mixed heritage.

She shivered. Even a year later, she could remember the scene in that restaurant. She couldn't ever go back there. Even if no one else recalled it, she would. She could still see the look on Dare's face—*trapped*—as the little old lady stood there.

Her nostrils flared as she remembered. Another surge of emotion flooded her, except this time, it was white-hot anger. The burning sensation of betrayal ripped through her, even though she couldn't have said why or how she had been betrayed.

Unaware of the melee of emotions in her, meanwhile, Lars looked around, satisfied. "Doesn't look crowded tonight," he observed. "Four," he said to the maitre d'. "The other two will be here in a few minutes."

"Let 'em find us when they get here," Kristin muttered.

Lars sighed. "Kristin—"

"What?" she said with a challenge in her voice.

He looked at her for a moment, his face blank, before he gestured down the polished wood floors of the hallway. "After you."

They followed the hostess and sat on *zabuton,* flat floor cushions, on the straw matting of the floor. Kristin tucked her feet under her and Lars sat awkwardly first in a half-lotus and then Indian style. They sat in silence, and before long, she heard a familiar voice and a soft shuffle of feet.

"Sounds like they're here," Lars observed. He looked at Kristin. "Now be polite," he said, his eyebrows rising in emphasis. "No matter what you may think of Dare, you've never met his friend."

Kristin didn't answer, instead straightening her back. But she didn't say a word.

Lars glanced at her. He shuddered. "Stop smiling," he ordered. "You're going to ruin my appetite."

She glowered, arranging her face into a mask of neutrality that would have done Switzerland proud. The door slid open partway, and their kimonoed hostess edged in, kneeled on the inside of the entryway and opened the door some more to let in the two people behind her.

A tall blonde woman came in, followed by Dare. The hostess bowed, Kristin bowed in return and the hostess reversed her steps to slide the door closed.

Once the door was shut, Lars unfolded himself and stood up to shake hands with Dare. "Glad you made it," he said. Then he turned to the woman and shook her hand. "I'm Lars Bergen," he said. "I'm a—a *friend* of Kristin's," he said, with a glance at her. "And you are?"

The blonde smiled, and in contrast her smile was real. It transformed an otherwise unremarkable face into a pretty one. She had an open face, with a happy look that Kristin at once found annoying and envied. "Dagmar Lundquist. I'm an old friend of Dare's, from Pascisci."

"Kristin Olafsson," Kristin said. "Welcome to Seattle."

Lars gestured for them to sit. Kristin glowered at him again, but he didn't notice. He was too busy doing his impression of a host. "Pascisci again! Pascisci's a long way from Seattle," he commented as the other two both folded themselves onto their own *zabuton*. "What brings you out here?"

"A job interview," Dagmar explained. "And since a mutual friend of ours knew Dare was out here, she suggested I look him up." She looked at Kristin. "My grandmother. She knows your grandmother too. I'm supposed to say hello to you."

Lars interjected, "Is your grandmother Ginnie Venderkash, by any chance?"

"I take it she has a reputation, even here in the big city?"

Lars nodded, smiling. Kristin suddenly wanted to slap his face. This was just too civilized for words, when all she wanted to do was go home and never see Dare—or his blonde—again. "Now, I don't know Pascisci, I've never been there, but I've heard a lot about your grandma. Amazing how she always assumes you're going to look people up for the sole purpose of saying hello to people you've never met," Lars commented.

"I've never met her, but I almost expect her to have someone from that town of yours call me up just to say hello!"

Politely, Dagmar and Lars laughed. Kristin rolled her eyes. Lars nudged her. "Are you awake? I'm so sorry," he apologized to Dagmar. "Kristin can be a trifle shy."

"Oh, I am not," she said crossly. "As for Ginnie, I've met her from time to time. She and my grandmother are friends."

The blonde smiled again. Kristin was getting tired of that white, perfect smile. She must have had years of orthodontia. "So hello. She wanted to make sure you were doing fine."

Kristin looked over at Dare, who had yet to contribute to the conversation, his expression unreadable. He watched her.

She stared back. Despite herself, Kristin could see the vein pulsing in his throat, and she could feel her own blood race through the delicate arteries of her wrists, speeding both away and toward her heart.

I want to go home. I want to go back to my apartment, and relax. I want to feel safe again. She turned back to Dagmar and smiled the most natural smile she could muster. "Has Dare shown you Seattle?"

The other woman laughed, glancing at Dare. "Oh, we've been busy. We went to Pike's Peak Place—"

"Pike Place," Lars murmured.

"And the Space Needle, and then we went to that festival today, where Dare ran into you. And yesterday we went down to the water—the pier. It's been exciting so far. And I don't even have my interview until Monday."

Kristin glanced at Dare again, her gaze questioning this time. He met her eyes and looked back, the question unasked and unanswered.

"So how does it compare to Pascisci?" Lars wanted to know, oblivious to the undercurrent. "I've heard so much about that town, and I'm curious to get another opinion."

Dare came back to life then, tearing his gaze away from Kristin. "Actually, Dagmar lives in Chicago. She probably gets back to town once a month or so — right?"

"Not quite, but more often than *you* get there," Dagmar said. "As for Pascisci — well, it's a quiet little town."

"Complete with small-town prejudices?" Kristin inquired, straight at Dare. And before she could stop herself, she rushed on. "How many lynchings? One a year? Two? Participate in any?"

The table hushed. She was horrified at herself. Dare stared at her, the muscles in his jaw visibly shifting. His expression was readable, and this time, it was not pretty. "That's your father's hometown," he snapped. "Remember? That's where your grandparents settled down. That's where you spent your summers when you were a kid."

Dagmar, to her credit, recovered quickly, although a hint of pink remained in her cheeks. "Well, there was Sven and his bunch," she interjected, glancing from Dare to Kristin to Lars, a hint of discomfort in her eyes. "They could be nasty. Wasn't he in our class, Dare? What was his last name?"

Kristin looked over at the other woman. "Olafsson," she said flatly. "He's my cousin."

The table was dead quiet now. The hint of pink in Dagmar's cheeks faded completely. "We don't speak," Kristin added. *Can I leave now? Can I avoid seeing these people ever again?*

Lars opened his menu. "What would you suggest, Krissy? I think I'll start with the miso."

"What a good idea," Dagmar exclaimed, flipping open her own menu. "You know, Pascisci didn't even have a Chinese restaurant until five years ago, let alone a Japanese place."

"'Krissy'?" Dare repeated. "Is that what people call you? That's such a cute nickname. It fits you."

In a pig's eye, Kristin thought. "Lars is the only one who calls me that," she said, her teeth bared. "And he gets away with it because he doesn't use it very often."

Dare didn't stop. "Someone named 'Krissy' should be perky," he continued, his mouth crooked to one side and turned down. "Someone bubbly. Someone pleasant."

"I'm quite pleasant, if you get to know me. And if you accept me for who I am."

"But if I recall, you have this problem with your bedside manner too. No wonder people don't like their doctors."

"Well, gee, maybe some people would like their doctors better if they were the right ethnic group."

"Maybe some doctors use that as an excuse for not learning how to be pleasant."

Kristin turned to Dagmar, whose eyes were wide as she pretended to study the menu. "Did you know his mother was Japanese?"

Dagmar's eyes were wary when she raised her gaze from the printed pages. Kristin didn't think it was possible for those blue eyes to get any wider, but there they were. "Really? You don't look it," she said to Dare. "In that case, can *you* recommend anything on the menu?"

Lars groaned. "Kristin—"

That was it. Kristin threw down her napkin and scrambled to her feet. "It was nice to have met you," she said to Dagmar. She dug into her back pocket, withdrew a business card and presented it to the other woman, who, to her credit, did not shrink away. "I'm sorry you had to be in the middle of all this. If you get the job, look me up and I'll make it up to you. But I have to go home now."

"Krissy, you drove!" Lars exclaimed. "How am *I* going to get to work?"

Kristin was already at the door. "I'm sure you'll find your way. Good night, all."

She carefully slid open the door and then just as carefully closed it, walking down the hallway. She could hear murmured, pleasant conversation from behind other closed doors. She only wished she could have joined in.

Kristin retrieved her boots at the front of the restaurant and tried to slip them on without breaking her stride. She couldn't. With a muttered curse, she sat on a bench and unzipped the first one.

As she finished yanking it on, a familiar step came down the hallway. "Are you coming with me?" she asked without looking up. "I'm in a hurry. I'm not going to wait for you."

"What the hell is wrong with you?" Lars demanded. "Kristin, behave like an adult."

"I am." She unzipped the other boot. "I'm behaving like an angry adult. What's your problem?"

"Jesus, Krissy, you could have just—"

"Don't call me that," she snapped. "Call me by my given name. After what he said —"

"You can dish it out but you can't take it?" another voice interrupted.

Kristin looked up. Dare was standing behind Lars. "I would have thought you were tougher than that," he said evenly.

Go away, she wanted to tell him. *Go back to your pretty blonde and leave me alone.* She was mortified at her behavior. She was embarrassed that, yes, she was jealous. They had parted on less than exemplary terms the year before, but once she had seen him with Dagmar—pretty, blonde, easygoing, and most of all free—she had been flooded with a jealousy that had nothing to do with reason.

Lars turned and put his hand on Dare's shoulder. "I'm sorry Kristin blew up like that," he apologized. "I don't know what's wrong with her."

"Can it, Lars," Kristin snapped. "As for you," she said to Dare, "I have nothing more to say. Go away."

Dare turned to Lars. "Could you leave us alone for a few minutes? We have to speak privately."

Lars looked at Kristin then at Dare then nodded reluctantly. "I'll be ordering dinner. And entertaining your guest. As for you—" He bent down and kissed Kristin on the cheek. "I'll talk to you later."

Dare waited until Lars disappeared down the hall before he sat down next to Kristin and slipped on his own shoes. "We need to talk, and we're going outside to do it."

Kristin finished putting up her boots. She stood up, heading for the door.

Dare grabbed her hand. She looked at him. "Ready?" he asked, not letting go. "Let's step outside."

Kristin's heart twisted. Not even attempting to get away, she nestled her fingers into his. His hand was warm, and suddenly, finally, she was willing to admit she was embarrassed. She nodded.

One by one, the streetlights illuminated the streets, the puddles on the ground reflected in the hazy glow. Dare led her out to the parking lot and watched her as she huddled in her jacket against the rising wind and rain.

"I assume this is your car," he remarked as he let go of her. "Unless you've switched cars in the past year."

She shook her head. Deprived of his warmth, her hand felt cold. She tucked it into her slicker. "This is still it."

"How does Lars fold himself into it? I had enough trouble doing it last year, and he's taller than I am."

"It's harder with crutches. And he drives his Volvo with the seat pushed way back."

"A Volvo, huh? Figures." He leaned against her car and looked her in the eye, his expression softened finally.

Kristin felt her eyes brim with tears. "I'm sorry," she said suddenly, her voice quavering. "I've made such an idiot of myself. I was so mad and so embarrassed at the same time."

Dare snorted. "We're even. I made an ass out of myself in front of your mother and grandmother. They probably tell you every day not to let me in the house."

She tried to smile. "Well, whenever I go over, at least." She blinked a couple of times. "And your poor girlfriend probably thinks I'm crazy."

"Her family lives next door to my father. And she's a sweetheart. She'll forgive you."

"Good. Tell her to look me up if she gets the job."

"I will. Kristin—" he paused. He leaned against the hood of her car.

"Yes?"

"I guess I ticked you off last summer."

She shrugged. Words weren't her strong point right now, so the less said, the better.

"How's Eric?"

She sniffed and leaned against the car next to him. "He's fine. He's taking summer classes right now."

"You said that."

"Oh. Sorry."

"I really ticked you off last year, didn't I?"

She sighed. "Yeah."

"I thought so," he said with a faint smile. "At least as far as I could tell from this dinner."

She smiled back unwillingly. "It was so horrible after you left last year, after dinner. I didn't know what to say to Mom or Marmar—and Eric kept saying, 'But he's not a bad guy, I know he's not!'"

"Well, at least someone in your family likes me."

Kristin snorted. "Eric's philosophy is that unless you try to hit him over his head, you've got to be okay."

"So he has all the forgiveness in the family?"

She stood stock-still. "I forgive you," she began slowly. "If you forgive me. But I don't think it's such a bright idea to see each other. We don't get along."

"We did before I screwed things up."

She shook her head. "Some things are a mistake, Dare. Can't you just take my word for it?"

"We can get over this. Can you take *my* word for that?"

"I have Lars to think of," she said, her heart hammering as her hands began to sweat, even in the chill of the evening.

"I get the feeling it's one-sided. And not on your part."

He grabbed her left hand and held it. He rested the tips of his fingers to her pulse, and she knew he could feel it race. "No ring," he observed. "Not even evidence of one."

"I just haven't worn it yet," she said, her voice trembling.

"I'll bet it fits. He doesn't seem like the kind of guy who'd give you one if he hadn't checked on the size first."

He traced the lines on her palm. The sensation of his hand on her skin was light, almost feathery. Her breathing almost ceased as she concentrated on his touch. "It fits," she whispered. She swallowed hard, took her hand back and pressed it against her heart. Her heartbeat was strong and she wished it was his hand there and not her own. "I'm going home now. It was nice seeing you again. Please relay my apologies."

She rummaged for her keys. Dare put his hand over hers, making her stop for a moment. "Give me a chance. Let's start fresh."

His eyes were dark in the dusk. Kristin wished she could lead him to one of the bright streetlights to read his expression, but she knew she couldn't.

She shook her head. "Not a good idea. I'll see you around." She grasped her keys.

He stood there as she started the car and eased it out of the parking lot. When she glanced in the rearview mirror, he was there still.

The wind and rain started back up again. The drizzle and drear reflected her mood.

Chapter Eleven

"Dr. Olafsson? That guy's on the phone again!"

Passing by, Kristin gritted her teeth. "Tell him I can't talk right now."

In point of fact, she could have. The emergency ward was slow at the moment, always a blessing—although it usually meant there would be hell to pay later. No, at the moment she was sitting, filling out a form a clerk could have filled out, but it gave her something to do to avoid the call.

She knew who it was. Dare Borodin was, if nothing else, persistent. After the first few times he called, she learned to avoid the phone. This was the ER. It was a busy place filled with, well, emergencies. Her family knew better than to call unless they had to.

It had been six long days since she bumped into Dare. It had been a quiet week, punctuated by calls she didn't take and regrets she didn't express.

After she left Dare in the parking lot, Lars called repeatedly, but she didn't answer. Instead, she went to see him the next morning at the hospital.

Orthopedics was so quiet in comparison to the ER that Kristin was tempted to have her hearing checked. The young nurse at the reception desk didn't quite whisper, but certainly her voice was lower than it would have been had she worked in the emergency room. Told that Lars would see her in a minute and she should wait, Kristin started to pace.

She knew what the problem was. All noise seemed to be muffled up there, and that made her nervous. Compared with the ER, which was as close to the outside world as possible, orthopedics was far removed from reality. Up there, she couldn't hear the sirens, the screeching of tires, anyone shouting. There just wasn't any commotion.

Lars hated commotion. He hated coming down to see her. The look of sufferance on his face pained her as much as it did him, mainly because it annoyed the daylights out of her. That, coupled with the commotion, made it much easier for her to come up to his tranquil world. It was a nice place to visit. She just didn't want to live there.

She cut to the chase when she saw him come down the hall. "I'm sorry. I should have returned your calls last night."

The slightly miffed look on his face eased slightly. "That's all right," he said, but the expression on his face belied the words. "You had enough to think about. Have you?"

"Been thinking? Yeah," she said slowly. She knew what he was referring to.

"Come to a decision?"

"Lars—" Kristin paused. She didn't want to talk about it, certainly not here. "No. I still have to think about it."

"Heard from what's-his-name?"

She stared at him in disbelief. "Who, Dare?" She could feel her pulse trip into fast-forward, and it was all she could do to stand still, not willing to admit how the subject of Dare Borodin affected her, even now.

"The guy yesterday?" Lars prompted. The look on his face annoyed her again, but she willed herself to remain calm. "With the pretty blonde? She and I had a very nice dinner while you and he were outside," he added. "Dagmar. Is everyone in that town Scandinavian?"

"Mostly," Kristin said, gathering her wits. "Why would I hear from him?"

Lars gave her a look of reproof. "Please. Because your phone's unlisted, he's not about to call your mother for your new number, and he knows you work here. Ergo. He has to call here."

"But I told him I wasn't going to see him again," she exclaimed.

Damn it! This was why she didn't want to get into it. She hated gossip and she knew Lars hated to be gossiped about.

Kristin lowered her voice. "I don't think—"

She stopped, her heart tripping when she looked at his eyes. As icy as a winter's rain. "He'll call," Lars predicted.

She shook her head. "You're wrong."

Lars was wrong about the timing. Dare had waited a day before he picked up the phone.

Kristin managed to avoid talking to him for nearly a week. Then, as she was coming back from lunch with Lars, Amy, one of the residents, called her over.

"Kristin? Lars is on the phone for y—" Amy trailed off, her gaze shifting from Kristin to Lars. "I guess not. Well, he *said* he was you," she amended.

Lars snorted. "I was wondering how long it was going to take for him to try this."

Kristin smiled, rueful. Amy was newly returned from vacation and hadn't spoken to Dare as often as some of the others on the shift. "Don't worry about it."

"Should I tell him it didn't work?"

Kristin shook her head. "I might as well get it over with." She glanced at Lars, whose expression gave her no clue or comfort. "At least he found a way for me to take the call."

"Provided you were talking to me," Lars said with a smile. "I'm going back to work. Tell me what happens."

She watched him go. Only after he turned the corner heading toward the elevator bank did she pick up. "Dr. Olafsson," she said. "Funny, Lars, you were standing next to me when the call came through. How did you manage that?"

"If you knew who it wasn't, why did you take the call?"

"To let you know it didn't work." She couldn't prevent herself from smiling. "Nice try, though."

"Would it have worked if he hadn't been standing there?"

"Most likely."

"What would it take for you not to hang up on me?"

"Going back in time and erasing everything that's happened between us."

"I skipped the time travel class. Besides that?"

"Just drop it, Dare. It's not going to happen. I have to get to work. Unless you want to talk to someone else here. Although I think Amy's a little ticked at you right now."

"There has to be something," he persisted. "For instance, I promised you dancing, but we never went. I was hoping I could invite you to a dance this Friday. How's that?"

Kristin thought for a second, chewing on her lip. "What makes you think Lars doesn't take me dancing every week? For all you know, he dances my feet off."

There was a pause on the other end. "I'd bet my life Lars is tone-deaf and couldn't dance if his life depended on it."

"You got that right," she admitted. This was a new twist…and it intrigued her. "Fine. I'll go dancing with you. But that's it. The next time we bump into each other, we can be polite and make noises about getting together and not do it, like normal people. Fair?"

"I'll pick you up on Friday at 7:30. Are you still living with your family, or have you moved?"

"I've moved out."

"What's the address?"

She paused. Oh, why not. She told him.

A minute later, she hung up, staring at the phone.

"So how did it go?" Lars inquired.

Kristin turned around. He had to have walked a complete circle around the floor to end up behind her. "Weren't you going back up?"

"I was curious. So how'd it go?"

"Better than I thought," she admitted. "Or at least less painful. He's taking me dancing on Friday."

"I thought you never wanted to see him again."

Blindly, she picked up a nearby file and opened it. "He reminded me he owed me a night out," she mumbled.

"Should I be concerned?"

His tone, as always, was even and disinterested. Kristin knew he was disturbed. But he would never admit to it.

She snorted but didn't look up, still toying with the folder. "I don't think Mom and Marmar would approve."

In response, Lars put his hands on her shoulders and leaned in. "Should I be concerned?" he repeated

Oh, give it up! Aloud, she said, "Not here, Lars." She moved away, not looking at him. She had had this conversation before with him but this time felt different.

Kristin had always confided in Lars, treating him more or less like a girlfriend. In turn, he had more or less tolerated it, until the past few years, when they were back in the same city again, and they were both adults, out of school, unencumbered. Now, he was getting insistent he was not a girlfriend.

She looked around. The rest of the staff, absorbed in their own activities, seemed to pay them no mind. What had to be done should not be in public but here it was.

She put down the folder in her hand and took a deep breath. "Lars, we've been friends for so long," she began, keeping her voice low. "And you know how my mother and my grandmother feel about you. You're a part of the family."

"You're not answering my question."

Later. Her stomach turned. She couldn't do this right now. "You're not going to be ousted from the bosom of my family, Lars," she said lightly. She refused to get any more specific than that. She had managed to avoid the Relationship Conversation thus far, and she certainly wasn't going to get into it now. "Mom and Marmar would never forgive me. How's that?"

Lars looked mollified—sort of. "It's a start."

The knot in Kristin's stomach eased. "If it makes you feel any better, you can go out with Dagmar when she shows up again."

He snorted but he looked away right then too. "Well, thank you, Kristin. Maybe we could double date."

There was that sarcastic bite to his tone again. "What a splendid idea. Let's keep it in mind." She looked up at him again with a grin, finally able to meet his eyes. Not terribly comfortable, but at least the tense moment was past.

But Lars was smiling. He looked as though he had forgiven her. He patted her cheek. "I'll be there if you need me." He picked up the folder. "I take it you really need supplies."

He held it open for her. She took it and looked at it.

Blank office supply requisition forms.

"I'll talk to you later, Krissy," Lars said, chuckling as he kissed her on her cheek.

Kristin watched him as he walked away. She shivered.

She didn't like this Lars.

To her and her family, he had always worn the most agreeable face. He had always been the ideal potential son-in-law to her mother and the ideal would-be grandson-in-law to her grandmother. He had always been the best of friends to her, and on occasion, even to Eric.

But she had always known he had another face. From time to time, she had seen the mean-spiritedness that possessed Lars and always wondered about it, but he had never directed it at her. So far.

* * * * *

On Friday she was late getting home. She raced in and straightened what she needed to—with the exception of the living room, which was always pristine, of course —before her own primping ritual.

Not that it took long. So she was more or less ready a few minutes later, padding around in stockinged feet and peering out the window. She glanced at herself in the mirror for what had to have been the tenth time in ten minutes. She still looked acceptable.

Could he find the place? The configuration of the apartment complex where she lived made it a challenge to find, she had to admit. She lived on Capitol Hill, a vibrant part of Seattle, not far from the hospital. The series of small apartment buildings where she lived were built in the early 1900s, long before the term "complex" was ever applied to living quarters. In fact, when the first working-class residents of the brick apartments moved in, the horse and buggy was the preferred method of travel, the world had yet to see its first modern global war and city dwellers could still see Vega and Altair on a starry summer night.

Kristin looked out the window above the sink. Dusk was approaching, throwing long shadows. Some of her neighbors were coming home, but no sign yet of Dare.

Then she let out a breath she hadn't realized she had been holding. He appeared at the entrance to the courtyard, looking at the apartment numbers on the doors. Then he saw hers — and her through the window. She waved. He waved back. She waited with the front door open, watching as he made his way.

"I'm sorry I'm late," he said as soon as he got into range.

She closed the door behind him. "It's tricky sometimes."

"I circled the block twice to figure out how to get in."

She paused for a moment to look at him. Her mouth was dry. Suddenly, she was acutely, painfully aware of him.

But she still couldn't believe this was a good idea.

Kristin nodded, answering his comment. "It confuses people the first time."

She looked at the dense clutch of bright dahlias in his hand, feeling the tension she could see in his muscles. "Are those for me?"

He looked at the bouquet. "They don't go with anything I'm wearing." He met her gaze. "But the red ones sort of match your cheeks at the moment," he added.

Kristin felt herself blush, shy for a moment. "Thank you. Do me a favor? Put them into a vase with water? I have a couple in the kitchen. I'll be right out."

"Sure. Nice apartment," he said as he disappeared into the kitchen.

"Thank you. I'll be ready in a few minutes," she called out as she hurried down the hall.

She closed the bedroom door and crossed to her cosmetics table. The three-mirror vanity, a gift from her Japanese aunts, was littered with rarely used cosmetics. She peered at her reflection, touched a finger to the edge of her lipstick.

Then she scowled. This was ridiculous.

"I can't find a vase. And—hey, snazzy living room. I never would have thought you would have a place like this," she heard.

She wrinkled her nose. That overdecorated, pristine living room. *Thanks again, Lars.* "I'm so scared I'm going to mess it up I spend most of my time in my study," she called out. Then, as she fastened an earring, a thought popped into her mind—one that made her head for the door.

When she came down the hallway, still without shoes and wearing only one earring, she found Dare standing in the living room. The look on his face was familiar, one that many of her first-time visitors wore for a few minutes—unease.

"You know, this room could be a model for one of those style magazines," he commented as she came in. "It doesn't have a magazine out of place. Everything sparkles. And it's the only home I've ever seen that didn't have at least one smear on a glass table. Even those shoes look as if they're there for show."

He started to lower himself into an ivory-brocaded club chair before he stopped, looked around and stood back up, flowers still in hand.

She stifled a smile. "Go ahead," she invited.

He shook his head. "I'll stand."

She knew what the problem was. The room was *too* perfect. "I make it a point not to come in here," she told him as she leaned against the doorframe. "And my cleaning service dusts it. You know—" she stopped.

"What's wrong?"

Kristin shook her head, embarrassed. He was dressed in a white Oxford shirt, jeans and sneakers that had seen better days. "I thought we were dancing."

His brow furrowed. "We are. Are you all right?"

"Are we going club-hopping? That kind of dancing?"

"No. I was thinking of…" His brow cleared. "It's the way you're dressed, isn't it? I think you look great."

Her face grew warm. She knew she looked good. The red silk dress, one of the few dresses she had, made her glow, and she was decked out in pearl earrings and choker, jewelry that had been gifts from her mother.

She was *way* overdressed.

He narrowed his eyes. "Are your feelings easily hurt?"

"No. Why? Do I look awful?"

He laughed, a short bark. "You're beautiful, Kristin, but you're overdressed for the occasion. Also for you." He reached into his shirt pocket and held out his hand.

She looked. It was a tiny gold ballotin of Godiva chocolates. "Thank you. Is there a punchline?"

"I figured I'd better give you the candy and flowers before I broke the news to you that we're going square dancing, and it's not an occasion that requires that dress, no matter how pretty you look in it."

Kristin looked at the flowers, at the box of chocolates and then at Dare. "Square dancing? Like in country western? Like I had to do when I was in junior high?"

He nodded again.

She took a deep breath. "Are you going to at least feed me afterward?"

He let out his breath. She allowed herself a quick smile. He had been nervous too. "If by that time you haven't insulted me, assaulted me, or done anything that requires calling 911, I was planning on it."

She looked down at her outfit and turned around. "I'll be out in a few," she said over her shoulder. Then she tossed the chocolates on the club chair, where the gold box gleamed, daring the room to quash its brilliance. "Try the shelf over the stove for a vase."

She hurried down the hallway again, carefully unhooking the other earring. "Square dancing," she muttered. "Great."

She had barely closed the door to her bedroom when she was already wiggling out of the dress. The shoes she had been planning to wear with the ensemble—a matching red, with a lower heel than those sitting artfully in her living room—she tossed to the back of the closet, where they hit the wall with a satisfying thump.

She yanked open her dresser, pulling out items she wore too seldom—casual wear, an informal shirt and jeans. Then she remembered something she had for shoes that could work. She opened the closet doors again.

"Are you all right?" she heard him ask.

She dragged on her jeans as she answered, "Hold on."

The buttons on the shirt became slippery and stubborn. Her fingers trembled. *What's wrong with me?*

There was a knock on the door. "I heard a thump. Are you sure you're all right?"

"Yeah. Hold on," she repeated. She zipped up the jeans and managed to close two of the buttons of the blouse.

"You know, the hallway looks like you," she heard.

The buttons slipped out of the buttonholes again. She bit off a curse and remembered why she didn't wear this shirt more often, but it was too late now. "Why, the woodblock prints?" she asked. She took a deep breath, wiped off her palms on her jeans and tried the buttons again.

"Yeah. They're pretty," she heard him reply as she reached for the doorknob. She was still fastening her shirt by the time Dare came into view, but when she looked up to meet his gaze, his eyes startled, she realized she hadn't buttoned up enough. She looked down. He got a healthy glimpse of her bare diaphragm and petal-pink bra before she finishing buttoning up the hot pink floral blouse.

She straightened the shirt, not bothering to tuck it in yet. "I threw my shoes to the back of the closet. That's probably what you heard. Did you find the vases?"

Dare tried to control the quirk of amusement around his lips. "I found one. I started to put your flowers into the one with a swirly pattern, but it's too small."

She nodded. "I've got others somewhere," she said, slipping past him. Still acutely aware of his presence, she walked past him, his faint musk dissipating as she kept moving.

She stopped in the foyer and knelt in front of a closed panel low to the floor, yanking it open. She pulled out a box after the door creaked open. "Here—shoot!" She fell back when the door came off its hinges, clattering to the floor.

He was beside her in an instant. "Are you all right?"

His scent was stronger now. She smiled. Like Irish Spring. "It still had one hinge working when I checked it last," she said, pushing away her impulse to bury her nose in his skin.

It was hard to remember he was just a guy. A guy with problems, even. But he smelled really, really good.

She picked the door up and peered at the hardware that was still attached. "Let me go find my screwdriver so I can take care of this before we go."

"Let me." He took the little door from her and produced a Swiss Army knife from his pocket. As she watched, he pulled out one of the tiny utensils from the knife's holder and reattached the door. "All done," he said, smiling at her.

"Thanks. I never realized how handy those things are. Or I guess you're handy," she answered.

"They're handier than I am." He gently touched the tip of her nose. "You've got *schmutz* on your nose."

"What? Where?" She crossed her eyes to try to see, and that made him laugh. Her eyes uncrossed to look at him.

Kristin could feel the rapid thrumming of her pulse. She wondered if he could hear it. In an idle gesture, he reached out and fingered the pendant around her neck.

The pendant. She'd forgotten.

She reached up and touched his hand before skittering off in doe-like shyness and finally resting on the necklace itself. "I forgot I had it on," she murmured.

The piece of jewelry was an intricate interplay of gold and pearls, wending closely around her neck before the chain met at the base of her throat and then trailed down in a dropped, entwined pearl and diamond figure, almost reaching the valley of her breasts. It was not something she would have worn with the casual attire, but she had forgotten to take it off.

And it attracted Dare's attention. "It's pretty," he said, still toying with it.

She could smell him, man and aftershave and soap. She loved the combination. "It was a gift from Lars," she said, her breathing quick.

Dare dropped the pendant.

"Sorry," Kristin whispered.

He was wordless as she went to the kitchen sink, still holding the dusty box under her arm. "Let me just put the flowers into water, and then we can go," she muttered.

She could almost taste his skin, he had been so close.

Kristin lifted the fluted crystal vase out of the box, her hands trembling. She kept a firm grip on it as the water ran around and between her fingers, lukewarm and soothing.

She hadn't felt the sensual swirl around her in ages. Now that she wasn't running from it, she welcomed it.

Then Kristin closed her eyes for a moment. *No. I'm not going to see him again after tonight.*

She shut off the spigot and jammed the flowers into the vase. She arranged the blooms, all the while listening for him. He had wandered back into the living room.

She heard him take a deep breath and then let it out. She didn't want to know what he was doing. She only wanted him to do what he had to do before the night, their night, was played out and they could be on their separate ways again.

She could hear the rattling of the Jelly Bellies—the pale ones, of course, part of the overall look—in the crystal dish in the living room as he picked up the velvet box from among the candy. "What's this?" He popped open the box.

She turned around, setting the vase on the kitchen table. She'd forgotten about the jewelry box. "That's the ring Lars has been trying to give me for the past six months. He's gotten into the habit of hiding it where he thinks I'm going to run across it. He still doesn't realize I don't go into my living room if I can help it."

He looked at her, then at the box. "Maybe I should go."

Their gazes met. He stood on the edge of the cover-model room. Then he glanced at the white velvet box in his hand.

"No," she replied. "I don't think so."

"You have a life without me." He looked at the box, his face expressionless.

"I also have a life without Lars. And I've been telling him that. Is it just me, or do the men I get involved with just refuse to listen to me?" she added, trying desperately to inject a note of humor, anything, into the conversation.

He didn't answer. Quickly, she wiped her hands on a towel and crossed the boundary between the kitchen and her living room, coming to a stop in front of him.

Wordlessly, Kristin put her hand over his, gently pulling the velvet box from him. She snapped it shut, walked over to the gleaming expanse of her coffee table and tossed it there. It blended in with the cream and ivory of the room, its paleness swallowed by the light, nearly becoming invisible.

"Tonight's not about Lars," she said. She reached out and grabbed his hands, turning him so his back was to the living room. "You and I are going out tonight, and we're not going to talk about him."

He stopped her with a hand to her arm. "Kristin."

His eyes were as dark as the shadows in the courtyard. "Am I one of the men you're involved with?"

"At the moment, you are."

He didn't answer. Instead, he dropped his gaze to the valley between her breasts. Slowly, he drew up the pendant hanging around her neck and over her head until she was free of it and it was twisting between his fingers.

"May I?" he asked.

She shrugged. As she watched, without glancing away from her, he flicked the pendant to the side, letting it bounce off the coffee table and skitter in a glittering pile onto the pale carpet.

He bent over and whispered in her ear. His breath stirred the fine hairs at the nape of her neck, and the shiver down her spine made her knees buckle. "I didn't think your outfit needed the extra jewelry."

Chapter Twelve
༨༠

"Where are we going?"

Dare hesitated. He considered not telling her until they reached their destination — but decided that honesty was best.

"The golf course." He kept his eyes on the road, not looking at her.

"The golf course?" He could feel her staring at him.

He glanced at the rearview mirror, at the speedometer, at the sky. Anything but her. He didn't have to look at her to know what her reaction would be. "The golf course."

Pause. He heard her settle into the seat. "So we're going to the golf course for, what, square dancing?"

He couldn't resist. He glanced at her.

She was smiling. Thank God.

"Unless you want to line dance, in which case we have to come back on Monday. Clog dancing's on Tuesdays and alternate Wednesdays."

She shook her head. "No, I don't think I'm going to be available on Monday," she said finally, and he could hear the amusement in her voice. "I have to work. What a shame."

"It is." Something else occurred to him that made him grin. "Do you realize this is the first time we've been in the same car but I've been driving?"

"That's true. Will I regret it?"

"When you and Lars go out, who usually drives?"

He could say the name without injecting any unnecessary emotion. Good. After the scene in Kristin's living room, he wasn't sure he could.

I didn't think your outfit needed the extra jewelry.

He had surprised himself, stripping the pendant from her. What hadn't surprised him was the surge of passion that swept over him as his fingers briefly held the delicate piece of jewelry in his hand, the warmth from her stealing through him.

She stared at him, clearly just as surprised.

"You're right, it doesn't," she gasped after a moment. He could see the pulse beat in her throat. It would have been so easy to touch it, to feel the flow of life.

"Lars usually drives," she responded to his question. He had almost forgotten he asked it. "In his car. He has to fold himself into a pretzel to get into mine."

"I'll bet he does. It was bad enough for me."

"And Eric, too," she added. "But that guarantees he doesn't take my car unless he really needs one." She grinned. "Next time, I'll get an even smaller car."

He laughed. "Carefully calculated."

"You bet. You don't have any siblings, right?"

"No."

"Well, Lars comes from a family of five kids. Whenever my mother and grandmother start talking, he can't get over how spoiled Eric and I were when we were growing up."

Was Lars going to be the topic of conversation all evening?

"When did you meet?" he inquired.

"It was my first day at the UW, and I was lost. He told me where to go, and I've known him since."

"A long time. Very romantic."

She looked out the window again. "He was Lars."

Bad idea, he thought with a trace of panic. Too much. He was losing her attention, and he had no idea what to do to get her to stop thinking about the elephant in the room. "Dagmar was always Dagmar," he offered. "We moved back to Pascisci, and there they were next door, all the Lundquists. I could have sworn there were five million of them."

"Didn't they ever ask you about Japan?"

He paused. In the back of his mind was a memory—Mrs. Lundquist, Dagmar's mother, fluffy, blonde and always cooking something cinnamony, asking a question. He remembered answering. "It was okay. Could I have another cookie? *Domo.*"

He'd been seven.

"Sure," he said, a little too loudly to his own ears. "But I was just a kid. How much could I remember?"

"We lived there when I was a kid, and I remember a lot," she said softly.

A drizzle started to fall. Dare flipped on the wipers and kept his eyes on the road, curbing his inclination to turn and watch her.

"There must have been a marketplace outside the base," she said. "Don't you remember the smell of the fish?"

The rain started to fall in earnest, fat drops splattering down the glass. "I don't remember," he said after a moment, hating himself for lying, but unable to stop himself.

"Didn't you ever go out to the market?" she asked, her voice soft. "I always loved the *osembe* store, with all those different kinds of rice crackers. And the bookstore. I couldn't read anything, but I liked hanging out there. I hated going back to base."

It was on the tip of his tongue to lie again, but his curiosity got the better of him. "You couldn't read anything?"

"I never learned how to read Japanese," she answered, her voice almost drowned out by the sound of the rain. "I spoke it when I was a kid, but I couldn't speak English. So Mom made sure I could speak and read English by the time we moved back to the States. Learning to read Japanese wasn't as important for an American."

"I can read it," he confessed.

"I thought you only spoke well enough to get around in subways and restaurants."

He winced. Hoist on his own petard. "Have you seen the Tokyo subways these days? Lots of English. You don't need Japanese anymore. I think of it as one more language in my arsenal of languages." Fortunately, this part was all true. "But it's not one I use as much as others. For instance, there's not much call for Japanese in, say, Munich."

"So you have traveled."

"Yeah." Now they were on more familiar territory. Now he didn't feel trapped in an emotional corner. "Every two years, like clockwork."

"Doesn't it get tiring, never staying in place?"

He shrugged. "I get a fresh start every two years."

"Where have you liked living the best?"

He pondered the question. "Here. It has you," he added.

She smiled. "Suckup."

He smiled. "It's the truth. The history in London was fascinating. The Parisians were a kick. New York was fun. Berlin—I drank a lot of great beer. But so far, I like Seattle best. You're right, that *does* sound like a line. I wouldn't trust me either."

He remembered the dinner at her mother and grandmother's house, gone horribly awry. "The suckup part of me just doesn't come out often."

"Same here," she assured him. "I've embarrassed myself more often than I care to admit. Isn't it annoying?"

"Yeah," he said, laughing. "So is this date tolerable so far?"

"So far. Now let's see how badly I square dance."

The golf course was not far from the highway. Previously, he had only been there in the daytime, checking it out. Noise had been part and parcel of the visit. But now, in the twilight, he could see the emerald courses lit by the occasional light, and what little sound he could hear from the highway was curiously incidental.

"I should take up golf," he mused as they walked into the clubhouse, which was bustling in contrast to the serene course. "You walk around in the grass, dressed in funny clothes, communing with nature. Sounds ideal, doesn't it?"

"It's only ideal until you start trying to hit the little ball. My dad was a golfer, but he didn't go out that often. It annoyed him, and he couldn't afford to get that upset."

The father. Damn it, he'd forgotten. "I'm sorry. Maybe we shouldn't have come. I didn't think. Did he—?"

To his relief, she shook her head. He admired the drops of water shimmering on the dark sheen of her hair, looking like crystals on black velvet, before he turned his attention to her eyes, dark and, at the moment, far away. "He had a massive heart attack one day out in the garden. He was gone by the time I found him," she went on. "But—" She shrugged. "It's one of the reasons I decided on emergency medicine. I've always wondered whether I could have saved him."

He watched for a second, looking at her profile, catching the glimmer of tears. He smoothed a strand of hair away from her face. She glanced at him but said nothing, not moving away from his caress, but not acknowledging it either.

Too much. Clearing his throat, Dare glanced at his watch. "We've still got a few minutes before the dancing starts," he said finally. "Let's go out back."

The night-lights flicked on as they stepped onto the covered concrete patio behind the clubhouse. Beyond the patio lay the golf course itself, lush and green even in the dim light.

Kristin leaned against a planter to admire the scenery. She sighed. "This is nice. Thank you."

His heart swelled. "I didn't know whether this would be your kind of thing, but I figured you probably hadn't done it."

"That's true," she admitted. "I've never seen a golf course at night. I haven't square danced since I was in junior high. And I've never been taken out to the golf course at night for square dancing, so you hit for the cycle. How's your knee?" Kristin inquired abruptly. She tucked hair behind her ear.

Dare watched her, but she was still looking out at the course. "It's fine," he assured her. "So's my wrist. I wouldn't have asked you out if they weren't. I owed you dinner and a dance."

She crossed her arms. If the movement was an unconscious attempt to protect herself from his gaze, it didn't work; it drew his attention instead. Her breasts were full, and if her arms hadn't been almost cradling them, they would have been straining the buttons on the blouse a little.

"Who am I to turn down free food and a Friday night out?" she asked.

Dare shrugged, not taking his eyes off her. "I thought you might like it. And I owed it to you."

"I hope that's not the only reason we're here."

He watched a solitary golfer under the lights on the green. "I wanted to have an evening out with you that didn't involve Lars or Dag."

She shifted. "Ex-girlfriend?"

"Girl next door. It's nice to see old friends."

She looked up at him. "Then I hope she gets the job."

"Do you really? Or are you being polite?"

"I'm being polite," she confessed. "I'm still so embarrassed."

"Don't worry about it. Dag has a short memory. Otherwise, I'd be in a perpetual state of embarrassment."

A breeze picked up just then—not cool, not warm, just a breeze. She shivered.

He straightened. "Chilly?"

She shook her head, but drew her arms around herself a little tighter. "Well, maybe a little."

Dare slipped an arm around her. "We'll be going in soon."

He immediately regretted having moved when his hand brushed against the curve of her breast. He hastily withdrew it.

He was torn between conflicting instincts. His body stiffened. "I'm sorry." He lowered his arm and took a deep breath.

So did Kristin. She stepped forward, just a little. "That's all right." Even in the dim light, he could see her swallow hard. "Let's go inside."

Dare followed her into the clubhouse, blinking at the harsh lights. They walked down the broad corridor that bisected the building, past a number of doors, until he stopped and peeked behind the doors with the loudest music, then gestured for her to do the same.

He knew what she was seeing, but he didn't know how she would interpret it. It was a large room, one that often was the site of wedding receptions, simple in style, ready to be decorated at a moment's notice—like now. There were brightly colored streamers hung from corner to corner, and at the other end of the room, there was a three-man band. He liked the lights, the activity—but most of all, he liked how happy the people looked as they walked around, waiting, men and women and even children, some of them dressed in Western-style clothing.

Kristin looked up at him, her eyes round. "It looks like the emergency ward on a blood-free day. Or maybe a Nordstrom's sale. All these people, milling around."

"In that case, it'll be a nice change of pace for you. Shall we?" he asked, offering his arm.

She hesitated, then she took him up on it.

As they did, the music burst forth, the fiddler fiddling energetically. The floor shook slightly as a group across the room stepped at the same time. "Good grief," Kristin breathed. "It feels like an earthquake."

"It's the boots," he told her as they crossed to a woman seated at a card table, cash box in front of her.

"You mean like these?"

For the first time, he looked down at her feet. She was wearing a pair of Western-style boots, white leather, fringe around the tops with a silver medallion on each.

"Nice boots. Remind me not to let you step on me."

"Thank you. Looks like a uniform around here."

"That's for sure." He looked around. "I may be one of the few wearing normal shoes."

Square dancing was lively. For Dare, whose experience in dancing was limited to a few spins around the floor during a few wedding receptions, it was an unusual occasion.

Dancing, he remembered only belatedly as he got into position, was a cheap excuse to touch. The first time he had been forced to square dance, he had been in elementary school and the entire experience had been a torturous affair, attempting to draw together two sexes who were barely able to socialize as yet without pummeling each other. The only saving grace was that neither side had to touch each other for long.

Of course, by the time their hormones kicked in a few years later, when touching the opposite sex was a reward, not a punishment, square dancing was a thing of the past—and the teachers struggled to keep them all apart.

Those phys-ed teachers would never have had any trouble getting the kids to learn square dancing, or anything that required touching, if they had just timed it right, he mused.

The more he thought, the easier it would be if society got back to square dancing as part of courting. He wouldn't have to worry about how close he was getting to Kristin, because it was never for very long and it wasn't frequent. But handing off the partner you wanted to touch got old fast when you found yourself looking forward to the next touch, then having to let go, grasping her around the waist, then letting go, twirling around—then letting go again.

He found himself craving the next time he was rewarded with the heat of her hand, the lushness of her waist and hips, shifting beneath the thin fabric of her shirt and jeans. He couldn't imagine—or maybe he could—the excitement the men of a few generations before must have felt when they could feel the girl's waist beneath the crinoline, the wired bodice, the petticoats—

Dare nearly misstepped. He remembered why going to the movies could be such an attractive proposition. It was dark. It was secluded. It was a temptation.

Kristin twirled close again. He held her hand, spun her around once, and then dipped her backward. His muscles tensed as he felt her lean into his arms. "Having fun?" he said, trying not to gasp.

She nearly stumbled, righting herself before he could grab her. "Sorry. I'm not used to this," she replied, raising her voice to be heard. He could feel her heart race as he came closer, then stepped back.

He splayed his fingers across the small of her back during the promenade. "Well, in that case, get ready," he whispered into her ear. He pressed her against his chest for a moment, his arms touching the length of hers. He could feel the smoothness of her cheek against the crook of his shoulder, her scent pervading his senses. He wanted to kiss her then, run his fingers through her hair, touch the length of her neck with his tongue, feel the heat of her body—

Then they separated again and Kristin smiled at him. The less than polite thoughts shrank away. Her sparkling eyes made him want to watch her dance, not take part in it. He saw her laugh in response to something that someone down the line said, and he wanted to be there with her.

Finally, it was time for the caller's break. The dancers broke, laughing and chatting.

Kristin had been at the other end of the line when the dance ended. "Would you care for refreshments?" he asked as he approached.

"Something to drink," she said. Her face was lit. "You know, this is fun," she remarked, grinning as one of the other participants waved on his way out. "I don't remember square dancing being fun when we were kids."

"That's because it wasn't," Dare retorted. "Where I went to school, we learned to square dance when we were still worried about cooties."

"If the schools waited until we were in high school, they wouldn't have been able to pull us apart." She wiggled her foot. "But I should have worn sneakers. I'm not used to doing any hoofing with these boots."

"Sit while I get you something to drink." He led her to the side, where metal folding chairs awaited resting dancers.

Now that he could touch her again for longer than a few seconds at a time, he was loath to release her. His right arm was across her back, his hand on her elbow, his left hand holding hers. Anyone who saw them might have assumed she wasn't feeling well, as opposed to being led by someone who couldn't let go of her. Or dancing.

But she also looked tense. "Relax," he whispered.

"I am. I'm just tired," Kristin said as she sat down.

For a moment, Dare's heart stopped. "I'm sorry," he ventured. "Do you want to go home?"

She shrugged. "I'm sorry. It's been a long week."

"In that case, let's get you food. Now that we're done with the dancing, we can go for food. Deal's a deal."

"You don't mind cutting this short?"

"Not at all," he said, and meant it. "I wanted to spend time with you. What would you like?"

She shook her head again. "I'm not that hungry."

"Did you have lunch?"

She started to open her mouth and then, with a shrug, said, "I can't remember."

Dare went into action. "You're not going to get a decent night's sleep unless you eat something." He pulled her up to a standing position. "The snack bar here has great barbecue. You'll love it."

"I don't know," she said, her voice fading. But she did allow him to pull her to the no-nonsense, extremely utilitarian counter of the snack bar.

She would like this, he knew it. "This guy's a genius," he told her. "The meat just falls off the bones. It's—two barbecues," he ordered, still holding her. He didn't want to let go unless he had to. "For here or to go?" he asked her.

She looked up. His eyes followed her gaze. There were plumes of smoke up high. They curled around, fighting with the tantalizing scent of the cooking. "Not here, I don't think."

He considered it for a second. "My place isn't that far. If you don't have a problem with that?" His voice dipped a little. Just possibly, it wasn't the sort of thing you asked on what was technically a first date.

She shook her head, eyelids drooping. Maybe she *was* tired.

Their orders arrived, and by then, it was clear Kristin really *was* tired. But she took a whiff of the bags and smiled. "This does smell good. I must be hungrier than I thought."

By the time they were on their way to the parking lot, Dare could guess she was hungry. She was rummaging through the sacks. "What else is there? Breadsticks? Something I could chew on until we eat? I'm starved."

He snorted. "I guess you're hungry."

She stuck her nose into one of the bags and breathed deeply. "This smells wonderful."

Dare stifled a smile. "Go ahead and dig around, but it's going to be messy," he warned, startled, as she found the cornbread and started to chew on a piece.

"How far away do you live?" she asked, chewing.

"About five minutes. Although," he said as he eased through an intersection, "at the rate you're going, you're going to be done with your meal by the time we get there."

Dare glanced at her. She looked happy munching. "I enjoyed myself. Thank you."

"Welcome. Maybe another time, even."

"I'd like that."

"You could even bring Lars."

She snorted. "I can't see Lars doing this. I can't even see Lars—" she stopped. "Never mind."

"I'm sorry. I shouldn't bait you like that."

She shrugged. "Lars and I don't have an exclusive relationship. At least I've tried to emphasize that to him."

It was almost difficult for him to breathe. "Good." He reached over and covered her hand with his.

He tried to tell her. "But I can't imagine someone not wanting that with you."

Chapter Thirteen
The lovers strained for each other, so close!

∞

This was too hard. She could spend an evening square dancing with him, but he was too close in the confines of an all-too-small vehicle.

"Thank you," she said finally. She tried to smile, but she couldn't do it. All the experiences of her life were converging, and she didn't know whether she was up to it.

An irritated honk from the car behind startled them. Neither of them had noticed the light change. Dare turned his attention to the road again and didn't say anything else until they eased into the spot in front of his duplex.

Kristin got out of the car, looking around. The night breeze smelled like the sea close by, and in the quiet of the evening, she could hear the lapping of the waves on the beach. She heard the cry of a raven, the answering cry of a seagull. The rain had become a mild drizzle, and above, the clouds were moving across the sky.

She shivered, but she wasn't cold. She hurried after Dare as he walked up the pathway with the bags of barbecue. "I'll take those," she told him, grabbing the bags. Flashing a grin at her, he fished out his keys and opened the door.

The light of the single lamp he had left on threw shadows in the apartment. She stepped in, looking around. Behind her, Dare closed the door.

Kristin felt her pulse start to race and her skin was clammy. *I'm actually nervous*, she thought in surprise. She was nervous about being in this man's apartment.

The first time she had been here, she was concerned with getting Dare off his feet. The second time, she was concerned with finding his first-aid kit. She didn't count the third time, when she and Eric picked Dare up.

Third time should have been the charm. This time, the fourth time, she had no qualms about his health—so far.

As far as she could tell, the apartment itself hadn't changed at all since the last time. The dining table was still covered with books. The living room was littered with newspapers. An empty pizza box was jammed into the garbage can.

"If I had realized you would be coming over, I would have cleaned up."

She looked up, startled. "Oh, no—I was just wondering if the stuff on your dining room ever got moved around, or whether it was on permanent exhibit."

"That's where I work at home." He started to pile the newspapers. "Let me clean up here, and then we can eat."

"I can help you."

"No need. All done. See?"

With just a few pickups, he had managed to clear the room of errant papers. "Wow, you're good," she said. Then she blushed. "You're really efficient."

His mouth crooked into a smile. "I know. I'm very good at what I do. Let's take the food out to the patio."

What did that mean, Kristin wondered as she picked up the bags of food again and followed him.

Then she looked out at Puget Sound, and any other thought she might have had vanished as she stared at the water.

She took a deep breath. "I didn't remember you lived on the beach."

Too many night shifts had made her forget how much power the sight of an evening sky could hold. The gibbous moon was peeking from among the clouds, hanging low over the mountains, the clouds its attendants as it climbed into the sky.

"*Tsuki-ohimesama,*" she breathed, a smile on her face as Dare set the table.

"The what? That sounds familiar."

Kristin turned. Dare had set up dinner on the table. He had not bothered to turn on the overhead light. Judging by the light from his apartment, there was no need.

"*Tsuki-ohimesama,*" she repeated. He sat down in one of the plastic chairs, and she did the same. "The moon princess. You can practically see her tonight. You know the story."

He looked up at the sky, then at her. "I remember," he said. "A foundling grows up and reveals she is the daughter of the moon queen, and she has to go home. And since then, her visage can be seen in the full moon.

"I don't think we look at nature enough, myself," he said, stretching out. "If we spent more time looking up instead of looking down—"

Her moment of fantasy over, Kristin finished the statement. "Wouldn't we spend a lot more time tripping over our feet?"

He grinned. "Maybe we'd be better people. If nothing else, we'd be more aware of our surroundings. Nature rules us, though we refuse to admit it. Why don't you start eating?" he suggested as he started to open the Styrofoam containers. "You were pretty hungry."

Kristin turned away from the moonrise and surveyed the sea of Styrofoam. Suddenly, her mouth watered.

"Thank you," she said as she slid one of the boxes to her. She took a deep breath. The spareribs were drenched with sauce, the vermilion pool a statement at the bottom. A small tub of sauce sat in the corner of the container. She pried it open and poured the contents over the ribs.

Her stomach growled. "Excuse me," she murmured as she licked a dab of sauce off her fingers and hummed her approval. "This sauce is wonderful." She glanced at him.

He was holding onto a dripping rib with two fingers and a thumb, carefully keeping it away from his white shirt. "Go ahead," he urged. "It's going to be messy. I'm not going to worry about it. But I may laugh at you behind your back," he added as he started to chew.

"Some gentleman you are."

"But I did warn you I was going to laugh at you."

Kristin wrinkled her nose at him. Daintily, she picked up her first rib, holding it between her index finger and thumb, and bit. She began to chew, her eyes half-closing in pleasure. She could feel the sauce trickling down her fingers and her chin and smearing across her cheeks, but she didn't pay any attention. "I was starving," she said in astonishment. "I don't think I had lunch."

"Shame on you. Would you approve of your patients doing that?" He pulled a tidbit off the bone.

But she wasn't paying much attention. "I beg your pardon," she said, chewing, running her tongue over the slippery surface of the sauce-covered bone. "I eat breakfast. Everyday."

She looked up to find him watching her. "He does breakfasts too, if you're wondering," he said. He picked up another rib and held it between his fingers, letting the sauce ooze onto the Styrofoam. "You're not shy about eating barbecue in front of me, are you?"

She swallowed. "Do I look it?"

His gaze dipped to her mouth. Her breathing slowed as he watched her tongue dart out and lick her slick, sauce-drenched lower lip, and all of a sudden she did feel self-conscious.

Then his eyes met hers, and her breathing paused.

He gestured to the side of his lips. "You have—"

"What?"

Reaching over with a napkin, he slowly dabbed at her mouth.

She watched his eyes. They were intent and she could feel his fingers through the rumpled napkin. Then he withdrew.

She sighed.

The spell was broken. Her heart pounded as she grabbed a napkin and rubbed her mouth to cover the way her hands and lips were trembling. "This is the problem with barbecue."

"I agree. Uh—" His eyes focused below her neck.

Kristin looked at the front of her shirt. Sure enough, her enthusiasm had left barbecue sauce, long, broad vivid smears down the hot pink cotton.

She winced. "The shirt was pretty new too," she commented dolefully. She picked up a new napkin, wet it with the edge of her tongue and dabbed at the stain. Then she stopped. "This isn't going to work."

"I don't think so."

She looked at him. "At least I'm not alone," she commented, smiling slowly. There was a splatter on the front of his white shirt, messier than hers. She glanced at his sleeves, and realized he must have accidentally rubbed his arm against the front of his shirt as well.

Dare looked at his shirt, then at her. "Guess not."

His gaze flicked down her face, the length of her throat and finally rested on her shirt. "If you'd like to try something, though—" he stopped. His eyes trailed back up almost languidly before resting on her face again.

Kristin felt her face grow warm. Her breathing became a little more uneven. "What?"

He nodded toward the beach. "Nature's way of taking care of things. If you want to try it."

The moonlight reflected off the waves. The breeze off Puget Sound had picked up. It was warm, with the salty scent of the water filling her senses. "Okay," she said after a moment. "I'll bite. What?"

"Take off your shoes. And your socks."

She stared at him. "Why?"

His eyes almost glittered. "Because you're going to be uncomfortable going into the water if you don't."

"What, go into the water? You've got to be kidding. This is Puget Sound. It's going to be cold. It—"

There was a glint of humor in his eyes. She looked down at the stain on her blouse. "Fine," she said, sighing.

Yet another napkin in hand, she started to wipe what was left of the barbecue sauce off her fingers before she looked down again. "Oh, to hell with it. In for a penny," she said, smiling suddenly. She licked the stuff off her fingers and gingerly heeled off her boots. "Now what?"

Dare had taken off his sneakers and socks. "I do this from time to time, and I don't know if it's going to get the stain out, but you'll feel better about it." He started to unbutton his shirt.

Kristin's eyes widened. "What—"

He looked up at her. His eyes were as dark as she had ever seen them, but there was a definite twinkle in their depths. "It's easier dunking the shirt into the water," he said as he shrugged it off. "But that's not something you may want to do on a first date. The wrong impression and all."

His T-shirt was white, untouched by the sauce. She could see the muscles of his shoulders and chest play and shift under the thin cotton, the ends tucked into his jeans.

Dare reached out for her hand.

She let him grab it before she started to have second thoughts. "We're really going in? Oh, I don't know—"

"You'll feel much better," he assured her.

"But this is the Sound. God knows what's in it. It's going to be cold," she wailed as he started to walk toward the sand's edge, dragging her along. "It's too cold. Come on, Dare! We can just go back and run some cold water on our shirts!"

He turned around and smiled, catching hold of her other hand and leading her, step by step, into the lapping waves. She couldn't look away. His gaze caught hers in their intensity, and now she felt as though she were drowning. "It's late August, Kristin," he reminded her. "It's a summer night. You're covered in barbecue sauce. Live a little."

He grabbed her around the waist and dipped her in.

She yelped before the water swirled around her. She struggled for a moment before she realized he was keeping her head above the waves.

Soon, she stopped struggling as her body adjusted to the temperature of the water. "This feels good," she said after a moment. The water, even in August, was only lukewarm, but it was soothing. The waves surrounded her, like a light blanket on an early spring morning—slightly caressing, slightly cool.

She closed her eyes. "This feels wonderful," she said after she got her breath back. The waves swirled around her.

Then she felt him stand her upright, his hands firm around her waist and back, supporting her. She opened her eyes.

They stood in waist-deep water, the currents buffeting them first one way and then the other, letting her sway.

Dare was in front of her, his hands on either side of her. She couldn't see his expression, but the combination of moonlight and the seeping light from the other apartments nearby gave her some idea; he was watching her. His shirt, the one he had shucked, was hanging from his shoulder, wet.

Kristin looked down at her shirt, now wet as well and, she realized, clinging to her. She looked up at him again. "Does it look like the stain's coming out?" She could feel the pulse in her throat start to race again.

His eyes shifted to the front of her shirt. "I don't know."

On impulse, she touched his chest. His T-shirt was wet up almost to where his heart was. She placed the palm of her hand against him, feeling the strong beat.

Beneath the wet cotton, his skin was warm. Beyond the smell of the water, the breeze around them and the lapping waves, she felt herself surrounded by sensation, of everything and of nothing. She couldn't think anymore. She could only feel.

Kristin spread her fingers against him, enjoying the feel of his muscles. He was wet and warm, and he smelled like all the good things in life.

"Good strong beat," she murmured hazily.

She heard him laugh. "You thought I didn't have one?"

His eyes were luminous. He trailed a finger down the curve of her cheek, her jaw, the length of her throat. She held her breath when his finger trailed down, stopping at the valley between her breasts.

She took another breath, quick and sharp, as the warmth of his skin heated hers. "Your skin is satin," he whispered.

His hand spread over her breast. Kristin didn't object. She could feel the heat of his fingers, warm and wet, through her. Her heart started to beat in unison with his pulse. Together, the pounding surrounded her.

"I think your stain's going to come out," he whispered.

She looked down. He was fingering the wet cloth of her shirt, which was clinging to her breasts. She could see the splash of errant color had faded.

Kristin smiled, feeling embarrassed. "I think it is."

But he tipped her chin up, forcing her to look him in the eye. Her gaze met his, and she forgot why she was shy. "May I?" he asked.

She remembered why. "Yes."

Her lips parted as she raised her face to meet his. Oh God, his eyes! She couldn't breathe. All her secrets seemed to be reflected in them. She couldn't have turned away if she tried.

Dare traced the outline of her face. He traced her cheekbone and ran a finger across the surface of her lips before his finger finally slipped into her mouth.

She moaned. Every muscle in her body sang with need. Her nipples stiffened as the muscles in her legs melted. Her mouth softened.

Her eyelids fluttered shut. She felt the warmth of his fingers as they stroked her throat, stopping again at the valley between her breasts. His tongue explored as his fingers spread, stroking her breasts.

Kristin murmured, unable to articulate any more than her delight. She trailed her hand down his back, feeling the heat of his skin through his wet shirt. Her fingers trailed past his waist and paused at the sodden denim covering his legs.

His jeans. The heavy fabric had to be uncomfortable to move in, considering it was waterlogged. But the jeans were molded to him, and her thoughts dissipated in the heat of his skin as she drew a lingering finger around the waistband of his jeans. Kristin could feel his tension.

"Do you think your stain's come out?" Dare gasped. His trembling reverberated through him and through her.

She couldn't answer. His thumbs were smoothing rhythmic circles on her shoulders. The contact threatened to steal any common sense she had left.

If she weren't in the water, she would have fallen to her knees by now. In the part of her mind still capable of clear thought, she tried to be upright. Why?

She couldn't remember. But she knew she should.

She murmured. "What?"

Through half-closed eyes, she sensed him lean forward and whisper in her ear. "Your shirt."

His finger trailed up her throat, lingering at the edge of her mouth. "Shirt?"

His fingers made their way to her ear, to stroke the delicate skin behind it. But then she forgot about that when she felt his lips on her neck, warm and exploring. She purred.

"Your shirt," he whispered again. She could feel his lips tracing the cord of her neck. "Clean enough? Your shirt?" He blew gently on the surface of her skin.

She shivered. Shirt. She remembered something about her shirt. "Yes," she said. She couldn't manage any more.

"Then let's go back in," he suggested, running his tongue on her neck. His hand was stroking her back, slow caresses that began at her nape and trailed all the way down her spine. His fingers made their way under her wet shirt, under her bra, stroking the skin there.

Go back in. Her eyes fluttered open.

"Back in?" She ran her fingers down his temple.

All of a sudden, her fingers slowed. Her heart began to trip a little less forcefully. A cold blade of uncertainty cut through the haze in her mind. The pit of her stomach twisted.

He took her hands again and began to walk backward, out of the water, onto the beach. She stumbled as she waded through the waves, her eyes open again. "Careful," he warned her, his voice hoarse. "Hold on to me."

She gripped his hands, ignoring the chill running down her back. "I'll be all right."

This was ridiculous. She was an adult. It was her choice.

Her heart clenched, and she didn't like it. She kept pushing through the water. It was no longer as cool, but somehow it seemed to be harder to move through.

Finally, the sandy beach was firm under her. Gently, she took away her hands from his and waded up onto the shore.

Kristin walked onto the sand and turned to look at the moon. The stars were starting to become visible through the clouds.

She turned to look at him, and this time, she met his gaze. She smiled tentatively. "I'm sorry."

Dare smiled back. His was rueful, and she knew he had forgiven her. "Sure."

He grabbed her hands again. This time, his skin was warm but not insistent, and the moisture from the Sound was already drying. "Still hungry? We have a lot of spareribs. I'll even give you a bib."

She wasn't hungry anymore, but... "Sounds good."

His eyes dipped down to gaze at her body.

She took a deep breath. She could feel her shirt plastered against her cooling skin.

She shivered.

"Before we do anything else," he said abruptly, "let's get into some dry clothes. It may be a warm night, but that's no reason to sit around wet if we don't have to."

He dropped her hands and turned toward the light of his apartment, leaving her to follow. In the distance, she could hear the lone caw of a raven.

Chapter Fourteen

So close — so close! the ravens cried. Could it happen? They held their breath, their wings tucked, in anticipation.

☙

Dare's bones felt as though they had melted during the evening and he hadn't noticed until now. His hair was finally dry after the dip into the Sound, and the back of his neck rubbed against the ribbed collar of the comfortably frayed polo shirt he had changed into.

A glance at Kristin, who was walking beside him, revealed her eyes were sparkling. Her feet were shod in borrowed *zori*, much too big for her, and she had had to roll up the bottoms of his sweatpants. The T-shirt she was wearing was knotted around her waist, and it went well with the ponytail that made her look about fifteen.

He paused as they walked along up the steps, resting his hand on her lower back, ostensibly to help her in a vaguely gentlemanly fashion, but in reality because he wanted to touch her any way he could.

After they rose from the waves of the Sound, he pulled out some dry clothing for Kristin to change into. He had taken the time while she changed clothes to bring their barbecued feast and spread it out on the coffee table in the living room, taking care to lay out large paper napkins to use as bibs.

She had gone into his bedroom to change. He hadn't looked over at the closed door as he moved the food inside. He still felt hot and cold by turns, as if he had a fever.

Warm. She had been warm and soft in his arms, and he was driving himself crazy thinking about it. He concentrated on laying out plates and containers. It wasn't easy. He had yet to change out of his own wet clothes.

The bedroom door opened. He looked up and smiled.

Kristin wasn't short, but the way she looked in his clothes, she might as well have been. The T-shirt that had seen better days suddenly looked as if their better days were still around, revealing just a shadow of the smooth skin of her waist underneath.

He never realized how seductive cast-off clothing could be.

No sooner had he closed the door to his bedroom, intending to change as well, than he unzipped his jeans, taking care to pull them off very, very carefully. He gasped when he managed to shove his underwear off. His eyes rolled in relief. He would never make the mistake of wearing cold, wet denim again if there was a possibility she was going to be anywhere around.

He closed his eyes for a second before he yanked a pair of jeans off a hanger in his closet.

"What's the thing on your dresser called?" Kristin's voice inquired through the bedroom door.

Dare paused and glanced at his dresser. "What thing?" he asked, mystified, trying to figure out what on his bureau was so exotic that someone would have to ask. What was there? His wallet, photographs of his mother and grandmother, the —

He'd forgotten. There was something else on his dresser, the only remaining item from his childhood before Pascisci, something he brought every time he moved but had not thought about in years.

Dar straightened. "You mean the *butsudan?*"

"Is that the thing the Japanese put incense and photographs and things in?"

Her voice got smaller and smaller, less and less certain.

"Yeah," he said, closing the closet door.

He stared at the *butsudan*. It wasn't big—small enough to fit on top of the bureau—but it was solid carved rosewood, almost a tiny armoire, with double doors that opened to reveal a space for, as Kristin had recognized, memorabilia for the deceased. "Your mother doesn't have one?" He yanked open a drawer of his dresser, then closed it. Socks? Nah. He zipped up.

"No," he heard her say after a pause. "She just has a photo of Dad on her dresser, like Marmar and Eric and I do. When I was here after you hurt your knee and you dozed off, I went to get a blanket, and I saw it, and it looked familiar, but I couldn't figure out why." She almost sounded wistful.

Dare opened the door. She sat on the floor right outside, and she looked up at him, her eyes surprised. His heart twisted. She looked so trusting. "You can come in now," he told her. "Especially if we're going to be talking about it."

Out of the corner of his eye, he noticed he had forgotten about the sodden clothing in the middle of the room. For some absurd reason, he didn't want her to see the mess. "Why doesn't your mother have one?" he inquired as he kicked the pile into the corner. She wasn't paying attention. She went straight to the *butsudan* after he had given her entry. She reached out and stroked it with a finger.

"She's never mentioned it, but I think it's because when she married my dad, she wanted to fit in as much as she could," she answered. Her tone was definitely wistful. "So I'd see stuff like this when we visited my relatives, but not at home."

He watched her face, trying to control his surprise. "It's a Buddhist family altar for paying respect to your ancestors. I never thought I'd teach *you* anything about Japanese culture."

She glanced at him. "You lived as a native, off-base. I always lived on base. I was always an outsider."

Dare gently pushed back one of the small, heavily carved doors of the *butsudan*. "This was the one thing of my mother's that my father didn't get rid of after she died," he said, his voice steady. "I don't think he knew what it was, but I did. The *obaasan*, the old lady who lived next door, told me I should respect my mother with it. I didn't understand half of what she told me then, but I just kept it with me, and—eventually—I did understand. My father thought it was a storage cabinet or something. And I made sure he didn't see it often after we got back to the States. I was a kid, but I knew."

Dare swallowed as he stared at the altar. The photograph of his mother displayed within it was yellowed even within its frame, and there was a small crack in the protective glass, courtesy of a rough handler at a long-forgotten airport somewhere. In it, his mother stood in front of a wooden gate, as tall as she was, bamboo trees peeking out over the fence. It must have been sunny, because she had a hand over her eyes acting as a shield, and she was dressed in a light skirt and blouse, typical of the period, with a round-brimmed hat on her head.

But it was her expression that always made him wonder. She was smiling, but she looked nervous, as though she were caught in the middle of something. One arm was down by her side, and it wasn't until you looked closely you could see her hand clutching at the fabric of her full skirt. If you looked closer still, you could see her knuckles were white.

But all he said was, "I think I was about two when this picture was taken. It's one of the two I have of her."

"I'm sorry," Kristin said after a minute.

He slipped his arm around her shoulder and squeezed. "It was over a long time ago." He could feel her warmth through the T-shirt. He smoothed the cotton over the upper part of her arm, bemused he was comforting her for—what? "Life goes on," he whispered in her ear.

As he did so, he knew that was a mistake. A flush of warmth flowed over his skin, and a swift, uncontrollable response from regions below his waist. It was all he could do not to look—impossible not to notice—that she must have taken off her bra as well, as her nipples were stiff and well defined under the T-shirt. Her ear suddenly looked like the sexiest organ he'd ever seen.

He would never look at that T-shirt the same way again.

But his polite nature got the better of him, and he stepped away. "You can get one downtown, if you're interested."

She nodded, taking a deep breath. He cleared his throat. "Why don't we finish eating now?" he suggested, gesturing toward the living room, toward the open door he was hoping to be on the other side of before he did anything rash and this first date ended up being the last.

He had a hard time remembering this was their first date.

He placed a light hand on her back, where her bra would have been. Yep. No bra. "Let's eat."

It got easier after they got back to the living room, which by then looked thoroughly lived in, with stacks of paper napkins tumbling off the table and sauce-oozing ribs sitting on larger paper napkins. Kristin didn't mention the *butsudan* again, but her face brightened when she saw the food.

Food was safe. Food held few memories—at least not barbecue. The mood between them could be light again. "You don't eat like this in public, do you?" he teased, reaching out again to rub a napkin against the edges of her sauce-smeared lips. A pile of used ones sat next to him.

She waved him off. "This is why I don't eat ribs in public." She rubbed at her mouth with her own napkin. "I'm sloppy to start with. I don't pay enough attention to what I'm eating to be able to do this like an adult."

"You're not doing such a bad job," he answered, watching her. And she wasn't. She had dropped nothing on her T-shirt this time, and only the tips of her fingers were coated with slick red sauce, and only the edges of her lips.

"Thanks," she said, tossing a rib, picked clean, into the trash container. Then she looked at him and cocked her head.

"What?" he asked, putting down the rib and reaching for his face. "Is there something on my f—"

She reached over and stopped him. "I don't know how you did it, but you have sauce on your cheek. It's right in the middle. Hold on."

He watched her lean across the coffee table. Later, he tried to imagine what his own expression must have been like—shock, delight, anticipation?

Kristin came closer, so slowly. His heart was pounding. He couldn't have looked away from her if he tried. Her eyes were the sky and the earth and the sea.

Her eyes fixed on him, she came closer, and somewhere along the way he noticed he had stopped breathing. Vaguely, he knew he should try to remember how. When he got a chance.

She came closer and closer, until she shifted slightly and placed her lips on his cheek.

He closed his eyes. The touch, light and brief, shot through him. He could feel her lips, and then, as if the entire incident had been in his imagination, he opened his eyes to see her backing away. "There." Her chest was rising and falling with a telltale speed. "All clean."

He swallowed. "Wouldn't it have been easier to tell me where I had some sauce?"

She laughed, and he had to laugh too. "But it wouldn't have been nearly as much fun."

"No, but my heart wouldn't have had quite the workout it just had." Napkin in hand, he reached out and swiped at the tip of her nose. They finished the barbecue, washing their faces and hands afterward.

"Thank you," Kristin said as she rubbed her hands dry.

Dare turned. Her hair, almost completely dry by now, floated in a cloud around her face. "For what?"

He reached out and smoothed an errant strand off her face. Even if there had been none, he would have done it anyway. It was only an excuse, and one he would invoke when he could.

"A good time." Her eyes were bright. "I didn't think I would, and I was so tired, but I had a lovely time. Thanks."

"I'm not as bad as you thought I was?"

She looked away, and then back at him. "No. And I'd like to do this again, if you could stand going out with me again."

"It would be a pleasure," he told her as he lifted her hand to his lips and kissed her palm. "With any luck, next time we won't need a pile of paper napkins or a change of clothes."

But she *was* tired, and her eyes *were* bloodshot, so after she bundled her wet clothing into a plastic bag, he took her home.

Their pleasant stroll back to her place after he parked the car was cut short when they came into her complex's courtyard. Someone was sitting on the bench outside her apartment—someone familiar. "You have a guest," Dare observed.

"Who—Lars? Is that you?" she called out.

It was. Damn it. "It's about time," Lars commented as they got closer. "I've been waiting for you." He glanced at Kristin, at Dare. "Well, thank you for seeing her home."

Startled, Dare didn't say anything. Then Kristin spoke. "Lars, what are you doing here?"

The tightness in Dare's heart eased. He touched her shoulder. "Why don't we take this inside?" he suggested. "Unless you don't mind being your neighbors' entertainment."

She nodded. He could see the tension in her neck. "Thank you," she said. She fumbled in her purse, only to stop when Lars pulled out his keyring. "I'll get it," he said.

Dare rolled his eyes. *How old are you, Lars?*

Old enough to feel threatened. Old enough to be adolescent about it. Old enough to not so subtly pull out his key to her apartment.

He could understand that.

But by the time Lars unlocked the door, Dare had forgiven the other man for the gesture. He was feeling charitable.

The fragrance of the flowers Dare had presented only hours before permeated the apartment. The blooms themselves were still on the table in the foyer, where Kristin had put them, a work of casual art. To his eyes, the flowers were brilliant and eclectic, bursting with color and life. Like her.

Lars saw them too. "Are you buying flowers for yourself, Kristin, or were these a gift?" he inquired, stopping to examine them. "A bit bright, aren't they?"

Do they pass inspection, Lars?

More important, are they what you would have bought? Because if they are, I'll go find something else. Right now.

"A gift," Kristin answered. She took a deep breath, a smile flitting across her face. Dare knew his flowers were the cause, and for a second he was absurdly happy. "So what's up, Lars?" she asked.

Dare was torn. He wanted to be there, to support her. But this wasn't any of his business. He had just brought his date home for the evening. It didn't matter she wasn't wearing the same clothes she had started the evening in. It didn't matter she was wearing his clothes and her own were in a plastic bag on the kitchen counter.

He lingered in the kitchen, pouring himself some water as Kristin and Lars continued, through the kitchen and into that perfect living room.

"I wanted to find out how your date went," Lars said, glancing first at her and then at Dare. Dare stared back, not changing his expression. He wasn't getting involved. At least not yet. "And I figured I'd wait for you. You didn't go out dressed like that, I assume."

Dare watched her. Her hair was bound with the rubber band that he had snatched off his newspaper. Her feet were getting dusty in the thongs he had produced, the bright red polish on her toenails dimmed by the sand. Her breasts quivered slightly under his T-shirt. Very nice to look at.

But Kristin didn't bat an eye. "Why does it matter?"

"Well, I just thought you'd like to look good in public." If Lars had had too much to drink, he was keeping it well under control. His speech was precise. He was also digging a nice hole for himself. Dare couldn't resist picking up the shovel. "She always looks nice," he interjected from the kitchen.

"Thank you, Dare," she said, not taking her eyes off Lars.

"This is none of your business," Lars snapped.

Dare took a sip of water. "Aren't you glad we're not doing this outside?"

"You could have just called tomorrow morning, Lars." Dare couldn't see the look on her face from where he was, but he knew her well enough to recognize that tone. He was glad it wasn't aimed at him. "And the date is ongoing, if it's any of your business."

Dare held his breath.

Lars shifted. "I see," he said, and now his tone flattened out. "I assume you've changed the sheets on your bed?"

Dare's eyes popped open. He put the glass down and started for the living room. *Lars, are you frigging nuts?*

Not that Kristin needed his help. "*I beg your pardon?*" Her voice was cool—that was to be expected. But there was a sliver of a crack there too that Dare could detect, one that might have been a hint of hurt. "Lars, repeat that question. I'm sure I didn't hear it right."

If there had been a hairline crack in her voice at the beginning, there was none that Dare could tell by the time she finished. By the time Dare reached them, Lars had bent forward, his face closer to hers. "How could you have led me on all these years?" he spat. "You damned tease."

Dare found himself behind Kristin. "You better go."

Lars ignored him. Dare placed a hand on his shoulder. Lars shook it off. "You're embarrassing yourself," Dare said.

"There's nothing much I can do if you're the kind of trash she wants to pick up."

"Careful," Dare said softly, stepping to her side. Kristin made a movement toward him, her eyes on Lars. "I don't care what you say about me, but be careful what you say about her."

Lars finally looked at him. "Stay out of this," he snarled. "Kristin, do you want me to tell your mother and your grandmother about this? You barely know him. And of all things, to invite him back with you—"

This time, Dare was in a position to see the change in expression on her face. Her eyes were narrowed in fury. "*Go*," she said, and nothing in her voice hinted at weakness. "Get out before I throw you out."

"Or what, is *he* going to?"

Kristin raised a finger, making him stop. Without saying another word, she walked from the living room, into the foyer, and opened the door. "Good night, Lars."

Lars stood, staring at her. Then he walked to the door and, without another glance at her or Dare, left.

Dare joined Kristin at the door, watching Lars walk across the courtyard. A minute later, in the still of the night, a car engine started up.

She closed the door. As an afterthought, Dare reached out and turned the deadbolt. He leaned against the door.

The apartment was quiet.

She stood in the middle of the kitchen, staring at him, but he knew it wasn't him she was seeing.

"I'm sorry you had to go through that," Dare said. He wanted more than anything to reach out to her, but he knew he couldn't. Not yet.

Her face looked as though it had become an ivory mask. Suddenly, he remembered a term he had never liked, because it implied all sorts of things, most of which he found offensive. The inscrutable Oriental.

Whoever coined that term had obviously never had to deal with a woman. Forget Asians. Women were the most inscrutable creatures on Earth.

"I'm sorry you had to be a party to that nasty scene," she answered. She turned away from him, bringing her hand up to her forehead. "Good God."

Suddenly, the blossoms in the vase seemed gaudy and tawdry, their scent suffocating. He should have brought roses. Roses were always safe. Or a living plant. He should—

He had to get out of there, before she threw him out too.

Dare opened his eyes. "Why don't I get going?" he suggested. "You're tired, it's been a long evening—"

"I did just change the sheets on my bed," she interrupted.

He froze, staring at the flowers. All of a sudden, he could see each and every pistil, every stamen of each and every flower in the riot of color. He could see the whorls of pattern of the wood of the table itself, gleaming in the dim light of the foyer. Was his hearing going? It had to be. "I beg—"

"You heard me. My sheets are clean."

Jesus.

His heart pounding, he turned to face her. He wondered if the expression on his face betrayed the thoughts darting through his mind. Shock. Trepidation. Wariness.

Anticipation.

The low light in the foyer made her glow like porcelain. Her eyes were unreadable, but it didn't matter. What drew his gaze was the curve of her mouth, slightly wicked, more than tempting, possibly inviting, open. Then her gaze met his.

"Are you sure you're not," he paused, trying to think of the right word, "doing this because you're angry at Lars?"

Her eyes shining, she reached up to her head and in a single motion snapped off the rubber band. Her black hair fell to her shoulders, in waves, her face as bright as her eyes.

There was an off chance this was not a dream. Kristin's fingers closed around his wrist and she placed a gentle kiss, featherlight, onto the palm of his hand.

"I don't think his name should be mentioned again tonight," she whispered. She started to nibble on the tips of his fingers, shooting bolts of almost painful sensation down his hand and wrist. "It's bad manners. I might get offended. I might get the wrong impression."

He stared at her, his mouth ajar, as she kissed her way down his hand, past his wrist. He groaned, partly in disbelief, as she nipped at the sensitive flesh on the inside of his elbow. "Are you kidding?" he gasped.

She looked at him. "Does it feel like I'm kidding?"

"No," he said, as he brought up his other hand to touch her cheek. "It's just hard for me to believe this is happening."

But he wasn't going to let the opportunity go to waste. Slowly, he tilted his head and touched his lips to hers.

Sweet as honey, soft as silk—for a moment, all he could think of were clichés. Her lips were warm, and had he not known better, he could have sworn she was feverish. He shut his eyes and felt her lips move under his.

Chapter Fifteen
The ravens fell silent.

෨

"I won't hold it against you if you change your mind."

Kristin stared at him, her mouth dropping open. "Am I sure?" She started to giggle. "You're asking me if I'm *sure*?"

The expression on his face was priceless. It was confused and amused and, most of all, aroused—and it endeared him to her the way nothing else could have.

Holding his head between her palms, she drew him closer. She looked into his eyes and took a deep breath. "Try me."

She held his gaze for seconds more, during which he focused on her until the rest of the world fell away, and nothing was left except the two of them, gaze to gaze, touch to touch.

His thumb trailed down her cheek until he came to her lips. Her lips opened just a little, and his thumb slipped in. She rasped her teeth, featherlight, on the edge of his thumb, and closed her lips around it in a kiss.

She could feel his pulse pounding. He drew his thumb out, and she kissed it again. Then she felt his hands caress her hair, running his fingers through it.

Her eyes drifting shut, she trailed her fingers around the curves of his ears. She found the cord of his neck and trailed her tongue down its length, stopping from time to time to nibble at the skin, slick with sweat. She could feel his muscles trembling.

She didn't know which one of them was trembling.

His hands began to knead the muscles of her shoulders, the warmth from his hands pouring over her skin. It felt good.

"You're so tense," he whispered, his breath sensitizing her nerve endings. "Relax. You were relaxed at my place."

She laughed and stretched her neck, inviting his hands to continue. "Oh, you're very relaxing. Don't stop now."

"I'll tell you what," he said, blowing into her ear.

She shivered. "What?"

"Let's go take a shower."

Kristin flattened her palms against the planes of his chest, felt the warmth through his shirt. "We just took a bath. In a very big, cold bathtub called Puget Sound. Remember?"

He blew into her ear, and she gasped. "I remember we just washed your shirt," he whispered. She felt a flick of his tongue around her earlobe, his teeth closed around it. The combination jumpstarted the blood through her veins. She was going to need a pacemaker if this kept up.

"I remember," she breathed. She arched her back, feeling her unbound breasts chafe against the cotton separating them.

"What about a bubble bath?"

"No bubble bath," she gasped. "Sorry."

"Then a shower." He ran the edge of his teeth on her ear.

She could feel her nipples tighten. "Oh, God," she whispered, trembling. Her fingers clutched at him for support. Her family thought he was crazy. Maybe she was.

This was her decision, one she made as soon as the door closed behind Lars and Dare was left in her apartment.

The man who had been willing to defend her from Lars. Who had willingly taken no for an answer, before at his apartment. Who made her feel as though she could melt into the stars. The man who held her in the Sound under the moonlight and made her shiver. And suddenly, she was afraid.

She wanted to take him into her bed but didn't know if she wanted to take him in the shower. That seemed—so intimate.

Then she met his eyes, and she had her answer.

"Should I go?" he asked.

She'd been a good student. She studied, she was reasonably bright and most of all, she was decisive when need be.

So why couldn't she come to a decision when she needed one?

"Did you change your mind?"

"No!" she cried out, and she was mortified at her tone of desperation. She grasped at his arms. "Stay. But I haven't cleaned my bathroom in a while. Don't look."

His face opened up. Then she closed her eyes for a second when he leaned in and gave her a kiss.

"I'm not going to be paying attention to the tiles."

She trembled. Neither would she.

Her legs were wobbly, but now that she had made the decision, she could take the steps. She looked up at him and realized she had never wanted anything as much. "This way," she said, raising his hands to her lips. A little rough, smelling a little like seawater.

So male. She squeezed his hands. He squeezed back. "And you've got to promise not to look at the sink. Promise."

Dare trailed a finger down her cheek, her throat, until finally he paused at her breast. His touch was light as he cupped it and stroked it, passed a finger over her erect nipple. "I promise."

She led him into the bathroom, trembling and aware they were both breathing harshly. She squeezed her eyelids shut and then opened them, letting her eyes adjust to the glaring light bouncing off the white tiles. "Here we are," she said, her voice sounding hollow as it echoed in the tiny room.

Without answering, he reached out and paused at the edge of her T-shirt, still tied. She could feel his fingers touching her skin. She quivered. "May I?" he asked, his voice ragged.

She breathed faster, unable to control the way her heart was pounding. "Please," she whispered.

A yank and the knot at her waist fell apart, the hem of the T-shirt tumbling down. He curved his fingers around her breasts, stroking, lightly squeezing, lifting them through the cotton. Her mouth dried and she couldn't breathe anymore.

Her mother had called him strange, and he had seemed it. But she couldn't walk away from him if she tried, not now.

"Wait," she finally managed. Taking a deep breath, she drew the T-shirt over her head. She stood in front of him, exposed and feeling shy...but not. She was pasty and out of shape and...oh hell. She wanted him to touch her.

His eyes didn't waver from hers as he caressed her breasts.

Her eyes closed. "Your hands are cold," she whispered.

In response, he kissed her nipple, skin to skin, flicking his tongue around her erect buds, until she wanted to scream.

She tangled her hands in his hair. He gave her breast a lingering kiss, so exquisite in the way he rolled her flesh in his mouth that she murmured in protest when he stopped.

Gasping, she leaned forward, ready to shove away the layer of fabric between them, only to have him stop her with a hand covering hers. "Not yet," he whispered.

"Let me," she gasped, the words almost pleading.

He shook his head, and his eyes danced in the shadows created by the overheads. "No. Time for a shower, remember?"

"Dare!" she wailed. She whacked him on his shoulder. "We can shower later!"

He gave her a kiss, demanding and hot, making her squirm. Reaching behind him, he turned on the spigots. A sprinkle of moist heat fell on her face and hair, misting the air. "I don't know if I can wait that long," she said, gasping as she broke off the kiss.

He was breathing as hard as she was. "Not yet." He kissed the tip of her nose. "A shower. A ritual shower to cleanse ourselves of all the bad karma."

At the back of her mind, she knew that made as much sense as anything. At the front of her mind, it wasn't something she cared much about. "Then let's make it a quickie," she breathed, kissing him hard. "Now."

She felt him tense, and she knew triumph. "*Now* can I take off your shirt?" She grabbed his shirt and began to shove the fabric up his chest, only to have him stop her again.

It took him a moment, but he covered her hands with his again, his eyes twinkling. "Allow me. I'm not sure how sturdy the cotton is."

"To hell with that," she said with a mock growl. She managed to get most of the shirt up to his neck.

He stopped her again, openly laughing now. He tested the gushing water, the heat fogging the room. "Hot enough."

"Yes," Kristin whispered.

As she watched, he grasped at the neck of his shirt and ripped it over his head. "It's time, don't you think?" he asked as his hands yanked at the cord of her sweatpants. The pants skidded down, pausing at her hips.

"It's about time," Kristin whispered. She spread her hands on his chest.

Oh, God, he's gorgeous, she thought. His chest hair was sparse, dark against his skin. The thunder of the water in the shower was nothing next to the way her heart was hammering.

"Why didn't I suggest skinny-dipping before?" she murmured, trailing her hands down to his belly.

He grinned. "What, in the Sound? Not even I would suggest that." His hands were at her hips now, massaging her skin. "Does hypothermia ring a bell?"

"I think so." *Control.* She wanted nothing more than to rake her nails down his chest, but she needed control. "But I want to see more."

He gave her a quick kiss. "Your wish is my command."

She shivered.

He reached out and shoved down her sweatpants, letting them freefall, until they ended in a dark puddle of fabric around her ankles, exposing her at long last. "Now you," she whispered, grasping the ends of his belt and yanking.

But he grabbed her again, holding her hands. His gaze was fixed on her nude body. "You weren't wearing underwear," he whispered.

"No. I didn't bother."

"Does this mean your underwear's balled up in that plastic bag?" His eyes glazed. "All that time and you weren't wearing underwear?"

She ran her tongue over her lips. "That's right. Come," she coaxed, pulling open her shower curtain and letting the clouds of moist heat escape. "Now take off your pants." She raked her fingernails down his chest, stopping when she approached his groin.

He murmured. His gaze drifted down from her face, and it seemed to Kristin that they were fixed on her breasts.

She reached up to caress his cheek.

"Have I mentioned you're beautiful?" he whispered.

Kristin smiled. "Not recently." She couldn't resist. She reached down and closed her hand around his penis.

"Stop that," he said unsteadily. He shoved her hand out of his way, groaned as she made sure her touch skittered across him. But obediently, her hand stopped on his hip and stayed there as his hands went to the zipper of his jeans. She watched him as he yanked the tongue down, wincing in his haste.

The wild look in his eyes made her suddenly frantic.

But he didn't move. "You're driving me crazy," she exclaimed, looping her thumbs into his belt loops. She splayed her hands around his hips, skirting as close as she could to his erection without touching it. He jerked once as she flexed her fingers, enjoying the tensing of his muscles. "And they say women tease." *Please,* she said silently to him.

He closed his eyes for a moment again. "I'm trying to control myself, I'll have you know."

His hands covered hers again, but this time, he didn't try to move them. *Soon, please,* she tried to tell him, her muscles softening. Somewhere in the back of her mind was a sense of wonder. "Do me a favor," she said in a whisper. "Don't."

She reached past his cotton briefs, and in a single, efficient motion, shoved.

Her breath stopped as the jeans and the briefs fell. *Oh God.* It was her turn to look.

Her mouth was bone-dry. "I should have insisted on skinny-dipping," she whispered.

His legs were defined from his running, and his shoulders made her want to stroke the muscles, nipping the taut skin. Her gaze drifted down his chest, skittering past his belly.

Oh, yeah. She wrapped her fingers around him, watching him tense. "It's time," she whispered.

He drew her closer. She rested her head against his shoulder and closed her eyes. Their skin touched, from breast to abdomen and beyond, their thighs brushing, heat against heat. She could feel his rigid length nestled in the juncture of her hips, and instinctively, her thighs parted.

Kristin's head began to swim, sensation sapping her of thought. She had had relationships before. But not one of them had made her feel like this. He held onto her buttocks, clenching and unclenching as he rocked against her.

She felt him place his lips to her ear. "Time for a shower," he whispered, nipping at her lobe. "Time to wash off bad memories. Start over fresh and new."

"Bed's closer," she tried to persuade him, her logic flawed. Desperately, she reached down and cupped him again.

She smiled when she heard him hiss. "Closer than the shower?" he said, but he was laughing. The shower curtain rustled and she opened her eyes to see him holding it for her.

He gestured toward the steam. "Your shower awaits."

She met his eyes. Eager. Anticipatory. And instantly, she was wet. "Thank you."

She stepped in.

The warm water hit her full. Closing her eyes, she raised her arms to take in the pulsing heat, threading the tension out of her muscles.

"Wonderful," she murmured. She felt Dare step in behind her, closing the curtains to form their own intimate world. She moved forward, letting the water gush past her and on him.

His hands drew her against him. "Just the water?"

The palm of his hand flattened low against her belly as the fingers of his other hand stroked the underside of her breast, glancing off the stiff nipple.

She arched her back again, thrusting her breast into his hand. "You're right up there," she breathed. Her hands went around him to feel his muscles flex, the water making his skin slick. The tension was building in him, echoing her own.

Then her hand brushed against something cold and hard and slippery — the soap dish attached to the shower wall.

She grabbed the soap and the washcloth hanging from the showerhead, turning both over and over until her hands and wrists were covered with suds. Her hands clenched and unclenched, picking up the rhythm of his hands on her.

A quick twist, and she was facing him again. He continued to stroke her. "If you insist on taking a shower, then we have to clean up," she whispered, kissing his Adam's apple. She felt the vibration of his groan and began to run the soapy washcloth over his chest, trailing large, round circles around his slick pectorals. The water was sliding off him. She wanted to touch every single inch of him, like the water.

She tried with the washcloth, soapy bubbles drifting across his skin. His hands tightened around her waist, trapping her hands between them. "I can't wash you if you do that," she said, breathless.

"That washcloth is deadly," he accused her. He brushed his lips against hers, his tongue tracing the shape of her mouth.

This time, the kiss was gentle, almost virginal. Her hand continued to rub in languid circles with the washcloth, releasing clouds of bubbles that slid down his shoulders, his chest, down his abdomen. "Deadly how?"

"It's rough. Haven't you noticed?" Before she could answer, his hand drew the washcloth from her fingers, mimicking the movement of her hands on him on her own skin.

She had forgotten. The washcloth was Japanese, designed to scrub and increase circulation. She had used the kind so long it had slipped her mind it was more abrasive than terrycloth.

She moaned. Tonight, it was more arousing than abrasive. His hands, one with the cloth and the other with the soap, drew slow circles on her, first with a stroke of the soap, then with a caress of the cloth that set her nerve endings tingling.

"It's not rough at all," she said with pleasure, rolling the muscles of her back with his hands. "It feels wonderful."

He caressed her from the nape of her neck to the curve of her back. She met his eyes as he bent to touch his mouth to hers. "So does this," he whispered.

Then he dropped the cloth and the soap, letting them swirl in the water pounding the floor of the bathtub. She wrapped her hands around his waist, deepening the kiss.

Her eyelids drooped as he drew her against him. He was stone hard now. He touched her belly and then slipped his hand between her thighs.

She drew a sharp breath, hazily noting the rising tension in her body was echoed by his groan vibrating through her. She kissed the plane of his chest, touching his skin with her tongue, teasing as his hips started to thrust, his shaft sliding between her smooth wet legs.

She twisted her hips, reveling in the sensation of his penis against her soap-slicked skin. She grabbed his arms, kneading them much the way he was kneading her gluteal muscles.

Then he stopped.

After a second, she opened her eyes. "Hey," she gasped.

He was breathing unevenly. She realized he was trembling again, though he had stopped moving.

Then he reached down to the edge of the bathtub and fumbled at the pocket of his jeans. Then he straightened again. He unrolled the condom on himself, letting her smooth it down.

He groaned and his eyelids started to drift closed. His hands tightened around her hips and lifted her as she wrapped her arms around his neck.

"Your legs around me," he whispered in her ear.

"One leg. I'm too tall and too heavy for this."

"Try it."

She did, tucking one foot under his *oshiri*, flexing her hips. Her other foot was still on the floor of the tub, but as he began to shift and flex the muscles of his thighs, she found herself leaving the ground.

"Aren't I a little too heavy for this?" she whispered. "Oh, my God. Oh," she moaned. Her knees tightened as his fingers slipped into her.

He blew in her ear. "I'll let you know if you're too heavy." He carefully, oh so carefully, slid into her.

So full. Her mouth opened. She paused, unable to breathe. "Are you sure?" She could feel him in her, filling her. "Oh, Dare."

He didn't respond. She could feel his muscles flexing as he began to rock within her. She felt the roaring of her pulse against the staccato beat of his heart as the water gushed around them.

He leaned her against the wet tile wall as he thrust into her more urgently. Faster and harder he drove into her, the thrusts reverberating through her body. She felt the rasp of his stubble, felt it scrape against her throat, and instinctively, she bit the corded flesh of his neck, feeling the trembling in his body run through her, making her tighten her legs around him and respond with thrusts of her own.

No more. She cried out, her body spasming once, twice, even as he thrust one last time, deep, harder, his shout inarticulate, his hands clutching at her. Her surroundings melted away, lost in a tidal wave of stars bursting across a summer night's sky, falling to Earth.

Dimly, she could feel him shift position.

Finally, she opened her eyes. Somewhere along the way, he had sunk to his knees to the bathtub floor, still within her. She was straddling him even as the water continued to hit their entwined bodies. "Oh," she said, her voice weak.

"Oh yeah," he said after a moment, his voice almost nonexistent, his arms tight around her waist again. He kissed her throat.

"We're out of hot water," she whispered as she kissed him.

His tongue stopped moving. "So we are." He grabbed her again and tried to stand up. "We also lost the condom."

Kristin opened her eyes and dreamily watched as the water at the drain made the latex sheath twitch and twirl.

Oh well.

It didn't really matter, considering. "Why don't we adjourn to my bed? Clean sheets and everything," she added drowsily, nipping his neck again. "And we can probably walk there."

"No." He stood up, helping her to her feet.

He turned off the water. He slid the curtain open and stepped out. He reached for her hand.

She cried out as he swept her up. "Now," he whispered as she met his eyes, "give me directions."

In the distance, faintly, she could hear a lone raven caw.

Chapter Sixteen

He didn't smell the sea.

That seemed wrong, somehow.

Rustling and murmuring. That sounded wrong, too. He could hear leaves rustling in a breeze, not the lazy, rolling *shuup* of the water hitting the rocky beach that he heard every morning. The rumbling he heard after that was an air conditioner—the roar of a car engine coming to life, people talking and laughing as they passed by. Instead, he smelled...what was that?

Apricots. Apricot shampoo?

Dare opened his eyes and he remembered.

Kristin's bed.

He turned his head and looked at her. She was fast asleep, sprawled on her stomach, her head turned away, her back ivory in the low morning light. He turned to face her, pausing when she murmured and shifted, blissfully unaware of his gaze.

Slowly, he slid the sheets down, taking care not to wake her. At this moment, fantasy was surely more enticing than reality. In reality, it was all too likely they would be awkward with each other in the harsh glare of morning, mumble something about a call, and that would be it. In fantasy—

He traced the curve of her back, from the arch of her neck, between the shoulder blades, coming to rest at her tailbone. He kept a wary eye on the gentle breathing motion of her back, which had not varied in its regular movement. Encouraged, he spread his hand over her hip, took a good look at the curve of her buttock. He stroked the fine skin there. He hadn't had a chance the night before.

He paused, lost in golden images.

"Don't stop," he heard her say, muffled.

Her voice was velvet. He resumed the caress. "I'm sorry I woke you up," he lied.

He heard her chuckle. "I've been awake and fell asleep again. Mm. That feels wonderful."

Encouraged, he continued to caress her, expanding his territory of touch. "Did you try to wake me up?" He moved his hand back up her spine again, smoothed her neck and shoulders. He kneaded her upper arms, stroked and swept her hair to one side, kissing the nape of her neck. She squirmed.

"Mm. No. I watched you sleep."

"Did you have fun?" He feathered kisses along her neck, trailing down the length of her shoulder. Her breathing quickened. Slipping his hand beneath her, he stroked the curve of her belly, slipped his hand up to her breasts.

"Yeah, but not as much as when you're awake." With that, she twisted to face him. Almost as if there had been no interruption, he continued to stroke her back, tracing the curve of her hip. "Good morning."

Her eyes looked as dark as her hair. He brushed his lips against her temples. "Good morning." He squeezed her warmly and briefly. The fantasy was over, so the reality might as well begin. First things first.

"Are you on the Pill, or do you have a 'morning-after' pill in your black doctor's bag?" he asked, his voice steady. "I have no idea when the condom came off last night."

He felt a hesitation before her breath resumed its cadence. "I can take care of it, but pregnancy isn't a big worry."

All he wanted to do was touch her at the moment, but reality was reality. "Tubes tied?" And he had to ask the other question of the modern age. "Have you been tested recently?"

He felt her smile against his skin. It was going to drive him wild. "You're so romantic," she said, her breath warm. "And I'm clean."

"Both questions have to be asked."

"True. I'll spare you the details and just tell you that I have reproductive organs with...problems that make it statistically unlikely I'm going to expect a baby anytime."

A flood of emotion swept past him, surprising him. For a split second, he was sorry.

But he wasn't going to think about it now. "Are you disappointed?"

He felt her tense for a moment, then relax. "I hadn't given it much thought. That's one of the reasons I always tried to discourage Lars. He's always made it clear he wanted a large family, just like the one he came from."

Dare thought for a moment. "Then you've never told him?"

She shrugged. "Over and over. But he's never listened."

"I'm honored you told me."

"You asked. And it might be important to you."

He changed the subject. "So are you a breakfast kind of person, or a just-coffee-until-lunch kind of person?" He trailed a finger down her spine again. Her skin was silk.

He felt her smile. Her hands started to echo his own, stroke by stroke. "Definitely a breakfast kind of person. You're staying, aren't you?" she asked, looking up.

Then she met his eyes, and he was startled. He wasn't expecting her to meet his eyes. Not the morning after.

Further, she actually looked as though she wanted him to stay. "Are you asking me to breakfast?"

"Depends on what I have in the kitchen. If everything there has mold on it, could I take you out to eat?"

"It's still part of the same date, isn't it? I'll pay," he answered, kissing her on the lips. They were pink and lush and could have been his breakfast on their own.

She snorted. "I'll pay. You discharged your responsibilities when you walked me to my apartment."

It was his turn to snort. "'Discharging' my responsibilities? You don't date much, do you?"

Her eyes became round, but there was a smile lurking around her mouth. She pinched his nipple. "I resent that. I don't deny it, but I do resent it."

He could barely feel her touch. "Ow," he said agreeably.

They remained that way for a while, curled up, her head on his chest. He hadn't felt this tranquil after sex in years.

The room wasn't especially big, but what it lacked in size it made up for in light. He saw in the corner, draped over the cherry-red overstuffed chair, two lengths of fabric. They seemed to have no apparent relation to the other fabrics in the room, not even a color in common, but still they were bright. They looked hand-stitched, even—

He took a wild guess. "Did you make those?"

Her hand, which had been caressing him, stopped. "No," she said almost reluctantly. "Well, yes."

"No or yes?" He was amused, but he wasn't going to tease her.

"I have a small loom in my study. I've been trying to weave off and on for years," she confessed. "I love the look, the feel—I've just never been able to get any good at it."

He suppressed a smile. Only Kristin would feel guilty about having a hobby. "That's still impressive. I know it takes a lot of work." He leaned forward. "Can I take a closer look?"

Her fist relaxed against his chest. "Be my guest."

Blinking at the bright light, Dare pushed back the comforter and got up, walking across the room. The woven fabric was less textured than he had originally thought, but that wasn't what had made him curious. The rough-looking texture had a hidden pattern. He squinted. It almost looked like stars.

"I was going for something, a specific pattern, and I couldn't manage it," he heard her say.

He looked at her. She had sat up, pulling the sheets up. "All of a sudden you're modest?"

Kristin smoothed the comforter around her. "Only when you're delving into my personal life." She paused.

They had just spent the night delving into highly personal areas, but this was different, he guessed. "Yes?" he asked, fingering the length of fabric in his hands. Vivid but diffuse, it seemed to change a little everytime he glanced at it. "It's a great effect," he said almost to himself.

When he realized she wasn't speaking, he looked up. "What?"

Blushing, she shook her head. "I was admiring the view." She put her hands underneath the comforter in a gesture of chagrin he found irresistible. "Cute *oshiri*."

He tried to look over his shoulder. "I'll take your word for it," he said. "I can't see it, myself."

Still holding the fabric, he got back in bed. "But you're not letting me have the same pleasure by being all tucked in, are you?" He leaned in to kiss the back of her neck. Her skin smelled like flowers on a summer's day. "I like yours too."

"I figured you'd remedy the situation if you were interested," she said breathlessly. Her hands emerged from beneath the comforter to touch his face.

"I thought you wanted breakfast," he whispered after a few seconds. He nuzzled her.

He met her radiant eyes. "It'll wait."

* * * * *

The heat of the sun hit his face. He shifted, eyes still shut, only to feel the sheets bunching around his waist. They were warm. Vaguely, he remembered they had been cool before.

He stroked the fabric. His hands felt the smooth, cool cotton first and then a fine, nubbled weave. Wool?

He opened his eyes. The morning light had mellowed as the sun made its way across the sky. He glanced at the sheets. The wool he had felt was the patterned fabric from Kristin's weaving, which had been forgotten after he had brought it back to the bed and other concerns had overcome them.

I fell asleep again.

He was alone this time. He touched the indentation on the other side of the bed. Still warm.

"You're awake!"

He turned. She was standing in the doorway, a flowered robe wrapped around her. It was short, exposing her legs.

And they were great legs, now that he had a chance to look at them.

"It's about time, I think." He sat up, stretching.

She leaned against the doorframe. Her feet were bare.

"So why are you all the way over there?" he asked in a burst of bravery.

She grinned. She brought her hand out of her robe pocket and showed him what she was holding.

A crumpled teabag. "I was going to make breakfast."

He regarded it with mild interest. "Not much you can do with that."

"We have to go out," she informed him with a shrug. "I don't have any coffee, this is the only tea I have left, my bread's moldy, the orange juice seems to have turned and all I have left is rice. And the Tupperware has stuff in it I don't recognize, and I should probably throw it down the toilet."

"When was the last time you went to the store?"

"About a month ago," she admitted. "I haven't had time. You should talk! I remember what you have in your refrigerator." She stuck her tongue out.

He distinctly remembered that tongue. Very talented. His groin was sore, but he twitched anyway.

"I know better than to offer anybody breakfast," he answered, turning back the covers and standing up.

He stopped in his tracks as he saw her face change. Her lips opened a little, pink and moist. Her gaze trailed up his body before meeting his.

"What?"

She shook her head. "I like watching you."

He paused as he looked around for his clothing. "Well, I like watching you," he answered, so honest he could feel the truth reverberating in his bones.

"That's good," she said, not taking her eyes off him.

"And I don't think it's fair you get to watch me naked while you're covered up," he added. He twitched again. Oh, yeah. He was sore but it was going to be worth it.

"Okay," she said, and promptly shrugged off her robe, letting it float to the floor. "We're even now."

Her cheeks were as pink as he felt. Her throat was as pink as her face. The tips of her nipples—

"If you just stand there, we're never going to leave this room," he managed to croak. He licked his lips.

His eyes met hers again. She bent and picked up her robe then tossed it onto the chair. She took a step toward him.

The tremor in her shoulders gave her away. *She's as nervous as I am.* She stopped in front of him, but not too close, as though she were wary of invading his personal space. He caressed the curve of her cheek. Her eyes closed. Her lips parted and his erection came back with a vengeance. With his other hand he stroked her hair, and finally brought her face close to his.

She was exquisite. Her skin was an undefinable shade between ivory and gold, her nose turned up infinitesimally, her lips full and begging to be made love to. A flourish of the finest freckles he had ever seen graced her cheekbones, and the tilt of her eyes completed how delectable she was—not quite Japanese, not quite identifiable. Except as herself.

Her eyes fluttered open and looked into his. "I've never felt like this," she whispered. Her hands crept around his waist, stroking his back.

He kissed the tip of her nose, then her lips. "Neither have I," he said, the truth of his statement almost hurting his heart.

Soft and sweet. His fingers stroked her neck, then her shoulders, before resting on her breasts. She moaned as he kissed the length of her throat, nipping and licking and—

Her stomach growled.

They froze.

With a sigh and a lingering kiss, he looked her in the eye. "Time for food?"

"I'm so embarrassed."

Her cheeks were a rosy pink. They were standing nude in her bedroom, after a night and a morning in which they had thoroughly explored each other, and she was embarrassed her stomach had growled.

"It's time we ate." He wrapped his arms around her, grateful for a little more time. "What time is it, anyway?"

"It's a little after one." He could feel her arms around him, and he felt a soft kiss on his chest. "And I'm starving."

Breakfast—brunch—well, no, definitely lunch by then—was a casual bagel place nearby, the morning crowds thinned out by then. The food was simple but satisfying, and it seemed to hit the spot for Kristin.

Saturday. It was Saturday morn—no, it was afternoon. They still had the entire weekend ahead of them.

For the first time in an eternity, he felt whole.

She smiled.

Chapter Seventeen

Two days later, Kristin was still smiling.

The carnation in her hand was pink, and it neatly matched the shade of the tip of her nose when she blushed. She knew that because Dare had told her the previous afternoon, right after he awakened her by kissing her on the nose after her nap, on Alki Beach. Then this morning, after he had kissed her until they were both gasping for breath. He had presented her with the carnation—she didn't know where he'd gotten it, and she didn't care—bopping her nose with it before he sent her home with a pat on her *oshiri*.

She sniffed at the posy and considered the situation. Her lover of all of a weekend—and it had been all of a weekend—had just given her a killer kiss and a flower and sent her home, claiming he had to go to work and so did she.

But at the moment, she didn't care. She would have stayed naked in his bed, living off pizza delivery forever.

She resisted the urge to start dancing, a soft-shoe right then and there on the sidewalk. It was bad enough she was grinning like an idiot. If she started dancing, she would probably be accosted by a battery of police officers with a straitjacket just her size before she made it back to her apartment.

Yes, she was feeling goofy. "I'm a goner," she said aloud.

Then she looked around, feeling silly. No one was around.

She was waving the flower like a baton when she turned the corner and started up the steps to the courtyard. Then there was a familiar sight sitting on the bench outside her apartment, and her skippy steps faltered and her baton became a flower again.

Lars.

Lars, sitting and reading a newspaper, a cup of Starbucks coffee next to him, waiting for her.

She didn't want to deal with him, not the way she was feeling. She wanted to jump and skip and dance. She didn't want to deal with Lars.

But she had to. She squared her shoulders, took a firm grip on her carnation and walked toward him.

The sunglasses he wore flashed in the early morning sun, obscuring his expression. He stood up as she approached. Ever the gentleman, she thought cynically. "Morning, Lars," she said, waving her flower. "I said I'd see you at work."

He made a production of folding his newspaper. "I know," he answered, his tone even. "But I got a call from your mother this morning, saying she hadn't heard from you all weekend, and she assumed I would know if you were all right."

Kristin winced. Bull's-eye. "What did you tell her?"

Lars shrugged. "I told her I'd seen you on Friday night and you'd said you had plans for the weekend. And that I thought the plans included Borodin, but I wasn't sure."

He sounded sullen. For a split second, she felt guilty, but she shoved the thought away. She'd known Lars a long time, but he had made the irrevocable break.

"Thank you, Lars," she said politely. "I'll call her before I leave for work."

Oh hell, she sighed to herself, *I'm in a good mood*. "I'm sorry we had to part on such bad terms on Friday," she began, quashing the voice inside her that was clamoring, *No, I'm not!* "But you said some horrible things."

She still couldn't see his eyes through the sunglasses. It occurred to her that possibly, since he had been drinking, his eyes were still bloodshot. "Yes, I did. And I must say I'm sorry."

Kristin was amused. She knew Lars well enough to know what that meant—"*I must say*"? He wasn't sorry at all—but he knew he had to say it. Further, the way he said it left enough uncertainty what he was sorry for.

Oh, Lars, you could have made this easy. We've known each other for such a long time, couldn't you be happy for me? "That's behind us, right?" she said, knowing it wasn't.

"Sure, Kristin." He picked up his coffee. "I'll see you at the hospital."

"Yeah," she said. "You want to have lunch tomorrow?"

She could have sworn his fingers tightened around the cup. "My schedule's pretty full, but I'll let you know," he said in that cool voice. His professional voice.

"You know the number," she replied in her own professional voice, reassuring and neutral. She gestured at the cup in his hand, slowly being squeezed. "Want to throw that out?"

He looked down at his hand. "Yes, I would."

She unlocked her apartment door. The smell of the flowers Dare presented her with on Friday night greeted her with an explosion of scent.

There was something else she had to do. She set the cup on the kitchen counter and went to the living room, looking around until she found it. The small velvet box.

It was on the floor under the coffee table, untouched since Friday evening. She picked it up and walked back to the kitchen, where Lars was throwing the cup into the trash in his usual precise way—first empty it, then rinse it, then crush it, then throw it out.

Dare would probably throw it out without a second thought.

"I'm sorry, Lars," she said. She held out the box. "I want to be friends. We've known each other for so long."

He stared at it, not reaching for it. Finally he did, pocketing it. "We're not friends," he said, each word distinct. "We never were. Goodbye, Kristin."

And with that, he turned and walked out, slamming the door.

His quick, staccato footsteps faded into the distance, and the sound of his car starting up was swallowed by the sounds of the morning symphony of Seattleites on their way to work.

Kristin sighed. Her stomach was roiling.

Just then the phone rang. With that new-lover's intuition, she knew who the caller was. Waving her flower, she picked up, chirping, "Good morning, and how are you?"

"I miss you," was the answer.

The sound of his voice flooded her body with remembered sensation. All of a sudden she felt shy. "I just left thirty minutes ago. Is your watch working?"

"It's been longer than that. It's been hours. Days."

She smiled. She couldn't help it. "I know." She tucked the carnation against her heart.

"There I was, about to button my shirt, and I realized it just felt wrong."

"Why?" she asked, more to hear his voice than anything else. She could hear the rustle of fabric, an occasional *plick* when a button hit the phone. She tried to imagine it. Dare with his white Oxford shirt half on, phone tucked under his chin, working at the buttons on his sleeves, tie hanging, ready to be slung around his neck.

"Because you should have been here to pick out my tie," he answered, his voice intense even as it tried to tease. "You should be here to unbutton my shirt as I try to button it."

Kristin felt her breathing pick up. "You're the one who patted me on my butt and told me to go to work," she returned, warming as she thought of unbuttoning his shirt. She had done just that the previous morning, unbuttoning his shirt even as he was buttoning it, and as it turned out—

"I'm not going to encourage you to skip work," he said with a laugh. The vibration of his chuckle sent a shiver down the back of her neck.

"Why would I blame you?" she said, just to keep talking.

"I'm just making sure. So how you doin'?"

"Okay." She added, "I miss you too."

There was a pause, during which she brought the carnation to her nose and smiled a smile she knew had to be gaggingly dopey. She was nauseating herself, and it was embarrassing. "So what time tonight?"

"Whenever you get off."

"Without you?" she teased. She was embarrassed at the juvenile innuendo, but again she couldn't help it.

But it was worth it to hear him laugh. "I'm embarrassed for you, Kristin," he rebuked her, but more with amusement.

"You should be. *I'm* embarrassed for me. I have to get a key made for you," she went on, switching gears as her floral baton began to swing again. "Because my hours aren't the usual eight to five most of the time."

She stopped then, surprised at herself. A key. A key to her *sanctum sanctorum*, her home. How many years had it taken her to finally give Lars one?

"Maybe it's time to change your locks," he commented, almost as if he were reading her thoughts.

"Maybe it is." She took another deep breath of her baton.

Another pause, and she knew neither of them would hang up first, not willingly. If they weren't careful, they would both end up late to work. Yet she stood, phone against her shoulder, her flower waving in the dim light of her kitchen. "Do you like spaghetti?"

"Sure. Is that dinner?"

"Would you like it to be?"

"We're going to be late," he pointed out.

"I'm already late. At least you're half dressed," she said. "I'm still standing here with my carnation in hand."

"Get off the phone!"

"You first."

Eventually they did. She danced through the day, and while she knew she would go home eventually, today it seemed to take forever.

She got off work, bought the makings of dinner and arrived home before she remembered to call her mother.

Kristin sighed as she set her groceries down. Briefly, she considered putting off the call, but then the image of Lars knocking on her door as she and Dare were having dinner spurred her to pick up the phone.

"*Moshi moshi*," she greeted when the phone was picked up. "It's me. *Daijoobu?*"

There was a pause, and then she heard Eric say dryly, "Thanks for mistaking my voice for Mom's, Kris. Everything's peachy-keen. Why do you ask?"

"Oh, I thought you were Mom. Lars said she called him because she hadn't heard from me, so—"

"Yeah. I think she's pissed, Kris."

"Why, because I didn't call? I don't call every weekend."

"But Lars doesn't tell her every weekend you're shacking up with someone she thinks is a *yottaro ahho*, too."

"He did *what*?"

"Okay, maybe it wasn't that bad, but that was the idea."

Kristin sat down, shaking her head. "He told Mom I was sleeping with Dare? What the hell's wrong with him?"

She heard a tap on the phone. "Uh, Earth to Kristin," Eric said. "Think about what you just said and figure out the motivations thereof."

"What are you babbling about? Those psych classes of yours—" She stopped. "I'm—oh, no."

"Getting a little clearer now? Aren't you the smart one?"

"I don't know what I was thinking of," she muttered. Lars, the faithful. Lars, the devoted.

Lars, having the last laugh.

It had probably seemed like an opportunity he couldn't pass up. Lars, the opportunist.

She sighed and started to think. "Is Mom around? Marmar?"

"They went to Costco. And I'm waiting for the guys to pick me up."

"Then just leave a message I called and said we'd be over for dinner tomorrow."

"'We'? As in you and Dare? Are you *nuts*?"

"Maybe," she said, and she was fairly sure about that.

"Hey, I don't have plans for tomorrow night. Mind if I stay around to watch the bloodbath?"

She snorted. "There won't be one. But I'm sure Dare would be glad to see you again."

Which was pretty much what Dare said when she informed him they would be dining with her family the following night.

"Sounds good," were his precise words.

That wasn't the reaction she was expecting.

"I needed to see your mother again anyway," he explained when she stared at him. "And it'll be good to see Eric again."

She was surprised but she shouldn't have been. "Why?"

"Because I have to make amends."

Then she knew that despite all his protestations, there was a thread of Old World traditionalism in him, an echo of the Japanese way she barely remembered most of the time, but she knew was buried deep in her own bones. The same ways that were buried in him but probably even deeper.

And he did apologize. He even brought a thoughtful, suitable gift and bowed deep. It was not a scene that played out in the most memorable fashion—Dare stuttered his heartfelt apologies, and Kristin's mother coldly accepted them—but it was done.

* * * * *

It was one thing for her to begin a new relationship, but quite another to end what she had viewed as an enduring friendship with Lars, and to watch Dare apologize to her mother in such form that she had never seen outside a traditional Japanese rite. Life was off-kilter as autumn officially began.

It was with all that behind her and between them they began their relationship. For some reason, neither found it worth noting they never solved many of their primary differences, but since it never came up, it seemed clear to Kristin the problem was no longer something to be dragged into the mud. Perhaps it had been beaten to death, she mused.

Of course, nothing ever remains the same.

It was about two months later when something came to her attention. At first it didn't occur to her. Then, it became clear that not only was it possible but that it had happened.

She was gripping the phone, her other hand open in a gesture of supplication. "How is that possible?" she repeated into the phone. "Amy, tell me how. I've had years—"

"Look, when you asked me, I thought it was unlikely too, but I did it. Then I ran it through twice."

"But how—"

Amy laughed. "If you don't know how—"

Kristin couldn't laugh along. "It's not funny."

"Are you okay?"

"Yeah. Yeah, I'll be fine. I'll talk to you later."

She hung up. She looked out her study window. It was a cool, sodden Sunday afternoon. The TV was on with a football game in progress, but neither she nor Dare were watching it.

Originally, she thought it was the flu, so she hadn't paid it much attention, other than cursing herself for not having gotten a flu shot. But then it went on long enough that she got concerned. With good reason.

She stared at Dare.

"Everything okay?" he inquired. He closed his book. She could see the title—*The New Official Guide to Japan.*

"Yeah. No. Maybe you should sit down."

He gave her a strange look. "I *am* sitting."

"In that case, I should sit down," she muttered.

"You *are* sitting."

"In that case, I have something to tell you."

He tossed the book aside. "What is it? Is it your mother? Your grandmother? Eric?"

She shook her head.

"What is it? You were talking to someone from the hospital," he said. His eyes widened. "What's wrong? You just had a checkup. Did something come out?"

She stared at him, feeling as though she had been turned to stone. "Yeah." She took a deep breath. "It did. I'm pregnant."

She could have cut the silence with a spoon. Heavy, thick. His mouth dropped open. "You're what?"

"You heard me."

He blinked. "But we've been careful. We—"

"No, we haven't. Not the first weekend," she reminded him. "Remember? The shower? The bed? The next morning? The kitchen? Until we bought more condoms?"

He was across from her, his hands on his lap, palms up—probably from shock, she mused. She didn't blame him.

She took a deep breath. That felt normal. She took another breath, and then she placed her hand across her abdomen.

That felt normal too, but obviously it wasn't.

Pregnant. After how many years of being told no, of studying the data herself, of coming to the same conclusion?

"This is downright embarrassing," she muttered, caressing her belly. "I'm never going to live this down."

"Pregnant," he echoed. His eyes were wide. "Our baby."

"Ours. Unless you're trying to imply something."

Kristin steeled herself. He could. It wasn't true, and they both knew it, but still, he could —

She wasn't even sure he heard her. "A baby. I thought—"

She raised a hand. "That's what I thought. I was wrong," she said. "Makes me wonder if I should change specialties. Obviously, there's research waiting to be done."

"A baby," he said again, his voice hushed.

"They ran the test three times. And I'm going to run a new one again tomorrow." She shook her head, mystified. "A baby."

She hadn't been feeling well, that was true. She had ascribed it to hay fever prevalent that time of year, or the flu. Clearly, like lawyers who represent themselves, doctors who diagnosed themselves were idiots.

"When is it due?"

"In about seven months. Dare, I'm questioning your math skills here."

"How soon can we run that test you can tell what sex the baby is? Not that it matters," he added, grabbing her hands. Then he reached out and caressed her abdomen. "Is it too early to go get a ball and a glove?"

She blinked. "It might be a girl."

"Are you trying to tell me a girl can't play catch? Hot damn. A baby," he repeated, and the look on his face reminded her of the Grinch, after his heart swelled three sizes big. It would have amazed her if it hadn't confused the hell out of her. "I think the box of stuff from my mother has one or two baby things from when I was a kid. Would you like some hot milk or something? No, you're allergic. What can I get you?"

She made a face, and she wasn't sure whether the reaction was to the idea of the milk or Dare's reaction to the news.

She wasn't sure whether she was ready for this, but he was.

"Not right now," she said, looking at him out of the corner of her eye. She looked down at his hand, warm against her belly still. "You're dealing with this pretty well. A lot better than I am."

"You're in shock. You've been told never to expect it. This is amazing. A baby," he breathed.

The transformation was almost eerie. "I never realized you liked kids so much."

"You don't understand. I never expected to be a father."

She stared at him. "You've had relationships before."

"Yes, but...not."

She found the conversation bewildering. "We're together, aren't we?"

He covered her fingers with his other hand. "Are we?"

"Yes." She blinked again, her throat closing when she looked into his eyes. "I hope so," she said, trembling. A flood of emotions assaulted her, making her shake.

He drew her close. She could feel his hands stroking her. "Hey," he whispered, "we're going to be parents." He tightened his hold on her just a little. She didn't move.

"Looks like it," she whispered back, her trembling continuing unabated. "If I'd known it was that easy to get pregnant, I'd—" she paused.

"You'd what?"

"I don't know." She tightened her own hold around him. "I don't know what I would have done. Worried more."

He stroked her back again, kissed her forehead again. "Me," he repeated. "I'm going to be a father."

"Are you trying to convince yourself or me?" She tried to chuckle, found she couldn't. In fact, she was feeling more and more uncomfortable.

"I'm sorry, honey." He kissed her hair again.

Honey. He had called her *honey.* He had never used an endearment before. "Oh, I don't mind," she lied.

He tilted her head so their gazes could meet. "You're terrified, aren't you? Poor sweetheart. What can I do to make you stop being so scared?"

"I don't know," she said, closing her eyes.

They held each other in the dimming light of the afternoon while the game on the television droned on and fans screamed as sooner or later, someone won, someone lost and the game ended.

"You feel any better?" he asked. His voice was rusty, as though he had been asleep.

"A little. I want to call my mother and grandmother."

He gave her one last little hug, firm, not hard, as though he were starting to take care of what he did already. "Do you think they're going to be ecstatic or upset?"

She stretched her back and tried not to think about the discomfort she would be in. Her feet would swell. Her back would hurt. "Why would they be upset?"

"Because—you know."

She caught his eyes. "No, I don't. What?"

"They'll be happy, but not that the father's not Lars. And we're not married."

She sighed. That was one end result of the events of the past two months. While Kristin's grandmother seemed to be willing to let bygones be bygones, Kristin's mother had accepted Dare's heartfelt apology only reluctantly. And both expressed dismay that Lars would no longer be a fixture.

She didn't know if she could take a comment about Lars, let alone that her mother and grandmother were going to be, respectively, grandmother and great-grandmother. "Let me think about this. I have to figure this out."

Dare grabbed her hand. "You're going to be a mom," he whispered, his eyes shining.

Yes, that's right. Get over it! She was feeling even more tired than she was before. But she didn't know whether it was emotional or physical. Aloud, she said, "Looks like it."

Dare leaned over her. "If you're not going to call them right now, let me use the phone."

"Who're you calling?" She couldn't think of anyone he would call with the news. "Dagmar?"

He laughed as he punched in numbers, in a combination that Kristin didn't recognize. "No. Hello? Dad? It's Dare."

Kristin blinked. She had forgotten he still had a living parent, because Dare never, ever mentioned him.

"Dad, I've got great news," he exclaimed. He reached out and squeezed her hand again. "I'm getting married. Kristin and me. The doctor. Ginnie told you about her."

Kristin stared at him.

When did we decide that? "We are? I wish you'd told me about this first," she whispered. Her stomach twisted.

Dare continued, his eyes bright, oblivious to her reaction. "We're going to have a baby. Isn't it great?"

Panic was sweeping over her in great waves now. "I don't know," she whispered.

Chapter Eighteen
And the ravens flew away, one by one.

෨

She didn't want to hear the rest of the phone conversation.

Kristin walked over to the windows. It was autumn, the beginning of two seasons of almost constant rain. In the distance, she could hear the screech of tires, car horns honking. She winced.

For some reason, every year when the rains began, Puget Sound natives had to relearn how to drive in the drizzle, relearn the fact the roads would be wet and slippery, as if it were a complete surprise, every single year.

Amid it all, those ravens would be hovering, and she saw them every single day. Sometimes they would be huddled on a branch, clustered together, protected against the rains. Sometimes she would see them individually, on a wire or even perched on a car, observing the activity and on occasion commenting—on what, she didn't know.

Kristin shivered. She looked around as Dare hung on the phone. By now, he wasn't saying anything.

He looked the way she felt. Her future had just been decided within minutes, without her input, and she didn't know if she liked that.

Kristin wandered down the hall. Over the past two months, the living room had lost its white and ivory decor. It had bursts of color now—a red pillow, a peach-colored handmade quilt brought in from the bedroom, a lime-green working phone that replaced the white French Provincial rotary that had never actually functioned. The place looked lived in, at long last.

In the coming months, there would be even more color. There would be colorful toys with bright patterns, and the living room would be as good a place as any to store them. The glass and wrought-iron coffee table would have to go. She had always been afraid she would trip and shatter it. Worse, spilling blood over the white carpet. Lars would be displeased.

A baby. She had never seen Dare so happy.

This was a surprise, one she knew would be unlikely to ever be repeated. And she was surprised, not reluctant. Just very, very…surprised.

Dare's voice had risen, and she could hear it all the way down the corridor. His tone as he spoke on the phone brought her out of her reverie. "I'm sorry you feel that way, Dad," he said. Then she heard nothing.

Bad reaction, she guessed. She decided to give him some privacy, so instead, she wandered into the kitchen. She rummaged in her cabinets until she found the dusty box of hot cocoa packets, only a year or two old.

She heard Dare put down the phone receiver and mutter something. "Are you talking to me?" she called out. She wandered back to her study. "Are you all right?"

She stopped at the door to the study. "Dare?"

This wasn't encouraging. He was holding his head in his hands. "Are you all right?" she repeated. She kneeled next to him, touching his arm.

His head came up and his eyes opened. "I'm fine." He smiled at her, and he seemed to have bags under his eyes he didn't have only minutes before. "I don't know why I thought he'd react any differently. I thought—I thought this was going to be it, the thing that finally brought us together. A grandchild. But no."

Kristin frowned. "I take it he wasn't as happy as you hoped." She squeezed his shoulder. "I'm sorry."

He covered her hand with his. "I'm sorrier than you are. He's coming out for a visit. He wants to meet you."

Festival of Stars

"Oh," she said. Should she be happy she was finally meeting his father? Or unhappy she was meeting someone Dare had avoided talking about the entire time she had known him? So she ventured, "You must be excited. When was the last time you saw him?"

An answer involving a holiday, that's what she was expecting—even the least-connected families tried a holiday get-together from time to time. Then he answered, "A few years ago. When I first met you." And she realized it was worse than she thought.

"That was *three years* ago. When did you talk to him last?"

Dare shrugged. "About two years ago. I thought I might have left some stuff at his house, and I needed him to check."

"Don't you even call him for Christmas? Father's Day?"

He shook his head. "I've tried. He doesn't like it. But I try on Christmas, and if I reach him, fine."

She looked at him. "Then why did you want to call him?"

He shrugged. "I thought about the reaction that your mother and grandmother are going to have, and I thought maybe he might be interested he was going to be a grandfather. I was wrong," he added. "But now he wants to talk to me in person."

Now her stomach hurt. "You told him about us, and me, and now he wants to talk to you. Not me, you."

"But he'll want to meet you too. After you meet him—"

"You're making me nervous."

"If I had known he would actually jump on a plane, I would have sent him a birth announcement instead," he said. The bitterness grew in his voice. "I wouldn't have wanted to inflict him on you, believe me."

"I have another question," she said, her voice level, even though her hands trembled. She crossed her arms.

"Now what?" Dare sounded tired. "I'm starting to think we should have kept this a secret."

"It's not too late," she answered, the quiver creeping into her voice. "We've only told one person so far. We could keep it at that."

"That's not what I meant!" he exclaimed. "I meant...I shouldn't have thought my father would care."

To her horror, Kristin's eyes filled with tears. "Don't say that!" She wiped at her eyes, more embarrassed than anything else. "That's a terrible thing to say. I'm sure he cares. He just doesn't know how to react."

Though she still had her own doubts, she reached out and put her arms around Dare. She closed her eyes against his shoulder. "I wish I could believe that," he whispered.

She rubbed her wet eyes against the flannel of his shirt. "You're making me afraid of whether I should tell my folks."

In response, he gave her a short, hard hug. "They're going to be so happy," he whispered into her ear. "Surprised, but happy. You'll see. They're getting their first grandkid."

As it turned out, they were both almost right.

It was almost time for dinner in the Olafsson household, and Kristin decided they were going to invite themselves for it. Her timing proved right. Her mother and grandmother were in the midst of preparations when they walked in, so she had taken a deep breath and blurted it out, bracing for the impact.

The looks on their faces were pretty much what she would have expected—shock, elation—apprehension. After all, that's what her own reaction had been.

"A baby, Kritchka," Solveig exclaimed. She placed her hands around Kristin's face and pinched her cheeks. "Your grandfather would have been so happy."

Moyo glanced past her daughter and stared at Dare. "*Itsu kekkon suru no?*" she asked pointedly. "When is wedding?" she repeated for the benefit of her English-speaking audience.

Kristin hugged her grandmother and turned. Her wave of positive emotion waned a little, however, when she saw Dare's face, looking like the proverbial deer in headlights. "Dare?" she asked. He had been so happy —

In a flash, he smiled and tried to look as though the glare his prospective mother-in-law shot him was nothing, and that the look of unease on his face was only in Kristin's imagination. But she knew it wasn't. "*Sugu.*" He bowed. "Very soon, Mrs. Olafsson."

He tried, Kristin had to give him that. He made a point of speaking Japanese to her mother whenever he saw her now. She barely responded most of the time. This was one of them.

Even Kristin, still in her grandmother's arms, could feel the chill between her mother and Dare. "Dare's father's coming in. We're going to talk about when then," she added desperately, not noticing the flinch on Dare's face at that.

Then the back door slammed and Eric's voice sliced the tension. "Hey, Kristin! Did you bring what's-his-name?"

Kristin glanced at Dare, whose frozen face had cracked a little. "Yeah, I did," she yelled back. "And we've got news."

They heard the thunder of Eric's footsteps as he skidded into the kitchen. "How's school?" Kristin asked, deceptively calm. But she reached out for Dare's hand.

"School's great! I don't know why anybody says that sophomore year's tough. So what's the news? Are you getting married?" He reached over and grabbed a handful of mixed nuts.

"Soon," Dare said, and again Kristin's stomach churned at his tense look. This was the second time he had mentioned marriage, but he had never spoken to her about it. Did he expect it to be a given? Or— "But the news right now is you're going to be an uncle."

"You guys are getting a dog? Get a big one. Those little ones are footballs, as far as I'm —"

"No, we're not getting a dog," Kristin interrupted.

Eric froze. A cashew that was about to bounce into his mouth reflected off his lips. "You're pregnant, Kris? You?" His handful of nuts slipped, spilling on the floor.

"Yeah," she snapped. "As opposed to Dare."

Eric choked. He promptly squatted to pick up the nuts. "Oh, wow," he said lamely when he stood back up, glancing at his mother. "But I thought—"

"That's what we all thought," Kristin interrupted. Somehow, this just didn't feel like good news. "Surprise."

"Congratulations. So when's the wedding? When's dinner?" he asked as he sat on a stool. He continued to pop the cashews from the dish after he threw away the ones that had been on the floor, but he was on automatic now. His unease was growing, Kristin could see that, as he realized he had stepped onto a minefield—and worse, he was related to both sides of the opposing forces. Whoever stepped on a mine first and exploded, he would regret it. She felt the same way.

For the first time in a while, she felt her own unease dissipate. It wasn't easy being on the battlefield, but it had to be even worse being a spectator.

"When is father coming?" Moyo asked Dare. Now that her mother had to speak directly to Dare, Kristin noticed she used English instead of the Japanese he had been using to speak to her.

Clearly uneasy, Dare shrugged. "As soon as he can."

"Shouldn't you start calling her 'Mom' or 'Mother Olafsson' or something?" Eric asked.

As Kristin watched, an almost identical shudder went through both Dare and her mother. "I'm not sure about that, Eric," Dare managed to say.

"You can call me 'Marmar', just like Kristin," Solveig said, pinching his cheek. For a second, Kristin saw the panicked look on Dare's face melt.

He was joining her family. A family that still had strong reservations—she thought it was fair to call it that—about him.

Even if he had been Bill Gates, her mother would have had the same expression on her face. Even if he had been the President of the United States, she would have done her best to make him flinch. That was her way.

"Thank you," Dare said to Solveig. Kristin could have sworn his eyes were brighter. "Thank you very much."

There wasn't much else to say. Dinner was quiet. In desperation, Kristin cajoled her brother into talking about his classes at the university. But now that her own news had been imparted, she found it difficult to talk about anything at all.

Not that her mother would have welcomed it at the moment. After she got used to it — then she would be happier.

At least Kristin hoped so.

It was going to take a while for it all to sink in. She and Dare had decided to leave after dinner, neither of them up for any more strained conversation.

Of course, if it had been her own kid who had done this — and with that thought she placed her hands on her abdomen — she would have been in shock too. She could imagine it — "Hi, Mom, hi, Dad, guess what? I'm pregnant when no one thought it was possible, and the father's someone you'd prefer not to have in the same state as you and did I mention we don't have a wedding date yet? Are you happy for me?"

Come to think of it, it was a miracle her mother had been as calm as she was. She herself wouldn't have been, not having had the training of years of polite Japanese society. No, she would have blown her top in good old-fashioned American outrage, and all hell would have broken loose.

What would her own father's reaction been? He had been the extrovert to her mother's introvert. He had always spoken first and thought later, of good soul and gentle spirit. For someone who never learned much Japanese, he had always managed to know what her mother thought.

She wanted that with Dare. To be able to guess his reactions — to be able to have his child come to them —

"Penny," she heard him say.

She looked up at him. "Pardon?"

He shot her a glance. They were on their way back to Seattle after dinner. The traffic on I-90 was, as usual, treacherous, but he presented her with a smile that calmed her nerves and made her feel a little better, even as he avoided being sideswiped by yet another idiot driving too fast with a cellphone attached to his ear.

"Penny," he repeated. "There's one in my pocket. You can have it if you tell me what you're thinking."

"Is this some sort of cheap attempt for me to feel you up?"

"Do I need a ruse for that?"

Smiling, she reached out and caressed his thigh. She watched his leg quiver before he patted her hand and placed it on the seat, away from him. "I was thinking about how my father would have reacted. My mother barely said a word."

"No, she just asked *me* when the wedding was. I almost wanted to promise my father wasn't going to bring his white hood. I swear that's what she was thinking."

Kristin grinned. "Be glad she's letting you in the house. I'd like to say that after the baby's born, she'll tolerate you a little more, but there are no guarantees."

"Thank God for your grandmother." He changed lanes to avoid a BMW veering between lanes on two tires. "Even Eric didn't seem to know what to say."

"Eric's nineteen. If you feed him, he'll be happy."

Dare shook his head. "It's not that easy, Kristin. He's not a dog. He's going to be less direct about sorting out his feelings about this than your mother was."

"Oh, I don't know, Dare. I've been his big sister all his life. I can predict what he's going to do."

"You're his big sister, but he's not your baby brother anymore. He's got his first taste of adulthood. Don't you remember being his age? Or were you always an adult?"

She sighed. "I was busy at his age."

"You've been busy all your life. Seriously. What were you doing in his place at his age?"

"Being shown the ins and outs of the university by Lars."

Silence. "I walked into that one," he muttered.

She waved it off. Lars was still a sensitive subject, despite her best efforts. "I was probably more mature at his age. He's still trying to figure out what he wants to do."

"Is that a crime?"

She smiled. "No. But he's still my little brother, and he's not going to form his own opinion about this yet. But he'll be fine."

"He seemed to be pretty happy about being an uncle," Dare said after a moment. "In a noncommittal kind of way. In a kind of in-shock-about-being-an-uncle kind of way."

She shrugged. "I don't think he's taking it that badly."

"I didn't say he was. I said he hadn't made up his mind yet. He's like you — wary and noncommittal."

"Oh, I am not."

He laughed. "Are we going to be doing this all our lives?"

"Discussions are a healthy part of a relationship."

"Discussions are. Blindly refusing to budge is not. My place or yours?" he asked, abruptly changing the subject. They had been splitting their nights between their apartments in the past few weeks.

"I have the midnight shift tonight," she reminded him. "Why don't you take me home and let me nap before I go in?"

He frowned. "How long are you going to be on that? You should be getting your rest. Did you eat enough at dinner?"

"I ate enough. I'm fine. I'm tired, though."

"Are you going to feel up to going in?"

She tensed. This over-concern routine was going to wear thin very quickly—and she still had how many more months to go? "I don't know. I'll have to see."

Dare delivered her to her apartment, kissed her good night, insisted on tucking her in—and then left, making sure the light was dim and the clock radio was playing classical music, her favorite way of falling asleep.

She waited until he left to get up, heading straight for the kitchen, digging out the pint of Ben & Jerry's chocolate fudge brownie frozen yogurt at the back of her freezer. Milk she didn't touch, but frozen dairy treats she would—and she now had a good excuse.

Kristin put her feet up in the living room. Her apartment was quiet, letting her unwind for the first time since that afternoon. She fiddled with the blinds. Outside the courtyard, she could see a few pedestrians hurrying in the steady drizzle, hear the shush of automobiles passing by, their tires slogging through the layer of rainwater on the road, oily from all the automotive traffic.

Pregnant. After all this time. One little accident and boom! Just like any other woman of child-bearing age. But were there truly and really any accidents?

It didn't matter now. It was done, and barring any unforeseen circumstances, she was going to be joining a club that she thought she would never be able to get the entry fee for—the Mommy Club. She had never paid any attention all those years when her friends would talk about their pregnancies, their labors, the sleepless nights—the little things that united them against the rest of the world.

It was as foreign to her as—she didn't know what. She had felt out of place in Pascisci, but at least she had spent her summers there. It was only after moving into the town as an adult she had felt uncomfortable. It was as foreign to her as the time she had received a certificate from the Daughters of the

American Revolution at her high school graduation, and realized with a shock when she had accepted it the blue-haired old ladies had expected someone, well, decidedly more blonde.

As foreign as that. And more.

She sleepwalked through her shift and went home, for once not letting the job get to her. Home again, she looked around and tried to visualize the changes that would be coming.

And she couldn't do it. She couldn't imagine how her living room, once fearsome in its *Architectural Digest* look, would look in just a few short months.

One way or another, it was going to happen.

Kristin decided to go to sleep, just as the rain started to let up and the autumn sun peeked through the clouds.

When the phone rang, her first thought, fuzzy and dream-ridden, was to ignore it. The dream had been fairly obvious in its symbolism—holding a baby, dropping it accidentally into a river, only to discover the river wasn't a river at all, but a river bed, bone-dry—and the sound of the ringing phone next to her bed jarred her into consciousness.

Part of her welcomed it. The dream had been scaring her, and if she woke up to answer the phone, she could abandon the panic that dropping the dream baby had given her. On the other hand, she was very tired, and she really could use the sleep.

On the third hand, she wasn't going to get any more rest by pursuing a nightmare. Blearily, she reached for the phone. "Yeah?"

"Good morning," Dare's cheery voice greeted her.

She closed her eyes again and smiled. "Good morning," she answered, her voice rusty and deep. "What time is it?"

"It's four-thirty in the afternoon. Did I wake you?"

His voice was filled with concern. She'd been in bed longer than she realized. "Hm. Yes, but I wasn't having a very good dream, so thank you for calling."

Despite her restless dreams, her discomfort was dissipating. Dare's voice was warm and reassuring. Thank God something was.

"I'm getting off in about half an hour, so I figured I'd get something for dinner and bring it over. How's that sound?"

At his mention of food, her eyes popped open. Her stomach, suddenly, was not feeling up to par. "'Scuse me—"

She ran to the bathroom and knelt in front of the porcelain throne, remembering one of the joys of impending motherhood—nausea.

It would have been one thing if this had been a recurring problem in her life, she thought resentfully as she upchucked dinner and everything else before, finally, it stopped—but this sort of thing was foreign to her.

One more foreign thing encroaching in her life. One more thing getting control over her.

She had no experience in this. Not when she got drunk during her college years. Not when she accidentally got kicked in her stomach during soccer practice in high school. Not when she ate spoiled tuna by mistake.

Her eyes closed and her stomach completely empty at long last, she pressed the lever and listened as the toilet came to life. *Welcome to a miserable few weeks*, she thought. Goodbye, peaceful mornings, as her system adjusted.

She shook off a flash of resentment as the idea of her orderly life being trampled flitted through her mind. It was one thing to always have hoped for this, always known it was possible. But for her, it hadn't been a likelihood, not since her teens. Now, it was just—a shock.

She washed out her mouth and brushed her teeth. She groaned. She felt frigging awful. How did women *do* this?

Finally, she went back into the bedroom and picked up the phone. "Sorry about that. I just f—"

Dial tone.

Kristin stared at the phone. "Great," she muttered. Then she hung up.

She heard her door open. "Kristin? Are you all right?"

Dare?

"I'm in here," she called out, perched on the bed. "What're you doing here this fast? I thought you were going to pick up dinner first."

The mention of dinner made her stomach roil again, but she decided to ignore it for a moment. But she wasn't going to stand up right away, either.

His shadow filled in the doorway. She winced as he flipped the switch and flooded the room with light. "Are you all right?" he repeated. He knelt next to the bed, taking her hand. "I heard you running—and then, nothing."

Kristin snorted. "Get used to it. I'm going to lie back down again." She closed her eyes. "I was throwing up. Welcome to the joys of pregnancy."

He didn't let go of her hand. "Are you all right?"

She laughed. "I'm fine. I was fine yesterday when I woke up. I was fine until I found out I was pregnant. Then, boom! All of a sudden, morning sickness. I'd swear it's psychosomatic." She squeezed his hand. He needed the reassurance as much as she did, if not more.

"Morning sickness? At four-thirty in the afternoon?"

She snorted. "At the moment, my system thinks it's morning. Did you speed all the way here?"

"Well, yeah," he said, and she smiled at his defensive tone.

"Is your car intact?" she asked idly, marking time before she could get up again. "Can you get me some crackers from the kitchen? If I have any? And bring me the box so I can keep it next to the bed."

"Sure." Squeezing her hand, he got up and left.

She took a deep breath. "I can't believe women go through this vomiting business voluntarily," she said aloud.

"What?" Dare called in from the kitchen.

"Nothing," she yelled back. "I was just muttering to myself," she said in normal tones as he came back in with a box of saltines. "I don't see how women go along with this vomiting business. It's really inconvenient."

"Isn't it normal?"

She shrugged as she took the box and tore open a sleeve of crackers. "Yeah. Hormones adjusting themselves." She shoved a cracker into her mouth. "And these help settle the stomach."

"Can you recommend any books I could read about this?"

He sounded shy. This was as new for him as it was for her. "I can dig up a few titles, but since we have to go in and talk to my OB/GYN, I'm going to let her do it."

"Kristin — we have to talk."

Her eyes opened, her nerves suddenly on edge. That didn't sound good. "What about?"

His expression didn't look good either. "About everything I haven't been telling you." He looked grim.

She didn't like this at all.

"I've got to tell you before my father shows up," he said. He squeezed her hand again, and she was frightened now. "I just need you to know."

Chapter Nineteen
The raven, alone now, sat and watched and waited.

ಐ

"I don't know how to tell you this."

Oh God. "What is it? Just tell me." She tried to sit up, decided against it, and instead turned her head to look at him.

His eyes were darker than the room. He looked terrified.

"I don't know how." His voice cracked.

"Whatever it is, we can work it out," she said, her own voice trembling. She didn't know what was going on, but he was starting to scare her. "Tell me." She reached out, but he was too far away for her to touch him.

He looked at her, at her hand. After a few seconds, she withdrew, and try as she might, she started to blink, willing the tears to stay in place.

Kristin tucked her hand under her blanket, and watched as he hunched down, holding himself close. "Remember I told you I didn't want to talk about my mother, or my father, and you respected that? And we haven't?" He looked up.

Remembering, she nodded. After first blush, she hadn't thought it was that important. As a matter of fact, it had slipped her mind.

"I just figured you and your father weren't that close," she ventured. "Was I wrong?"

He shook his head—then nodded. "No, you're right. If not for the fact that my grandmother made me promise to check on him once in a while, I would have cut off ties with the old man the day I graduated from high school. If not for Gram, I wouldn't have spoken to him after that day."

The bitterness in his voice permeated his words. She did not like this. "This isn't a minor disagreement, I take it."

"No." He settled on the floor, against the side of the bed. He reached out and grabbed her hand then, entwining their fingers. After a second, she squeezed his hand. "Let me tell you why things are the way they are."

He leaned back against the bed, tilted his head to nestle against her thigh, and began.

* * * * *

Some of the young soldiers who landed in the postwar Japan were eager to see the world, like Eric Olafsson. Some of the young soldiers who landed there were not.

Like Eric Olafsson, John Borodin was a young soldier, one who had not quite been old enough to enlist as the war drew to its end. He did join the armed forces afterward, and when he had been assigned to Occupied Japan, he thought nothing of it. The Navy was a job and he was going to serve his time and then by God he was going home to Indiana. He thought nothing of the fact that from the first day he stepped onto Japanese soil, he hadn't liked it.

John Borodin's frame of reference had never been especially broad, and another country, another culture, half the world away, was more of a shock to him than it was to most of the occupying forces.

It was the little things. One by one he could have dealt with them, but altogether it was nearly unbearable. It was hotter in Tokyo than in Indiana. It was crowded, and on occasion he found his surroundings to be repellent, considering chunks of the country had been bombed nearly out of existence, a marked change from the quiet farming town of Pascisci.

And the people! He couldn't believe the people. It was a sea of dark hair and unreadable eyes. Before coming to this foreign land, he had only seen one Asian face in his life, on a trip to Chicago, in a restaurant. Further, the boy from the Midwest kept running into the endless expanse of water the base was built against. It was disconcerting. It was bewildering.

Nor had he ever been the most outgoing of young men. The difference was, if he didn't socialize with anyone on base, then he had to go off—and he ran into that problem with people who didn't look like him or talk like him.

But he was an American boy who was lonely, and far away from home. He met Keiko one day when he wandered into a fishmonger in an attempt to find a decent American hamburger—why he thought he could find one off-base, no one knew—and found that the language barrier was worse than stiff. Depending on circumstance, it was impenetrable.

And that was how he found himself shouting in a vain effort to be understood when pretty, young Keiko walked in. The elderly fishmonger had never before in his life spoken to a nonnative, let alone someone who didn't speak his language. John's loud voice and erratic hand gestures were bewildering to him, and considering John was nearly a foot and a half taller, intimidating.

Keiko's English—only faintly accented by then, thanks to her study of the language—worked perfectly to calm the American soldier down. And since she wanted to continue to improve her English, she tried to help him.

Better she had kept walking instead, but she hadn't. Once the confusion was settled — the elderly fishmonger had no hamburger, had never seen hamburger, sold only fish, which John despised—Keiko found herself being peppered with more questions, all in English. She kept staring at him. He was the most exotic person she had ever seen—he had hair that was almost white! His eyes looked like the sky!

Despite his disdain for the darker people he was surrounded by, he was also desperately lonely, and a desperately lonely young man with the attention of a young woman who spoke his language was not likely to give it up. It wasn't anything he had to worry about, he told himself. It was a mild flirtation, one that mirrored the flirtations that surrounded him among his GI buddies. And she was a native, so it didn't matter.

The mild flirtation with Keiko stretched from that afternoon to months, and by then her father *did* know—and was livid his daughter, his previously obedient daughter, had forsaken her duties and chosen to consort with the enemy, the enemy against which her own brother had died honorably, crashing his plane into a US battleship as a *kamikaze* pilot, as had her uncle, her father's brother.

And then her sister, who had been raped by an American soldier early in the Occupation and had refused to step outside their house since, committed suicide.

Then Keiko discovered she was pregnant, and expected John to marry her—not unexpected. But John Borodin resisted.

Marry a native girl? The thought appalled him. But it wasn't as though he had a girlfriend back home. He had fully expected, however, that he would find one when he got back home, and get married then and only then.

Marry a Jap? It was a ludicrous idea.

What John Borodin didn't count on, however, was his own mother. His mother, who had raised him since his father's death, was insistent he marry Keiko. Unlike her son, she had no problem with the fact her potential daughter-in-law was not white. She had waited a long time for a grandchild, and by God, her son was not going to deprive her.

So John reluctantly married Keiko in a ceremony witnessed by two strangers off the street. Afterward, he went back to the base and she went home—and was promptly thrown out when her father disowned her for marrying the white devil.

John refused to apply for married enlisted men's housing, so Keiko moved into a tiny apartment outside the base. John dropped by when he was in the mood and basically ignored her when he was not. He was on duty when Keiko gave birth, and when he received the news, he went to visit his newborn son, whom he named after his mother's hometown and after his own father, also his own name. And so it was that Darien John Borodin was first graced with the presence of his father.

Near the end of his tour, John received word his mother had had a stroke. He was going home, albeit a little earlier than expected. As he was packing, he received word that Keiko had been killed in a car accident, the victim of a hit-and-run involving a Jeep inside base limits.

He never did find out what happened. He did find out, much to his dismay, that his plan to present and dump his son onto his late wife's family hit a snag. They disowned her when she married John, and they had no desire whatsoever to claim, let alone acknowledge, the half-breed son of a wayward daughter.

Meanwhile, his mother, recovering from her stroke, was insistent he bring his now-motherless son back to the States, claiming it could be her only chance to hold a grandchild. John was trapped between his mother and a hard place, and in the end, he chose the wishes of his mother.

So he went home, accompanied by a little boy, who carried his own suitcase and clutched the few toys and mementoes he was allowed to take. By the time they arrived in Indiana, the long and tiring trip involving more plane changes than he could care to remember, the little boy was tired beyond measure, bewildered and longing for his mother, the only parent he had known, really.

Darien John bonded quickly with his grandmother. It was she who gave him his nickname, since he was willing to try new things. John's mother and John's son got along famously. John's mother and John's son got along much better than they did with John himself.

Soon, between John's silence on the subject of his late wife and his mother's reluctance to expound on same, the topic of

Dare Borodin's mother became a moot point. She was dead, and the boy was here. And that was that. People forgot.

And with that, Dare grew up, avoiding his father when he could, never referring to his earliest memories, knowing instinctively he had to avoid talking about it. He became the essence of the all-American boy.

Dare's grandmother died when he was in his mid-teens. By then, his relationship with his father, never good, crumbled completely. As his grandmother lay dying, while Dare's first inclination would have been to run as far as he could, she made him promise to finish his studies, go to college, and—hardest of all—speak to his father on occasion.

* * * * *

Dare was standing at the window now, looking out at the dark, sodden scenery. "The time before last I spoke to my father, I met you. I thought there was a nice symmetry there." He ran a finger along the blinds. "I pieced together a lot of the story. My grandmother told me parts—I remember some of the neighborhood kids telling me some other parts when I was a kid—and some I actually got from my father, usually when I was arguing with him after Gram died."

Kristin wiped her eyes. "Why didn't you tell me before?"

He shrugged as he turned to face her. "There was no good time. If I could have figured out a way, I would have."

Kristin frowned. "So when you called your father—"

He took a deep breath. "When I called Dad, I figured it was worth a try. But now I'm going to inflict him on you, and I am so sorry."

She was quiet for a moment. "When is he coming out?"

Closing his eyes, he said. "He's arriving Friday. Do you think you'll be up for it?"

"Depends on what time. I have to go to work," she reminded him. She reached toward him. "But I'll be there for you as long as I can."

He smiled briefly. "Thank you. I just hope you don't regret it when you meet him."

"He's your father," she reminded him. "He may not be the most lovable person in the world, but the fact that he's your father counts for something. And who knows? He might have softened up over the years. He's getting old. He's alone. He never remarried, did he?"

"No."

"That's a long time."

"He never remarried because he's an objectionable old man. You'll see."

The week slipped by. Despite her misgivings, Kristin began to, little by little, relax into the role of expectant parent. She bought books and consulted with Dare and her OB/GYN, and she accepted little items from friends and her grandmother, who presented her with mementoes from when her father was born. From her mother she received, with surprise, a book of baby names—in Japanese.

She came home one morning after her shift to find that Dare had acquired a baby's mobile, one that wound up, decorated with red and pink and yellow birds and horses bobbing around as it spun slowly to a pretty little melody. He had fastened it to the ceiling in a corner of the living room near the windows, and when the sun came out, the colors of the plastic sparkled into life. She spent half an hour watching it spin, her eyes moist, embarrassing herself.

She didn't see as much of Dare that week, considering her work schedule. But his anticipation was plain. The books she found lying around were more detailed and complex than the simple books she had given him, and she could tell he was intent on finding out as much as he could.

"If he could figure out how to speak fetus, he would," she muttered to herself as she woke up early Friday afternoon. Dare's father was scheduled to come in later, and she knew Dare wanted her to greet his father with him. She showered and dressed. Dare would pick her up as soon as he got off work.

At least the rain had abated. The more it rained, the slicker the roads, and considering the area attracted out-of-towners from drier climates, the driving could get tricky.

She sat down in her living room. Her previously white-on-white room was now not only splashed with vivid color, it was gaining items that—gasp—did not necessarily belong there. A pile of thick books was stacked in the corner, where they had mysteriously migrated from Kristin's study, and the mobile bobbed above it, waiting for a breeze or a twist of its key to start its gentle melody.

Kristin rubbed her forehead. She didn't want to meet this man who apparently had no desire to recognize his son for the unique human being he was. Because of him, Dare had been isolated, touched by humanity only through his grandmother and even, she knew now, his neighbors.

But she was going to meet him and be polite and pretend he was the most wonderful person in the world, because Dare, who didn't believe that his father was that any more than she did, wanted her to. And Dare was the father of her baby.

She still found it hard to believe. But Dare didn't. Whereas she was too tired to do any planning, he was planning up a storm. It was disconcerting to discover he was actually making the lists that brides did, and he was starting to gather real estate brochures, because he had decided they should start off their new life together in a house—Mom, Dad and Kid.

In fact, he was orchestrating her life as much as Lars had. And she didn't like that thought at all.

And it didn't do much good to find out from her younger brother that Lars had, after an absence, started to show up at her mother and grandmother's house once more, as if he were still the prospective son-in-law. It didn't help that his own family only lived a few blocks away.

She sighed. If she had her druthers, she would suggest to Dare they elope. Or run away from home and drop a postcard in the mail to tell everyone they were alive and well and they were never, ever coming back.

That fantasy was tempting.

The sound of a key being fit into the lock startled her. "Dare?"

"Kristin? Are you up?"

"I'm in the living room," she called out. She looked up as he walked in. It still surprised her he could look so good in a gray suit. Today, he even had on a conservative tie, his school emblem the motif and a pearl tie tack. "Hi," she said as she raised her face for a kiss. "You look so distinguished. I look like such a slob." At best, her shirt and chinos were serviceable.

He looked tired but he smiled anyway. "You look comfortable. I suspect your patients would prefer that." He kissed her forehead. She closed her eyes. His lips were warm, almost as if he had a fever.

Kristin held out her arms for him to pull her up, and he complied. "Ready to meet your future father-in-law?"

"I'm ready to meet your father," she emphasized. "And is there anybody else in your family you'd like me to meet?"

"He's the only one left," he told her, bracing her as she found her balance. She hadn't gained so much weight yet she needed the aid, but she did like the emotional boost.

"Good. I'm pretty nervous about meeting this one."

The traffic was as bad as it could have been. The rain had abated, but residual oil on the roads caused a skid now and then.

The airport was, as always, busy and confused. Dare was starting to tense up, she could tell—his hand, entwined with hers, was starting to feel colder, clammier, stressed.

"Hey," she whispered as they got on an escalator. "Calm down. They just touched ground."

"I know," he answered, looking around, as if his father had gotten off the plane before it touched ground and now was waiting for him. "I'm just getting ready."

By the time they got to the baggage claim area, incoming passengers were already clustered around the carousel, which had yet to disgorge their belongings. Kristin and Dare stopped at the edge of the group and waited along with everyone else.

"Where is he?" she asked. She tried to imagine what Dare's father looked like. Was he dark, was he fair?

"He's probably still on his way here. He doesn't move quickly anymore," Dare answered, his eyes darting around.

Finally, the carousel began to move and the waiting travelers started to claim their things. As Dare and Kristin waited, the travelers, reunited with their bags, left with friends and loved ones. Some of the travelers were children, traveling alone, looking around as they searched for someone to meet them, and happily leaving with them when they found them.

Kristin's stomach clenched as she watched them. Dare might have been like that at that age—tired and almost lost and searching for something he didn't know.

She glanced at him. His arms were crossed on his chest as he leaned against a column, watching the down escalator as the next load of passengers came off and headed for the carousels. He took a sharp breath and stood up.

She guessed. "Is that him?"

Dare nodded. His mouth tightened as a white-haired man walked off the elevator nearby, aided by a walker.

Kristin's breath caught. "I hadn't realized he needed help walking. We could have made arrangements, seen if we could have met him up there."

She saw a muscle twitch in Dare's cheek. "He would have hated that," he said. "Let's wait until the other passengers clear out. It's too crowded."

Kristin's first glimpse of John Borodin sparked neither awe nor antagonism. He was, essentially, a Caucasian male in his seventies. His white hair was shot through with strands of what looked like a dulled brown, making him look as if he were platinum blond and graying slowly.

He must have been tall in his youth, she mused, looking out over the heads of the postwar Japanese. Due to the increasingly Western diet, Asians were much taller now than they would have been when John Borodin arrived in the Far East, and for someone who had been young and homesick, the short, dark-haired people who surrounded him must have been an additional confusion.

The next crowd of incoming passengers heading for the carousels blocked her view for a moment. When she could see him again, she saw the old man catch sight of Dare.

Neither of them made a move to meet each other, simply staring at each other for a moment.

Kristin could see Dare in his father. She could see the son in the shape of the father's jaw, the line of his nose, the slant of his cheekbones. And certainly in the twitch of the muscles in the cheek.

They didn't have any choice now. The passengers thinned out, their luggage firmly in hand, to the extent there was no one between father and son.

Reluctantly, Dare stepped forward, extending his hand. "Dad. Did you have a good flight?"

"If you consider two stopovers of an hour each time 'good', yes," John Borodin said. He glanced at Dare's extended hand.

"Mr. Borodin, I'm glad to meet you," Kristin said, stepping forward and extending her own hand. "I'm Kristin Olafsson. Dare's told me so much about you."

John didn't even twitch. "I have two pieces of luggage," he informed his son.

Perhaps he was deaf. "Mr. Borodin, I'm K—"

The older man glanced at her. "I know who you are. I was speaking to my son," he said. "I have no reason to speak to you."

"Dad, that's inexcusably rude," Dare said angrily.

"I came out here to talk to you, not her," John Borodin shot back.

That twisting clench in Kristin's stomach came back right then. She closed her eyes.

"Welcome to Seattle," she whispered as her lover and his father started to argue.

Chapter Twenty
The lone raven could wait no longer, and soon, it too flew away.

∽

After the initial, furious argument between father and son, startling travelers and airport personnel alike, Dare shut up. He was gasping as though he had run too far and too fast, but he pressed his lips together when he saw Kristin look away.

She was embarrassed. He couldn't blame her.

"This is neither the time nor the place, Dad," he said as evenly as he could. "Let us take you to your hotel."

His father looked at him with a similar evenness. Why not? Dare thought bitterly. Like father, like son.

On occasion, he wondered if there would ever be a way to replace DNA. That way, he fantasized, he could replace the DNA in him that was the product of his father and truly proclaim they were no relation.

He really should have kept going to that psychiatrist. This was not healthy at all.

"I have two bags," John Borodin repeated. "I will retrieve them and then we can go."

"Then let's get your bags," Dare answered. "I'm sorry, Kristin."

Gratitude flooded through him when she smiled. Suddenly weak, he had to ignore the urge to sink to his knees and thank God she could still smile like that, when all he felt like doing was walking away.

"That's all right, Dare," she said, squeezing his hand.

He blinked, trying to ignore the burning in his eyes. His day still had rays of sunshine, and she was one.

She was the only one, come to think of it.

And she kept trying. "We've had nothing but rain here for the past few days, Mr. Borodin," she said as they went on their way. "I hope you've had better weather in Indiana."

Don't even bother to try, Kristin! Just ignore him and maybe he'll go away.

Of course, John Borodin ignored her and kept walking.

But that didn't stop her from trying again. "Mr. Borodin, my father's family's from Pascisci. How long has your family lived there?"

Oh, Kristin, don't do it. Please, just ignore him.

"Tell your—*friend*—I'm not interested in small talk."

Dare stopped in his tracks, blinded by rage. He couldn't speak for a moment. He glanced at Kristin, who stopped as well. Her cheeks were flushed, and her hands were clenched.

Damn. Damn. Damn. "Dad, stop it," Dare said, teeth clenched.

"Don't worry, I can deal with it," Kristin snapped. "Your father is obviously a man of strong convictions and few words."

"Oh, he can talk for hours when he wants to," Dare answered. He looked around. Fellow airport users were passing by, with only a shifting of a gaze or two to show the conversation was being carefully ignored. "Let's go."

The conversation—one-sided though it was—ceased as they proceeded to the baggage carousel. Dare shook his head, taking a deep breath from time to time. Then he grabbed Kristin's hand, tucking it under his arm. He met her gaze and he was glad to see she was smiling.

"Hush," he said as she opened her mouth. "I just want this moment to last right the way it is." He lifted her hand to his lips, both because he wanted to and also because he knew his father would notice. It was childish but he couldn't help it.

There was a good reason why he avoided going home.

She smiled and whispered, "Why don't you try some gossip about Pascisci? I'll wander away for a while."

Dare's heart felt as though it would burst. "Stay." He squeezed her hand and turned to his father, who must have seen it, for he had a grimace on his face. "So how are the Lundquists?" Dare managed to say, feeling a little better.

"Dagmar was home for a weekend last month. She stopped by as the family was going to church," John Borodin said. "She said something about finding a job in Oregon."

"Not far from here," Dare said pleasantly. "We'll have to visit. How about Ginnie Venderkash? Have you talked to her?"

It was working, he realized. The innocuous conversation seemed to be working. Kristin was keeping mum, even though the expression on her face clearly stated it was taking great strength of will to do so. He wanted to reach out to her and caress her cheek, thank her for her understanding.

After all, it wasn't as though she had anything riding on this. It was her future father-in-law who had something riding on it—his grandchild. A real family.

Suddenly, Dare craved it all, the idea of it. A real family, like one he never had, like one his grandmother would have liked to have had. Like the one Kristin had, with a kid brother and a mother and a grandmother. It didn't escape his notice her family lacked the one element that he had and categorically didn't want, a father.

A father, like he was going to be.

"There's one," John Borodin said, pointing to his luggage. "The brown one. And the second, right after it."

"Got 'em," Dare said, letting go of Kristin's hand to grab the two pieces off the carousel. His hand felt cold without her, but she tried to make up for it by rubbing his back.

He smiled at her. "Is that it?" he asked his father. A flood of gratitude swept through him. This wasn't going to be the easiest of visits—he didn't even know how long it would be—and he had to make sure he had her support.

He hoped he still had it by the time his father went home.

The two bags were all Dare's father had brought, so they headed for the car. Quietly, Dare let Kristin take the second suitcase, smaller, soft-sided, after a short, wordless discussion. He took the bigger one.

Christ. The man had insulted her and ignored her but she still carried his suitcase.

And she was carrying his grandchild.

Alarmed, Dare shot her a glance, but she didn't see it. She seemed to be all right, though, and the suitcase didn't look as if it were overwhelming her, no strain.

He spotted his car and started toward it, John Borodin following him at a distance, dependent on his cane. "My shift starts in a few hours, so why don't you drop me off," Kristin said to Dare in a low voice as they reached the car.

He glanced at her as he unlocked the trunk. "I'm sorry."

In response, he heard her laugh softly. "I figure I'm better off out of the way."

"I wish I could be," Dare muttered. He swung the larger bag into the cavern of his trunk, then nestled the smaller one next to it, slamming the hood shut.

"And I'll sit in the back."

He shot her a glance. "Sit in the front, please."

"No, I'll sit in the back. I'd prefer to be looking at the back of his head and not have him glaring at the back of mine."

Dare nodded. She had a point. In the same situation, he would have done the same.

He allowed her to climb in the back just as John Borodin was approaching the car.

"I'll take you to your hotel after I drop Kristin off, Dad," Dare said as he started the car.

"Good."

It was amazing how much and how little a simple word could imply. Dare edged the car out of the space and onto the exit ramp. With that simple word, his father managed to convey, "That's the way it should be, sending the woman away before we start discussing matters like real men."

Or he could have been imagining it all about the single-word response, but he didn't think so.

It was going to be a long visit.

Dare caught sight of Kristin's gaze in the rearview mirror as he slowed to pay parking fees. She smiled, letting him remember he had a wonderful life to look forward to.

Just as soon as his father was gone.

None of them said a word on the freeway. When Dare finally stopped in front of Kristin's apartment complex, she took the opportunity to lean forward, kiss him as close to his lips as she could considering she was in the backseat, said breezily she would talk to them soon—"them"— and then leapt out.

He had to applaud her for not running away.

He felt like running.

"Hotel next, Dad. Would you like dinner?"

"Yes."

Dare gritted his teeth. The nightmarish days after his grandmother died were coming back to him, and the relief he felt the day after he graduated from high school. He had spent the summer before college taking courses at the local college, anything to keep away from his father.

"So what would you like to eat?" Dare asked as they were on their way again, this time through congested city streets.

"I'm not here to try out the local cuisine."

Dare took a deep breath. "Then we'll have dinner at the hotel restaurant. Maybe some nice fusion cuisine," he said through gritted teeth. "What about the Museum of Flight?" he asked, knowing full well what the answer would be.

Some things were predictable. "I'm not here to sightsee."

Calm down, Dare told himself. *It's not going to do any good to try to strangle the old man while you're driving. You've got a child to support.*

A flood of bitterness rushed through him then. "Then what *are* you here for, Dad?"

"I'm here to stop you from making a mistake, *son.*"

"I'm not making a mistake, Dad," Dare said. He kept his hands on the steering wheel. He kept his gaze on traffic. He kept his temper.

"You are. You just don't realize it yet."

"I don't know if you've noticed, Dad, but you don't exactly have a sterling record of great decisions."

"That's how I recognize a bad one when I see it."

Red light. Step on the brake. Watch the traffic signal. Take note of the pedestrians. Beware of the bicyclists. Count to ten before answering. "We're not getting anywhere talking about this right now, so let's not," Dare suggested. "Let's just get you checked in, you can unpack, we can have dinner and then you can just relax for the evening."

And I can get away from you until tomorrow.

"How's the hip?" Dare asked, trying to be as polite as he could. "Still doing the physical therapy?"

"I fired her," his father answered. "How's the job? Still speaking different languages?"

Dare remembered how infuriated his father had been when he learned his son's job was something that required close and involved contact with "foreigners", as he put it. Not to mention the talent that came naturally, speaking all those languages. One should be good enough.

The truth was, Dare had kept the job all these years because he liked it and he was good at it. It had nothing to do with the fact it annoyed his father. Not even he could have kept a job for well over a decade just to spite the old man.

"Same job, new place every couple of years, maybe a new language to pick up one of these days," Dare added.

That was for spite. It was true. He'd been considering a new language, but with the upcoming change in his lifestyle, he'd put it on hold — but he really didn't have to mention it.

"English is still good enough for me," his father said.

"I know."

More silence.

The hotel was finally in front of them. It was in midtown. Dare booked it for a number of reasons. One, it was far enough from his own office that lunch wouldn't be convenient if the old man stayed on for longer than a few days, and two, the hotel was across from a Japanese restaurant and a Thai restaurant. He hoped the old man's room had a good view.

He had a lot of anger issues, he conceded.

Dare waited until his father checked in, then accompanied him to his room — old-fashioned, luxurious, comfortable — and waited until his father had unpacked.

They kept their conversation to a minimum. There wasn't anything they wanted to talk about. Not right then.

"If you're tired, do you want to just order room service?"

He was hoping, and this time, he got his wish. "I believe that is what I will do," John Borodin said. "I will speak to you tomorrow."

"I'm sure you will," Dare said.

The drizzle had become a full-blown squall by the time he got back to his apartment. Its dark mess was a depressing contrast to the duplex next door, where the windows were ablaze with light. He could hear music and laughter from within.

He grabbed a beer and sat on the patio looking out at the beach, despite the chill in the air. He could see the waves, lapping at the sand.

The water would be frigid.

The phone rang, breaking into his blue funk. "Hi," he heard after he answered it. "How did it go?"

He smiled. He sank into his chair and put his feet up. In the background he could hear the hustle and bustle of an evening in the ER. "Okay. How're things there?"

"Not crazy. Did you make sure your father got checked in? Did you feed him?"

"Yes, he's checked in and he said he was going with room service. So I said good night and came home."

"Did you talk much?"

Yes, we did, Kristin, he wanted to say. *We talked and he insisted I'm making a mistake. I told him he wouldn't know what a good decision looked like. I stopped myself from slugging him. Is that what you want to hear?*

What he wanted to say and what he would, of course, were two different things. "A little. We'll talk more tomorrow."

"Has he decided what he'd like to see here?"

Yes, Kristin, he'd like to see you and our baby as far away from me as possible. But he wasn't going to say that either. "I don't think he has. I was going to take him to the Museum of Flight. I figured he should like that."

"Good idea. Didn't you say he used to be an aeronautical engineer? My day off's tomorrow, why don't I go with you?"

Bad idea, Kristin. Bad, bad idea. Run. Better yet, work double, triple shifts the entire time he's here. Save yourself. "If you want to. If you want to come along, why don't you meet us there?"

There was a pause. "If you think that's best."

There was a note of hurt in her voice. *It's for your own good, Kristin. You don't want to be in the same car.* In the back of his mind, he knew he should be stating his opinions, not thinking them, but he didn't want to express his comments, not when they were so dark. They had no touch of light in them.

"Are you getting along any better?"

"I'm used to him," he answered carefully. *I don't want to have to tell you he's your worst nightmare. I don't want you to know what kind of horror you're marrying into.* "He's not easy to get along with."

"I noticed."

"So if you don't want to come tomorrow, that's fine."

She was quiet. Then, "What are you doing?"

"I'm not doing anything," he denied. *I'm just trying to keep you from getting infected by what's left of my family.* But he couldn't tell her that, either.

For the first time in months, he found himself unable to tell her what he meant. He was nauseated by the realization.

A longer silence this time, and then, "I figure I should try to get to know your father, so why don't I show up just for a while?" she suggested. He heard the wary tone in her voice, as if she were afraid of what he might say next.

If truth were told, so was he.

"That's fine," he said quickly, before she suggested something that would kill him, like lunch with the old man.

After an even more stilted exchange, he hung up and went back to staring at the Sound.

Dare kept forgetting to ask how long his father was going to be in town. But as he knocked on the hotel room door the next day, he realized it didn't matter. No matter how short, it would still be too long.

He could hear the old man in the room before the door opened. "Good morning," Dare said pleasantly as he stepped in. "Sleep well?"

John Borodin closed the door behind him. "Well enough. It's quieter than Chicago, at any rate."

His father used to travel to Chicago for business, Dare remembered. He wondered when he had retired—at least he assumed the old man had retired—then realized he didn't care. "So how long are you staying?" he asked, not caring the question came out of the blue.

"Until I can talk some sense into you," the old man said almost pleasantly. "Barring that, anytime after Saturday."

"My mind is made up," Dare shot back, wanting to be anywhere but there. "And I have a lot of sense. I could retire next year on what I've saved. See? You've taught me well." The sarcasm was a bit much, but he couldn't help it.

John Borodin snorted. "Either you're trying to get me off topic or you're sadly mistaken talking about your good sense. You know damned well I'm not talking money. Money is not the issue here. The issue is the rest of your life. I may not have been the best father, but by God, I'm going to make sure you don't ruin your life the way I ruined mine."

"We're getting married and we're having a family, Dad," Dare snapped as they got into the elevator. He could feel his blood pressure rising and his heart pounding. "The sooner you accept that, the better you'll be."

"It wasn't like when I was your age, boy," the old man said, leaning on his cane. "You've got choices. She can get rid of it. She can go back to her family. Put it up for adoption, for God's sake. I didn't have those choices. Nobody wanted to deal with half-Jap babies back then. Her family didn't want to deal with her."

"We don't want to get rid of it, Dad," Dare said, taking another deep breath. He leaned his forehead against the elevator wall. His head was pounding.

Frankly, he was surprised it took this long.

"We want to have the baby, have more, settle down, live happily ever after, and we'll do it with or without you." The elevator doors slid open, and they stepped out. "Have you had breakfast? Do you want any?"

"White should marry white, boy," the old man said, ignoring his son's question. "We should stick to our kind."

That comment, uttered a little too loud, elicited gasps from passersby. Dare felt his face turn red, wished he could call out, "He's just had a stroke! He's also claiming he's Napoleon!"

Actually, his father would be easier to deal with if that were true.

"Welcome to the shrinking world, Dad," Dare said, gritting his teeth. "The human race is intermarrying at a rate that's going to give you a stroke." Was that too hopeful? "And you forget, I'm not white. In your own twisted logic, I'm marrying my own kind. Or did that escape your notice?"

"You're my son, and that makes you white!"

"I'm also the son of my mother, and that makes me nonwhite, according to census standards. Actually, according to census standards, I can be whatever I want to be, and I think I'll just be an American, thank you very much. Now why don't we drop the subject. Where would you like to eat?"

Of course, the subject never was dropped. It took a break from time to time, but it was never retired. By the time Kristin showed up at the museum, Dare's head was pounding. He had forgotten she had planned to meet them there. Hell, he wished *he* could leave.

But he gave her an affectionate kiss, unusual for either of them in a public place—whether it was to trigger a response in his father or because he was so grateful to see her, he didn't know—but she seemed to like it.

God knew, she kept trying. "So did you sleep well, Mr. Borodin?" she asked.

What did one call one's future father-in-law, one who was openly hostile? Of course, in his own case, he called Kristin's mother "Mrs. Olafsson". But Marmar was "Marmar".

He had one hell of a headache.

John Borodin was using a wheelchair for the museum viewing, so he had to glance up. But that was all he did. "I slept fine, young lady. It would have been even better if my son listened to me."

Round one, Dare thought. *He comes out swinging.* But at least he had spoken to her, answered her question.

"Dare's an adult and he knows his own mind, Mr. Borodin," Kristin replied. "Perhaps you hadn't noticed."

She dances back from the opening challenge and exhibits some fancy footwork of her own.

"He doesn't *know* his own mind. He hasn't gone through what I have."

"And you haven't gone through the experiences he has," she answered, a little less sweetly. "Perhaps you should both listen to what the other has to say."

Dare's head swung. He stared at her. *But I know what he has to say,* he wanted to shout. *I heard it for the better part of eighteen years before I could get away from it.*

"I've been telling him for the better part of his life what I have to say," John Borodin said through clenched teeth.

Thanks, Dad. I'm glad you said it and not me.

"Why won't you understand he's made his decision?"

"That's because you made his decision for him!"

They weren't being loud, but Dare wished he could be far, far away. Pascisci would do...if his father weren't there.

Dare's headache wasn't getting any better.

"This is the kind of decision every person, man and woman, makes for him- or herself," Kristin pointed out. "Remember back. You made your decision. All you're saying now in essence is that you're unhappy about the decision you made."

"What I'm saying is he—and you—will be unhappy about the decision, I can guarantee it," John Borodin said intensely.

"Then that's our mistake to make, sir," Kristin snapped. Dare wanted to reach out, try to calm her down. Her cheeks were turning a bright red and her eyes were flashing.

If the topic weren't so distasteful, she would be attractive. Unfortunately, the topic made him want to vomit.

His father, meanwhile, had wheeled on to the next exhibit. Kristin was behind him, and Dare trailed the both of them.

"You know, I was at the Smithsonian last year for a conference," she commented, still trying to talk to John Borodin. Dare wanted more than anything to make all this up to her. "That was the first time I'd seen the Air and Space Museum. It was fascinating."

Don't do this, Kristin. Let's just dump him and go home and hold each other, Dare pleaded silently. That headache was mushrooming into a cloud that leached into his very bones.

John Borodin actually answered. "The *Enola Gay*'s there, I assume you saw it. It's there to be viewed by Americans and others alike."

Dare's head whipped around. The *Enola Gay* was the plane that had dropped the atomic bomb on Hiroshima, marking the beginning of the end of World War II. He stared at the back of his father's head in horror.

"Yes, sir, I did see it," Kristin answered evenly. But Dare knew her well enough to know she was getting to the point that she wanted to beat over his head. "I'm as American as anyone else born on US soil, Mr. Borodin, since I was born here. I don't see what your problem is, considering your own ancestors came to the United States the same way."

"How my ancestors came here is not the subject of your concern," John Borodin snapped back. "My concern is solely with my son's decision to marry outside his ethnic group."

Kristin smiled, and it wasn't a very nice smile anymore. In fact, it was the smile that Dare ran from when he saw it. "We are both of age, sir, and all you can do is to keep your comments to yourself."

That was it. They were going to be shouting at each other anytime now. Dare stepped between them. "That's enough," he said pleasantly, showing his own teeth, smiling a smile where the humor never got anywhere near his eyes. "This is neither the time nor the place. This is not good for the baby."

Kristin looked away, sighing. "I thought I could do this," she muttered. "I've got to run a few errands, sweetie," she told Dare, kissing him.

Dare appreciated the kiss, but did not appreciate the cool tone that accompanied it. He hoped it was aimed at his father and not him. "I'll talk to you later."

Don't leave me here with him, he wanted to shout. *Take me with you.*

She started to walk away, then turned around. "I forgot to tell you—" she paused. Dare did not like the expression in her eyes. "My mother and my grandmother want to have a little celebration. You'll meet my family," she added.

Dare shivered. That was a wind that blew no good.

"I'll call with details, Dare. I'll see you there, Mr. Borodin."

And then she was gone.

Once she left, Dare felt as if the energy had been sucked from him. Now he had to spend the rest of the day with his father, and converse the best he could without ending up in a shouting match.

Then it struck him. He could speak multiple languages, was contemplating learning another, but he had never been able to communicate with his father, in any language.

His father only spoke English. He wondered if that were significant somehow.

It didn't matter.

Chapter Twenty-One
The ravens were gone, every one.

೧೦

Kristin fumed as she turned onto her mother and grandmother's street. No matter the language, the conclusion was still the same. Having a celebration was fine. Having John Borodin there was not.

Having John Borodin anywhere in town was not.

"Oh, no," she groaned when she recognized the gray Volvo sitting in the driveway. Having Lars at a celebration dinner marking her engagement to Dare was not. Of all the people she didn't want to see...

Whose idea was it? she wondered in a fury as she got out of her car, grabbing the coleslaw she had brought. Her mother's, her grandmother's? She was assuming it wasn't Eric but it could have been. Maybe it had been all three.

Funny. She never thought any of them would take her relationship with Lars that seriously. But she never thought Lars would take their relationship breaking up the way he did.

Funny. She never thought she would find herself unmarried and pregnant, with a prospective father-in-law the likes of John Borodin.

Funny. She'd always been forthright about her ambitions and her intentions. She never thought she'd find herself so— ambiguous in her desires.

Funny.

But clearly, Dare wanted to get married. He wanted to have a family in a way he never had. She could understand that. In a very real way, he was pushing away his father's choices.

Now if only she could understand her own reluctance. She knew she also wanted to get married...or at least expected to. She wanted to relish the opportunity to have a child, the way she never thought she would. She wanted to revel in a family.

If she could do it without John Borodin, she'd be happy.

"I'm here," she called out as she came in through the kitchen and placed the wrapped bowl of coleslaw on a counter. "Anybody here? Mama? *Doko?* Marmar? *Var ar du?*"

She took off her jacket before she started in the direction of the sunroom, where she guessed the gathering would be. In preparation for the event, everything sparkled and gleamed. Through the windows, she could see the sheer whiteness of the laundry hanging and fluttering in the breeze. From previous experience, this time of year, she knew that by the time the wash was dry, it would also be stiff from the cold.

After all these years, not to mention top-of-the-line dryers, her mother still preferred to dry the laundry outside, under the sun. Kristin had always been confused by the preference—it wasn't as though her mother had anything against appliances—until she found out it was a longstanding tradition, so long that it was almost instinct, to appease the willful nature of the Japanese sun goddess, Amaterasu. It didn't matter if any one person believed anymore. It was just something one did.

Kristin smiled to herself, touching her stomach. Maybe someday she herself would, with a family of her own. Maybe it could happen.

A babble of voices floated out toward the sunroom. She recognized Eric's voice, laughing about something. She heard a deeper voice, chuckling. She heard her grandmother say something to her mother, and her mother tell something to Eric.

It sounded like a family, except it wasn't, not quite.

"Hey," Kristin said, stopping at the doorway. "Hi, Lars. I didn't know you were going to be here."

Clearly masquerading as one of the party-givers, Lars was wearing an apron as he stood in front of the well-used Weber grill, fiddling with the controls. Eric had been handing him the barbecue utensils, and stopped in the middle of threatening to toss a towel at his mother. The sliding glass doors stood wide open, letting the crisp, cool autumn air into the sunroom.

Her mother and grandmother were sorting the wicker and paper plates and the host of beverages. And judging by their strained looks, despite the laughter Kristin had heard, she guessed inviting Lars hadn't been their idea.

"Did I see the heavy silver out? Don't tell me we're using those for a barbecue." Her eyes swept over to the men, one of whom continued to fiddle with the barbecue—the one she wasn't related to—while the other, younger one—the one to whom she was—nervously played with the utensils and condiments. Neither, she noted, looked at her at first.

But finally Eric did. He wiggled his eyebrows and glanced at Lars. He, too, had a surprised look on his face.

So that left— "I haven't seen you in a while, Lars," she said as she perched on a stool.

He still wasn't looking at her. "I hear the ER's been busy," Lars said as he twisted a dial. Then he looked at her.

His eyes were cold when he wasn't smiling. She'd never noticed that before. But then she had never really looked. *Oh, Lars, please don't do this.* "Yeah, it has," she replied aloud. "The traffic's been horrible on drivers."

"I can imagine. I just dropped by to return a measuring cup, and I got invited," he explained. "You don't mind?"

Mind? Of course I mind, but you know that. "Of course not," she said, her tone dry. "You'll get to meet Dare's father. He can tell you more about Pascisci."

"I can't wait. Congratulations, by the way," he added.

Kristin shrugged, lips thin. She had discouraged him for years because of her presumed infertility, although he had never paid attention. But the few times they had slept together, she had made sure she had protection. This was as awkward as it could have gotten. "Summer due date," she said briefly.

The others retreated. Not that she blamed them. She wished she could too. But it would be rude to ask Lars to leave, as dearly as she would love to.

She turned to her mother. "Mama, can I do anything?" she asked, pointedly in English. She wasn't going to let Lars annoy her. She even tried to rationalize he had been almost a member of the family for so long he might as well get treated like one, even if it was for the last time.

Her mother flashed a rare smile. "*Lemoneido tsukutte*," Moyo said promptly, with a knowing glint in her eye.

Kristin hid a smile of her own. Making lemonade was a time-consuming job since she made it with fresh lemons, and it would take her into the kitchen, far away from Lars. All of a sudden, despite her exhaustion, she was filled with gratitude. If she hadn't been so tired, she would have reacted more sharply to Lars' presence.

"Sure," she said. "Any particular pitcher?"

Her mother shook her head. "*Iie. Domo.*"

"You're welcome," Kristin said as she made her way to the kitchen.

She got out the lemons and the juicer, but she didn't start right away. Instead, she leaned against the counter for a while, eyes closed, wishing she had enough energy to bring over a stool. But she was too tired for that.

So tired. She was exhausted—Lars was right. The ER had been busy lately—but she was not going to let either Lars or John Borodin annoy her.

After the confrontation with Dare's father, Kristin had decided to go into work early, and she did again the following day. Not only that, she had stayed past her shift to help out.

And she didn't want to talk to Dare just then. The argument with John Borodin had upset her more than she would admit. She had never encountered such blind hatred in her life, and it infuriated her as much as it sickened her.

How had anyone grown up with that man? How could she fall in love with someone *related* to that man?

Sighing, Kristin opened her eyes and dragged a stool over to her work area to perch on as she cut up the lemons. A good night's sleep ought to do the trick.

Making lemonade was a boring but soothing occupation, allowing her to decompress. She had left a message on Dare's machine, telling him what time to be at the house, but otherwise she had had no contact with him. She missed him, but she also knew she needed the space. She hadn't had much time to herself in a while and she desperately needed it.

What was the problem? Intellectually she knew her pregnancy was something to be happy about...but it felt as though it had been foisted on her—no, that wasn't it. She felt tricked. If she had yearned for a baby, if she had never been told she was infertile, that would be one thing. She would have been dancing a jig.

But now...now she felt as though she had been duped into a situation she hadn't planned and worse, didn't *understand*.

The sound of a car coming into the driveway startled her. That had to be them. She measured sugar into the pitcher and stirred, waiting for Dare to come to the door. She was too tired to do anything else.

She was filling the pitcher with water and ice when the expected knock came at the back door. She looked over her shoulder and saw two silhouettes through the smoked glass. "It's not locked," she called out.

"Hi." She smiled as they walked in. "Have a good day?"

Still in dress shirt and slacks from his half-day of work, Dare looked tense, but brightened when he saw her. She lifted her face for a kiss. She might have been reticent before, but not anymore, certainly not in front of John Borodin. She felt the brush of Dare's lips, the itch of his five-o'clock shadow. It felt good, so long as she didn't turn to look at the old man glaring at them. To hell with him.

"Not bad," Dare said, smiling back. His eyes looked tired too, their sparkling hazel obscured at the moment. She saw fine lines in his face she had never seen before. "We went on the Underground Tour. I figured at least I'd never been, so — "

So at least one of us would try to have a good time. She guessed the rest of the statement. "Did you like it, Mr. Borodin?" she asked, not without a touch of malice. He wouldn't have liked it.

She was right. "The entire city should have been ripped down and started over. Sightseeing is not why I came here," John Borodin insisted.

Kristin sighed. He was as stubborn as an infant and far less cute. He refused to listen to anything other than his own words, no matter his words were ignored by everyone else.

She suppressed a shiver of distaste. "Mr. Borodin, why don't you relax. Maybe talking to my family will make you feel a little better about something you can't stop."

"Why would talking to *your* family make me feel better?"

Because otherwise I'm going to deck you, that's why, she thought before she bared her teeth at him. "Maybe Prozac in your food might help. Or rat poison. But I could get hold of the Prozac a lot easier."

That finally got through to him. He reared his head back, surprised at the rejoinder, as though it never occurred to him that someone might stop humoring him.

"That's funny, Kristin." Dare stepped in.

"Yes, it is," she answered sweetly. "But I wouldn't do that. Rat poison is traceable and I wouldn't slip Prozac into your food unless I knew something about your medical history. Here, Dare," she said, picking up the pitcher, "why don't you take the lemonade out to the sunroom and take your father?"

Dare reached out and took the pitcher from her, still watching the standoff. "Sure. Dad? This way."

Go with him or I'll bash you over the head with a pan. But she watched them go without making another comment.

After they were gone, Kristin sat again, refusing to fight the tears that blinded her. She wiped her eyes.

She was tired and she wanted to go home to her own apartment and most of all, she wanted John Borodin to go home. She had too much to do to let this bother her. And suddenly she resented Dare, resented him for his placating his father, with a white-hot, vicious resentment that constricted her breathing for a moment.

But there wasn't anything she could do. She had to endure the evening, smile a little, eat well and live well — the perfect revenge. So she made her way back to the sunroom.

The scene when she arrived could have been a melodrama. There was the villain of the piece, his lips curled, as the young innocent — perhaps Eric wouldn't appreciate that description, but that's what he was — stood frozen with surprise, his hand extended in greeting. That John Borodin had out-and-out rejected the proffered handshake Kristin had no doubt. *Son of a bitch.* Doing that to her good-natured baby brother. Her mother stood nearby, her eyes as furious as Kristin had ever seen, as if she herself would be willing to bash the man over the head, rules of hospitality bedamned.

Added to the scene were her grandmother, a shocked expression on her face, hand raised to her mouth, and in the corner, Lars, watching the tableau, a look of surprise on his face as well — but there was something else. Something she didn't recognize, and didn't like.

Last but not least, there was Dare, caught between Eric and his father, a look of desperation on his face. As if he would, if given a chance, run.

She wouldn't blame him if he did.

Kristin entered calmly, pretending the scene in front of her was nothing out of the ordinary, and the fathers of her lovers always rejected her little brother.

Play it cool. She walked over to the buffet table and found room for her coleslaw before she turned around.

The scene wasn't static anymore, but it was just as bad. The look in Dare's eyes hadn't changed, but the look in Eric's had, from surprise to pain.

I'm so sorry you have to be subjected to this, kiddo. "John — I can call you John, can't I? — this is my younger brother, Eric. Eric, this is Dare's father, John Borodin."

By the looks on the faces of her brother and John Borodin, the exchange had already begun — and been stopped short. The bile rose in Kristin's throat. She smiled again, less nicely. "Shake his hand, John. He won't bite. He's trained."

John Borodin wasn't having any. "I don't have to deal with this," he said, his face suffused with anger. His hand remained where it had been, raised and away from Eric.

"Do it or I'm going to kiss you," Kristin said sweetly.

"You will not."

"Try me, old man."

"You must be Dare's father," Lars said as he stepped forward, whipping off his apron and offering his hand. He smiled that smile, the one Kristin knew from long experience was calculated to calm. It was a politician's smile. He had missed his calling. "I'm Lars Bergen, Kristin's old — friend. And a friend of the family," he added, after the deliberate pause. "I'm glad to meet you."

The look on John Borodin's face reflected confusion. But he shook Lars' hand. "Hello."

"Let me introduce you to Kristin's family," Lars went on. "You've met her younger brother, Eric," he said, nodding in the younger man's direction.

By this time, Eric was staring at John Borodin and Lars as though they were a newly discovered species. "And this is Kristin's mother, Mrs. Olafsson the junior," Lars continued, his voice almost mesmerizing. Kristin was surprised when her mother started to bow, then stopped. "And this is Mrs. Olafsson the senior. From Pascisci," he added. "And I'm sure you have people in common."

John Borodin ate it up. Kristin watched, amazed, as the unpleasant old man came alive, patting Lars on the back and greeting Solveig as though they were old, dear friends.

For her part, Kristin's grandmother was taken aback at the man's abrupt effusiveness. She nodded a few times at his questions, and mostly listened. But her eyes were wary.

Watching became too much for Kristin. She edged toward Eric, who had stepped back, toward the door.

"Why did you bring him here?" he asked Kristin angrily, not bothering to lower his voice. "He's the rudest s—"

"It wasn't my choice, believe me," she interrupted.

"I'm sorry," Dare said. Kristin looked up. He had come over and she hadn't noticed. "I can't tell you how sorry I am."

"Then get him out of here," Eric snarled. "He's insulted Kris, he's insulted my mother, he's—"

"He's insulted everyone," Kristin said.

"I mean, what's his problem? Dad—"

Kristin raised her hand to quiet him. She understood what was bothering him now. "Dad was one end of the spectrum. Dare's father is the other end."

"But what's his pr—" Eric stopped. He stared at her for a second. "He doesn't even know us," he said, bewildered.

But John Borodin thought he did, Kristin wanted to tell him. He could not get past his own experiences, his own memories and because of it, he could not see anything at all. Whereas Eric Olafsson Sr. had arrived in war-torn Japan after the end of World War II eager for new experiences, John

Borodin had not—and though their experiences in some way may have been similar, their reactions had been very different.

"You've lived a sheltered life, kid," Dare said, echoing Kristin's thoughts. "There are a lot of people like him. Not necessarily in Pascisci, but it's a big world filled with people who can't see past their own backyard."

"I'm sorry, Mr. Borodin, but I think they're old enough to make up their own minds." Solveig's soft voice cut into their conversation. "And I like your son. I think he and my granddaughter will be quite happy."

"You're wrong. They should stick to their own kind," John Borodin insisted.

"Dad, I *am* sticking to my own kind," Dare cut in sharply. "No matter how much you wish otherwise, my mother was Japanese. I'm half-Japanese. Kristin's half-Japanese. She *is* my kind."

"What's wrong with you?" Eric finally burst out. "You're a sad, pathetic old guy, and just because you aren't happy, you want to make sure no one else is. Why don't you go home!"

"Eric!" three female voices cried out. Then two of them shut up when Moyo's voice, quiet and edged in steel, continued. "Eric, get fruit salad from kitchen. *Ima.*"

His face scarlet, Eric quickly left.

The sunroom fell silent. Kristin could see the dust motes dance in the diminishing sunlight of the afternoon.

"Dad, I wish you would reconsider," Dare said, breaking the silence. "I'm not going to change my mind. Insulting your hostesses for this evening isn't going to change anything. And you're embarrassing both of us."

"Then think about why you brought me here. Why did you?"

Dare hesitated. "I was hoping you would be civil for the evening. That was too much to ask, I guess."

"See here," John Borodin said, turning to Kristin.

She stared at him for a second. "Me?" she asked, making sure. "You're talking to *me* all of a sudden?"

"Yes, you," he said impatiently, just as Eric came back in with a large crystal bowl filled with fruit salad. Kristin glanced at him. His cheeks were still red, but he looked calmer, despite the glare he shot toward Dare's father.

"What?" she asked, avoiding her mother's gaze. On top of everything else, she did not want to feel as though she were being scolded for this situation.

"I'll give you money if you break it off with my son," John Borodin said, his eyes glittering. "What would it take?"

Too much. Her mouth dropped open and she stared at him, not hearing the gasps, not hearing even Dare's *"Dad!"* Dimly, she knew Lars stepped forward and restrained Eric. Dimly, she knew it when both her mother and grandmother staggered for a second.

"I mean it," John Borodin insisted, his face pale, the veins in his forehead bulging. "I want to spare my son the hell I went through. I should have married my own kind. I didn't and see where it got me."

Finally, Kristin formed a coherent sentence. "You're a very sad man." She shook her head.

John Borodin snorted. "From the first I knew I shouldn't have done it," he went on, oblivious. "We didn't have anything in common. We were lands apart in everything that mattered," he said, the accidental pun not registering. "But I couldn't get away from her. And if I had just waited until I got back to the States, I would never have had this problem."

Problem? What was the problem, his son marrying her or was Dare the problem to start with?

For the life of her she couldn't work the hard knot in the pit of her stomach loose. "I'm sorry you had a bad marriage. But that doesn't have anything to do with Dare and me. Just because you were unhappy doesn't mean we'll be."

"There's nothing to say he'll be happy, either."

Kristin bit her lip, then went on, trying to keep her tone gentle. "Mr. Borodin—John—you might have had the same problem if you had married a girl from Indiana. Sometimes there's no way around it. Sometimes you make a mistake."

"I will sign over your entire inheritance to you now if you give her up," John Borodin said, turning to his son.

Kristin opened her mouth, to try to reason with him. But she couldn't do it. She caught Dare's gaze. She was surprised by the pinched, miserable look.

Defeated. That was it. He looked defeated. A frisson of fear leapt up her spine. She had never seen him look that way.

"How about it?" John Borodin persisted. Kristin turned to look at him. The old man's face was pinched and pale too, but the glint in his eyes scared her.

He twisted his mouth. "You've got to make up your mind right now, boy. Right now."

Dare stared at his father for a minute—two minutes—three minutes. Finally, he spoke, but it wasn't to his father.

"I'm sorry, Kristin. About everything."

She stared at him. "I'm sorry about your father, too. But what else would you have to be sorry about?"

Dare reached out and stroked her hair. "Dad and I can't stay here right now. It's not good for you, it's not good for the baby. We're going to leave."

She didn't know what to say. *No, please stay? Please leave? Please push your father into the Sound and make sure he stays there?* She pressed her hand against her forehead, trying to stave off the headache that was coming. She had to be coming down with the flu. She felt lousy. That had to be it.

She wanted to be away from there, from them. She wanted to be back at work. At least she could do something constructive, not be pummeled from all sides.

Kristin looked out the open door, at the gardens beyond. The afternoon had abruptly faded. The rain had begun to fall, hitting the glass in streaks. Autumn in Seattle.

Great. On top of everything else, she was going to drive home in lousy weather. And she loved driving as it was.

Enough. That was it. She didn't feel well and now this nasty old man had thrown the rest of her day in the trash. "Go," she said. She wasn't going to let her voice crack. She had some pride left. "Go, and take him with you."

She stared at Dare. He looked back, and the look on his face seemed blank of emotion. She didn't know what that meant, and at that moment, she didn't care. She just wanted John Borodin out of there.

"All right." He turned away. "I'll talk to you later."

She sat down on the wicker sofa, put her feet up on the wicker table and closed her eyes.

There wasn't a word spoken in the sunroom. Then, when she heard the door open and close and Dare's car start up, she stood up again. "I'm going out to the garden. Okay?"

Her mother and her grandmother were fitting plastic lids and stretching Saran Wrap over the food, while Eric was tearing sheets of aluminum foil into strips and Lars was shutting off the grill. The celebration was over.

"That's fine, dear," her grandmother said. Her mother said nothing, simply looked at her with sharp eyes.

"*Tiyado?*" Moyo inquired. Japanglish—yes, she was tired.

Kristin nodded. "I'm exhausted, Mom. I just want some peace and quiet."

"Call if you want something, Kristin," Lars said as he turned off the grill and closed it up.

"Sure, Lars," she said, surprised. "Thanks."

She grabbed her jacket and slipped out the back door.

Once she was outside, the solitude of the early evening comforted her. She looked up. Although the skies were weeping a little, she knew the stars were up there, waiting to show themselves. In the distance, she imagined she could even hear a raven caw, but she knew that the ravens had not been in evidence for some weeks now.

Kristin made her way to the walled Japanese garden her father had built for her mother, so many years ago. She slipped inside the gate and sat down on the bench in front of the pond.

The only sounds she could hear were an occasional bubble bursting on the water's surface, with the bamboo rustling in the damp breeze. After a few minutes, she began to cry.

She wanted to curse at John Borodin and Dare both, but she couldn't. She could have cursed at one, but not both. John Borodin she could curse at, but she also had to feel sorry for the man. He had led a miserable life, one of his own making, refusing to recognize the path that had led him to where he was today, alone and cut off.

Dare Borodin she could curse at for less obvious reasons. He didn't have to bring his father. He didn't have to deal with his father.

He didn't have to deal with her, either.

Kristin took a deep breath, willing the tears to stop. She didn't know if she wanted to deal with him at all at this stage. Then the idea made her cry a little more, until she was sobbing, the sound reverberating through the gardens.

Her sobs drowned out the squeak of the garden gate, so it was not until her grandmother placed a hand on her shoulder that she realized Solveig was there.

"Sweetheart—" Solveig said gently.

Kristin's sobbing abruptly ceased, and she nearly had hiccups trying to stop it. She crossed her arms across her stomach, and she rocked a little. "Marmar."

"*Mitt lite flicka*, don't cry," Solveig said, smoothing her hair. "You're just tired. Maybe you should take a nap."

"I just want it all to go away, Marmar," Kristin cried. "I just want it all to not be a problem any more."

"Whatever you do is going to have a problem, sweetheart," Solveig soothed. "You know that's the way things are."

Her grandmother's gentle lilt fluttered through her. "Mom didn't come out with you, did she?" Kristin asked. She wasn't ready to have a conversation with her mother.

"No, she didn't," Solveig said. "She's not very happy right now. But she wanted to make sure you were all right."

"Considering you don't really speak the same language, Marmar, it's amazing how much you understand each other."

"We're both mothers, that's why," Solveig said, smiling. "We know what it feels like to have our children hurt."

At the mention of mothers, Kristin started to tear again. She was horrified. She hadn't cried this much since her father died. "I'm sorry," she sobbed. "I can't seem to stop."

Solveig gave her shoulder a squeeze. "It's the baby, dear. It does that to you."

"The hormones. I know. But knowing doesn't help any."

"Be patient, *flicka*. It'll be better soon. I promise."

"I know, Marmar. It just doesn't feel like it right now."

"*Ja*. Ready to go in now?" Solveig coaxed. "My old bones are chilly."

Kristin looked up. The mist had dissipated and the clouds had parted. She could see the faint sparkles of the stars.

"Yes, Marmar," she said, reaching out and holding her grandmother's hand as she stood up.

They walked along the path. By the time they arrived at the back door again, Kristin had calmed down a little.

Lars was on the phone when they came in the kitchen. She heard, "I'll tell her you said that." After a minute, he said, "I'm sorry. I know the family was hoping it would work out."

What?

Her stomach was churning, and she didn't like it one bit. "Who is that?" she asked. Lars frowned and shook his head.

Eric, who was stacking Tupperware in the refrigerator, answered. "It's Dare," he burst out, his eyes wide.

Her heart leaped. "You should have called me," she answered. Just then Lars hung up, his expression blank. He picked up a platter and started to rinse it.

She stopped taking off her jacket. "Why didn't you come out and get me? What did he say?"

"I talked to him. He said not to bother you," Lars said, his face still blank, "and that he was sorry."

"He already said that. But why would he be talking to you?" Her stomach was threatening a revolt. She didn't know if she was starving or threatening to lose it.

"He said he was at the airport, and he'd be talking to you."

She let the jacket fall off her shoulders. "That's it? That's all he said?"

Lars shrugged. "I said you weren't feeling well and you needed some rest. And—" he stopped.

Her heart seemed to pause. "What?"

"I got on the phone because Eric—well—" Lars paused, glancing at the boy. "Eric was getting a little upset."

Kristin knew what that meant. Eric was still at the age where everything was in black and white. Lars had probably stepped in and taken the phone. "What did he say?"

"He said he was with his father at the airport. He said he had to go with him and he'd see you. That's what he said," Lars added. "It just sounded—unfortunate. I'm very sorry."

Kristin stood there, trying to think. No. It couldn't be. "I'm sure it just came out wrong." Her mouth trembled. "I'm sure it did. What else did he say?"

Lars looked at her. His eyes were wide and they stared into hers, still devoid of emotion. "I told you. He said he was at the airport, with his father, and he said goodbye. Kristin...Indiana *is* his home."

This couldn't be happening. "What, are you trying to say he's dumping me?" she exclaimed. She felt woozy, as though she were going to faint. *Not now*, she told herself. *Later*. She grabbed the edge of the counter to keep her balance. "You're wrong. You're just saying that."

"Why would he do that?" Eric asked in horror.

"That's what his father wanted to do to his mother," she answered, her stomach churning. "But he couldn't."

"Why would he want to do *that*? Kris, his dad's—"

"At least they'd have something in common," Lars murmured, almost under his breath.

Her heart twisted. "But he wouldn't do that to me. He wouldn't."

She couldn't breathe. She wanted to cry again but she couldn't do that either.

"Maybe I misunderstood. Call the airline, find out if there's a reservation in their names," Lars suggested.

"They're not going to give out that information," Kristin said, thinking frantically of the alternatives. "But I can find out if there's a flight out to the county airport."

So she did. She looked up the number and called, and she was calm and efficient. She was calm as she hung up. And then she wasn't anymore.

She started to cry as her stomach started to roil all over again. "He wouldn't do this to me. He couldn't."

He wouldn't take his father up on his offer. He wouldn't.

Or maybe he would. Blood would tell, wouldn't it? Like father, like son. Except this time, the pregnant woman had a family to fall back on. "He could. He did," she whispered to herself. "Oh, God, he left me."

Chapter Twenty-Two

Kristin covered her eyes with the palms of her hands. "He's gone back to Indiana."

"Oh, you don't believe that," Lars said. He patted her hand. "I'm sure you're mistaken."

"Why would I be? His father tried to dump his family. Why would his son be any different?"

"Because they're different people," Lars said. "That should be clear. I think you've emphasized that point."

"Why would he do that?" Eric asked in distress.

"What else am I supposed to believe?"

"You can't really believe that crap!"

She shook her head. "We haven't been talking since—that man—came into town."

"Why don't we go to the airport?" Eric asked, brightening. "He just called. He can't be leaving yet, right?"

Kristin glanced at Lars, whose face was still oddly frozen. "No," he said, then added, "this is a terrible time of night to be on the freeway. You'd never get there in time."

Even in her pain, Kristin knew the look on Lars' face troubled her, but she didn't have the time to think about it. "This doesn't make any sense. I don't understand what he's doing. I'm not going to sit around and wait for something to happen. I have to go to the airport. I don't know if I can drive right now, Eric. Will you drive me?"

Her brother's face lit up. "Sure."

"Are you sure you don't want to think about this?" Lars persisted.

"No. I want to settle this." Her stomach felt like hell, but she had to do this. "Can you tell Mom and Marmar where we went?"

"I'll tell them," he said. He stared at her. "Don't go, Krissy. The weather's hideous, and neither one of you likes to drive when it gets like this."

"I have to. Ready, Eric?" She wrapped her arms around her stomach and willed it to calm down. It didn't work.

This just didn't make any sense. What was he *thinking*?

Eric had the car started and moving so fast Kristin barely had time to buckle her seat belt. They were already headed toward the freeway on-ramp when Eric snapped his fingers. "We're going to be driving into the sunset. Do you have a pair of sunglasses in here, Kris?"

Her eyes closed—she was so tired—she said, "I don't think so." She rested her head against the window.

"Damn," he muttered. "I'm going to have to squint."

The setting sun was glaringly bright as they merged into traffic. Kristin was only vaguely aware of the cars zipping past them, despite the slickness of the road.

The car skidded a little as Eric sped up. Her eyes snapped open. "If you can't keep up, stay to the right!" Kristin said with a gasp. She reached out and grabbed the dashboard.

"I'm trying to get to the right, but no one's letting me," he said tensely, glancing in the rearview mirror.

The pit of her stomach was twisting. Trying not to think at all, she looked out the window, trying not to focus on the high-speed ins and outs in front of her as drivers in a hurry weaved through the traffic, veering from side to side.

How dare he.

He made me want this. I was perfectly happy with my life until he came along. Damn him, damn him!

Don't think about it. The sun had almost set. All she could see was the brilliant sliver of light poised over the Olympics.

She shivered. Maybe it was the weather. She reached over and switched on the warm air.

"Kris, please turn that off," Eric said, strained. "The air's hitting my eyes and I can't afford to have my eyes tear."

"I'm sorry," she said, her voice faint. "I forgot." She switched it off and huddled in the corner.

"We should be okay as soon as we hit I-5," he answered, his teeth clenched. "The road's a little slick here."

Kristin looked out the front. To the left of them, a BMW skidded a little before regaining control, and beyond it, an older sedan did the same before slowing down. "Just keep away from the idiots with the cell phones attached to their ears."

"I know. And not only that, the sun's going to be full in my eyes in the next few seconds."

Kristin looked up. At that moment, the sun seemed to burst in its brilliance before it finally set behind the mountains.

And it was blinding, glaring vermilion in its intensity. Kristin winced as the sun hit her eyes, and then realized what it had to be doing to her brother, whose eyes were more sensitive than hers. "Eric, can you see?"

The answer was a second in coming. "Yeah," he said, strained. "What I can't believe are these idiots who aren't slowing down with the sun right in their eyes."

It was true. Despite the congestion and the ice, despite the glaring sunset, the speed of the traffic didn't slow at all—or get any safer. "Just keep an eye on that nutcase who keeps weaving," she said, her teeth clenched.

"I am. Jesus!" Eric shouted as the BMW that had been marking pace in the next lane decided to move over, not bothering to signal. Eric swerved, then tapped the brakes. He breathed a sigh of relief.

"Idiot," she muttered—at the BMW, not her brother. Her heart was pounding like a trip-hammer. "Not a semi," she groaned as she realized what had replaced the BMW on their left. Eric, not an experienced driver, hated semis.

"I see it. I'm keeping an eye on it."

"You'd better," she warned as she gripped the armrest. "He's going too fast—"

"Fuck!" Eric yelled as the semi, without signaling and clearly not looking, began to move over into their lane. "Damn it!" He hit the horn, but its urgency was swallowed by the traffic and the screeching of the tires on the wet pavement.

The car began to hydroplane. "Eric, look out!" Kristin screamed. She grabbed hold of the dashboard as he began to pump the brakes and tried to steer into the skid. She couldn't even close her eyes.

The white steel barriers that divided the freeway came closer as the car slid sideways.

No! No...

They were going to slam into the barrier.

That wasn't the only thing she realized. Even as the barrier came closer, she doubled over as a spasm hit her body. Even as the screech of the car's tires deafened her and the impact of the crash knocked her out, she knew without a doubt she was miscarrying.

Then the car behind them hit them, jerking her and Eric forward. Her forehead hit the dashboard, she heard the sound of breaking glass, a vicious pain slashed through her and then, nothing.

* * * * *

There wasn't anything else to say.

By the time Dare got back to his apartment from the airport, the sun had been swallowed by the shadow of the mountains. By the time twilight fell, his father would be on his way home, only one of the two tickets he had purchased put to use.

And he felt bad about that.

True, they didn't get along. True, they avoided speaking to each other. But Dare had always assumed they would speak again. For no other purpose than to assure and be assured no funeral arrangements were necessary at the current time.

But not anymore.

Dare didn't bother turning on the lights. The brilliant colors of the sunset flooded the apartment. For some reason, the elongated, twisting shadows that was the setting sun's last gasp made him uneasy.

He sank into his club chair and closed his eyes, feeling both the heat of the setting sun through glass and the chill of the autumn evening.

He still couldn't get over it.

There was no way he and his father were getting past this.

Dare knew, had always known, his father had tried to forget the part of his son's genes that didn't come from Pascisci stock. But he never knew it went so far. If he had to choose between his father and his child, he was going to make the only choice he could make.

"I mean it," his father's voice rasped, ripping through his memory. "Everything I have, I will turn over to you if you give her up. I have a ticket for you to come back with me, if you give up this idiocy."

Dare had rolled his eyes. "You refused to hire that caregiver you were supposed to," he retorted. "Was this why? You bought me a ticket to go back to Pascisci with you, because you need someone to help you? What were you thinking?"

His father's nostrils flared. "I assumed you would be reasonable about this."

"I *am* being reasonable. What am I, five? I didn't want to go with you when I was seven, but I had no choice then. Now we're definitely going to have to get to the airport in time to get you on that flight, and I can arrange for someone to meet you at the other end. That wasn't smart, Dad."

Dare shook his head. That also meant he'd better call Kristin and tell her he wouldn't be seeing her tonight, depending on how long it took—the books he had been reading emphasized the importance of sleep and rest.

"Haven't you been listening to me, boy?"

"You haven't said anything intelligible. You keep saying the same thing over and over."

"Do you want your children to be little slant-eyes, boy? Do you want them to be beat up by the other kids? Give her up."

Dare stared at him for a second. "Dad, no one ever called me that. Not even Sven ever called me that."

"Of course not! They all thought you were white!"

"But I'm not," he said, exasperated. "Any kid I have, with Kristin or not, would be part Asian. Dad, we're going around in circles," he said finally. "And you're living in a past that, frankly, sounds pretty scary." He knew it still happened now, but from the sounds of it, his father might as well have put on a white hood, the way Kristin suggested once.

"This is for your own sake!"

"No, you're doing this for *your* sake. Isn't that it? You managed to wipe out for the most part any clue you had a son who wasn't, in your own words, 'All-American', but you couldn't keep kidding yourself about it if we showed up one day with a kid in tow who looked more Asian than not?"

The conversation—or argument—continued as they drove to the airport, as they headed toward the ticket counter. "Fine," the old man finally spat as Dare set down his bags at the end of the long line. "Make the same mistake I did."

"You know, Dad," and here Dare's voice dropped, "I'll bet you wish more than anything right now I had turned out to be gay. At least that way you could have kidded yourself. Isn't that true?"

John Borodin stood, mute, staring at him.

It took a while, but the line moved, the ticket refunded, and John Borodin's own flight confirmed.

And there was nothing else to say. Dare accompanied his father as far as he could go, with arrangements for John in a wheelchair—had he had a chance to tell Kristin his father was going home early?

Then his father's turn came. "Goodbye, Dad," he said. "I'm sorry it had to end like this."

His father glared at him. Dare realized the elder Borodin had aged badly. The years of solitude were written on his face, and the bitterness of those years had twisted him. "I didn't have to bring you back, you know. I could have just left you in the streets, no matter what your grandmother said—a lot of babies ended up that way. I could have told her you died, I couldn't get you out of the country—anything."

Dare felt something faint stir in him. Compassion? "I know." He managed a smile. "Thank you."

And that was that.

By the time he walked into his apartment, he was tired and depressed. When the phone rang, he nearly fell out of the chair. Only when the phone shrilled for the second time did he realize he had dozed off. He glanced at the clock. He had been asleep for two hours and some.

He picked up the phone and mumbled, "Yeah."

"I hope you're satisfied," the caller said viciously.

"What?" Dare said, foggy-brained. The voice was familiar, but he couldn't figure out why. "Who is this?"

"If it weren't for you, none of this would have happened."

The voice was familiar. So was the background. Coming awake, Dare tried to place it. The soft bells, the announcements—his eyes opened. "Lars?"

"She's in surgery. Thanks to you."

He knew who Lars was referring to, but— "What is she doing in surgery? She's not a surgeon. Why—"

Then he knew. The cobwebs vanished, replaced by a surge of adrenaline and a vibrato of dread. He couldn't breathe. He couldn't swallow. He could barely echo, "*Surgery*? But—"

"She was chasing after you and she got slammed by a semi."

Dare's stomach roiled. "*Jesus*. When? B—" His heart twisted. "Which hospital?"

"Don't bother," Lars snarled. "The last thing the Olafssons need is you. Go away. We were fine until you came in."

"Tell me where she is, damn you!"

"She's at Pacific, if that makes a difference," Lars shot back. "Keep away from her."

"Go to hell," Dare snarled. He threw down the phone and ran for the door.

God no, he kept praying to a deity he rarely called upon. *No, please. Not Kristin.*

Please no, he kept chanting as he darted in and out of traffic, not hearing the blares of the car horns around him. *It can't be.* Horrifying images flooded his mind as he had last seen Kristin, trying her best not to cry, as he hurriedly ushered his father out.

I did that to you, he thought, at one point forced to stop for a light, pounding the steering wheel in frustration. *Now you're paying for it.*

At the hospital, he veered into a parking space—two—because he couldn't take the time to straighten the car. The front desk took its time in processing the information he gave them. He stood, his hands twitching at his sides—until the receptionist gave him directions.

He didn't even bother to mumble his thanks. He ran for the elevators. By the time he found himself on the right floor in the right wing, he had to stop for a moment and squeeze his eyes shut for a second. He couldn't stop the hot tears from forming behind his eyelids. Long-held control he had spent most of his life enforcing was slipping away, but he couldn't deal with it, not right now —

He strode down the hall, searching for the nurses' station. When he found it, he came to an abrupt stop, but as soon as he opened his mouth, he turned — and saw familiar faces.

He started toward them, pausing only briefly as he realized, much to his dawning terror, they were crying.

Please, no.

Solveig and Moyo were holding each other, sobbing, and Lars stood over them. Dare noted he was dry-eyed.

Irrational rage boiled into his chest. *Unfeeling son of a bitch.* He didn't know why or how, but he just knew.

"What are you doing here?" he heard behind him.

Dare turned around. Eric was standing there, tear-stained, his arm in a cast, his other hand clenched.

"Lars called me—"

"This is your fault," Eric snarled.

Dare stared at him, puzzled. "Lars called. Where is she?"

"If you hadn't decided to run back to your father, none of this would have happened. You—"

"You should leave, Dare," Lars said behind him.

Dare turned around. He was confused, but one thing was clear. "I want to see Kristin. Where is she?"

"She's still in surgery, you sorry—"

A man garbed in green scrubs approached Solveig and Moyo. Then neither Eric nor Lars made any difference. "Kristin," Dare started.

The doctor looked at him wearily. "And you are?"

"My name is Dare Borodin. I'm Kristin's fiancé. What happened?"

The hallway became silent. Dare found himself holding his breath, trying to read the man's expression.

"I'm sorry, Mr. Borodin," the doctor said.

"What? What happened? Is she alive? Tell me she's alive."

"She's recovering. She miscarried when her car was involved in the pile-up on I-90. She also suffered other injuries when her side of the vehicle hit the railing. She lost a great deal of blood. And the driver of the car was also injured."

That explained Eric's cast. But that was not the point. "Is she going to be all right?" Dare asked tensely.

The surgeon straightened. "She should be fine," he said, addressing not just Dare but Solveig and Moyo as well. "But she's going to be with us for a while."

Dare closed his eyes. "Thank God."

"You can see her in a few hours. But for the time being, I'd suggest you go home."

Afterward, Dare slumped against the wall. "Miscarriage," he whispered to himself. He leaned against the wall.

"Go away," he heard Eric say again. "You've done enough."

"I'll just wait here until she wakes up," Dare insisted, opening his eyes.

Eric was standing in front of him. The family resemblance was strong right then. His jaw was flexed and his chin was raised. He looked remarkably like his sister in a bad mood.

"You're not seeing her. If it hadn't been for you, none of this would have happened."

Dare stared at him. "What?"

Moyo and Solveig rose from their seats, their eyes red-rimmed. "*Erikku,*" Moyo said, a hand on her son's shoulder. "Don't."

"Not now, Eric," Solveig added.

"I want to figure this out now. If it hadn't been for him, none of this would have happened."

Dare stared at him. "What are you talking about?"

"If it hadn't been for you, we wouldn't have had to go racing out to the airport and get caught in that mess," Eric said angrily. "If not for that, she wouldn't be in there!"

"But why would she be going out to the airport?" he asked, still stupefied. "She wasn't feeling well. I figured she'd take a nap, go home. I don't underst—"

"Dare, go home," Lars interrupted, his voice soft. "I think you should go home, not antagonize the Olafssons."

Dare stared at Lars. This didn't make sense. Why would—

The call. Lars had taken the call. Lars had answered the phone when Dare had called to say he was at the airport.

What had he said?

"You," he breathed. *"What did you say?"*

Lars stared back at him. "I think you've done enough. Go home. Stay away from the Olafssons."

That was it.

Dare snapped. All the sorrow he had felt and witnessed through the years, the tiny shining light...all extinguished now. *"You—"* and then he lost it, couldn't remember what happened next, only that he was against the wall once more, Eric held back by Lars. Solveig and Moyo stood nearby, exclaiming in languages that, much to his irony, only he, the outsider once again, could understand.

He raised his hand to his mouth, to discover a streak of blood when he took it away. He stared at it. He didn't remember what happened, when, how.

But he could figure out who. The look of triumph on Lars' face caused another eruption of rage to bubble through him,

"Get out," Eric yelled. "You're nothing but trouble."

"I'm not going anywhere until I can talk to Kristin," Dare said, his voice steady.

"I don't think that's such a good idea," Lars answered.

Dare turned to Solveig and Moyo. "I love her more than I can tell you," he said. His voice was low, almost shaking. "I need to talk to her. Please."

Amazing. For two women from two such disparate backgrounds, he never would have believed they would have an ounce of similarity between them. But they did. The expressions on their faces echoed each other as they stared at him, wide-eyed and ashen-faced.

"Please," he said, his voice cracking. He looked first at the older woman, then at the younger. He could have sworn he saw compassion. But right then, the doors at the end of the hall opened and out came a bevy of green-garbed folk surrounding someone on a gurney they were pushing. He forgot about Solveig and Moyo and cried out, "Kristin?"

And then there was an outcry as Eric lunged at him again, but Dare avoided him, running instead for the gurney. "Kristin?" he said as he got to her side.

She looked up at him, and his throat closed. Her face was dazed, and even through the blurry look in her eye, he could tell she was having none of it. "Go 'way," she slurred.

"I'm sorry about the baby, Kristin," he said, trying to stay beside her as the gurney was pushed along. "Talk to me."

"Sir, she's not in any—" one of the green-garbed folk began. But he ignored them, stopping only as they paused at the elevator.

Kristin stared at him, dazed. "Go. Away. I. Don't. Want. To. See. You. Again."

Dare stared at her. "You can't mean that."

"Yes, I do. Go away." Much to his horror, a tear welled in her eye and trickled down her cheekbone, disappearing into the mass of her pinned-back black hair.

"But—"

"What's it going to take for you to go? I was happy before you! I had a good life! *You made me want it all and I knew damned well I couldn't have it!*"

"What are you talking about?!"

"I *knew* I was never going to have a baby and you—you—"

"Later, sir," a nurse said. The elevator doors opened.

"Go to hell!" Kristin yelled.

Dare stared at the doors as they closed, unwilling to accept or believe. The bubble of emotion in his heart shattered.

"Go," Lars said behind him. Dare turned. Beyond Lars was Eric, who was alternately hugging his mother and grandmother. They seemed to have forgotten he was there.

Dare watched for a second. The day before, he had a father he avoided and a future that involved a child. That centered on Kristin.

Today, he had no father. He had no child to look forward to. He didn't even have Kristin.

He had a future, but not one he looked forward to.

"I'll go," he finally said.

Chapter Twenty-Three
Fourth Year:
Gathering together once more, the ravens spread their
wings and bridged the River of Heaven.

೫ಿ

The apartment was emptied, the bathroom cleaned and he was packed. He didn't have anything left to do. He thought about taking a walk on the beach, but it was mid-summer, and he didn't feel like dealing with the crowds. Besides, beaches were beaches, and for the most part they were all the same.

It had been a long winter.

He took a last look out the patio door, then decided to take a drive around the city, thinking of what he would remember about Seattle.

It had been a winter filled with bursting frustration and searing bitterness. He tried, day after day, to gain access to see Kristin in the hospital, only to be turned away, until he found out he had even been barred from the floor, orders of Lars Bergen, M.D. Eric threatened him more than once. Moyo and Solveig had simply hung up when he tried to call.

Eventually, he stopped trying. It was clear what he thought was a simple mistake was true. She didn't want to see him again.

Then the time had come for him to decide on his next assignment. Until then, he had assumed he would request a permanent position in Seattle—but then his plans had changed. He had flipped through his choice of assignments and chosen one he would have shied away from not so long ago.

So now he would be on his way in a matter of hours, but first, he was playing tourist. It wasn't until he had driven through the International District and gone beyond it he realized he was near the Japanese Buddhist church.

He had managed to avoid it for the past six months. But he might as well see it one last time.

A sign caught his attention, and he slowed down to ponder his next move, coasting to a stop at the red light. *Bon Odori.*

The festival of the dead.

Dare rubbed his jaw. He had no reason to go visit the festival. He'd never been all that interested. Further, he would be inundated by fairs and festivals again soon enough, and it was quite possible he would be sick and tired of them by the time he finished his next rotation.

But the *Bon Odori* was special this year. The Dance of the Dead, the Japanese celebration where the spirits of one's dead relatives dance with the living, was a notable occasion among the Japanese.

He made his decision just as the light turned green. He flicked on his signal and turned left.

They'd never even discussed names. He didn't even know what the sex of the baby would have been.

Three months after his final words to his father, he had received his final communication from him. One last photograph, yellowed and fragile, water-stained and slightly torn at the edges, of his mother and himself as a baby.

Two weeks after that, he received word from his father's lawyer, for all further communication to be made through him. And that was that.

The baby would have been born just about then. It was only appropriate to commemorate its life and death here.

He found on-street parking not far from the temple. Walking along the tree-lined streets and cutting through the park across from the church, Dare stopped when he got close, just to admire the festival decorations. Small booths lined the street, which had been closed off for the occasion, just like the ones he remembered when he was a little boy—but it looked as though the organizers were still setting up. That made sense. The *odori* itself, the dancing, took place after sunset, after the lanterns were lit and the drummers began. Until then, the festivities mainly consisted of food at the booths and knick-knacks.

He decided to take a walk around. He had never explored the area during his stay in Seattle and this was his last chance. Then it occurred to him he had seen a bagel shop around the corner. This could be his last chance to taste a bagel for two years, so he went for it.

He was already down the street when he realized the bagel he had just bought was uncut. He decided to cut it himself, using the blade on his Swiss Army pocket knife.

Stopping at the edge of the festival and holding the knife carefully—it was, after all, very small—he cut into the bagel.

Just then, a cacophony of squawks exploded nearby. He jerked, dropping the bagel and his knife.

He looked up. A murder of ravens were clustered on the power lines up above, energetically cawing and flapping their wings, saying something in their own ravenish way.

His hand was moist, and he looked down. He cursed. As the blood began to trickle down his wrist, he realized he had managed to gash his palm open.

"Oh, hell," he groaned. "Just what I need."

Now that he was paying attention, it *hurt*.

"Damn it," he muttered.

Dare saw a man dressed in a *yukata*, a casual summer kimono, approach the festivities. "Excuse me. Do you know where the nearest hospital is?" he called over, holding up his hand to slow the loss of blood.

The Asian man looked comfortable and cool in his blue cotton garment, with a black-and-white patterned cloth tied around his head. He didn't look that surprised at Dare's injury, but asked, "Cut yourself? You should be careful."

He picked up the knife, folded it up, and gave it back to Dare. "Looks nasty."

"Yep. And the blood's going to be a mess," Dare added as the red smear began to seep through the brown bag he had jammed against the wound.

"I'd give you my headband to stanch it," the man added, "but it's a family thing."

Dare shook his head. "I just have to get it taken care of before I lose too much blood and I miss my flight." The pattern of the man's headband looked vaguely familiar, although he couldn't figure out why. Then he remembered—ravens. The pattern was of ravens in flight. And today of all days, there were a lot of ravens around.

The man in the *yukata* eyed the scarlet mess. "There's a first-aid station at the other end of the festival," he told Dare. "They could probably take care of you. Flying today, eh?"

"Supposed to be."

"Don't suppose you could take a later flight?"

"Only if necessary," Dare answered, holding his hand away from him before it started to drip and soak into his shirt. "Thanks anyway."

Even without the sign with the big red cross out front, he would have been able to figure the tent. It had all the earmarks of one, complete with a bench out front and boxes of what looked like medical supplies alongside it. The tent flap was open, so he stepped into the cool dimness.

He stopped when he saw the figure bent over a small table, taking out containers of what looked like bandages from a large box. For a second, he forgot why he was there.

"Gimme a second," the young man said as he scribbled on the clipboard in front of him. "Yeah, can I h—"

They stared at each other for a second before Eric Olafsson finally spoke. "Hey."

Dare smiled faintly. The lump in his throat dissipated. "Hey. How're you?"

Eric had grown up a little. He was beginning to look more like the pictures of his father, less like his mother and grandmother. "Not bad." He nodded at Dare's hand. "Hurt yourself?"

Dare glanced down. The red was seeping through the paper bag. "Yeah. I cut myself while I was slicing a bagel."

Eric snorted as he examined Dare's hand. "You came to a Japanese festival and sliced yourself with a bagel?" Then, "You visiting from Indiana?"

Dare was momentarily confused, but just shook his head. "I haven't been in Indiana in two or three years."

"Oh, I thought—" Eric stopped. He started to clean the wound, quickly, efficiently—he'd had practice, Dare guessed. "I thought maybe you went back with your dad. "

Bizarre thought. Once again, Dare shook his head. "I haven't spoken to my father in six months."

Eric pressed a gauze pad into Dare's hand. He seemed vaguely uncomfortable.

Dare wanted desperately to ask, but couldn't, not directly. So he tried the indirect route. "How's your mom and grandmother?"

"They're fine," Eric answered instantly. "Marmar's learning how to make sushi and Mom's learning how to make lutefisk. It's hysterical. Kristin says—" he stopped again.

The silence filled the tent before Dare broke it again. "How is she?"

Eric chewed on his lip for a second. "She's okay."

"That's good," Dare said. The next question was the tougher one, one he didn't want to know the answer to, but like taxes, it had to be done. "Is she seeing Lars?"

He was surprised at the reaction to the question. Eric shook his head. "She said she was tired of being manipulated and threw him out of the house. You know, I really thought you were living in Indiana."

It was Dare's turn to snort. "My father disowned me. I don't see any reason to go back anytime soon."

"He disowned you?" Eric exclaimed. "Keep your hand up."

"We communicate through his lawyer these days."

They stared at each other. "I'm sorry, man. Maybe Lars was more manipulative than we thought," Eric ventured.

Dare smiled wryly. He had come to that conclusion months ago, for all the good it did him. "I could have told you that."

In fact, he had tried, but that was all in the past.

Eric turned and called to the back of the tent. "Hey, I'm taking a break. We got a bagel gash," he called out. Then he turned back to Dare. "Good luck, man. And I'm really sorry."

Dare shook his head. "Don't worry about it, kid."

With a thumbs-up, Eric slipped out, closing the flap behind him. He left Dare waiting, staring toward the hidden part of the tent.

Dare knew who was back there. He knew she would be coming out. His heart started to hammer. *Wait*, he told himself. *Wait*.

He could hear the raucous cries of the ravens again.

Kristin came in from the back, her arms filled with packets of adhesive bandages, not looking at her next patient quite yet. "I'll be right there," she said, still counting the packets under her breath.

The closed flap cut off the noise from the festival.

It was just the two of them again—the outside world cut off, irrelevant.

Her arms finally free of the bandages, Kristin turned around toward her patient, holding a single packet. She was holding it with two fingers when she finally focused on him. "Now let's take a look at th—"

The packet slipped from her fingers. Dare looked away, unable to look her in the eye. Instead, he caught the packet on its way down. "Oh, my God," he heard her whisper.

He looked at her finally, unable to avert his gaze any longer. "It's been a while."

Her eyes were wide, looking even wider in a face that was noticeably thinner. She was trembling.

He offered her the packet in his unbloodied hand. "I think you dropped this."

Kristin stared at it and then at him. "Yes. Thank you."

She let her hair grow out. Instead of the determined flip he remembered, it was hanging below her shoulders now, almost straight. He recognized the red and white batik top she was wearing under the white jacket. Instead of fitting on her curves, it hung loose.

"You look tired," she said after a minute.

Dare imagined he did. "So do you. You've lost weight," he answered. Before he could stop himself, he reached up to touch her face—only to remember his bleeding hand.

She noticed it too. "There are easier ways to get my attention, Dare," she said with a faint smile. "Let's see it."

She touched his hand, moving it closer to the light on the table. Her skin was cool, as though she were in shock. "How do you get bagel gash at *Bon Odori*, Dare? You can't do this with a chopstick, and that's the deadliest thing around," she murmured as she took away the gauze for a look.

He couldn't take his eyes off her as she delicately straightened his fingers. Her free hand went for the box of latex gloves, but didn't quite reach it.

Her hair was falling over her shoulder and blotting out part of the light from the standing lamp, but he didn't care. He could have been in complete darkness at that moment and he wouldn't have cared. He was so close he could smell her warm scent, of apricots and the soap she loved. He was so close he could almost touch the pulse in her throat. "I bought a bagel around the corner. I tried to cut it open with my pocket knife," he answered, his lips dry. "I missed."

She looked up to meet his eyes. "Guess so." She flashed a smile, and he marveled at how she could still light up the darkest tomb. "Don't worry. We can take care of this in a jif."

She reached out to the medical supplies at her side, the fingers of her other hand still resting on his. "Visiting?" she asked, her voice shaking a little. "How's your father?"

"I don't know. I haven't talked to him in months." He watched her, waiting for a response.

She turned back. "But don't you live—"

"Until tonight, I live here. I got a posting overseas. But never mind that. How are you?"

She was staring at him now, her dark eyes puzzled. She was possibly the most beautiful, most exotic he had ever seen her. "I'm fine," she whispered. "I thought you went back to Indiana."

"My father disowned me. Basically, when I took him to the airport after the barbecue."

"But—" She stared at him, then away.

He reached out with his good hand and touched her. "Are you all right?"

"I'm fine." She swallowed, then took his hand. "I'm going to clean this. And you're going to need stitches."

"That figures. Can you do that here, or do I have to go to the hospital?"

"I can do it. So how have you been? You're leaving tonight?"

He didn't want to talk about this with her, but he had to. "My rotation was up, so I chose an overseas assignment."

"So how did you end up here? At the *Bon Odori?*"

He didn't want to talk about this. Really, he didn't. "It seemed like an appropriate time to say goodbye to the baby before I left the States," he said, his voice barely a whisper.

Her hands were trembling. "I hope you're not going to stitch me up with your hands shaking like that," he said, covering her hands with his good one, trying to joke about it.

"You never went back to Indiana? But—"

So many questions unasked, unanswered, so many of them answered now without a word. "I know. I'm sorry about everything."

"I'm sorry too," she quavered, and he could tell she was trying not to cry. "I've made such a mess of things."

"It wasn't you," he told her. "Don't cry. Things just— happened."

She started to shake. "But they didn't have to."

"I dragged you through all this, and I'm so sorry about that."

"No, I dragged you. You were living a very nice life on your own until I made you come into mine," she said, her voice quavering.

"But you made it better." He paused, and took a deep breath. "Because of me, you lost your best friend—"

"He's no friend. He never was," she interrupted, sniffing, wiping her eyes and examining his hand again.

Her touch was so warm now, and so light.

"I ruined your life. I came into it, you lost a friend, I turned your life upside down—"

"But I liked it," she protested.

He laughed. "There's something to be said about that."

She whispered, "I'm sorry too."

He didn't have to ask for details. "You were just out of surgery. You just lost—"

"I miscarried," she filled in. Her voice was steadier now. "I shouldn't have believed what anyone else had to say without talking to you."

"I nearly slugged Lars at the hospital."

"Especially Lars," she agreed. "You should have. I threw a bedpan at him about a week later. Empty," she added.

He laughed out loud. "Well, I would guess you got your point across."

"Yeah, I did. But I wanted to throw one at you, too, for leaving me."

This felt good. It felt easy.

He smiled. "If I thought I could get within ten feet of you, I would have been glad to show up so you could aim at me. But I got barred from the floor."

"You wouldn't have had to worry even if you'd managed to figure out how to get in. I have terrible aim."

He tried to tell her. "Maybe you'll forgive me someday for everything that happened, but I just want you to know I'm always going to care about you."

She was silent for a while. "How?"

His heart stopped. "I'm always going to want the best for you," he managed.

"That's not what I meant."

He knew. "I'll always love you, Kristin," he whispered. "If you threw yourself at me, I'd always catch you."

She was still holding his wounded hand. "I felt so empty without you. With the accident and the miscarriage, I thought I had lost my soul somewhere, and you went home to Indiana."

Too much. "You were the only home I had," he said, barely steady. "I was born in one country, raised in another, and for a living I went from place to place—and wherever I

317

went, I was always looking for a home. But I never found one, not until I met you."

He closed his eyes as the tears started to well. They were hot and he didn't particularly want them to land in her hair. Her hair deserved better.

"I have a question," he said.

"What is it?"

"After I get settled in my new assignment—would you consider coming for a visit? I'll get you a hotel room, if you want," he added. He didn't want to screw this up, not this time.

She shook her head. "I stay with you."

A tendril of joy wove through his heart. "The apartment only has one bedroom. One bed. I think it's one room, even."

"How many do we need?"

"You may not be able to find work," he warned.

She smiled wistfully. "I've been thinking about research instead of emergency medicine. In fertility. I wasn't much interested before, but I really need a change now. And I can start the reading on that off-site. So where are you going, anyway?"

He laughed. "You'll love this."

"What?"

"I'm going to Iwate. In the northern part of Japan. They have a big cattle industry in that area. Not only that, did you know there's a museum there devoted to cattle?"

She stared at him in disbelief. "Your next assignment's in *Japan*?"

"I thought it was about time to take a look at the part of my life I shut away. There weren't any openings in Tokyo, but there were up north. Are you still interested?"

"I've never been up there. I can't wait."

He couldn't speak for a minute. "May I?" he asked, turning toward her and lowering his face to hers.

"Please do," she said, smiling.

He kissed her then, feeling her soft skin and hair overwhelm him. "I love you, Dare," he heard her whisper.

The tears were trickling down his face, but he didn't care. He kissed the tears falling down hers. "I love you, too. I don't think I've said that before, have I? I assumed you knew."

"You never did. I always thought—"

"And I never really asked you to marry me, so would you?"

"I would," she said. She closed her eyes and shook her head. "Thank you for asking."

"Anytime."

"Now let's get that hand stitched up before you do anything else to it," she said. She wiped her eyes with the side of her hand. "Honestly, there are easier ways to see me, you know."

"Yeah, but this has always worked like a charm," he told her. He laughed.

"You're going tonight?" she asked. "I may need you for overnight observation."

"I can catch the flight another day," he told her.

Outside, the raucous cries of the ravens filled the air.

Also by Eilis Flynn

ebooks:
Festival of Stars
Hunters for Hire: Echoes of Passion
Introducing Sonika
The Sleeper Awakes

Print Books:
Introducing Sonika
The Sleeper Awakes

About the Author

Eilis Flynn has spent a large share of her life working on Wall Street or in a Wall Street-related firm, so why should she write fiction that's any less based in our world? She spends her days aware that there is a reality beyond what we can see - and tells stories about it for Cerridwen Press. Published in other genres, she lives in verdant Washington state with her equally fantastical husband and spoiled rotten cats.

The author welcomes comments from readers. You can find her website and email address on her author bio page at www.ellorascave.com.

Tell Us What You Think

We appreciate hearing reader opinions about our books. You can email us at Comments@EllorasCave.com.

Why an electronic book?

We live in the Information Age—an exciting time in the history of human civilization, in which technology rules supreme and continues to progress in leaps and bounds every minute of every day. For a multitude of reasons, more and more avid literary fans are opting to purchase e-books instead of paper books. The question from those not yet initiated into the world of electronic reading is simply: *Why?*

1. *Price.* An electronic title at Ellora's Cave Publishing runs anywhere from 40% to 75% less than the cover price of the exact same title in paperback format. Why? Basic mathematics and cost. It is less expensive to publish an e-book (no paper and printing, no warehousing and shipping) than it is to publish a paperback, so the savings are passed along to the consumer.

2. *Space.* Running out of room in your house for your books? That is one worry you will never have with electronic books. For a low one-time cost, you can purchase a handheld device specifically designed for e-reading. Many e-readers have large, convenient screens for viewing. Better yet, hundreds of titles can be stored within your new library—on a single microchip. There are a variety of e-readers from different manufacturers. You can also read e-books on your PC or laptop computer. (Please note that Ellora's Cave does not endorse any specific brands.

You can check our website at www.ellorascave.com for information we make available to new consumers.)

3. *Mobility.* Because your new e-library consists of only a microchip within a small, easily transportable e-reader, your entire cache of books can be taken with you wherever you go.

4. *Personal Viewing Preferences.* Are the words you are currently reading too small? Too large? Too... ANNOYING? Paperback books cannot be modified according to personal preferences, but e-books can.

5. *Instant Gratification.* Is it the middle of the night and all the bookstores near you are closed? Are you tired of waiting days, sometimes weeks, for bookstores to ship the novels you bought? Ellora's Cave Publishing sells instantaneous downloads twenty-four hours a day, seven days a week, every day of the year. Our webstore is never closed. Our e-book delivery system is 100% automated, meaning your order is filled as soon as you pay for it.

Those are a few of the top reasons why electronic books are replacing paperbacks for many avid readers.

As always, Ellora's Cave welcomes your questions and comments. We invite you to email us at Comments@ellorascave.com or write to us directly at Ellora's Cave Publishing Inc., 1056 Home Avenue, Akron, OH 44310-3502.

Make each day more *Exciting* With our

Ellora's Cavemen
Calendar

☥ www.ElloRasCave.com ☥

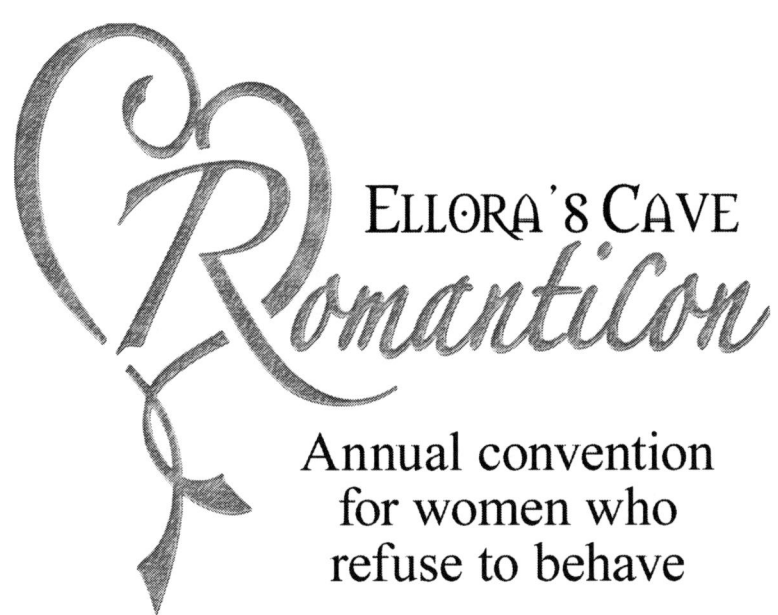

ELLORA'S CAVE
Romanticon

Annual convention for women who refuse to behave

www.JasmineJade.com/Romanticon
For additional info contact: conventions@ellorascave.com

Discover for yourself why readers can't get enough of the multiple award-winning publisher Ellora's Cave.

Whether you prefer e-books or paperbacks, be sure to visit EC on the web at www.ellorascave.com for an erotic reading experience that will leave you breathless.